fire after dark

Sadie Matthews is the author of six novels of contemporary women's fiction published under other names. In her own work, she has described decadent worlds of heady escapism and high drama. This is her first novel to explore a more intimate and intense side of life and relationships.

She is married and lives in London.

fire
after
dark

SADIE MATTHEWS

HODDER

First published in Great Britain in 2012 by Hodder & Stoughton
An Hachette UK Company

1

Copyright © Sadie Matthews 2012

The right of Sadie Matthews to be identified as the Author
of the Work has been asserted by her in accordance with
the Copyright, Designs and Patents Act 1988.

A CIP catalogue record for this title is available from the British Library.

ISBN 978 1 444 76550 2

Printed and bound by Clays Ltd, St Ives plc

Hodder & Stoughton policy is to use papers that are natural,
renewable and recyclable products and made from wood grown
in sustainable forests. The logging and manufacturing processes
are expected to conform to the environmental regulations
of the country of origin.

Hodder & Stoughton Ltd
338 Euston Road
London NW1 3BH

www.hodder.co.uk

To

X. T.

THE FIRST WEEK

THE FIRST WIFE

CHAPTER ONE

The city takes my breath away as it stretches beyond the taxi windows, rolling past like giant scenery being unfurled by an invisible stagehand. Inside the cab, I'm cool, quiet and untouchable. Just an observer. But out there, in the hot stickiness of a July afternoon, London is moving hard and fast: traffic surges along the lanes and people throng the streets, herds of them crossing roads whenever the lights change. Bodies are everywhere, of every type, age, size and race. Millions of lives are unfolding on this one day in this one place. The scale of it all is overwhelming.

What have I done?

As we skirt a huge green space colonised by hundreds of sunbathers, I wonder if this is Hyde Park. My father told me that Hyde Park is bigger than Monaco. Imagine that. Monaco might be small, but even so. The thought makes me shiver and I realise I'm frightened. That's odd because I don't consider myself a cowardly person.

Anyone would be nervous, I tell myself firmly. But it's no surprise my confidence has been shot after everything that's happened lately. The familiar sick feeling churns in my stomach and I damp it down.

Not today. I've got too much else to think about.

Besides, I've done enough thinking and crying. That's the whole reason I'm here.

'Nearly there, love,' says a voice suddenly, and I realise it's the taxi driver, his voice distorted by the intercom. I see him watching me in the rear-view mirror. 'I know a good short cut from here,' he says, 'no need to worry about all this traffic.'

'Thanks,' I say, though I expected nothing less from a London cabbie; after all, they're famous for their knowledge of the city's streets, which is why I decided to splurge on one instead of wrestling with the Underground system. My luggage isn't enormous but I didn't relish the idea of heaving it on and off trains and up escalators in the heat. I wonder if the driver is assessing me, trying to guess what on earth I'm doing going to such a prestigious address when I look so young and ordinary; just a girl in a flowery dress, red cardigan and flip-flops, with sunglasses perched in hair that's tied in a messy pony-tail, strands escaping everywhere.

'First time in London, is it?' he asks, smiling at me via the mirror.

'Yes, that's right,' I say. That isn't strictly true. I came as a girl at Christmas once with my parents and I remember a noisy blur of enormous shops, brightly lit windows, and a Santa whose nylon trousers crackled as I sat on his knee, and whose polyester white beard scratched me softly on the cheek. But I don't feel like getting into a big discussion with the driver, and anyway the city is as good as foreign to me. It's my first time alone here, after all.

'On your own, are you?' he asks and I feel a little uncomfortable, even though he's only being friendly.

'No, I'm staying with my aunt,' I reply, lying again.

He nods, satisfied. We're pulling away from the park now, darting with practised agility between buses and cars, swooping past cyclists, taking corners quickly and flying through amber traffic lights. Then we're off the busy main roads and in narrow streets lined by high brick-and-stone mansions with tall windows, glossy front doors, shining black iron railings, and window boxes spilling with bright blooms. I can sense money everywhere, not just in the expensive cars parked at the roadsides, but in the perfectly kept buildings, the clean pavements, the half-glimpsed maids closing curtains against the sunshine.

'She's doing all right, your aunt,' jokes the driver as we turn into a small street, and then again into one even smaller. 'It costs a penny or two to live around here.'

I laugh but don't reply, not knowing what to say. On one side of the street is a mews converted into minute but no doubt eye-wateringly pricy houses, and on the other a large mansion of flats, filling up most of the block and going up six storeys at least. I can tell from its Art Deco look that it was built in the 1930s; the outside is grey, dominated by a large glass-and-walnut door. The driver pulls up in front of it and says, 'Here we are then. Randolph Gardens.'

I look out at all the stone and asphalt. 'Where are the gardens?' I say wonderingly. The only greenery

5

visible is the hanging baskets of red and purple geraniums on either side of the front door.

'There would have been some here years ago, I expect,' he replies. 'See the mews? That was stables at one time. I bet there were a couple of big houses round here once. They'll have been demolished or bombed in the war, maybe.' He glances at his meter. 'Twelve pounds seventy, please, love.'

I fumble for my purse and hand over fifteen pounds, saying, 'Keep the change,' and hoping I've tipped the right amount. The driver doesn't faint with surprise, so I guess it must be all right. He waits while I get myself and my luggage out of the cab and on to the pavement and shut the door behind me. Then he does an expert three-point turn in the tight little street and roars off back into the action.

I look up. So here I am. My new home. For a while, at least.

The white-haired porter inside looks up at me enquiringly as I puff through the door and up to his desk with my large bag.

'I'm here to stay in Celia Reilly's flat,' I explain, resisting the urge to wipe away the perspiration on my forehead. 'She said the key would be here for me.'

'Name?' he says gruffly.

'Beth. I mean, Elizabeth. Elizabeth Villiers.'

'Let me see . . .' He snuffles into his moustache as he looks through a file on his desk. 'Ah, yes. Here we are. Miss E. Villiers. To occupy 514 in Miss Reilly's absence.' He fixes me with a beady but not unfriendly gaze. 'Flat-sitting, are you?'

'Yes. Well. Cat-sitting, really.' I smile at him but he doesn't return it.

'Oh yes. She does have a cat. Can't think why a creature like that would want to live its life inside but there we are. Here are the keys.' He pushes an envelope across the desk towards me. 'If you could just sign the book for me.'

I sign obediently and he tells me a few of the building regulations as he directs me towards the lift. He offers to take my luggage up for me later but I say I'll do it myself. At least that way I'll have everything I need. A moment later I'm inside the small elevator, contemplating my heated, red-faced reflection as the lift ascends slowly to the fifth floor. I don't look anywhere near as polished as the surroundings, but my heart-shaped face and round blue eyes will never be like the high-cheek-boned, elegant features I most admire. And my fly-away dark-blonde shoulder-length hair will never be the naturally thick, lustrous tresses I've always craved. My hair takes work and usually I can't be bothered, just pulling it back into a messy ponytail.

'Not exactly a Mayfair lady,' I say out loud. As I stare at myself, I can see the effect of everything that has happened lately. I'm thinner around the face, and there's a sadness in my eyes that never seems to go away. I look a bit smaller, somehow, as though I've bowed a little under the weight of my misery. 'Be strong,' I whisper to myself, trying to find my old spark in my dull gaze. That's why I've come, after all. Not because I'm trying to escape – although that must be part of it – but because I want to rediscover the old me, the one who had spirit and courage and a curiosity in the world.

Unless that Beth has been completely destroyed.

I don't want to think like that but it's hard not to.

Number 514 is halfway down a quiet, carpeted hallway. The keys fit smoothly into the lock and a moment later I'm stepping inside the flat. My first impression is surprise as a small chirrup greets me, followed by a high squeaky miaow, soft warm fur brushing over my legs, and a body snaking between my calves, nearly tripping me up.

'Hello, hello!' I exclaim, looking down into a small black whiskered face with a halo of dark fur, squashed up like a cushion that's been sat on. 'You must be De Havilland.'

He miaows again, showing me sharp white teeth and a little pink tongue.

I try to look about while the cat purrs frantically, rubbing himself hard against my legs, evidently pleased to see me. I'm inside a hall and I can see already that Celia has stayed true to the building's 1930s aesthetic. The floor is tiled black and white, with a white cashmere rug in the middle. A jet-black console table sits beneath a large Art Deco mirror flanked by geometric chrome lights. On the console is a huge white silver-rimmed china bowl with vases on either side. Everything is elegant and quietly beautiful.

I haven't expected anything else. My father has been irritatingly vague about his godmother's flat, which he saw on the few occasions he visited London, but he's always given me the impression that it is as glamorous as Celia herself. She started as a model in her teens and was very successful, making a lot of money, but later she gave it up and became a fashion journalist. She married once and divorced, and then again and was widowed. She never had children, which is perhaps why she's managed to stay so young and vibrant, and she's been a lackadaisical godmother to my father, swooping in and out of his life as it took her fancy. Sometimes he heard nothing from her for years, then she'd appear out of the blue loaded with gifts, always elegant and dressed in the height of fashion, smothering him with kisses and trying to make up for her neglect. I remember meeting her on a few occasions, when I was a shy, knock-kneed girl in shorts and a T-shirt, hair all over the place, who could never imagine being as polished and sophisticated as this woman in front of me, with her cropped silver hair, amazing clothes and splendid jewellery.

What am I saying? Even now, I can't imagine being like her. Not for a moment.

And yet, here I am, in her apartment which is all mine for five weeks.

The phone call came without warning. I hadn't paid attention until my father got off the phone, looking bemused and said to me, 'Do you fancy a spell in London, Beth? Celia's going away, she needs someone to look after her cat and she thought you might appreciate the chance to stay in her flat.'

'Her flat?' I'd echoed, looking up from my book. 'Me?'

'Yes. It's somewhere rather posh, I think. Mayfair, Belgravia, somewhere like that. I've not been there for years.' He shot a look at my mother, with his eyebrows raised. 'Celia's off on a retreat in the woods of Montana for five weeks. Apparently she needs to be spiritually renewed. As you do.'

'Well, it keeps her young,' my mother replied, wiping down the kitchen table. 'It's not every seventy-two-year-old who could even think of it.' She stood up and stared at the scrubbed wood a little wistfully. 'I think it sounds rather nice, I'd love to do something like that.'

She had a look on her face as if contemplating other paths she might have taken, other lives she might have lived. My father obviously wanted to say something jeering but stopped when he saw her expression. I was pleased about that: she'd given up her career when she married him, and devoted herself to looking after me and my brothers. She was entitled to her dreams, I guess.

My father turned to me. 'So, what do you think, Beth? Are you interested?'

Mum looked at me and I saw it in her eyes at once. She wanted me to go. She knew it was the best thing possible under the circumstances. 'You should do it,' she said quietly. 'It'll be a new leaf for you after what's happened.'

I almost shuddered. I couldn't bear it to be spoken of. My face flushed with mortification. 'Don't,' I whispered as tears filled my eyes. The wound was still so open and raw.

My parents exchanged looks and then my father said gruffly, 'Perhaps your mother's right. You could do with getting out and about.'

I'd hardly been out of the house for over a month. I couldn't bear the idea of seeing them together. Adam and Hannah. The thought of it made my stomach swoop sickeningly towards my feet, and my head buzz as though I was going to faint.

'Maybe,' I said in a small voice. 'I'll think about it.'

We didn't decide that evening. I was finding it hard enough just to get up in the morning, let alone take a big decision like that. My confidence in myself was so shot, I wasn't sure that I could make the right choice about what to have for lunch let alone whether I should accept Celia's offer. After all, I'd chosen Adam, and trusted him and look how that had turned out. The next day my mother called Celia and talked through some of the practical aspects, and that evening I called her myself. Just listening to her strong voice, full of enthusiasm and confidence, made me feel better.

'You'll be doing me a favour, Beth,' she said firmly, 'but I think you'll enjoy yourself too. It's time you got out of that dead-end place and saw something of the world.'

Celia was an independent woman, living her life on her own terms and if she believed I could do it, then surely I could. So I said yes. Even though, as the time to leave home came closer, I wilted and began to wonder if I could pull out somehow, I knew I had to do it. If I could pack my bags and go alone to one of the biggest cities in the world, then maybe there was hope for me. I loved the little Norfolk town where I'd grown up, but if all I could do was huddle at home, unable to face the world because of what Adam had done, then I ought to give up and sign out right now. And what did I have to keep me there? There was my part-time job in a local cafe that I'd been doing since I was fifteen, only stopping when I went off to university and then picking it up again when I got back, still wondering what I was going to do with my life. My parents? Hardly. They didn't want me living in my old room and moping about. They dreamed of more for me than that.

The truth was that I'd come back because of Adam. My university friends were off travelling before they started exciting new jobs or moved to other countries. I'd listened to all the adventures waiting for them, knowing that my future was waiting for me back home. Adam was the centre of my world, the only man I'd ever loved, and there had been no question of doing anything but being with him. Adam worked, as he had since school, for his father's building company that he expected one day to own himself, and he was happy enough to contemplate living for the rest of his life in the same place he'd grown up. I didn't know if that was for me, but

I did know that I loved Adam and I could put my own desires to travel and explore on hold for a while so that we could be together.

Except that now I didn't have any choice.

De Havilland yowls at my ankles and gives one a gentle nip to remind me that he's there.

'Sorry, puss,' I say apologetically, and put my bag down. 'Are you hungry?'

The cat stays twined around my legs as I try and find the kitchen, opening the door to a coat cupboard and another to a loo before discovering a small galley kitchen, with the cat's bowls neatly placed under the window at the far end. They're licked completely clean and De Havilland is obviously eager for his next meal. On the small white dining table at the other end, just big enough for two, I see some packets of cat biscuits and a sheaf of paper. On top is a note written in large scrawling handwriting.

> Darling, hello!
> You made it. Good. Here is De Havilland's food. Feed him twice a day, just fill the little bowl with his biscuits as if you were putting out cocktail snacks, lucky De H. He'll need nice clean water to go with it. All other instructions in the useful little pack below, but really, darling, there are no rules. Enjoy yourself.
> See you in five weeks,
> C xx

13

Beneath are typed pages with all the necessary information about the cat's litter tray, the workings of the appliances, where to find the boiler and the first aid kit, and who to talk to if I have any problems. The porter downstairs looks like my first port of call. My porter of call. Hey, if I'm making jokes, even weak ones, then maybe this trip is working already.

De Havilland is miaowing in a constant rolling squeak, his little pink tongue quivering as he stares up at me with his dark yellow eyes.

'Dinner coming up,' I say.

When De Havilland is happily crunching away, his water bowl refreshed, I look around the rest of the flat, admiring the black-and-white bathroom with its chrome and Bakelite fittings, and taking in the gorgeous bedroom: the silver four-poster bed with a snowy cover piled high with white cushions, and the ornate chinoiserie wallpaper where brightly plumaged parrots observe each other through blossomed cherry tree branches. A vast silver gilt mirror hangs over the fireplace and an antique mirrored dressing table stands by the window, next to a purple velvet button-back armchair.

'It's beautiful,' I say out loud. Maybe here I'll absorb some of Celia's chic and acquire some style myself.

As I walk through the hallway into the sitting room I realise that it's better than I dreamed it could be. I imagined a smart place that reflected the life of a well-off, independent woman but this is something else, like no home I've ever seen before. The sitting room is a large room decorated in cool calm colours of pale green and stone, with accents of black, white and silver. The era of the thirties is wonderfully evoked in the shapes of the furniture, the low armchairs with large curving arms, the long sofa piled with white cushions, the clean line of a swooping chrome reading lamp and the sharp edges of a modern coffee table in jet-black lacquer. The far wall is dominated by a vast built-in white bookcase filled with volumes and ornaments including wonderful pieces of jade and Chinese sculpture. The long wall that faces the window is painted in that serene pale green broken up by panels of silver lacquer etched with delicate willows, the shiny surfaces acting almost like mirrors. Between the panels are wall lights with shades of frosted white glass and on the parquet floor is a huge antique zebra-skin rug.

I'm enchanted at this delightful evocation of an age of elegance. I love everything I see from the crystal vases made to hold the thick dark stems and ivory trumpets of lilies to the matching Chinese ginger pots on either side of the shining chrome fireplace, above which is a huge and important-looking piece of modern art that, on closer inspection, I see is a Patrick Heron: great slashes of colour – scarlet, burnt orange, umber and vermillion – creating wonderful hectic drama in that oasis of cool grassy green and white.

I stare around, open-mouthed. I had no idea people actually created rooms like this to live in, full of beautiful things and immaculately kept. It's not like home, which is comforting and lovely but always full of mess and piles of things we've discarded.

15

My eye is drawn to the window that stretches across the length of the room. There are old-style venetian blinds that normally look old-fashioned, but are just right here. Apart from that, the windows are bare, which surprises me as they look directly out towards another block of flats. I go over and look out. Yes, hardly any distance away is another identical mansion block.

How strange. They're so close! Why have they built them like this?

I peer out, trying to get my bearings. Then I begin to understand. The building has been constructed in a U shape around a large garden. Is this the garden of Randolph Gardens? I can see it below me and to the left, a large green square full of bright flower beds, bordered by plants and trees in the full flush of summer. There are gravel paths, a tennis court, benches and a fountain as well as a plain stretch of grass where a few people are sitting, enjoying the last of the day's heat. The building stretches around three sides of the garden so that most of the inhabitants get a garden view. But the U shape has a small narrow corridor that connects the garden sides of the U to the one that fronts the road, and the single column of flats on each side of it face directly into each other. There are seven altogether and Celia's is on the fifth floor, looking straight into its opposite number, closer than they would be if they were divided by a street.

Was the flat cheaper because of this? I think idly, looking over at the window opposite. No wonder there are all these pale colours and the reflecting silver panels: the flat definitely has its light quota reduced being close to the others. *But then, it's all about location, right? It's still Mayfair.*

The last of the sunshine has vanished from this side of the building and the room has sunk into a warm darkness. I go towards one of the lamps to turn it on, and my eye is caught by a glowing golden square through the window. It's the flat opposite, where the lights are on and the interior is brightly illuminated like the screen in a small cinema or the stage in the theatre. I can see across quite clearly, and I stop short, drawing in my breath. There is a man in the room that is exactly across from this one. That's not so strange, maybe, but the fact that he is naked to the waist, wearing only a pair of dark trousers, grabs my attention. I realise I'm standing stock still as I notice that he is talking on a telephone while he walks languidly about his sitting room, unwittingly display-ing an impressive torso. Although I can't make out his features all that clearly, I can see that he is good looking too, with thick black hair and a classically symmetrical face with strong dark brows. I can see that he has broad shoulders, muscled arms, a well-defined chest and abs, and that he is tanned as though just back from somewhere hot.

I stare, feeling awkward. Does this man know I can see into his apartment like this while he walks about half naked? But I guess that as mine is in shadow, he has no way of knowing there's anyone home to observe him. That makes me relax a little and just enjoy the sight. He's so well built and so beautifully put together that he's almost unreal. It's like watching an actor on the television as he moves around in the glowing box opposite, a delicious vision that I can enjoy from a distance. I laugh suddenly. Celia really does have it all – this must be very life-enhancing, having a view like this.

I watch for a while longer as the man across the way chats into his phone, and wanders about. Then he turns and disappears out of the room.

Maybe he's gone to put some clothes on, I think, and feel vaguely disappointed. Now he's gone, I turn on the lamp and the room is flooded with soft apricot light. It looks beautiful all over again, the electric light bringing out new effects, dappling the silver lacquer panels and giving the jade ornaments a rosy hue. De Havilland comes padding in and jumps on to the sofa, looking up at me hopefully. I go over and sit down and he climbs onto my lap, purring loudly like a little engine as he circles a few times and then settles down. I stroke his soft fur, burying my fingers in it and finding comfort in his warmth.

I realise I'm still picturing the man across the way. He was startlingly attractive and moved with such unconscious grace and utter ease in himself. He was alone, but seemed anything but lonely. Perhaps he was talking to his girlfriend on the phone. Or perhaps it was someone else, and his girlfriend is waiting for him in the bedroom and he's gone through there now to take off the rest of his clothes, lie beside her and drop his mouth to hers. She'll be opening her embrace to him, pulling that perfect torso close, wrapping her arms across the smooth back . . .

Stop it. You're making it all worse.

My head droops down. Adam comes sharply into my mind and I can see him just as he used to be, smiling broadly at me. It was his smile that always got me, the reason why I'd fallen in love with him in the first place. It was lopsided and made dimples appear in his cheeks, and his blue eyes sparkle with fun. We'd fallen in love the summer I was sixteen, during the long lazy days with no school and only ourselves to please. I'd go and meet him in the grounds of the ruined abbey and we'd spend long hours together, mooching about, talking and then kissing. We hadn't been able to get enough of one another. Adam had been a skinny teenager, just a lad, while I was still getting used to having men look at my chest when I walked by them on the street. A year later, when we'd slept together, it had been the first time for both of us – an awkward, fumbling experience that had been beautiful because we'd loved each other, even though we were both utterly clueless about how to do it right. We'd got better, though, and I couldn't imagine ever doing it with anyone else. How could it be so sweet and loving except with Adam? I loved it when he kissed me and held me in his arms and told me he loved me best of all. I'd never even looked at another man.

Don't do this to yourself, Beth! Don't remember. Don't let him keep on hurting you.

I don't want the image but it pierces my mind anyway. I see it, just the way I did on that awful night. I was babysitting next door and had expected to be there until well after midnight, but the neighbours came back early because the wife had developed a bad headache. I was free, it was only ten o'clock and they'd paid me for a full night anyway.

I'll surprise Adam, I decided gleefully. He lived in his brother Jimmy's house, paying cheap rent for the spare room. Jimmy was away so Adam planned to have a few mates round, drink some beers and watch a movie. He'd seemed disappointed when I said I couldn't join him, so he'd be delighted when I turned up unexpectedly.

The memory is so vivid it's like I'm living it all over again, walking through the darkened house, surprised that no one is there, wondering where the boys have got to. The television is off, no one is lounging on the sofa, cracking open cans of beer or making smart remarks at the screen. My surprise is going to fall flat, I realise. Maybe Adam is feeling ill and has gone straight to bed. I walk along the hallway towards his bedroom door; it's so familiar, it might as well be my own house.

I'm turning the handle of the door, saying, 'Adam?' in a quiet voice, in case he's sleeping already. I'll go in anyway, and if he's asleep, I'll just look at his face, the one I love so much, and wonder what he's dreaming about, maybe press a kiss on his cheek, curl up beside him . . .

I push the door open. A lamp is on, the one he likes to drape in a red scarf when we're making love so that we're lit by shadows – in fact, it's glowing darkly scarlet right now, so perhaps he's not asleep. I blink in the semi-darkness; the duvet is humped and moving. What's he doing there?

'Adam?' I say again, but more loudly. The movement stops, and then the shape beneath the duvet changes, the cover folds back and I see . . .

I gasp with pain at the memory, screwing my eyes shut as though this will block out the pictures in my head. It's like an old movie I can't stop playing, but this time I firmly press the mental off switch, and lift De Havilland off my lap onto the sofa next to me. Recalling it still has the capacity to floor me, to leave me a sodden mess. The whole reason for coming here is to move on, and I've got to start right now.

My stomach rumbles and I realise I'm hungry. I go through to the kitchen to look for something to eat. Celia's fridge is almost bare and I make a note that grocery shopping will be a priority for tomorrow. Searching the cupboards, I find some crackers and a tin of sardines, which will do for now. In fact, I'm so hungry that it tastes delicious. As I'm washing up my plate, I'm overtaken suddenly by an enormous yawn. I look at my watch: it's still early, not even nine yet, but I'm exhausted. It's been a long day. The fact that I woke this morning in my old room at home seems almost unbelievable.

I decide I'll turn in. Besides, I want to try that

amazing-looking bed. How can a girl not feel better in a silver four-poster? It's got to be impossible. I go back through to the sitting room to turn out the lights. My hand is on the switch when I notice that the man is back in his sitting room. Now the dark trousers he was wearing have been replaced by a towel tucked around his hips, and his hair is wet and slicked back. He's standing right in the middle of the room near the window and he is looking directly into my flat. In fact, he is staring straight at me, a frown creasing his forehead, and I am staring right back. Our eyes are locked, though we are too far apart to read the nuances in one another's gaze.

Then, in a movement that is almost involuntary, my thumb presses down on the switch and the lamp obediently flashes off, plunging the room into darkness. He cannot see me any more, I realise, although his sitting room is still brightly lit for me, even more vivid than before now I'm watching from the dark. The man steps forward to the window, leans on the sill and looks out intently, trying to see what he can spy. I'm frozen, almost not breathing. I don't know why it seems so important that he doesn't see me, but I can't resist the impulse to remain hidden. He stares a few moments more, still frowning, and I look back, not moving but still able to admire the shape of his upper body and the way the well-shaped biceps swell as he leans forward on them.

He gives up staring and turns back into the room. I seize my chance and slip out of the sitting room and into the hall, closing the door behind me. Now there are no windows, I cannot be seen. I release a long sigh.

'What was all that about?' I say out loud, and the sound of my voice comforts me. I laugh. 'Okay, that's enough of that. The guy is going to think I'm some kind of nutter if he sees me skulking about in the dark, playing statues whenever I think he can see me. Bed.'

I remember De Havilland just in time, and open the sitting-room door again so that he can escape if he needs to. He has a closed litter box in the kitchen which he needs access to, so I make sure the kitchen door is also open. Going to turn out the hall light, I hesitate for a moment, and then leave it on.

I know, it's childish to believe that light drives the monsters away and keeps the burglars and killers at bay, but I'm alone in a strange place in a big city and I think that tonight, I will leave it on.

In fact, even ensconced in the downy comfort of Celia's bed and so sleepy I can hardly keep my eyes open, I can't quite bring myself to turn out the bedside lamp. In the end, I sleep all night in its gentle glow, but I'm so tired that I don't even notice.

CHAPTER TWO

'Hey, excuse me, can you tell me where I can find Lie Cester Square?'

'Sorry?' I say, confused, blinking in the strong, morning sunshine. Above me the sky is a clear blue with only the faintest suggestion of clouds in the distance.

'Lie Cester Square,' she repeats patiently. The woman's accent is American, she's wearing a sunhat and big dark glasses, in a touristy uniform of red polo shirt, loose trousers and trainers, with the obligatory small backpack, and she's holding a guidebook. Her husband, dressed almost identically, is standing mutely behind her.

'Lie Cester?' I echo, puzzled. I've made my way from Randolph Gardens to Oxford Street, one of London's main shopping thoroughfares, and am strolling along it, watching the crowds of people out even at this relatively early hour, and gazing in the shop windows. It's hard to believe that all this bustle and commerce is going on just a five-minute stroll from Celia's flat. 'I . . . I'm not sure.'

'Look, here it is,' the woman says, showing me her map. 'I wanna see the statue of Charlie Chaplin.'

'Oh – Leicester Square, of course . . .'

'Lester?' she repeats, puzzled, and turns to her husband. 'They say it Lester, honey. Honestly everything's a trap around here if you don't know.'

I'm about to tell her that I'm a tourist myself but somehow I'm a little flattered that she thinks I know my way around. I must look like a Londoner. I take the map and look at it carefully, then say, 'I think you can walk there from here, look. If you go up to Oxford Circus, then down Regent Street to Piccadilly Circus and turn left, it's a straight line across to Leicester Square.'

The woman beams at me. 'Oh, thank you so much, that's so kind of you. We're kind of lost. It's so busy, isn't it? But we're loving it!'

I smile back. 'You're very welcome. Have a lovely stay.'

I watch them go, hoping they'll find their way to Leicester Square all right and that the Chaplin statue lives up to their expectations. Maybe I should try and find it myself, perhaps it's worth a look.

I fish my own guidebook out of my shoulder bag and look through it as people swarm by in both directions. All around are large department stores and big chains: Gap, Disney, mobile phone shops, fashion outlets, chemists, designer glasses stores, jewellers. Along the wide pavements are stalls selling souvenirs, luggage, knick-knacks and snacks: fruit, caramel-roasted nuts, waffles, cold drinks.

My plan is go to the Wallace Collection, a free museum nearby that holds an extraordinary amount of baroque art and furniture, and then maybe grab some lunch somewhere and see what the afternoon brings me. I have that delicious sense of freedom: there's no one to answer to, no one to please but myself and the day stretches ahead, full of opportunity and possibility. London has more to offer than I can ever take advantage of, but I plan to see all the big sights, especially the ones nearest to me: the National Gallery, the National Portrait Gallery and the British Museum. My degree is in History of Art and I'm practically salivating at the thought of all the things I'm going to see.

The sun is bright and the sky clear. I'm feeling almost jaunty. The number of people about is overwhelming but there's also something liberating about it. At home, I can't go anywhere without meeting someone I know and one of the reasons I found it so hard to venture out is that I knew that everyone would be talking about Adam and me, and what had happened. No doubt they even knew what we'd said in that final tearful interview when Adam had confessed that he and Hannah had been sleeping together for months, since before I'd returned from university. That had probably been the subject of hot gossip, too. And I came back, innocent of all of it, thinking that Adam and I were still one another's soulmates, the centre of each other's world. They must have been laughing at me, wondering when I would finally find out and what would happen when I did.

Well, they all know now.

But no one here does. No one around me gives a

damn about my humiliation or my broken heart or the fact that I've been betrayed by the man I loved. I smile and breathe in the fresh summer air. A big red bus rumbles by me and I remember I'm in London, the great capital city, and it's spread out before me, waiting for me to discover it.

I set off, feeling lighter than I have for weeks.

It's late afternoon when I finally return to Randolph Gardens, a heavy carrier bag of groceries cutting into my palm, ready for a cool drink and keen to take my shoes off. I'm exhausted but pleased with everything I've achieved today. I managed to find the Wallace Collection and spent a very happy morning delighting in the rococo art and furniture within the extraordinarily beautiful Regency house. I revelled in the pink and white magnificence of Boucher, drank in Fragonard's gorgeous floral fairytales and sighed at the portrait of Madame de Pompadour in her lavish gowns. I admired the exquisite statues, ornaments and furniture, and lingered over the collection of miniatures in the galleries.

I found a nearby cafe for lunch, where hunger helped me overcome my general shyness at eating alone, and then decided to see where I would end up if I simply wandered. Eventually I found myself at what I discovered was Regent's Park, and spent a couple of hours walking around, sometimes through manicured rose gardens, sometimes along paths bordered by green expanses and shaggy trees, sometimes beside lakes or playgrounds or sports fields. And then, to my astonishment, I heard the trumpeting of elephants and saw in the distance the dappled neck and small head of a giraffe: I was near the zoo, I realised, laughing. And after that, I turned for home, stumbling onto a very smart street as I went that had, alongside chic boutiques and homeware shops, things like cash points and a branch of a supermarket that meant I could stock up on some food and other necessities. As I made my way back to Celia's flat, with only a couple of stops to consult my map, I felt almost like a real Londoner. The woman who'd stopped me that morning had no idea I knew the city as little as she did, but now I was a bit more seasoned, and already excited about what I might do tomorrow. And the best thing was, I had barely thought about Adam. Well, not that much. But when I did, he seemed so far away, so distant and removed from this life I was living, that his power over me was distinctly diluted.

'Good afternoon, De Havilland,' I say brightly to the familiar dark body awaits me inside the door. He's delighted to see me, purring nineteen to the dozen, rubbing himself against my legs in ecstasy, not wanting to let me walk a step without him pressed close to my calves. 'Have you had a lovely day? I have! Now what have we here? Look at this, I've been shopping – I can cook dinner. I know, I know, it's beyond exciting. I bet you didn't know I could cook but actually I'm all right and tonight we're going to have a delicious seared tuna steak with Asian dressing, rice and stir-fried greens, although I'll bet you that Celia doesn't have a wok, so we'll have to make do with whatever we can find.'

I chatter on to the little animal, enjoying his company and the gaze of his bright yellow eyes. He's only a cat, of course, but I'm glad he's there. Without him, this whole exercise would be a lot more daunting.

After dinner, which I managed to cook perfectly fine without a wok, I wander through to the sitting room, wondering if the man in the apartment opposite is going to appear but his flat's in darkness.

I go over to the bookcase and start inspecting Celia's library of books. As well as a wide range of novels, poetry and history, she has a wonderful collection of fashion books on everything from the history of famous fashion labels, to biographies of celebrated designers and large photographic volumes. I pull some out, sit on the floor and start flicking through them, admiring the stunning photographs of twenti-eth-century fashion. Turning the large glossy pages of one, I stop suddenly, my attention caught by the model in one particular photograph. It is an image from the sixties, and a girl of startling beauty stares out, her huge eyes made feline by the bat-wings of eyeliner on her lids. She's biting her lip, which gives her an air of intense vulnerability that contrasts with her polished beauty, the carefully styled dark hair, the amazing lace mini-dress she's wearing.

Tracing my finger around the girl's face, I realise that I know this woman. I glance up to the framed photographs that cover a nearby side table. Yes, it's unmistakeable. This is Celia herself, a modelling shot taken in the earliest days of her career. I turn the other pages quickly: there are three more shots of Celia, each with that delicate air alongside the high-fashion look. In one, her dark locks have been cut to a close crop, a gamine style that makes her look even younger.

That's weird, I think, puzzled. *I always imagined Celia as a strong woman but in these photos she looks so . . . not exactly weak . . . Fragile, I guess. As though life has already dealt her a blow. As though it's a big bad world out there, and she's facing it alone.*

But she came back from it, didn't she? Other photographs around show Celia at varying stages of her life and as she moves through it, that vulnerability seems a little less evident. The Celia, glowing and laughing in her thirties, is definitely stronger, more confident, more prepared to take on the world. She's sophisticated and knowing in her forties, glamorous and experienced in her fifties in a world before Botox and fillers when a woman's age showed whether she liked it or not. And age looks good on Celia.

Maybe she just realised that the blows will always come. It's how you deal with them, how you get up again and carry on.

Just then, the silence is shattered by a shrill ring and I jump with a gasp, before realising it's my phone going off. When I answer, my parents are on the line, wanting to hear how I am and what I've been up to.

'I'm fine, Mum, really. The flat is gorgeous. I've had a lovely day, it couldn't be better.'

'Are you eating properly?' my mother asks anxiously.
'Of course.'

'And have you got enough money?' my father says. I can guess he's on the sitting-room extension while my mother is sitting in the kitchen.

'Honestly, Dad, I've got plenty. You don't need to worry.'

Once I've recounted everything to them in minute detail, told them my plans for the next day and assured them that I'm completely safe and able to look after myself, we say goodbye and I'm left in the strange buzzing silence that descends after lots of chatter and noise abruptly stops.

I get up and go over to the window, trying to quell the loneliness I can feel growing inside. I'm glad my parents called, but they've unintentionally brought me down again. It feels all the time as though I'm struggling as hard as I can to get out of the black misery that's swamped me since the night I surprised Adam; it takes all my strength to get just a few steps away, and then the lightest touch sends me straight back into its depths.

The flat opposite is still in darkness. Where is the man I saw last night? I realise that I've unconsciously been looking forward to getting back here and seeing him again; in fact, he's been floating through my mind all day without my really being aware of it. The image of him half naked, the way he moved so gracefully about his sitting room, the way he stared so directly at me – it's all burned itself onto my retina.

He looked like no man I've ever seen before, not in real life at least.

Adam is not a particularly tall man and although he's strong from the work he does for his father's building company, it's made him stocky rather than defined. In fact, the longer I've known him, the more solid and squarish he's become, perhaps because he gets his energy from a greasy-spoon diet of endless fried food and cooked breakfasts. And in his down-time, he likes nothing more than to sink several beers and make a late-night trip to the chip shop. When I saw him that night, raising himself on his elbow and gazing at me in horror, with Hannah's frightened face on the pillow below him, my first thought was: *He looks so fat.* His white chest seemed podgy and his naked stomach hung down pendulously over Hannah, who matched him in ripeness with her big breasts, an expanse of pale belly and full hips exposed.

'Beth!' he'd gasped, his expression flicking between confusion, guilt, embarrassment and, unbelievably, annoyance. 'What the fuck are you doing here? You're supposed to be babysitting!'

Hannah said nothing but I could see her initial bewilderment becoming a nasty kind of defiance. Her eyes glittered at me as though she was spoiling for a fight. Caught in the sordid act, she was going to take me on. Rather than play the role of the wicked seductress, she was going to recast me as the lumpen fool intent on standing in the way of Romeo and Juliet's true love. Her nakedness was becoming a badge of honour rather than shame. 'Yes,' she seemed to be saying, 'we're fucking, we're mad about each other, we can't resist it. So what the hell are *you* doing here?'

Don't ask me how I knew all that in those few seconds between walking in and realising what I was seeing, but I did. Female intuition may be a cliché but that doesn't make it untrue. I also knew that everything I'd believed in approximately one minute before was now utterly defunct, and that the horrible pain I felt was my heart being beaten and mauled to within an inch of its life.

I managed to say something at last. I looked at Adam imploringly and said only, 'Why? *Why?*'

I sigh heavily. Even a day losing myself in the hugeness of London can't seem to stop me replaying the whole miserable scene. How can I escape it? When will it all end? Because the truth is, misery is so bloody tiring. No one ever talks about how exhausting it is being sad.

The flat opposite is still in darkness. I guess the man must be out, living his glamorous life, doing endlessly exciting things, hanging out with women like him: beautiful, sophisticated and high maintenance.

'I need ice cream,' I decide suddenly. I turn away from the window and say to De Havilland, who is curled up on the sofa, 'I'm just going outside. I may be some time.' Then I grab the keys and head out.

Outside the flat, some of the confidence I've acquired during the day seeps away, like air escaping slowly from a punctured tyre.

Around me the buildings are high and forbidding. I have no idea where I am or where to go. I'd planned to ask the porter on my way out, but the desk was empty as I passed it, so I head back towards the main streets. There are shops all right, but none that has anything to offer me and anyway they're all closed, their windows grilled and locked. Behind the glass are Persian rugs, vast china vases and chandeliers or exquisite clothes. Where can I buy ice cream? I walk without direction through the warm summer evening, trying to remember where I've come from. I pass bars and restaurants, all smarter than anything I've seen before, with burly men in black jackets and earpieces standing outside. Behind manicured box hedges, people in sunglasses, with that unmistakeable air of wealth, sit at tables, smoking over ice-coolers of champagne, white plates of delicious-looking morsels abandoned in front of them.

I begin to quail inside. What am I doing here? What makes me think I can survive in a world like this? I must be mad. It's ridiculous. I don't belong and never will. I want to cry.

Then I see a bright awning and hurry towards it, full of relief. I emerge from the corner shop a few minutes later with a tub of very expensive ice cream in a bag, feeling a lot happier. Now all I have to do is find my way back.

It occurs to me I've not yet seen a television in Celia's apartment, or a computer, come to that. I've got my aged laptop with me but goodness knows if there's an

Internet connection. Probably not. I'm not sure I can imagine eating ice cream without watching something on the telly at the same time, but I guess I'll survive somehow. It will still taste the same, right?

I round the corner into Randolph Gardens and I don't know exactly how I manage to do it but the next moment I've almost walked smack into a man on the pavement in front of me. He must have been ahead of me and stopped without my noticing so I kept right on going until my nose was practically pressed into his back.

'Oh!' I exclaim and step backwards, losing my balance. I stumble off the pavement and into the gutter, dropping the bag with my ice cream in it. It rolls away and comes to rest on a dusty drain stuffed with litter and dead leaves.

'I'm sorry,' he says, turning around, and I realise I'm looking straight into the handsome face of the man from across the way. 'Are you all right?'

I can feel myself flushing scarlet. 'Yes,' I say, sounding breathless, 'but it was all my fault. Really. I should watch where I'm going.'

He's quite mind-blowing close up, in fact I can hardly look at him, concentrating instead on his beautifully cut dark suit and the bunch of white peonies he's carrying. *How weird*, I think, *he's holding my favourite flower*.

'Let me get your shopping,' he says. His voice is deep, low and his accent is well educated and cultured. He steps forward as if to get down into the gutter to get my ice cream for me.

'No, no,' I say quickly, blushing an even hotter scarlet. 'I'll get it.'

We both bend and reach out at the same time and his hand lands right on top of mine, warm and heavy. I gasp and pull away, and promptly stumble forward. He instantly clasps my arm in a strong grip, stopping me from falling forward flat on my face.

'Are you all right?' he asks as I try to regain my balance. He isn't letting me go, and my face is flaming with embarrassment.

'Yes . . . please . . .' I say faintly, only aware of the iron fingers round my arm holding me up. 'You can let me go now.'

He releases me and I bend down to retrieve my bag with the all-too-obvious tub of ice cream in it. Bits of old leaf stick to my bag. I rub a hand across my face and feel the grit of dust there. I must look a fright.

'Just the weather for ice cream,' he says, smiling. I look up shyly. Is that a teasing note in his voice? I suppose I'm just some random girl in the gutter with streaks of filthy dust on her face, holding ice cream like a little kid with her treat. But he is something else. His eyes are so dark they're almost black but it's his eyebrows I really notice: strong black lines with a devilish hint about the arch. He has one of those straight noses that have a kink at the bridge that, oddly, only adds to its perfection, and below that is a full, sensual mouth, although at the moment the lips are curving into a smile and revealing straight white teeth.

All I can think, weakly, is *Wow*. All I can do is nod. I'm completely speechless.

'Well, good night. Enjoy your ice cream.' He turns and heads quickly up the steps of the apartment building, vanishing inside the front door.

I watch him go, still in the gutter, now feeling the grit between my toes. I breathe in, a long, desperately needed breath. I've been holding it while he looked at me. In fact, I feel really strange, a bit overwhelmed, with a kind of buzz in my head.

Slowly, I walk into the apartment building and make my way back up to Celia's flat. When I get there, I go straight to the sitting room. The light in the flat opposite is on now, and I can see him quite clearly. I fetch a spoon from the kitchen and go back, pulling a chair up to the window, close enough so that I can see out easily but not so close that I'm visible. I open my tub of ice cream and watch as the man moves about, going in and out of his sitting room. He's taken off his jacket and tie now and is walking about in a blue shirt and dark trousers. He looks effortlessly sexy, the shirt emphasising his broad shoulders and the trousers his lean masculine form. It's as though he's dressed for a fashion shoot in a men's magazine. I notice that he has a dining table and chairs in his sitting room. That makes sense. If the apartments are identically laid out, then his kitchen will be, like Celia's, a narrow, galley affair. While eating clearly doesn't matter enough to Celia for her to bother with more than the tiny two-man table in her kitchen, this man wants something a little more civilised.

Does he cook? I wonder. *Who is he? What does he do?* I need to give him a name, I decide. 'The man' isn't quite evocative enough. What shall I call him? Well, Mister something, obviously, as we haven't been introduced and first names are so peculiar to an individual. It would be weird to call him something like Sebastian or Theodore, and then discover his name was Reg or Norm or something. No, I need something that's mysterious and flexible, something that can contain all possibilities . . .

Mr R.

Yes, that's it. I'll call him Mr R.

As in Randolph Gardens. It kind of suits him.

Mr R walks back into his sitting room carrying an ice bucket and a couple of glasses. A promising-looking gold foil top pokes out of the bucket. Two glasses – so he's expecting company unless he intends to have a drink in each hand. There's no sign of the flowers. I sit back on the chair, crossing my legs like a school kid, and take the lid off my ice cream. I curl a long bit up onto the spoon and suck it off slowly, letting it melt on my tongue, savouring the sweet, cold trickle down my throat. It's plain vanilla, just the way I like it.

Mr R disappears again, and he's gone a long time. I've managed to eat about a quarter of the tub, and De Havilland has nested in the gap between my knees and slipped instantly into purring slumber. When he comes back, he's obviously showered and changed – he's now wearing a pair of loose linen trousers and a blue T-shirt, which look, needless to say, amazing – and he's not alone.

I gasp when I see her and then mentally roll my eyes at myself. *So what, he's not allowed a girlfriend? He doesn't even know who you are! You've spent two nights having a good old look at him, and now he somehow belongs to you?*

I almost laugh at my own craziness and yet, somehow, the weird intimacy of being able to see inside his flat like this has made me feel like there's a connection. That is clearly in my imagination, but still, I can't quite shake it. I lean forward to get a better look at the girlfriend.

Okay. Just as I thought. I'm way, way off course if I think I'll ever be able to compete with a girl like this.

Girl? She's a woman. A proper adult, grown-up woman, the kind who makes me feel like a gauche and scruffy child in comparison. She's tall and slender with the kind of elegance that can't be learned, and she's wearing a pale linen trouser suit with a white T-shirt underneath the jacket. Her dark hair is cut into a wavy bob, and she's wearing red lipstick in a way that indicates style, rather than tartiness. I can see that she's fine-boned and lovely, as though she's stepped out of the pages of Paris *Vogue*. She's the kind of woman who would never look tatty or sweat-stained or have a ponytail that hangs limply down her back. She'd never trip into gutters or walk about with a streak of grime on her face.

She is the kind of woman who is given white peonies and champagne in a Mayfair apartment. I bet she never ate ice cream with only a cat for company because her boyfriend preferred to shag someone else.

39

Just the thought of Hannah (my God, I'll never be able to forget seeing her lying there naked, her breasts bare with dark nipples crowning them, her belly damp with sweat) and the ice cream curdles in my mouth. I put the tub down, annoying De Havilland by leaning across him. He stretches out his claws and sinks them lightly into my bare leg, just enough to let me know he doesn't like my change of movement, and then relaxes them.

'Ouch, you naughty puss,' I say, but not crossly. The little pinpricks of his sharp claws are not unpleasant and, in a way, they bring me back to the present. 'Stop it. I'm sorry. I won't disturb you again. Now, I want to watch.'

Mr R is taking the bottle out of the ice bucket. The woman picks up the glasses from the table and holds them. She's laughing and saying something as Mr R rips the foil from the bottle neck and starts untwisting the wire cage around the cork. He's laughing too. No doubt she's witty and intelligent as well as beautiful and stylish. How come some people get all the good fairies turning up and loading on the blessings? It's just not fair.

It's weird observing them but being able to hear nothing. I've got visual with no audio and it's making me want to find the remote and check I've not muted the volume by mistake.

The cork pops silently, white spume erupts from the bottle. The woman holds out the glasses and Mr R pours the froth into each of them, waiting for it to settle into golden liquid. He puts the bottle down, takes a glass and they raise the flutes to one another before sipping. I'm watching so hard that I can almost feel the prickle of bubbles across my own tongue as they drink. What is their toast? What are they celebrating?

In my imagination, I hear him say, 'To you, my darling.' I bet she thrills to the sound of his voice saying something so intimate and sexy. I want to be a part of their world so much, it's all I can do to fight the impulse to jump up and wave, and then, when they notice and open the window, to ask if I could come over and join them. It looks so calm, happy, so adult. I watch them drink and talk, move to the sofa and sit down while they talk some more, and then watch Mr R go out of the room, leaving the woman on her own. She takes a call on her mobile phone, leaning back on the sofa as she speaks and listens. Then her face suddenly changes. Her expression is harsh, cruel and proud, and she begins to talk rapidly and, I sense, loudly. After a quick tirade into the phone, she ends the call with an emphatic tap of the screen and a toss of her head.

Mr R comes back into the room carrying some dishes of food. Surely he could hear her, she was obviously talking loudly, if not actually shouting – but they are quite normal, still smiling at one another. She gets up off the sofa and comes over to the table to inspect the food, while he goes out again and returns a second later with more dishes. I can't see what they contain but four seem to be enough. They begin to settle down at the table, and I watch them almost longingly, wishing somehow I could be there. Not just with them, but part of a different world altogether, one with more grace and style than my own ordinary existence.

The evening light is fading and the room I'm staring into is getting brighter and more vivid as the twilight deepens around it. Then Mr R gets up, walks over to one side of the window and looks out. I hold my breath. He's looking straight at me, surely he must be able to see me . . .

What's he going to do?

Then, suddenly, the view is gone. A white blind has dropped down, softly but sharply, blanking out my view just like that.

I breathe out, feeling bereft. They've gone. I didn't switch them off, they switched me off. Behind that blind, their charmed life goes on while I'm left outside by myself.

I can't believe how alone I feel. I lay my hand on De Havilland's body, feeling its warmth, trying to get some comfort from the serene sleep pulsing through him. But I want to cry.

CHAPTER THREE

The next day I sleep late, which is unusual for me. When I push back the curtains, the sky is a flawless blue and warm sunlight floods everything. I spend a lazy morning doing odds and ends, singing along to the old transistor radio as I finally finish unpacking my bags and tidy up the kitchen. I had meant to make my trip to the National Gallery and then walk down to Westminster Abbey, but somehow the morning slips away. At lunchtime, I make a sandwich and grab an apple and decide to find a way into the gardens down below and eat my lunch there.

The porter is friendly and tells me how to get through the back door to the gardens. The only way in is through the apartment building so the gardens are exclusive to the people who live there. I head out, walking along the shadowed gravel walkway, my gaze flicking up to where Celia's flat is, and across to where Mr R lives, but soon I'm out in the sunshine. The building widens out around the large green space that has been made into a magnificent garden, like a miniature park. There's a well-tended area with flower beds and plants laid out with benches and a fountain, and then a stretch of grass that's been allowed to grow a little long and hazy, like a lazily tended lawn that's on the brink of becoming a meadow. Beyond that is a pair of tennis courts, well kept and evidently often used. A couple of ladies are gently knocking a ball back and forth to one another.

I take my rug, found in Celia's hall cupboard, and put it down on the cool grass near the tennis courts. The thwack of the ball on the strings and the occasional shout of 'sorry!' is rather comforting, and I settle down to my lunch and my book as the sun blazes down, the light moving slowly across the lawn, dousing first my toes and then my calves in sunshine. By the time it reaches my thighs, I've finished my lunch and am lying sleepily on my rug, half reading my book and half dosing. I'm only vaguely aware that the ladies have gone and that their gentle ping-ponging of the ball has been replaced by a different, forceful hitting, and masculine grunts and shouts.

'Good – follow that forehand through. Come in to the net! Volley, volley, volley! . . . Excellent, good work.'

It's a tennis coach shouting instructions at his pupil. The voice floats over my consciousness. I'm mostly aware of the brightness of light on my closed lids and the heat of the sunshine, and don't even notice when the voices and the shots stop. The first I know of it is when the light on my eyes darkens and I feel the slight coolness of a shadow falling upon me. I open my eyes, blinking, and realise that someone is standing over me. It takes a second or two before I can focus: whoever it is is glowing like an angel and I realise that it's because they're wearing white. Tennis whites.

Oh my God. It's him. Mr R.

Before I can do much more than stare upwards at him, noticing that his dark hair is pushed damply back and that his nose is glistening with beads of sweat – *he's even more breath-taking like this* – and that he's staring straight at me, he speaks.

'Hello again,' he says, and smiles.

'Hi,' I say, breathless, as though I'm the one who's been playing tennis, not him.

'You're the girl I saw yesterday, aren't you?'

I struggle up into a sitting position, not wanting to talk to him while lying flat, but I still feel at a distinct disadvantage as he towers over me. 'Yes,' I manage.

He comes down to my level, crouching beside me. Now I can see close up those amazing eyes under the strong black brows, and he seems to be taking in everything about me. I feel very vulnerable to his gaze. He says, 'And you're staying in Celia's flat. I've made the connection now, I saw you there a couple of nights ago.' His smile fades and his expression becomes concerned. 'What's happened to Celia? Is she okay?'

His voice is low and musical and in that smart, well-educated accent, I can catch a slight foreign intonation but I can't place it. Maybe that explains his dark looks. As he moves, I get a wave of warmth from his body heat. It's sweet and salty with his exertions at the same time.

'Yes, she's fine. She's gone away for a while and I'm looking after her flat.'

'Oh, okay.' His face clears. 'I was worried there for a moment. I mean, I know she's amazing for her age, but . . . well, I'm glad to hear she's all right.'

'She's . . . fine,' I finish again lamely. *Come on, talk to him, impress him!* But the picture that floats into my mind is that of the polished woman in his flat the night before. Lying on my picnic rug, still dazed with sleep, I'm pretty far from that.

'Good.' He sends me another dazzling smile. 'Well, I hope you enjoy your stay. Just let me know if you need any help.'

'Okay,' I say, wondering if I'd ever have the courage to do such a thing.

'I mean it. Don't be afraid to ask.'

'Yes . . . thanks . . .'

'Goodbye for now.' He stands up, regards me for one long moment, almost as if waiting for me to say something else, then turns away.

'Bye.'

Was that the best I could manage? I want to groan out loud. *Talk about making an impression, Beth. You had marginally more conversation than the park bench over there. He'd have got more sparkling wit from the fountain.*

But, honestly, what do I really think is going to happen? A man like that will be interested in me? I can't even keep my boyfriend and anyway, I remind myself, he's taken.

Then, as he walks away, heading back towards the building, his tennis lesson over, he suddenly stops, turns round and looks at me again. His stare lasts only a few seconds before he turns back on his way, but it's long enough for me to feel a pleasurable thrill spreading out over my body. Is it my imagination or did his look mean something more than just friendliness? His proximity is having a strong effect on me. My drowsiness has gone and the buzzing summer life around me makes me feel lighter than I have in a long time. I squeeze my toes in the cool tickling grass as I watch him disappear into the door of the apartment block, then look back towards the tennis court where the coach is retrieving tennis balls.

Lucky tennis balls, being whacked by Mr R, I think, and laugh. *Okay, so I've got a crush. I might as well enjoy it. It adds a little something to my summer. And it can't do any harm, can it?*

That tiny exchange creates a golden glow to my whole day. In the afternoon, I go for a walk and discover the grandeur of Piccadilly, with the imposing and famous institutions along it: the Ritz, Fortnum & Mason, the Royal Academy. I wander down St James's Street, passing old-fashioned shops: milliners, vintners, purveyors of leather luggage and cigars; I walk between grand, castellated houses and find myself on the wide expanse of the Mall. At one end I can see Buckingham Palace, while before me is an idyllic-looking park. I've found the heart of tourist London, the dream of red, white and blue and monarchy. There are so many different aspects of this enormous city, and this is just

47

one. I walk through the park, watching children scampering about, feeding ducks, playing on the swings, and then find another face of London: the Houses of Parliament, dark, gothic and craggy, sitting alongside the ancient pale majesty of Westminster Abbey, where I'd planned to come this morning. Tourists mill around the area and queue to get into the church. I decide not to join them, but watch for a while, wondering what they make of this place, before I head for home, returning the way I came.

That evening, she's back.

The blinds are up now, and I can see clearly again, so I eat my supper sitting in my chair by the window, watching as Mr R and his girlfriend carry on their silent movie for my entertainment. They sit at the table and share a delicious-looking meal, talking and laughing together. I'm prepared for this to follow the same pattern as last night – the sudden dropping of the blinds just when it might get interesting – when something unexpected happens. They get up from the table, the woman picks up a jacket and puts it on and the next moment, they are heading out of the sitting room, Mr R switching off the light as they go.

Where are they going? What's happening?

I'm startled by the sudden change of expected events. And then a crazy impulse overtakes me. I jump up, tipping a sleepy De Havilland off my lap, and run to the hall cupboard. I've already seen that Celia has a motley collection of hats and coats there, and I grab a vintage Burberry trench coat and run out. The little lift is on my floor and a moment later, now in my improvised disguise with my hair loose and the coat collar high, I'm stepping out into the foyer just in time to see the front door close and Mr R and his girlfriend heading down the steps towards the streets.

What am I doing? I'm a spy now? I feel excited but also aghast at myself. What if they see me? What if he recognises me and wants to know what the hell I'm doing following him? Can I bluff it? Who knows – but it's too late. It's madness but now that I've started, I'm going to see it through. I want to know where they're going. I feel, strangely, as though I'm part of their life now, and they're part of mine. Besides, they'll probably hail a cab any moment and roar off away from me and I'll head back to the flat and try and regain my sanity.

But they don't.

Instead they walk through the back streets, talking to one another in voices that I can't make out, taking what is evidently a familiar route though it's completely foreign to me.

If I lose them, I'm going to be in trouble. The map is in my bag back at the flat and I don't have the faintest idea where I am.

The darkness makes it all the harder to distinguish direction and take note of landmarks, particularly when I'm intent on keeping their figures in my vision without getting too close. I'm lurking behind them at what I hope is just the right distance. I have no idea whether I'm fading into the background or sticking out like a sore thumb. Let's hope they don't decide to turn around suddenly . . .

They walk on, the woman's high-heeled shoes tapping loudly on the pavement. She's wearing a dark dress today with a well-tailored jacket over the top, while Mr R has kept on his business suit, not needing a coat or jacket in this hot weather. In fact, I'm the one who looks conspicuous in a raincoat, considering that most people around us are in T-shirts and light tops.

Never mind, I'll just have to pretend to be your typical British eccentric if anyone asks.

No one will ask, I remind myself. No one gives a damn. That's what's seductive about this city. I can be whoever or whatever I like. It's so different from home, where a change of hair colour can spark a frenzied debate that grips the entire populace.

We walk through dark streets and then come out onto a busy main road with cars, buses and taxis whizzing along it. We cross it and then are in some chic, pedestrian byways, with unusual boutiques and bars and pubs buzzing with young people standing about on the pavements, drinking and smoking. I'm worried I'll lose Mr R and the woman as they weave through the crowd but they're moving at a regular pace, obviously utterly unaware that they're being followed. We're heading into a different part of the city and I soon see bars of a more vibrant nature. Rainbow flags hang outside some – they're gay bars, I recognise the emblem – others have discreetly curtained entrances. I realise that I can see women dressed in miniskirts and bustiers standing outside doorways that hang with glittering streamers.

The red-light district? I think disbelievingly. *This is where they're going?*

We pass a couple of seedy-looking shops and just as I'm wondering what on earth is happening, we come out in a busy, vibrant area with yet another identity. This has a curious mixture of business and play: everywhere I can see work buildings, the kind devoted to media pursuits of film, television, advertising and marketing, but around them are countless bars and restaurants. There are people everywhere, in all kinds of dress, from sloppy and casual, to sharp and very expensive. They are dining on food of all kinds in every sort of restaurant, or drinking wine, beer or cocktails at tables on the pavement. The air has a curious aroma of a summer evening mixed with the bitterness of petrol fumes and cigarette smoke, and the cooking smells of hundreds of restaurants. This place is humming with activity of a kind that won't begin to lose momentum until the early hours, long after theatres have closed and the pubs have shut.

But I can see that this isn't just a place devoted to work and consumption. There's something else going on here too. The first indication is when I walk past a sex shop, one of those high-street ones that seem mostly to sell feather boas, naughtily shaped chocolates and saucy underwear to hen parties. Although they've got their fair share of brightly coloured vibrating plastic, they only seem interested in sex itself as a phwoar-style joke. But soon I see another shop selling gear of a different order altogether. The mannequins in the illuminated window are wearing shiny plastic boots, zipped or laced, with vertiginous heels, fishnet stockings, crotchless lace panties, studded garter belts and leather bras, some studded, some spiked, all with holes for the nipples. The models wear leather caps or masks, and hold whips in their hand. Inside the shop, I see rails of outfits and more underwear and for a moment I'm tempted to move inside and touch some of them.

Hardly have I taken this in than I'm passing another kind of shop, this time a bookshop. In the window are displays of artistic-looking black-and-white volumes, but they are unashamedly devoted to the naked human body, the human body in all sorts of exotic sex gear and the human body locked in embrace with another human body . . .

Mr R and the woman are still walking ahead of me, and the pavements are busy with people. I'm trying to keep them in sight while also taking in the fact that I'm now passing a sex shop, beautifully presented and with gold angel wings over the door, but a sex shop all the same, cautioning anyone who's entering that they must be over 18 and not offended by adult material.

I know where I am. This must be Soho.

I'm not such an innocent that I haven't heard of the famous red-light district of London, but its seedy days are clearly long behind it. There's nothing furtive or grubby about all this. The streets are awash with money and glamour, filled with all sorts of people and entertaining every sort of lifestyle, and none of them seem the least perturbed by the flagrant display of sexual paraphernalia. It simply exists alongside all the other aspects of human indulgence.

But still, I feel like a country bumpkin among all of this. The truth is, I've never seen anything like it, and I feel strange even looking at such things in public. Adam and I felt self-conscious about holding hands, and even alone we hardly ever discussed exactly what we were doing with one another. I can't imagine walking into a place like these shops and casually picking up bits and pieces that would announce to everyone that I was in the habit of having sex, of putting on gear like that or of using the toys and gadgets they had on offer. I mean, chocolate body paint is one thing, a huge throbbing vibrator something else entirely. I picture myself standing at the till, handing over a sex toy and then paying for it without dying of embarrassment. There's only one way I'm going to use it, after all, and the idea of having someone know that is almost more than I could bear.

Just then, Mr R turns a sharp left and we cross a dark square, then another road and take another turn along a small street that's lit only by one lamp burning orange in the night. It's like stepping back in time: tall Regency houses set back from the path behind iron railings, each with a metal staircase leading down to a basement. I can't tell if these are private houses or hotels or businesses, their elegant paned windows are mostly shuttered, some with a golden line showing there is light and life behind them.

The couple in front of me go straight to one of the houses of dark red-brown brick and descend the stairs, their steps resounding on the metal, and a moment later a door opens and they disappear inside. When I'm sure that they're well and truly in, I go to the railings and peer over. Below are two large windows, not shuttered as they look out below street level, and I can see that the room beyond is dimly lit and figures are moving inside. What place is this? A bar? A private house?

I have no idea, and I'm far too shy to find out more. When a deep voice says 'Excuse me' and a man in a smart suit goes by me, marching smartly down the stairs with absolute purpose and going through the door, I step back, feeling foolish. I can't follow them any more and I can hardly wait around for them. I'm going to have to find my way home on my own. I have a feeling that Oxford Street is nearby and if I can locate that, I'll be able to get home from there.

You're acting really strangely, I tell myself sternly. But I can't help it. I have the sense of a world of adventure existing somewhere very close nearby which I long to be a part of. It's closed to me, but open to Mr R and his girlfriend. Somewhere, they're living a life a thousand times more exciting than mine, than anything I've ever known during my quiet, provincial life. I ought to leave them to it, but I can't. It's as though I've stumbled on a small shining thread and I can't help pulling it, no matter how much it might cause my life to unravel.

I take off my raincoat.

It's time to go home.

I walk back the way I've come, looking at street names until I see some I recognise from looking at my map earlier. As I follow the way I believe leads back to Oxford Street, I see a shop that is still open alongside some small cafe bars and restaurants. It looks like a bookshop but with pretty knick-knacks as well, and on impulse I step inside.

A smiling grey-haired woman greets me as I come in and then makes a point of leaving me to myself as I begin to browse. I can see why: the books cover all manner of topics but principally they are erotic – saucy novels, pictures and poems. I wander about, glancing at titles and resisting the impulse to open the covers. I can't, not with someone here to see what interests me. I move away from the books and inspect the beautifully drawn sketches on the wall, then gasp and flush, casting around quickly to see if I've been noticed. The pictures are graphic depictions of sex. The bodies are headless, the artist concentrating on only the torsos of the subjects and the way they are joined together: a woman sits straddled on a man, her back arching and her hands on his chest; another is kneeling forward on a divan, a man engulfed in her bulging sex and thrusting into her from behind.

I'm scarlet. Wherever I look, I see something else:

hands holding a huge erection, a woman bending over it as if in worship; the most intimate parts of a female spread open and inviting, fingers parting them to give full access. A woman and two huge penises, one penetrating at the front, one at the back . . .

Oh my God. What is all this?

I look about for something else to focus on and move towards a large walnut glass-fronted cabinet with beautiful objects on the shelves. I can see carved marble and jade and crystal, fine leather and velvet.

I gasp again. I'm so many different kinds of fool. I'm looking at a wide variety of obscenely beautiful sex toys. I can see handwritten cards beside each one:

Jade pleasure-giving dildo £545

Crystal butt plug £230

Marble eggs £200 for the three

A string of onyx love pearls £400

On the shelf beneath is a collection of slender leather riding whips and an antique walking stick with a carved handle which, as I look harder, I can see is the long shaft of a phallus, its testicles tucked up at the base.

At the bottom are some metal implements that baffle me until I see the little cards beside them: they are nipple clamps and vices for seizing the tenderest parts of the body. Beside them are handcuffs in black leather lined with white fur, and slender plaited ropes in different colours.

'Are you looking for something in particular?' asks a voice. The woman is standing near me now, looking friendly, but I am immediately full of confusion.

'Oh . . . no, thank you . . . I'm just looking.'

'Okay.' She looks at me as though she completely understands my embarrassment and at once I feel a little more relaxed. She gestures to shelves on the other side of the room. 'There are some other bits and pieces over here if this is a little pricy for you. This really is our *objets d'arts* range. Those are more affordable.'

She leads me over to them. There are a huge variety of rubber and latex toys here, some like enormous rockets with all manner of projections, some smooth and slender like stylish pens in bright greens, blues and pinks. 'You'll probably have heard of some of these before.' She sees where I'm looking. 'Those thin ones are more for anal use, if you're wondering. The traditional vaginal ones are these larger ones. This, for example' – she picks up one of the monsters – 'is quite famous, and one of our bestsellers.'

I stare and draw a loud intake of breath without meaning to. It's so long and thick. Can it really be accommodated in . . . *in there*? I've never used a sex toy, never even really imagined it, and now I can't envisage how it would fit anyone, let alone me. I've only ever had sex with one man and though he was perfectly well endowed, he certainly wasn't anything like this size.

The woman indicates one of the larger protrusions on its shaft. 'This is the clitoral stimulator. You can leave it just as it is, or . . .' She flicks a switch on the base and the little thumb-like swelling starts to hum and move in a grinding motion. It also flickers with little lights inside it, as though it's dancing at its own personal disco. She smiles at me. 'This works a treat. It's one of the reasons it's our bestseller. And look at this.' She presses another switch and the whole shaft begins vibrating, a large inner ring pulsing up and down it, bulging in and out. It hums in a low, rhythmic way that reminds me of De Havilland's purring, which makes it seem like rather a happy thing. It looks strangely alive, especially with the lights glowing inside it – like some extraordinary and dense jellyfish. I can't help almost gulping at the sight. After a moment, the woman switches it off and puts the monster down. 'We've got plenty of others as well. Just ask me if you'd like any more explanation. I'm here to help.'

'Thank you.' I stare at the range of vibrators and feel a strange sense of excitement building in me. People do this. Normal people. Not perverts or nymphomaniacs, but normal women with sexual urges. The truth is that sex is one of things that I've been mourning over. Without Adam, I've lost not just my friend and the man I've given my heart to, but my lover, the man who touches me, kisses me, hugs me. The man who desired me, who longed to caress my breasts and run his hands over my hips, who wanted to know my intimate places and love them, with his tongue, his fingers and his cock. Now he's gone and my body is already crying out for his attention. When I've cried into my pillow at night, weeping over Adam's betrayal and the knowledge that he's now doing all those things with someone else, I've also been grieving for the loss of physical love and the pleasure it brought me. Could these things – the little buzzers to be held to that most tender nub, the bobbled, battery-powered rubber shafts with G-spot tantalisers – be the answer?

You could buy one. There's no one else here. The woman is friendly and anyway, you'll never see her again. She doesn't care what you want to do with it . . .

If there was ever a place to explore and experiment, then the solitude of Celia's flat is the place to do it.

Then I remember. I came out without my money. I don't have any way of buying anything. All the deliciously enticing thoughts disappear and suddenly I feel that I want to be at home.

'Thank you,' I call to the shop lady, and I turn, thrusting my hands deep into the pockets of my overcoat, and hurry out, the shop bell chiming behind me as the door closes.

I concentrate on finding my way back to Randolph Gardens, but even as I stride towards the busier street, I'm aware that something has changed. I'm alive in a different way, tingling, aware even of the breeze against my cheek and the way it tickles. Beneath my coat, I'm hot and needy.

CHAPTER FOUR

I'm still buzzing the next day. It's a rather luxurious feeling, as though I want to rub myself against the sheets on the bed, or stand naked at the open window and feel the breeze on my skin. For a moment, as I lie in bed, my hand brushes down over my belly to the patch of soft hair between my legs. The tip of one finger strokes gently over the small but intensely sensitive spot that protrudes slightly from the lips there. The effect is electric. It springs to life, swelling under my fingertip as if begging for attention, and a pleasant sensation spreads outward from my belly.

The image of that throbbing, pulsating shaft with its tantalising grinding little thumb placed exactly in the right spot, and the pictures I saw last night, float into my mind. I swallow hard and pull in a deep breath. A hot wetness is spreading through my groin. I see Mr R first in his tennis kit, damp with sweat, and then naked to the waist, wrapped in a towel. My fingertip sinks deeper into the warmth and I twitch just a little in response. My clitoris is stiff now, making its presence known, every nerve ending wanting stimulation.

Shall I?

I've brought myself to a climax before, of course.

The long months at university without Adam had taught me the merit of that particular solitary pursuit. But since that night, I haven't been able to bear it. I can't touch myself. I've felt too rejected to be able to lose myself in the pleasurable imaginative space that would allow me to come.

But now? Can I . . . ?

I flick my fingertip back over my swollen bud and this time a shudder ripples down my legs and up over my belly. My body is longing for it, begging me to give it release. I rub again and then again, gasping a little at the intensity of feeling it creates.

Then, it happens. I see that goddamned awful picture in my mind again: Adam turning to face me, revealing Hannah lying below him. I see his flabby belly with the rough patch of coarse brown curls at the base, and I see Hannah's spreading legs, the triangle of damp and flattened hair. I see again, with horror only a little dulled by repetition, the way they are joined together, his dark red shaft poking deep into her glistening ruby lips.

I groan. The desire that a moment ago was racing through me vanishes.

Why the fuck did I have to see that? Why the fuck can't I forget it? That image will always haunt me. The vision of their panting, animal desire kills my own arousal. The sight of Adam's cock, once my own prized possession, our shared joy, plunged into Hannah's body, has made my desires wither up and disappear.

I touch my clitoris again and it buzzes hopefully

beneath my finger. It's no good. My flesh might still be willing, but my spirit is crushed. I get quickly out of bed and wash away all that hot arousal in the shower.

Despite being unable to satisfy my body's evident longing for an orgasm, I can't shake the sense of luxuriousness. I had a very worthy day planned, one of cultural sightseeing in the art galleries and museums, and I'd planned to wear sensible clothes and sneakers and take a picnic lunch with me so I didn't have to eat in a high-priced tourist-trap cafe. But today, I don't feel quite in that frame of mind after all. In fact, the huge department stores along Oxford Street keep appearing in my imagination. Just a few days ago, when I arrived, I would have been far too intimidated to consider going in to such places on my own, but now something has subtly changed.

I chatter to De Havilland as I make some coffee and put some cereal in a bowl. In response, he saunters over to a scratching panel that Celia has put on a cupboard door and spends a happy few minutes ripping it to shreds with his claws while I bore him with my witterings.

'Do you think London is really making me brave again?' I ask him, as he digs in and then tears out his claws. 'I used to be brave, believe it or not. I went off to uni on my own, knowing absolutely no one and ended up making loads of friends.' I think wistfully of Laura, a fellow student who became my closest pal. She's travelling in South America, spending her last few months of freedom there before starting a job in London with a management consultancy company. She promised to send me emails whenever she passed an Internet place, but I haven't picked up my emails for a while now. It's strange that I've barely thought about them either. Usually I'm glued to my laptop, surfing the net, catching up with what everyone's up to, getting gossip. Now it's sitting abandoned in a bag in the bedroom and I've forgotten all about it.

Today I'll see if I can get a connection, or at least take the laptop somewhere I can log on. Every cafe has Wi-Fi these days, after all.

As I get dressed, I wonder what Laura would make of my break up. She'd be sorry for me and sympathetic, but I know that, deep down, she'd be glad. She tried to like Adam for my sake but when they'd met on the one occasion Adam had visited me at college, staying over in my shared student house, she'd not taken to him. I'd seen that look in her eyes while they talked, the one that showed she was barely keeping in her irritation. Afterwards, she'd tried to bite her tongue, but eventually she'd said, 'Don't you think he's a bit . . . a bit boring, Beth? I mean, he talked about himself all night and never once about you!'

I defended him, of course. All right, Adam could be a bit egotistical, he could ramble on a little – but he loved me, I knew that.

'I'm just worried that he doesn't love you quite enough. He takes you for granted,' she said, concern in her eyes. 'I don't know if he deserves you, Beth, that's all. But if he makes you happy, then fine.' Laura hadn't said any more about what she really thought of Adam, but when a third-year law student had shown a bit of interest in me, she'd urged me to spend some time with him and see what happened. Of course I hadn't. I was taken.

Thinking about Laura makes me yearn for some company. I've been alone for a while now and I need some interaction. Instantly my plan takes shape. As for wandering alone in galleries – well, that can wait for another day.

'Oh, that looks wonderful on you, really wonderful!'

I'm sure it's just sales patter – the assistant says it to all the customers, I expect; no doubt everyone looks marvellous in her company's clothes – but there's something frank in her gaze that makes me believe her.

Besides, if the mirror can be trusted, I do look surprisingly good in this dress. It looks like nothing on the hanger, and even on it's a fairly ordinary black dress, but it seems to bring my hidden charms to life in the way it fits so well across my bust and follows the curve of my waist and hips in such a perfect smooth line down to my knees. The fabric is some kind of silk mix that means it's clingy but substantial at the same time, with a subtle shine.

'You've got to get it,' breathes the assistant, hovering at my shoulder. 'I mean it, it suits you soooo perfectly.' She smiles at my reflection. 'Is it for a special occasion?'

'For a party,' I lie recklessly. 'Tonight.'

'Tonight?' Her eyes widen. She senses some kind of interesting story of why a girl would be shopping for a party dress on the very day of the event. 'Are you having a makeover day?'

I stare at myself. The dress is so pretty. I feel amazing in it, sexy and sophisticated. What's bringing it down is my bare face, undone hair and lack of shoes. A makeover day? How much would something like that cost?

I've always been a prudent person, careful with my money. I'm not exactly a splurger and I've never shopped for recreation. In fact, unlike most of my fellow students, I came out of university with no debt on top of the usual student loans, and my savings still in a healthy state.

Why not live a little? asks a voice inside my head. *Why not be reckless for once?*

'I suppose I could,' I say slowly.

The assistant claps her hands with glee. This kind of thing is clearly right up her street. 'Ooh, let me help you. First, you've got to get the dress, and I'm not just saying that. You look beautiful in it. You can leave it here and I'll look after it. You know we've everything you could possibly need in this place – beauty spas, treatments—'

'Let's not go too far,' I say hastily.

'—the hair salon, the nail bar.' Her eyes are shining at the thought of moulding my imperfect body into something worthy of the dress. Then her expression becomes concerned. 'But they might all be booked up. I'll make some calls for you, I'm sure I can pull some strings.'

Before I can stop her, she's hurried to the sales desk and picked up the telephone. I semaphore that I don't want any beauty treatments but she waves me away and books a facial. 'You'll love it,' she says confidently as she dials another number, 'and I was thinking your skin is fabulous but it's looking a bit dry. Do you use night cream? You should, I know a lovely lush one that will really restore inner moisture and replenish sub-epidermal hydration.' Before I can say anything, she's connected to the salon and is making me a cut and blow-dry appointment, her gaze flicking over my hair as she says, 'I do think a few highlights would help, actually, Tessa, if there's time.'

By the time she's off the phone, I've got several appointments, the first of which is only a few minutes off.

My assistant is clearly in her element and having a whale of a time. She gets someone to cover her till while she takes me down to the lower ground floor and the treatment rooms. It's all so good-natured that I'm carried along on the wave of enthusiasm, and when I'm handed over to Rhoda in the beauty centre, I've surrendered all control over my day. Before long, I'm lying on a bed with Rhoda massaging my face, spreading some kind of clay mixture on it, putting cool discs on my eyes and leaving me to bake for a while. It's a wonderfully relaxing experience, the kind of thing I've always assumed is meant for other people and not for me, but as the gentle fingers begin to wipe away the mask and anoint me with unguents and creams, I think: *Why not me? Why shouldn't I have this?*

'All done,' Rhoda says, handing me a sheaf of complimentary product testers. 'And you look great.'

I catch a glimpse of my face in the mirror as I pay – it's not exactly on the house, even if I have had some strings pulled for me – and I do seem to be glowing. Or is it my imagination? Who cares? The whole experience was amazing.

'You're expected on the top floor,' Rhoda informs me. 'For your hair.'

A short lift ride and before I know it, I'm ensconced in a high chair, a black nylon cape clipped around my neck and a pile of the latest glossies in front of me. A slender young man in a black T-shirt and with an improbable swoop of blond hair over his forehead talks me through what we might do with my hair. I've experimented with colours and cuts in the past but for the last few months, I haven't bothered. The result is that I have a gradation of colour, from dry straw at the ends to dark mouse at the roots, and any attempt at a style has long since grown out into shaggy ends.

Cedric takes me in hand. With practised ease, he paints my hair with the contents of some little plastic dishes, and folds it into tin foil, then leaves me with a magazine to amuse me while I cook under a revolving neon disc. After half an hour, he passes me on to a girl with delightfully soft hands who rubs and rinses and massages all the chemicals from my scalp and replaces them with something that leaves my hair slippery smooth and smelling of coconut.

Cedric reappears, brandishing scissors. Now it's time to comb and snip, and he chats away as he lifts long dark ribbons of hair and slashes into the ends with the slender blades. I watch myself in the mirror, wondering what is going to greet me at the end of all of this. When the cutting is done, Cedric sprays my hair with something, picks up his hairdryer and says, 'How glam do we want to go?'

I look at myself in the mirror and say, 'Glam.'

In my mind, I'm meeting Mr R for dinner. Tonight, he doesn't want that woman I've seen him with. Tonight, he's going to see me and gasp. 'Are you the girl from Celia's apartment?' he'll say, amazed, unable to believe his eyes. 'That little girl from the fifth floor opposite my flat? But you're . . . you're . . .'

I'm lost in a happy dream as the dryer roars around me, burning the tips of my ears bright red and singeing my scalp. Cedric is busy now with a spiky brush, rolling my hair hard, pulling it tight, blasting it with hot air and then releasing it with a twisting movement that leaves behind a loose ringlet. When he's worked his way all around my head, I have a halo of golden, glimmering waves. He sprays hairspray into his palm, rubs his hands together and then scrunches my hair, smoothes it, pulls it back and releases it. I have a long bob, a fringe that sweeps down over my face and falls seductively over one eye. It's a rich, shimmering gold.

'Do you like it?' asks Cedric, stepping back, putting

his head to one side and examining his work critically.

'It's . . . beautiful,' I say, a little choked. I'm remembering what I looked like only very recently, when I stared in my bedroom mirror after a fit of crying over Adam, and saw a lank-haired, puffy-eyed, dull-skinned girl with nothing left of her sparkle. She seems very far away now and I'm relieved to see the back of her.

Cedric smiles. 'I'm thrilled, babe. I knew I could make something of you. Now . . . apparently you're due on the ground floor. You've got some make-up and nails coming your way.'

I don't care, I don't care what it costs, I think recklessly as I hand my debit card over at the till. They're all being so lovely to me. They don't have to, but they are. And it's bloody fantastic.

When my lift arrives on the ground floor, I feel like royalty. Someone is there to meet me and take me over to the make-up counter that's been selected for me. Then a whole other session begins. A young make-up girl, looking old beyond her years in the store uniform and the obligatory pancake-thick cosmetics, gets to work. She moisturises my skin, applies serum and sprays my face with ionised liquid, then begins with tinted moisturisers, foundations and secret concealers. All the while, she murmurs compliments about my skin, my eyes, my lashes, my lips. It's all I can do not to believe that I've somehow become one of the most beautiful women on earth, but even while I retain a healthy scepticism, it's a seductive feeling.

Colours are applied to my brows, my lashes, my cheeks and my lips. I'm given glow and shimmer and something called 'pops' of colour. Eventually, when all that can be painted has been painted, the girl stands back happily and tells me I'm finished. Then she hands me the mirror.

I gasp. Then I tell myself – *it's their job to make you look like this and buy their products. These people are make-up artists.*

But still, I look nothing like I've ever looked. My blue eyes are defined in a way I've never managed with my trusty kohl, with long swooping dark lashes, and they glitter appealingly. My cheeks are flushed with pink-gold and my lips are an invitingly moist cherry red. I feel like I've stepped from the pages of a magazine.

I buy quite a lot of what has been applied to my face, which is no doubt the idea, and then I'm taken across to have my nails painted bright red while an animated girl from the East End tells me all about her boyfriend troubles. I hardly listen, to tell the truth. I'm thinking about Mr R. I'm lost in a fantasy world where I'm walking towards him across the restaurant, and he's rising to his feet, his mouth dropping open in amazement, and then, as I come to him, he's unable to resist taking me in his arms and . . .

'All done, love!' announces the nail girl, satisfied. 'Now leave it for twenty minutes to be on the safe side, yeah?'

There's one last task to be done before they release me from their care. I've got a pair of shoes to buy, something that will go with the black dress. My debit card already feels hot in my hand from the amount I've used it, but I've come so far that I have to go on. A stint in the shoe department brings me a pair of high black shoes with pointed toes, and then, after everything, I'm back where I started with my original assistant.

'Oh!' she exclaims, clapping her hands together. 'You look . . . *amazing*! I really never thought you'd look this good. Honestly, it's a transformation.'

She's right. I know she is. When the dress is on, the shoes, along with the hair and make-up . . . well, my confidence soars. Perhaps there is life after Adam. Perhaps someone else might love me, want me, desire me . . . Mr R, of course, is a pipe dream, but someone might.

'Thank you,' I say with deep sincerity. 'You've been so kind. I appreciate it so much.'

'Don't be silly, you deserve it.' She leans in towards me with a conspiratorial smile. 'Now go out there, enjoy your party and knock them dead!'

I leave the department store feeling like everyone is looking at me, admiring my new dress and my freshly done hair. Three days ago I arrived in London sweaty and shabby. Now look at me: I hope I look like someone Celia would be proud of.

I chance upon a small square hidden down an alley off the main road, and decide to have something to eat in one of the restaurants that line it. The whole process has taken hours and I'm so hungry that I don't care that I'll be eating alone. As I devour a plate of delicious pasta, I remember how, when I arrived, I was far too frightened to even think about doing such a thing. Well, look, here I am eating alone and nothing awful has happened. No one has stormed in to ask me how I dare do such a thing, no waiter has turned his nose up at me with a sneer and refused my order. I've been treated with quiet respect and it feels rather nice.

Afterwards, I'm not quite ready to go home even though it's now late afternoon. I wander north, back towards the chic area I discovered on my first day where I went food shopping. I'm not meeting Mr R of course, that little dream only exists in my imagination, but I don't want this pleasant flight of fantasy to end. It's only because I'm in this mood that, when I see the card in the window, I have the courage to go in. Behind the window is a large, light, blond-wood-floored gallery, its white walls adorned with large pieces of modern art. My eye is drawn to it at once because part of my degree focused on the development of Expressionism and art between the First and Second World Wars. The paintings here look as if they might be directly influenced by that era.

In the window is a white card, handwritten in beautifully neat lettering:

Experienced gallery assistant required.
Temporary position. Please enquire within.

I stare at it for a moment, seeing my own shadowy reflection in the glass. I came to London with the idea that I would look for some kind of summer job to keep me busy and perhaps to be the first step on a new path. After all, I can't stay working in my home-town cafe for ever, and so many friends are moving to London to start the next phase of their post-uni lives that it makes sense to see if I can find a future for myself here. I felt that I had missed the boat by not sorting anything out but maybe it's not too late. Laura asked me to come and live with her in London and share a flat or a house, but I hadn't seen how I would afford the rent without a job, and anyway I intended to stay with Adam.

I see a movement inside the gallery and catch a glimpse of a tall thin man with high cheekbones and an aquiline nose. He's in a dark suit and moving about near a desk halfway down the gallery. Has he seen me?

I decide to walk away and forget about it but something stops me. I'm as polished and primped as I'll ever look. If I can't impress a future employer looking like this, I never will. Before I really know what I'm doing, I've pushed open the door and am walking confidently towards the man, my high heels tapping on the wooden floor. He turns to look at me, and I can see that he has short blond-grey hair cut to a speckled stubble at the sides and with a neat bald patch on top. His grey eyes are hooded and beneath the impressive jutting nose, he has thin lips and a well-shaped chin. He wears a pair of gold-framed spectacles so discreet they're almost invisible. His hands are extremely graceful, and overall he projects an air of elegance and culture.

He says nothing as I approach but raises his eyebrows enquiringly.

'I saw your card in the window,' I say in my most confident voice. 'Are you still looking for someone? I wondered if you might consider me for the position.'

His eyebrows rise even higher as his gaze flickers quickly over me, taking in the dress, shoes and make-up.

'Yes, I am still looking, but I have some interviews later today and' – he smiles in a friendly but distant way – 'I'm afraid I am looking for someone with experience.'

I can see that he doesn't think for a moment I'm up to it. Maybe my appearance is actually working against me. He thinks I'm a bimbo, too interested in lipstick to know anything about art. This annoys me. Surely any modern man should know that a woman shouldn't be judged on her looks alone? Surprises come in a variety of packages after all.

I can feel a spark of my old confidence come back. 'If it's experience with people you need, I've spent years working with customers in a retail environment.' This isn't strictly true – is a cafe a retail environment? But we did sell some knick-knacks, postcards and a motley collection of antique china, so perhaps it counts. I continue without missing a beat: 'And if it's knowledge of the subject you're after, my degree is in the History of Art, and I concentrated on the early twentieth-century schools, the pre-First World War movements of Fauvism and Cubism and their growth after the war into a variety of Expressionist movements and Modernism. I can see from the artist you're showing here that you might be interested in this area too. This artist is definitely influenced by post-Expressionism and the Bloomsbury Group: I love those simple shapes and faded tones, the naivety. That painting of a chair and the vase of flowers could be a Duncan Grant original.'

The gallery owner is staring at me, then a smile creeps around his thin lips and the next moment he has burst out laughing. 'Well, you're certainly enthusiastic, I'll give you that. History of Art degree, eh? That's a good qualification. Sit down, we'll have a chat. Can I get you a cup of coffee or tea?'

'Great.' I beam at him and sit down where he's indicated. From then on, we get on very well. He's easy to talk to – charming, in fact, with beautiful manners – and I don't feel any interview nerves at all. It's more like a pleasant chat with a kindly teacher, except that he has miles more style than any teacher at my old school. He's extremely good at getting information out of me without my really noticing it and I tell him all about my degree, my life at uni, my favourite artists and why I've always been drawn to art even though I'm rubbish at drawing and painting.

'The world needs people who love things as well as those who do them,' he remarks. 'Theatre, for example, isn't just made of up actors and directors. There are the agents, the producers, the impresarios and financiers, who keep the whole thing running. Books don't exist simply because of writers, but because of publishers and editors and all the people who run bookshops for the love of it. Art, of course, is the same. You don't have to paint like Renoir to appreciate art and to work in the delicate but important business of promoting artists and buying and selling their work.'

I feel enthused about the possibility of a career in the art world, and I suppose he can see my excitement because he looks at me over the top of his gold-framed spectacles and says not unkindly, 'But all these worlds are very difficult to work in because the competition is intense. Getting your foot in the door is vital. I've already had a dozen answers to my card in the window. People know that it's an excellent opportunity to get experience.'

I must look deflated because he smiles and says, 'But I like you, Beth. And you clearly adore your subject and know a lot about it. As a matter of fact, I know one of the tutors on your course, he's an old friend of mine, so I know you'll have an excellent grounding in modern art. I tell you what. I'm seeing some other people later but I'll certainly remember this conversation.' He looks serious for a moment. 'I must stress that the position is a temporary one. My full-time assistant has been unexpectedly taken into hospital and will be away for several weeks, but he'll be returning to the position when he's recovered.'

I nod. 'I understand.' I don't tell him that I'm a temporary Londoner myself. I can work all that out if I get the job, which doesn't sound very likely.

He hands me an ivory business card engraved with navy copperplate. It reads:

James McAndrew
Riding House Gallery

Below are his contact details. I give him my mobile number and email address which he writes down on a pad on the desk. His writing is, like him, measured, elegant and a little old-fashioned.

'I'll be in touch,' James says, with another of those wise smiles of his, and a moment later, I'm back on the high street, feeling jubilant. I grin at my reflection in shop windows as I pass them, still getting used to my blonde waves and the curvaceous figure my black dress gives me. Even if I don't get the job, I'm pleased that I had the courage to walk in off the street and give it my best shot. I decide that, no matter what, I'll go back and see James and get some advice on what I should do next if I want to work in the art world.

I'm surprised when I look at my watch and see that it's getting late. I head back for home. Amazing how much time shopping and preening can take if you let it.

The flat opposite is in darkness. I stare at it for a while, hoping that the light will suddenly go on and reveal Mr R there. I'm desperate to see him. He's been buzzing around in my mind all day, constantly there, almost as though he's the one who's secretly watching me as I go about my day. Tonight, I feel ready for him in a different way. Even before I go into the sitting room to see what's happening opposite, I've refreshed my make-up, run my fingers through my hair and smoothed my dress down over my hips. I feel sophisticated and sexy, as though I made a tiny step towards being as polished as his girlfriend.

Like he's really going to notice!

So when his apartment stays resolutely in darkness, I feel the sting of disappointment. The window opposite remains opaque all the way through my solitary supper and afterwards. There is something very lonely about an empty flat, the way it sinks into a blank slumber without an inhabitant to bring it to life. Nothing has a meaning without someone to look at it, use it, live in it. De Havilland is cross with me because I won't let him sit on my lap, but I don't want cat hairs all over my new dress. He goes over to the sofa sulkily, curls up with his back to me and pointedly ignores me.

Then a plan that has been subtly brewing in my head all day almost without my realising it comes to fruition.

CHAPTER FIVE

Beth Villiers – master spy.

No. How about . . . *Beth Villiers, the Mata Hari of Mayfair.*

I laugh at myself. I'm out walking in my high heels again. My feet should be killing me but they're not. I'm wrapped in Celia's trench and rehearsing lines in my head.

Oh, what a coincidence seeing you here! Yes, I'm meeting a friend, his name is James. James McAndrew. He owns a gallery nearby and suggested we meet for a drink in this bar. I've no idea why he's so late. You'd like to buy me a drink? Why, thank you, that would be marvellous. This dress? It suits me? You're very kind . . .

Mr R and I are getting on famously in my imagination as I reach the brightly lit and bustling Soho streets. I've remembered the way very well. In fact, I can trace my steps exactly. I can even recall what shop windows I looked in and the faces of people I passed. This must be why the police make people do crime scene re-enactments as soon as possible after the event, before memories become hazy and clouded.

I take a turn into the dark, discreet little side street

lined with Regency houses. It's a funny place to have a bar. You'd have to be in the know to stumble across it, and even then, it doesn't look like the kind of place you'd walk in from the street, tucked away as it is below ground level.

Standing by the iron railings, I take a deep breath. I draw on all the confidence that has built up in me today.

I'm going to do it. I'm going to seize the day. I won't be afraid.

I walk down the metal staircase, my footsteps ringing with more assurance than I actually feel. At the bottom I can see in through the windows but whatever is beyond is dimly lit. I make out people sitting at tables, flames flickering on each one. Other shapes are moving around the room. I look at the front door. It is jet black and on the front is painted in white letters THE ASYLUM.

Too late to back out now. Let's hope there aren't lunatics waiting for me inside.

I'm tingling with apprehension, my fingers shaking slightly as I push the door open. It's unlatched and moves slowly and heavily under my force. Inside is a small lobby. A lantern in the shape of a star hangs from a chain, sending out a muffled light. There is a small printed notice, framed: *Abandon hope, all ye who enter here.*

What is *this place?*

I take a few steps inside. No one is there to stop me, though there is a chair and a table with a leather-bound book open on it, a silver pen in an old-fashioned holder and an inkwell. There is also a black tin box with *The Asylum* written on it in gold lettering.

The doorway to the bar is clear, and I advance cautiously, blinking to get used to the dimly lit interior beyond. There are people, very smartly dressed and sophisticated, drinking at the tables, and there is the faint murmur of conversation. Wine glasses, champagne flutes and cocktail tumblers glint where the candlelight catches them. But my eye is drawn beyond that, to the back of the bar, where I can see a line of cages hanging from the ceiling from chains. Inside each one, there is a person. I peer through the shadows.

Am I seeing what I think I'm seeing?

I'm looking at a woman, dressed only in black underwear, her wrists in cuffs that are joined by a long chain. She has high stilettos on, leather straps criss-crossing up her legs. Her face is half covered by a mask that glitters and shines with encrusted metal, and her hair is tightly bound. She is grasping the bars of her cage, moving subtly and sensuously, stretching out her limbs as much as she can in the confined space. The others in the cages are similar: women in very little, their faces covered, all shackled in some way. One is a man, his torso bare, wearing a minute pair of leather shorts. He is chained by a spiked neck collar to the roof of his cage and he stares constantly at its floor.

As I watch, still trying to take in what I'm seeing, a man in a smart business suit approaches one of the cages. The girl inside sits up and holds herself so that she can be examined. The man leans forward and mutters something to her, and she bows her head, then sinks down into a kind of obeisance in front of him. He talks more through the bars and she subtly nods. A moment later, he is opening the cage, and pulling her out by the chain between her wrists. She goes with him without resistance, following as he leads the way between the tables.

What's happening? Is this some kind of brothel? Is that really the kind of place Mr R and his girlfriend like to hang out?

'What are you doing here? Who are you?'

The voice is sharp and aggressive. I jump and turn to see a man. At first sight he seems ordinary enough – medium height and dressed in black – but he is terrifying. His head is shaved bald and one half of his face and scalp is tattooed all over in a swirling, primitive pattern. The effect is freakish and frightening. His eyes glow at me, furious and threatening. They are so pale that they are almost white.

'How did you get in here?' he demands. A few people nearby turn to look, but evidently have no interest in what's unfolding at the door. Perhaps they're used to this sort of thing.

'I . . . I . . . the door was open . . .' I stammer, flushing. I can feel my hands begin to shake again. 'I thought . . .'

'This is a private club, members only,' he hisses. 'You are expressly forbidden. Now get the hell out and stop nosing around where you don't belong.'

His gaze is white hot with scorn. I feel like a naughty child, humiliated in front of everyone. I cower under his threatening attitude, a helpless fool.

'You heard me,' he says in that nasty hiss. 'Get out *now*, or I'll escort you out myself.'

I find the power to move from somewhere and stumble past him, into the small lobby and out of the door. I'm climbing the staircase towards the street, tears stinging my eyes, trembling, horrified by what's just happened.

What's the point? Why did I bother thinking I might be able to find a place in this horrible city? Why did I spend all that money on trying to pretend I'm a proper woman when I'm so stupid?

It all seems so hopeless. Adam was right to dump me. I'm never going to be able to become what I long to be. As I stand under the lamppost on the street level, I begin to cry in earnest, grateful that there are so few people about. I'm scrabbling in the coat pocket, hoping I'll find a packet of tissues there, as tears roll down my face. I sniff hugely and wipe the tears away with the back of my hand. All it's taken is a few unkind words and I'm a mess, lonelier than ever.

'Hey, are you okay?'

I look up at the source of the voice but I'm blinded by tears. It's familiar, though. Surely I've heard it before . . .

'You're crying. Can I help you? Are you lost?'

I look up and see him, his face illuminated in the light from the street lamp and the concern obvious in his eyes. Just as I realise who I'm looking at, and my stomach is taking a graceful swoop and dive towards my shoes, his expression changes. Mr R frowns and smiles at the same time, looking bemused. 'Hey, you're the girl from Celia's flat. What on earth are you doing here?'

'I . . . I . . .' I blink up at him. He's incredible close up, and his nearness robs me of the power of rational thought for the moment. All I can think about is how beautiful those eyes are, so intense and powerful under the strong black brows, and how perfect his mouth is. What must it be like to have those lips kiss you, to caress that handsome face? I want to reach out and stroke my finger down his strong jawline and feel the roughness of the dark shadow of stubble I can see there.

'Are you lost?' He looks concerned.

I nod, trying not to sniff again. 'I came out for a walk,' I manage to say. *Oh God, don't let me get the hiccups, please . . .* 'I must have come further than I thought.'

'Hey.' His dark eyes seem to glitter in the light from the streetlamp. 'Please, don't cry. It's going to be all right. I'm going to take you home.'

'But . . .' I'm about to ask if he's going into the club when I remember that this will be a dead giveaway '. . . aren't you busy? I don't want to interrupt your evening.'

'Don't be silly,' he says almost brusquely. 'I'm not leaving you here alone. I said I'll take you home.'

I'm worried I've annoyed him. He pulls a phone from his pocket, taps out a message and sends it, then looks back at me. His expression is strangely stern. 'There. All done. Now let's get you back where you belong.'

My tears vanish as I realise, to my astonishment, I'm walking back through the streets of Soho with Mr R. He's in one of his immaculate business suits, and as he walks beside me I guess he's over six feet tall – tall enough to tower over my five feet and six inches. He walks easily at my side, making sure that he doesn't stride on too far so that I have to trot to keep up. I've got a sensation of warm lightness that feels like helium inside a balloon. Any moment now, I'm going to start floating if I'm not careful.

When we go through a crowd of teenage tourists standing outside some fast food joint and filling up the pavement, he puts a hand in the small of my back and guides me through them. As we emerge the other side, I can barely speak with the excitement that courses through me at his touch. When he takes his hand away, I feel bereft.

'You really came a long way,' he says, frowning. 'Didn't you bring a map? Do you have a map function on your phone?'

I shake my head, feeling silly. 'Stupid of me.'

He almost seems to glower at me for a moment as he mutters, 'Really very stupid. It can be dangerous out here you know.' Then he appears to relent. 'Well, something tells me you're not used to London.'

'No. It's my first time.'

'Really? So how do you know Celia?' If he was angry with me, he seems to have put it behind him now. His eyes look warmer.

'She's my father's godmother. She's been in my life for as long as I can remember but I don't know her very well. I mean, I've only seen her a few times and I've never visited her before. I was amazed when she wanted me to look after her flat for her.'

'I can understand why you leapt at the chance.'

Do people assume we're together? Maybe they think he's my boyfriend . . . could they? He's so incredibly gorgeous, though . . .

As we walk along heading west towards Mayfair, I can't help taking in everything about him. His hands are beautiful: strong and broad with long squarish fingers. I wonder what they would be like on my skin, how they would feel on my bare back. The thought makes me shiver lightly. His clothes are all very expensive-looking, and he carries himself easily but without a trace of the kind of arrogance you might expect from a man who looks like him.

He starts to talk about Celia, how he's got to know her through the fact that their flats face each other.

Really? No kidding!

I try to look innocent and it doesn't seem to occur to him that I might have been watching him.

'Her apartment is incredible, isn't it?' he says. 'I've had coffee there with her once or twice. Amazing woman. So interesting – the stories she has to tell about her career!' He laughs and shakes his head and I laugh too. It seems that he knows her much more than even my father does. The way he speaks of her makes me want to get to know Celia properly.

'She's the kind of person I'd like to be when I get to her age,' he continues, 'ageing gracefully but holding on to that zest for life. But I worry about her too. No matter how energetic she seems, she's getting on. She'd hate to admit she's the slightest bit vulnerable, but I keep a quiet eye on her, just in case anything should happen.'

He's kind as well. Oh God, kill me now!

'But you know Celia,' he says jokily. 'She's seventy-two years young, right? I have a feeling she's going to be just fine. She'll probably outlive us all, and still be climbing Mount Everest when we're too tired to climb the stairs.'

The atmosphere between us has lightened now that my tears have vanished, and the anger he seemed to feel at my lost state has gone. We're coming closer to Randolph Gardens. I slow my pace a little, hoping to draw out the time we have together. Any moment now, we're going to be home and then we'll go our separate ways. I don't want it happen. I'm enjoying the crackle of electricity I am sure I can feel between us.

Then he stops and turns to face me. 'You're all on your own, aren't you?'

I nod. He gazes at me for a moment with a searching expression, then says softly, 'Why don't you come up to my flat? You look like you could use a cup of coffee, and I don't want you going back to Celia's place still feeling upset. Besides, I've been talking so much, I don't know anything about you.'

I loved listening to his voice. It's warm and pleasant, a deep, capable voice. *Would I like to come up for coffee?* My heart starts to beat faster, a shakiness possesses me. 'That would be very nice,' I say, my voice coming out a little higher than I intended. 'Yes, please.'

'Good, that's settled. Let's go in.' He turns to lead the way up the steps and then stops, and looks back at me. I'm petrified in case he's about to change his mind, but he says, 'I don't even know your name.'

'Beth. It's Beth.'

'Beth. That's nice.' He smiles at me, one of those heart-breaking smiles. 'I'm Dominic.'

Then he turns and carries on into the apartment block, and I follow behind.

Once we're in the lift, I find the closeness of our bodies so electric that I can hardly breathe. I can't look up at him, but I'm intensely aware of the way his arm is brushing mine and that with the tiniest of movements we'd be pressed against one another.

What if the lift stopped? What if we were trapped in here? I see him suddenly in my imagination, his mouth hard on mine, his arms pulling me tightly to him. *Oh God.* It makes all sorts of weird fireworks go off in my belly. I steal a glance at him from under my lashes. I feel almost sure that he's feeling something of this strange electricity too.

I'm almost glad when the lift judders to a halt and I can breathe properly again. I follow him out into the corridor. It's very odd to be on the opposite side of the building. Now that we're inside and away from the street, I'm feeling shyer by the minute. Add to that the fact that everything here is the same but the other way around. It's an Alice-through-the-Looking-Glass feeling as he leads me to the front door and unlocks it.

Dominic smiles. 'Come on in. And don't worry, I meant to say earlier – I'm not an axe murderer. Not on Thursdays, anyway.'

I laugh. It never occurred to me for a second that I might not be safe with him. He's Celia's friend, isn't he? I know exactly where he lives. It's fine.

Inside, the first thing I see is my own reflection in his hall mirror, and the expression of horror that greets me when I clock what's happened to my sophisticated look. My hair, so beautifully twirled and waved earlier, has dropped and is hanging limply around my face. My make-up has worn off and I'm pale-cheeked, with swollen pink eyes and some lovely inky mascara effects underneath. Great. So much for Miss Sophistication.

'Oh,' I say out loud.

'What's wrong?' he says as he shrugs off his jacket, giving me a tantalising glimpse of the outline of muscled arms beneath his shirt.

'My mascara is everywhere, I look a mess.'

'Here.' He comes up close to me, and then, to my astonishment, he puts the ball of his thumb under my eye and rubs gently.

89

I gasp. His touch is warm and soft. I realise that he's staring into my eyes now, his expression intense. His thumb stops moving, his fingers rest on my cheek. I think he's going to caress my face and I can't imagine anything I'd like more. I blink and inhale softly; instantly he seems to snap back to himself. He takes his hand away, and his gaze slides away too, as he says, 'I'll make some coffee.' Then he goes through to the kitchen, leaving me alone to recover.

Was that my imagination or did we just have a moment?

'How do you like your coffee?' he calls, as the kettle begins to heat up.

'Uh – just with milk, thanks,' I reply, turning to the mirror and frantically running my fingers through my hair, but he's already on his way back so I have to leave it.

'Let me take your coat. It's rather warm for this, isn't it?' He lifts the coat from my shoulders. I feel as though he's being purposely businesslike, in case of a repeat of that odd little moment we just had.

'I . . . er . . . feel the cold,' I reply lamely. 'I'm very sensitive to the weather.'

He leads me into his sitting room and indicates a long square modern sofa. 'Take a seat. I'll just go and finish making our drinks.'

I go slowly over to the sofa, looking around. I've already got a sense of this room from the view opposite but it's quite different to be inside it. For one thing, it's much more luxurious and stylish than it appears from a distance. I suppose that it's no surprise a man who can afford a flat in this part of town can also afford to decorate it with the best. It's very modern, and everything is in shades of taupe and grey, with accents of black. The sofa is that off-white stone colour with plump grey and white cushions and it's L-shaped, placed around a large glass coffee table that appears to be balanced on hunks of granite, and two elegant black armchairs face the sofa from across it. Vast glass lamps with black shades sit on polished pale-wood side tables. Placed around the room are elegant pieces of pottery – trios of white vases in varying sizes, a large dome-like ornament with black swirls all over it – and tribal art. A carved mask in black wood takes up a part of the main wall, along with a very big black-and-white picture that I think is an abstract painting until I realise that it's an enormous photographic print of a flock of birds in flight, their wings and bodies blurred by the speed of their motion. The walls are covered in fabric rather than paper – a kind of rough, hemp-like material. The floors are carpeted in the type of thick pale wool you can dream of using only if there is no question of small children or pets coming anywhere near it. A large flat-screen television hangs over the fireplace, which is full of huge church candles, unlit at the moment. A well-stocked drinks table stands near the window.

I sit down, taking it all in.

Wow. This is a bachelor pad, all right.

It's masculine, but not oppressively so. Everything is in extremely good taste. Actually, I expected nothing less.

My eye is drawn by a strange piece of furniture. It looks like a stool or a low seat, but it isn't quite that. Instead of an armrest on each side, it seems to have two at one end, placed quite far apart, and at the other is a kind of broad rest with a scrolled back.

That's a weird-looking object. What's it for?

A picture floats unbidden into my mind. It's a flash-back to the scene inside the club earlier this evening. I see the girl in the cage, writhing against the bars, her eyes glittering from behind the studded mask. I see her following the man, docile as a tamed pony. That's the place that Dominic went to with his girlfriend. I feel the first stirrings of something like doubt. I've been so entranced by his looks, by his aura and by the kindness he's shown me, but maybe he's not as straightforward as he seems on the surface.

At that moment, Dominic comes in holding a tray with a coffee pot, a jug and two cups on it. He places it on the glass table and sits down on the sofa adjacent to mine so that we're close but not exactly cosy.

'So,' he says, as he pours out the coffee, adds milk and passes me the cup, 'tell me about yourself, Beth. What brings you to London?'

It's on the tip of my tongue to say, 'I got my heart broken and I came here to mend it' but that seems a little too personal, so I say, 'I've come for some adventure. I'm a small town girl and I need to spread my wings.' The coffee is hot and aromatic. It's exactly what I need. I take a sip; it's delicious.

'You've come to the right place.' He nods wisely. 'This is the greatest city in the world. I mean, I like New York and Paris, and I'm a big fan of LA no matter what people say, but London . . . nowhere else comes close. And you're right in the heart of it!' He gestures out of the window. Hundreds of windows in buildings all around us glow bright yellow in the summer darkness.

'I'm very lucky,' I say honestly. 'Without Celia, I wouldn't be here.'

'I'm sure you're doing her a favour too.' He smiles at me again and I feel that odd tension. Is he flirting with me?

I'm enjoying the sensation of being close to him. The nearness of his broad shoulders beneath the white shirt is disconcerting. I can sense the brown warmth of his skin radiating towards me. The shape of his mouth is making my breathing shallow and a small buzz of something like excitement flutter in my stomach and circle my groin. God, I hope he doesn't notice the effect he's having on me. I take another sip of the hot coffee, hoping it will ground me a little. When I look up those black eyes are staring at me and I can hardly hold in a gasp.

'So, tell me about how you've found London so far.'

I shouldn't be so shy but there's something about his magnetism that is making me into the old gauche Beth I've been trying to leave behind. I start to tell him about what I've seen in the city, stumbling over my words and searching for the right way to describe things. I want to talk impressively about works of art and the places I've seen but I sound like any other tourist reeling off a list of sights. He is utterly charming though, asking me interested questions and appearing fascinated by what I'm telling him. He doesn't realise he's only making my clumsiness worse.

'And I loved the collection of miniatures in the Wallace Collection, and the portrait of Madame de Pamplemousse,' I say, trying to sound knowledgeable.

He looks puzzled. 'Madame de Pamplemousse?'

'Yes . . .' I'm glad to be able to show off my knowledge. 'Louis XV's mistress.'

'Oh!' His expression clears. 'You mean Madame de Pompadour.'

'Yes. Of course. Madame de Pompadour. That's who I meant.' I feel awkward. 'What did I say?'

'Madame de Pamplemousse.' He bursts out laughing. 'Madame Grapefruit! That's brilliant.' He's properly laughing now, throwing back his head, showing his perfect white teeth, the deep rich sound booming around.

I laugh too, but I'm also mortified to have said something so stupid. I'm scarlet with embarrassment and as I try to laugh it off, I realise my eyes are stinging again. *Oh no, don't! Just don't! Don't start blubbing, this is ridiculous.* But the more sternly I talk to myself, the worse it gets. I've made a fool of myself and like a baby, I'm going to cry about it. I use all my strength to stop myself and keep it in, biting the inside of my cheek hard.

He sees my expression and stops laughing at once, his smile fading. 'Hey, don't be upset. It's okay, I know who you meant. It's just funny, that's all, but I'm not laughing *at* you.' He reaches over and puts his hand on top of mine.

The moment our hands touch, something strange happens. The sensation of his skin on me is electric, almost burning. A kind of current flows between us that almost makes me shudder, and I look up, astonished, into his eyes. For the first time I really see him, and he stares straight back at me, his expression surprised, almost disconcerted, as though he's also feeling things he didn't expect to. I feel as though I can see his real self, unmasked by politeness and convention, and that he can see right back into me.

Every day, as we go about our lives, hundreds of faces slide by, flickering in and out of our consciousness. We meet the glances of people on trains or buses, in lifts or on escalators, in shops, at counters, on the way to work and back again, and we make a tiny half connection that is broken and lost almost at once. For an instant, we recognise someone else's existence, grasping the fact that they have a life, a history, a whole past that has brought them inexorably to this moment where we connect with them, and then, just as swiftly, we disconnect, our eyes turn away and we go on our separate paths, forward to different futures.

But right now, as I look into Dominic's eyes, it's as though I know him, even though he's a stranger. As though our different ages and life experiences don't matter a bit. In some strange way, it feels like we know each other.

The world beyond us falls away and disappears. All I'm conscious of is his hand on mine, the torrent of excitement that's racing through my body, the deep sense of connection. I am staring into eyes that seem to penetrate to the core of my being, that seem to know me intimately. I have the instant conviction that he understands me. I am certain he feels it too.

It seems as though we're frozen like this for an age, but it must only be a few seconds. I begin to grasp our situation, coming back to reality like a swimmer breaking the surface after a long dive, and I wonder with a kind of shivering anticipation what's going to happen now.

Dominic looks both awkward and amazed, as though something he never imagined has just happened. He opens his mouth, and is about to say something, when we hear a sound in the hallway. Dominic's gaze shifts at once to the door, and I turn as well, just in time to see a woman marching in. She's wearing a long dark fur coat despite the warm evening, and her expression is cross.

'Where the hell have you been?' she demands as she walks in, and then stops dead when she sees me, looking me up and down with a rapier gaze. 'Oh.' She turns to Dominic. 'Who's this?'

The spell, our connection, is broken. He hastily removes his hand from mine. 'Vanessa, let me introduce Beth. Beth, this is my friend Vanessa.'

I murmur a quiet hello. This is the woman I've seen before. So that's her name. Vanessa. It suits her.

'Beth's staying just across the way,' Dominic goes on. He's very self-possessed but I can pick up the slightest hint that he's a little flustered under that calm surface. 'I've been neighbourly and asked her in for coffee.'

Vanessa nods a greeting at me. 'How gallant,' she says coolly. 'But we were supposed to meet two hours ago.'

'Yes, I'm sorry, didn't you get my message?'

I notice he doesn't mention coming to my rescue in the dark Soho streets.

She stares back at him, obviously telegraphing that she doesn't want to talk about this in front of me. I get to my feet at once.

'Thank you so much for the coffee, Dominic, it was terribly kind of you. I'd better be getting back now, I mustn't leave De Havilland on his own for too long.'

'De Havilland?'

'Celia's cat,' I explain.

Vanessa looks amused. 'You've got to look after the cat, have you? How sweet. Yes, well, don't let us keep you.'

Dominic gets up too. 'If you're sure, Beth. Don't you want to stay and finish your coffee?'

I shake my head. 'No, I don't think so. Thank you anyway.'

He walks me out into the hall and as he hands me my coat, I look into those dark eyes again. Did that moment between us just happen? He appears just as he did before it: a kind, polite stranger. And yet . . . something in those black depths is still there.

'Take care, Beth,' he says in a low voice as he sees me out. 'I'll see you soon, I'm sure.'

Then he leans towards me and brushes his lips over my cheek very lightly. As our faces touch, it's all I can do not to turn to him so that he can kiss my lips, which is what I'm longing for him to do. As it is, my skin burns where he's touched it.

'I'd like that,' I reply almost on a sigh. Then, as the door closes, I head back down towards the lift, wondering if my weak knees will manage to carry me all the way back to Celia's flat.

CHAPTER SIX

My inbox is full of messages but most are rubbish. I scroll through, deleting as I go, wondering why I subscribe to so many gossip and shopping sites. A large frothy coffee sits cooling beside me, the chocolate powder on the top melting into the milky foam. I've found one of those coffee chains where everyone is sitting with a half-drunk cup and a laptop, taking advantage of the free Wi-Fi. There's a message from Laura, though, and I click on that. She's travelling in Panama now and has sent an email with several attachments showing her bent under a huge backpack, grinning at the camera, a jungley greenness behind her, and some incredible views.

Missing you loads, she writes. *Can't wait to see you when I'm back. Hope you're enjoying your summer and are totally loved up with Adam. Hugs and kisses, Laura.*

I stare at it, wondering what to tell her. She thinks I'm still at home, working as a waitress during the day and hanging out with Adam in the evening. I've come so far from that, and something tells me that my own adventure is only just beginning. For a moment I consider writing it all down and telling her, but I'm not quite ready to share yet. My secret is too delicate and strange, and it doesn't quite exist in the real world. If I talk about it, maybe I'll inadvertently kill it.

I shiver with a sweet deliciousness as I recall the moment I had with Dominic last night. (Amazing how quickly he's become Dominic to me – the name Mr R seems ridiculous and childish now.)Just remembering that look, the strange and immediate intimacy sets everything in me swirling crazily, as though my innards are taking their own personal rollercoaster ride around my body. It's half pleasant and half unbearable.

But then . . . there is Vanessa. His girlfriend. The one I've seen him with and who was expecting him to meet her.

But he didn't tell her that we met in Soho, or that he stood her up for me.

That doesn't mean anything, you idiot.

Even so . . . a girl can dream, can't she?

I type out a quick message to Laura, saying how much fun she must be having and how I can't wait to see her and tell her everything that's been going on. As I'm writing, I see another message slip into my inbox, and when I've sent Laura's on its way, I click to see what it is. It's from james@ridinghousegallery. com. *Who?* For an instant I'm confused and then it all comes back. *Oh my God, my interview at the gallery.*

I open the email.

Dear Beth

It was a real pleasure to meet you yesterday. I saw some other candidates after you, and I have to admit that none of them had your enthusiasm or the certain something that makes me think we'd enjoy working together. If you're still interested, I'd love to talk about you taking the gallery assistant job over the summer. Let me know when it's a good time to chat and I'll give you a call.

I'll look forward to hearing from you,

Best wishes, James McAndrew

I stare at the message and read it three times over before it sinks in. James is offering me the job. *Oh wow! How fantastic.* I'm delighted, triumphant. So yesterday wasn't a total disaster – my new look paid off in one respect. I know I've fallen on my feet, finding a job in a proper gallery just like that.

Who knows where it might lead?

Quickly I send back a reply saying that I'm definitely still interested, and very keen to work for him. He can call me any time on my mobile. I've hardly sent it off when my phone, sitting on the table next to me, rings.

I sweep it up. 'Hello?'

'Beth, it's James.'

'Hi!'

'So, are you going to be my new assistant?' I can hear a smile in his voice.

'Yes, please!' I'm smiling broadly back.

'When can you start?'

'How about Monday?'

He laughs. 'You're certainly enthusiastic. Monday is great.' He tells me a little about the job and the salary – which is hardly more than I earn as a waitress but I suppose that's the reality of foot-on-the-ladder jobs – and says he's looking forward to seeing me on Monday. After thanking him profusely for the opportunity, I ring off feeling buoyed up and positive. Is London really starting to open its doors to me? I dash off a quick email to my parents telling them the good news and reassuring them that all is going well. Beyond the coffee shop window, golden sunlight is blazing down on the city.

My last days of freedom before I start working – I'd better go out and take advantage of it.

I finish my coffee, pack up my laptop and head back to the flat. After dumping my stuff, I head out to visit the National Gallery and some of the other must-sees on my list. Everything seems radiant and exciting. *It's amazing how a change of mood can affect everything.* The gallery is far too big to take in on one visit, so I go and see the twentieth-century European rooms to prepare for my new job, and then take in some magnificent Renaissance masterpieces to finish everything off with a huge dollop of dramatic scale and vivid richness.

Venturing back into Trafalgar Square, with its black lions sitting guard over the fountains, I think it's a crime to spend the rest of this summer day inside. I thread my way through the groups of tourists and visitors, and walk back to the flat where I collect my rug, sunglasses, a book, a bottle of water and some fruit. Then I head to the garden at the back of the building, and take my old place near the tennis courts. Dominic isn't there, the courts are empty, and I'm obscurely disappointed even though I told myself he'll be at work. I wonder what work he does. He was playing tennis during the day earlier in the week, so perhaps he has flexible hours. Who knows?

I lie down with my book and start to read, relishing the warmth of the sun on my limbs. No matter how I try to concentrate on my book, my thoughts keep drifting back to Dominic and that moment we shared last night. He must have felt it too, I'm sure of it. I recall the way he looked confused, baffled by the strength of the connection between us, as though he was thinking *this girl? But . . . that's not supposed to happen . . .*

I sigh luxuriously, putting my book down, my eyes closed, giving in to the recollection of his face, his eyes, his touch on my bare skin and the way it sent a juddering electric current flashing through me.

Beth.

I can hear his voice as clearly as if he's standing right beside me. It's hard not to thrill to the sound of it, deep, low and musical. I sigh and brush my hand over my chest, wishing he were really here.

'Beth?'

It's louder now, more questioning. I open my eyes and gasp. Dominic is right there, standing beside me, smiling down. 'Sorry to surprise you,' he says.

103

I sit up, blinking. 'I didn't expect to see you here.'

He's wearing jeans, loose fitting, and a white T-shirt. He looks adorable – the casual look suits him just as much as the business one. In his eyes is a curious, unreadable expression. 'I don't know why I'm here to be honest,' he says. 'I was working upstairs when I just had the strongest feeling I should come down to the garden and that I would find you here.' He spreads his hands out. 'And here you are.'

We gaze at one another, smiling, a little awkward but only in a superficial way. That connection from last night still fizzes between us.

'So, what are you doing?'

'Just sunbathing. Enjoying the gorgeous weather. Being wickedly lazy, really.'

He stands there, looking down at me. 'I've had enough of work for today. Would you like to come out with me? I know a fantastic pub near here with a garden, and they do a mean Pimms. I can't think of anything more wickedly lazy than being there, with you.'

'I'd love to.'

'Good. I can show you a bit of London that you might not find on your own. I'll just go upstairs and get a few things. Shall we meet by the door in twenty minutes?'

'Fabulous.' I beam up at him, feeling light and joyous.

Twenty minutes is just enough time to change from my shorts and T-shirt into my flowery summer dress, and slip off my plimsolls in favour of some sparkly flip-flops. After a moment's hesitation, I take a lacy shawl from a hook in Celia's cupboard and sling it around my shoulders. With my newly blonded hair gathered up in a ponytail and my sunglasses, I look a little bit sixties. I have a feeling Celia's shawl will bring me good luck, though I have no idea why. Would she want me to form some kind of relationship with her neighbour? Actually, something tells me she'd be delighted. I can almost hear her whispering, 'Go for it, Beth. Enjoy yourself! Why not?'

Dominic is waiting for me at the door to the building. He's also wearing sunglasses, square black Ray-Bans, and is reading a message on his phone, when he looks up and sees me. Instantly his face brightens with a huge smile and he tucks the phone into his jeans pocket. 'You're here. Wonderful. Let's get going.'

We talk easily as we stroll through the hot Mayfair streets. Dominic knows where we're going and I put myself entirely in his hands as we walk along quiet back routes, through cool alleys and into small hidden squares. People are sitting on the pavements in front of cafes and bars, windows and doors open to the slight breeze. Bright flowering baskets hang from brackets, bringing flourishes of scarlet and magenta to the facades. I love the feeling of walking beside him, as though we belong together, some of his glamour transferring itself to me – at least, that's what I like to think.

'Here we are,' Dominic says as we approach a pub. It's a traditional building and its exterior is a riot of climbing greenery and colourful blooms. He leads the way inside where it's clean and modern in a pared-down way, through the shady bar and out into a courtyard that's been transformed into a beautiful garden, with potted trees, tubs of flowers and wooden tables shaded by green umbrellas. A waitress comes out and Dominic orders a jug of Pimms. It arrives almost at once, the colour of cold tea, full of ice and fruit. Sliced strawberry, apple and cucumber, and sprigs of mint float in the frothy surface.

'It isn't summer without Pimms,' Dominic remarks, pouring out a tall glass for me, the ice and fruit plopping in with a satisfying sound. 'It's one of the things the English do best.'

'Sometimes, from the way you talk, it sounds like you're not English yourself,' I say shyly. 'Your accent is English but sometimes I think I can hear a vestige of something else.' I'm dying to know more about him. I take a sip of my Pimms. It's delicious: sweet and aromatic, fresh and tangy with mint. I've tasted it before, but none as nice as this. It's dangerous stuff, I can tell. There's hardly a hint of the alcohol I know is there.

'You're perceptive,' Dominic says, looking at me thoughtfully. 'I am English, as it happens, born right here in London. But my father was in the diplomatic corps and was constantly posted abroad, so right from my youngest days, I've moved around. I spent a good deal of my childhood in South-East Asia. We lived in Thailand for some years and then my father was sent to Hong Kong, which was great fun. But just when I was starting to take some interest in the world around me, I got sent back to England.' He makes a face, something like a grimace. 'Boarding school.'

'Didn't you like it? I've always thought that boarding sounds very romantic.' I remember how, when I was growing up, I longed to go to a boarding school and was thrilled by the idea of midnight feasts and dorms and all the rest of it. Being an ordinary pupil at the local school and walking home every day with my bag loaded with homework always seemed so dull in comparison to what went on in storybooks.

'It wasn't that.' Dominic shrugs. 'But there's always the distance, you see. Being put on a plane to go home for the holidays is all right. Being put on a plane to go back to school is about the most bloody thing you can imagine.'

I can see it in my mind: a small boy, trying hard not to cry, attempting to be brave, saying goodbye to his mother at the airport. He's taken away by a stewardess as his mother, proper in a hat and gloves, waves farewell. When she's out of sight, he can't stop a few tears escaping but he doesn't want the stewardess to see how much he cares. Then he's put into his seat to begin the long, lonely journey back to England. A stern-faced, big-bosomed matron, her grey hair in a tight bun, meets him at the airport and accompanies him back to school. I picture it as a forbidding place, out on a desolate moorland with nothing and no one for miles, just boys missing their mothers. Boarding school suddenly doesn't seem as romantic as once it did.

'Are you all right?'

Dominic is peering at me closely.

'Yes, yes, I'm fine.'

'You've got the most tragic look on your face, that's all.'

'I'm just thinking about you having to go back to school, missing home so much, being so far away . . .'

'It wasn't that bad once I got there. In many ways, I had a marvellous time. I shared a room with two other boys and we had our duvets from home and posters on the walls, our favourite books on the shelves. And I loved games and there was plenty of that. Most weekends I was playing rugby, football or cricket for the school.' He smiles with the memory. 'One thing you can say about English boarding schools is that they tend to be well equipped with swimming pools, tennis courts and art departments and whatever, and I made the most of it.'

The Dickensian gothic castle of misery in my imagination disappears to be replaced by a kind of cheerful holiday camp. Boarding school sounds brilliant again.

He goes on. 'But much as I loved my school, when it came to university, I decided I wanted to spread my wings. So I went abroad.'

'Back to Hong Kong?'

He shakes his head. 'No. I decided to go to the States. I went to Princeton.'

I've heard of that. It's one of the best American universities, like our Oxford and Cambridge. The Ivy League, that's it. 'Did you enjoy it?'

He smiles. 'I had an amazing time.'

As he speaks, I can hear the faintest American twang in his voice, as though the memory of Princeton has brought back some of the accent he picked up there but was rubbed away by the London years.

'What did you study?' I sip my Pimms again. A piece of strawberry bobs against my lips and I open my mouth and let it sit on my tongue. It's deliciously flavoured by the drink. I eat it slowly while I imagine a younger Dominic, sexy in an American-preppy outfit, sitting in a lecture theatre taking notes as a professor talks animatedly about . . .

'Business,' Dominic says.

. . . business. The professor is enthusiastic about his subject and Dominic is now wearing a pair of dark-framed glasses that make him look like a particularly gorgeous version of Clark Kent. He's concentrating hard, frowning slightly so that his glasses sit in the furrow on the bridge of his nose. While he carefully notes down his professor's words of wisdom on the nature of large corporations and the function of regulation, a nearby girl is staring with unashamed longing, unable to concentrate because his nearness is sending her nerve ends into a shivering orbit . . .

I move unconsciously, my mouth opening slightly as I imagine what she must be feeling. Something a little like I'm feeling now maybe. One of my legs moves against the other, the warm skin tingling under its own touch.

'Beth? What are you thinking?'

'Uh . . .' I spring back to the moment. He's leaning forward, his black eyes glittering with amusement. 'Nothing. I was just . . . thinking.'

'I'd love to know what about.'

Heat creeps up my face. 'Oh, nothing really.' I curse my vivid imagination, it's always doing that, pulling me into another universe that seems so real I can almost touch it.

He laughs gently.

'So what did you do after Princeton?' I ask hastily, hoping he's not psychic. *That would be really embarrassing*.

'I did a year's postgraduate study at Oxford, and I made some connections there that brought me into the job I'm currently doing. I spent a couple of years in a hedge fund first, getting some practical experience of finance.'

'How old are you?'

'I'm thirty-one.' He looks wary. 'How old are you?'

'Twenty-two. I'm twenty-three in September.'

He looks faintly relieved. I guess that he suddenly worried that I might be one of those girls who look old for their age.

I take another sip of my Pimms, and Dominic does the same. We are so easy in one another's company, despite the fact that everything we say reveals what strangers we actually are.

'So what is your job?' I ask. I guessed it must be something in money, something that could make a man so comparatively young able to live in Mayfair. Unless he inherited something, of course.

'Finance. Investments,' he says vaguely. 'I work for a Russian businessman. He has a great deal of money and I help him to manage it. It takes me all over the world, but it's mostly based here in London, and it's very flexible. If I need to take an afternoon off – like today' – he smiles at me – 'then I can.'

'It sounds interesting,' I say, though I'm still really none the wiser about what he does. The fact is, anything Dominic did would be fascinating to me.

'That's enough about me, I'm very dull. I want to know a bit more about you. For instance – does your boyfriend mind you being here in London on your own?'

I have the feeling he's being mischievous with me, enjoying my discomfort as my treacherous cheeks burn scarlet again. 'I'm single, actually,' I say awkwardly.

He raises his eyebrows. 'Really? I'm surprised.'

It's hard to tell if he's teasing me or not – those dark eyes can be rather opaque. I hope I don't sound like I'm offering my single status as an invitation. I'd be mortified if he thought that. Besides, he's taken. As soon as I think that, I wonder if this is my chance to find out more on that particular topic.

'So,' I say, hoping my face is cooling down a little, 'how long have you and Vanessa been together?'

Immediately I worry that I've gone too far somehow. His expression closes, as though all emotion has been shut off. The friendly openness vanishes, replaced by something cold and blank.

'I'm sorry,' I stammer, 'I've been rude. I didn't think . . .'

111

Then, it's as though a switch is turned back on. The coldness disappears and it's the Dominic I've come to know sitting across from me, though his smile seems just a little forced. 'Not at all,' he says. 'Of course you haven't been rude.'

I'm swamped with relief.

'I just wondered what made you think she and I are together.'

'Well, you know . . . she had that air about her, like you and she are very close, very familiar, like a girl-friend and boyfriend would be . . .' *Oh God, I'm so clumsy at expressing myself when it's important.*

After a moment's pause, he says, 'Vanessa and I aren't together. We're just very good friends.'

I get a flashback of the private members' club. I know they went there together. They must be very good friends indeed to go to a place like that. I still can't quite reconcile what I saw there with Dominic's outwardly normal demeanour. It's a mystery I file away for later.

He looks at the table and runs his finger along its smooth wooden surface. He says slowly, almost thoughtfully, 'I won't lie to you, Beth. Vanessa and I were together once. But it was a while ago. We're just friends now.'

I remember the way she walked in last night. She didn't even knock. She has her own key. Are they really just friends? 'Okay.' My voice is small and shy. 'I didn't mean to pry, Dominic.'

'I know. It's fine. Listen.' He evidently wants to

change the subject. 'Let's have another drink here and then I'm going to take you out for dinner. Okay?'

'Well . . .' I wonder what the correct form is. I can't let a man I hardly know take me out, can I? 'That would be very nice but I'll pay for myself, of course.'

'We'll talk about that later,' he says in such a way that I guess he isn't going to let me. But I don't care. All that matters is that I've got the whole evening with Dominic to myself, and unless something very strange happens, there's absolutely no worry that Vanessa will march in and take over.

I sigh happily and say, 'At least let me get the next round.'

'You're on,' Dominic replies with a smile, and I get up to order the drinks.

It's the most blissful evening. I love being close to Dominic, feasting my eyes on his dark good looks. Not only does he make me happy just looking at him but he also seems genuinely interested in me. It makes me think that perhaps I wasn't as happy with Adam as I've led myself to believe. Before we split, Adam hadn't made any effort with me at all. When I got back from uni, it was obvious that he expected me to fit into the life he had made for himself and his circle of friends, a life of the pub, television, beer and takeaways.

As we sit together in that pretty pub garden, the late afternoon sun sinking into a golden evening, Dominic says, 'So, Beth – what are your dreams for the future?'

'I'd love to travel,' I say. 'I've hardly gone anywhere. I want to expand my horizons.'

'Really?' His expression is unreadable but there's the hint of something dangerous in the way his black eyes glitter. 'We'll have to see what we can do about that.'

My stomach swoops. What does he mean? I swallow quickly and try to think of something amusing to say, but as I chatter on about countries I'd like to visit, the excitement burning inside doesn't die down.

As the alcohol floats through my bloodstream, I begin to relax properly and the last vestige of my shyness melts away. I make jokes, telling Dominic about life at home and some of the more ridiculous stories about my time as a waitress. He laughs uproariously as I describe some of the local eccentrics who frequent the cafe and their general craziness.

When we leave the pub and walk to the restaurant, I'm so enraptured by the way I'm amusing him that I don't have a clue where we're going. It's not until we're sitting at another outdoor table, this one under a canopy of vines, and the smell of barbecued meat makes me realise how hungry I am, that I become aware we're at a Persian restaurant, with a bottle of chilled white wine on the table and a salad of deliciously fresh vegetables and herbs, a plate of hummus, and some flat bread hot from the oven, in front of us. It's all wonderful, and we both start eating hungrily. I'm already stuffed by the time the next course arrives: aromatic grilled lamb, more of the incredibly fresh salad and rice that looks plain but tastes fantastic, sweet and salty at the same time.

As we talk over dinner, our conversation becomes a little more personal. I tell Dominic about my brothers and my parents, and what it was like growing up in my small hometown, and why I was drawn to the history of art. He tells me that he is an only child, and describes something of what it was like to be brought up in a culture of servants and nannies.

In the atmosphere of confession, it feels natural to tell him a little about Adam. Not much – I don't mention that terrible night and the ghastly sight of Adam and Hannah together – but enough so that he understands that my first big relationship has recently come to an end.

'It's a tender time,' he says gently. 'It's one of the sad things we all have to go through. It feels like the end of the world at the time, but things do get better, I promise.'

I gaze at him. The wine and the intoxicatingly beautiful evening have made me brave. 'Was it like that when you finished with Vanessa?'

He's startled and then laughs, but not easily. 'Well . . . it was different. Vanessa and I were not one another's first love, or childhood sweetheart, or whatever you want to call it.'

I press on, leaning towards him. 'But you ended it?'

There is a glimpse of that shutter that I'm learning can fall so easily over Dominic's face, but it doesn't quite drop. 'We agreed to end it. That we were better off as friends.'

'So . . . you fell out of love with each other?'

'We discovered that we weren't as . . . compatible . . . as we'd thought we were, that's all.'

I frown. What does that mean?

'We had different needs.' Dominic looks over his shoulder for the waiter and gestures for the bill. 'Really there's no big story. We're friends now, that's all.'

I realise he's getting just a tiny bit tetchy and the last thing I want is for this intimate, almost romantic evening to be spoiled.

'Okay.' I think of how I can change the subject. 'Oh, I got myself a job today.'

'You did?' He looks interested.

'Uh huh.' I tell him about the Riding House Gallery and he's clearly thrilled for me.

'That's great, Beth! Those jobs are really hard to get, the competition is intense. So you'll be busy from now on, will you?'

'No more lying in the garden for me,' I say with mock despair, 'not during working hours anyway.'

'I'm sure there'll still be time for fun,' he says, and his eyes twinkle while a dark eyebrow raises. Before I can ask him what he means, the waiter has appeared with the bill, and Dominic is paying it, waving away the offer of my debit card.

It's almost dark as we walk back through the streets towards Randolph Gardens. The air is rich with the smell of a summer city night: the fragrance of flowers, the scent of cooling asphalt, the dry dust of the day blowing in the evening breeze. I feel so happy. My gaze slides to Dominic.

I wonder if he feels as blissed out as I do? I suppose there's no reason why he should. It's just dinner with a girl who's around for the summer, providing a bit of novelty distraction from the hedge fund business, or whatever it is he does.

In my heart, I wish that it's not just that, but I don't want to get my hopes up.

As we get closer to home, the atmosphere between us becomes more charged. After all, this is such a romantic thing to do, returning home together after a delicious meal and wine. Surely it should end with something like . . .

I can hardly dare to think of it.

A kiss.

After all, he's single, he's told me himself. And he's straight because he went out with Vanessa. And . . . surely I can't be alone in feeling the chemistry between us?

We're in Randolph Gardens now. Dominic stops at the bottom of the steps and I stand next to him. Once we're through the door, nothing can happen. The porter will be there, watching, putting an effective stop on any unexpected goodnight embraces.

I turn to look at him, my face tipped up towards his, aware of the breeze gently lifting strands of my hair. *Now, now,* I'm urging him, desperate, longing for a touch of that beautiful mouth on mine.

He's staring down at me, his gaze moving over my

face as though he's memorising it. 'Beth,' he says in a low murmur.

'Yes?' I hope the yearning isn't too obvious in my voice.

There's a long pause. He moves fractionally towards me and I'm filled with a dark excitement. *Is this it? Please, Dominic, please* . . .

'I'm busy tomorrow,' he says at last, 'but would you like to spend Sunday together?'

'I would love that,' I breathe.

'Good. Me too. I'll pick you up around twelve and we'll do something.'

He stares at me just long enough to make me wonder if it's going to happen, then he bends quickly and brushes my cheek with his lips. 'Good night, then, Beth. Let me see you to the lift.'

'Good night,' I whisper, not sure how I'm going to deal with the geyser of desire that's just exploded inside me. 'And thank you.'

His dark eyes are inscrutable. 'You're very welcome. Sleep well.'

If I can sleep at all, it will be a miracle, I think, as we go inside.

CHAPTER SEVEN

In the event, I sleep very well, no doubt because of the excitement coupled with the wine. I dream a hectic, exciting dream where Dominic and I are at a party. There are people in glittering masks everywhere, and I keep losing him in the crowd, spotting him and trying to get to him, knowing that if I can only reach him, something beautiful will happen. After hours of trying to catch him, I finally find him and just as he is about to sink his lips on mine, I wake up, flustered.

I wonder if I should go back to that shop and ask the lady to sell me one of her vibrators so that I can work off some of this frustration that's plaguing me, but before I can do anything to sort it out on my own, De Havilland comes in, jumps on the bed and starts clawing at me to get his breakfast for him. By the time I've done that, the moment has passed.

I decide that today I'll go shopping for something to wear for my new job and set off towards the main streets. But it's a very different experience to the delightful personally tailored day I enjoyed earlier in the week. On a sunny Saturday, Oxford Street is packed with people and in the shops, the assistants are hot and hassled despite the air-con. It takes hours to find anything and by the time I return with my purchases, I'm feeling as harried as the assistants looked. Randolph Gardens feels like a haven of tranquillity compared to the throng of humanity I've had to fight through. Not for the first time, I bless Celia for providing me with such a lovely place to live in. I might have been at the mercy of buses and underground trains, sharing a cramped house miles away from the centre, or in a lonely bedsit somewhere. Instead, I've got an oasis of calm to enjoy.

And, I remind myself as I unwrap my new things, I've also got tomorrow to look forward to.

As well as the sensible skirt and shirts I've bought for my job, I couldn't help getting something a little more exciting for whatever Dominic and I are going to do tomorrow. It's a dress, demure with its pink-and-navy painterly print and silken fabric, but sexy in the way it's belted in tight at the waist, and in the way the cap sleeves fall in ruffles over my upper arms. The boat neck drops just enough to hint at the beginning of a cleavage.

I put it on and admire the reflection in the mirror. Yes, I think this is just the thing. And I've spotted a vintage-looking straw hat in Celia's wardrobe which will go with it wonderfully. Satisfied, I take it all off again and have a long soak in the bath to get rid of the city dust. Afterwards, when I'm wearing a silk robe from the back of Celia's bathroom door and wandering about the apartment, doing odds and ends, I don't consciously decide to leave the lights off in the sitting room but somehow I allow the dusk to invade and darken the room anyway. My gaze constantly slides to the dark square opposite, where I hope at any moment to see Dominic. I want to see it burst into golden light so that I can revel in the familiar sight of him moving about. I'm desperate to see him. I've been aware of him throughout the day, sometimes even talking to him in my imagination. Now I'm hungry to see him again.

I have my supper – a simple pasta dish with artichokes, peppers and goat's cheese that I picked up in a deli on the way home – give De Havilland some of the attention he wants, and then sit down on the sofa with a few of Celia's fashion books on my lap and a glass of wine beside me. I don't usually drink alone and it feels very grown up to sip the cold, flinty liquid while I turn the pages.

I manage to lose myself in the photographic history of Dior and the New Look and it's some time before I look up again, but when I do, I gasp.

The flat opposite is lit, at last. The lamps on the side tables have been switched on, I can see them glowing. For the first time, though, I cannot see inside. The blinds are still up, but the diaphanous curtains, unnoticed when I was in the flat, have been pulled across the entire length of the window. The effect is to create a room of silhouettes, slightly distorted and oddly sized but still recognisable. I can make out the furniture, the table and chairs. Everything has a different character when seen this way: something quite ordinary can appear exotic and unusual. I see a strange shape, a low rectangle with thrusting upward spikes, like an animal lying on its back with spindly legs in the air, and it takes a moment before I remember that it is the low seat I noticed when I was there.

I get up and move quietly and slowly over to the window. I'm sure that I'll be invisible to the flat opposite, and whoever is there certainly couldn't hear me, but I'm careful just the same.

Two shapes come into the room. One is a woman and one a man, that much is obvious, but it's impossible to know who, although the man must be Dominic. They are black shadows against the white veil of the curtains, walking about, sitting down, moving easily. There must be a window open somewhere, for the curtain shifts and moves as if in a breeze, which further distorts the shadows. It hangs still for a while, allowing me to get a fix on what I'm seeing, and then it wrinkles and billows, and I lose sight of them.

'Goddamn it!' I say under my breath. 'Stay still!'

It's unbearably tantalising, to know that Dominic is there with someone. Who is it? It must be Vanessa, that's who it's always been in the past. But the shadows are so undefined, I simply can't make out whether it's her or not. I know it's a woman because I can see her outline and the shape of her dress, but everything else is vague. It's very frustrating.

De Havilland has woken up and jumps up onto the windowsill beside me. He sits down, curls his tail around his feet, blinks and watches some pigeons fluttering about from the roof to the trees. Then he sticks out a paw and starts cleaning it. I wish I could be so serene and calm, but I'm glued to the action opposite, trying to make out what's going on over there.

Am I jealous? Of course I am!

Nothing that's happened between Dominic and me has gone further than a date, but even so I can't help a feeling of raw possessiveness flood through me. Last night we had dinner and talked and he told me it was over with Vanessa. So why is there a woman in his apartment with him?

But . . . I never asked him whether he was seeing anyone else.

The thought hits me like a bucket of icy water, and I gasp. What an idiot I am to assume he must be single. When I virtually begged him to kiss me at the end of the evening, lifting my face towards him, my lips parted hopefully, I'd thought the tension between us was sexual, but maybe it was just awkward embarrassment on his part, as he realised I have a massive crush on him.

Perhaps he's telling her all about it right now.

'Yes, she's sweet enough but I think I've been a little unwise,' he's saying, as he pours his companion a glass of ice-cold champagne. 'She obviously thought I was going to kiss her last night. I hardly knew what to do, so I gave her a peck on the cheek. I offered to take her out tomorrow – she's a girl on her own, I thought she'd like someone to show her around. I was just being friendly, but I'm worried now that I'm leading her on.'

His girlfriend laughs as she takes the glass. 'Oh Dominic, you're too kind-hearted for your own good! You might have known that a naive little thing like that would fall in love as soon as look at you!'

He's bashful. 'Perhaps . . .'

'Oh, come on, darling. You're rich, successful and handsome – she's going to think you're her Prince Charming if you so much as smile at her.' She leans forward, her perfectly made-up lips in a knowing pout. 'Put her out of her misery, darling. Tell her you're very sorry, but tomorrow's off.'

'Maybe you're right . . .'

I'm gasping at the vindictiveness of this mystery woman, boiling with anger and ready to go over and defend myself, when there is a change in what is happening behind the curtain. The breeze drops for a while and I can see more clearly. The people behind the curtain look different somehow, and I realise that the man – Dominic – is now naked, or wearing very little, at least. I can tell from his outline that his torso is bare. I can't tell whether the woman is dressed or not, but if she is, she is wearing something very figure-hugging. Her silhouette is smooth but perfectly defined. The shapes are close together, examining something, as far as I can tell.

My anger at the imaginary conversation disappears. My heart is racing but now it's with horrified apprehension. *He's naked? But why?*

Why would a man be naked with a woman? You don't even need three guesses. One is going to do it.

Unless it's massage . . . ? I think hopefully. *Yes, maybe that's it. Maybe it's a massage.*

Certainly their behaviour doesn't seem to indicate they're about to start making wild love to one another. They seem to be calmly discussing something. Then, abruptly, the atmosphere between the two figures changes. I sense it immediately. The man kneels down and bends his head before the woman. She towers over him, her hands on her hips and her nose haughtily in the air. She's saying something. She begins to walk around him, circling him, but he doesn't move. This goes on for some minutes. My breathing is shallow and I stay stock still as I watch them, wondering what the hell they're doing, and what's going to happen next.

I don't have to wait too long. The woman goes over to the curious seat and sits down on it. The man goes onto his hands and knees and crawls over to her, whereupon she speaks to him, her attitude stern and unbending. He's at her feet. She puts out a foot and he obediently leans forwards and seems to touch his mouth to it. Then she picks something up from the side table. She holds it out to him. It's the shape of a hand mirror, with a long handle and an oval top. He leans forward again and does the same thing, putting his lips to whatever it is.

Is he kissing it?

I can't even frame my thoughts. All I can do is watch.

The next moment he has dropped at her feet again but now he has clasped her legs and appears to be crawling up her. He lays himself out across her lap, so

125

that his back is across her thighs, his shoulders, neck and head drop down on one side of her, and his bottom is exposed to her right hand.

She takes up the implement and, in a soft, almost gentle movement, she brings it down. He stays completely still. A moment later, she repeats the action, bringing the implement down with a sure, steady movement. She does it several more times.

Okay, I'm not imagining this. She's spanking him. She's spanking him with a hairbrush or something.

My mouth has gone dry, my thoughts are whirling. From this distance, I can't make out everything that is happening, especially when the breeze makes the curtains flutter and obscure my view, but it is still the strangest thing I've ever seen. From my perspective it seems ridiculous: a grown man, bending his great body over a woman's knees and allowing her to smack him over and over again. I've heard vaguely of such practices but they're the stuff of jokes, aren't they? Or enjoyed by whimpering upper-class inadequates who've never gotten over being punished by Nanny or caned by the science master. But that sort of thing doesn't happen any more. And not to men like Dominic – rich, handsome, powerful . . .

I'm confused, suddenly almost tearful. What's he doing over there? The spanking is moving up a notch, I can tell that. The woman is developing a rhythm and her strokes are growing in force. I can almost hear the steady thwack as she brings her paddle down. It must hurt and hurt horribly. How can anyone stand it voluntarily? What kind of person wants *that*, for goodness' sake?

Things change again, quite suddenly. The man is pushed off her knee, and she opens her legs. He kneels between them, so that this time he is leaning over her left knee, with his feet tucked behind her right leg. She is picking up a fresh implement, a larger, flatter one. Now she starts her work again, bringing the paddle down hard on the cheeks of his bottom. Each time it hits, it looks like a castanet and I realise there are two flat heads slapping together when they land. They must cause an incredibly painful, stinging sensation as he absorbs each blow, but still he doesn't move, lying prone and accepting the punishment. He seems to be clutching her left thigh in absolute surrender to what she's doing. For at least twenty minutes she hits him with a regular, almost clocklike rhythm; I can hear the blows in my mind as she raises and beats, raises and beats.

Then it changes again; he rolls to the floor and lies there, while she gets up and walks around. She must be stiff, I expect, from his weight leaning on her. She is speaking again. The man raises himself up onto the seat and lies down on his stomach, one leg on either side. He lifts his arms and puts them on the two strange spiky rests I noticed when I first saw it. So that's what they're for. That's why there are two on the same side of the chair.

The woman stalks over to him, picks up some scraps of cloth from the side table – scarves? – and swiftly binds his wrists to the armrests. Then, from the table, she picks up another tool. This time it is a long strap, like a belt except that I cannot see a buckle on it. She swishes it through the air a few times, no doubt creating a whistling sound for the added torment of her victim. I know what's coming next and I can hardly bear to watch it, but somehow I can't stop myself. The length of the leather flicks upwards and then comes down hard on the exposed buttocks of the man on the stool. Once, twice, three times, and on she goes, whipping with a steady hand. I can only imagine what the bite of that leather into the skin must feel like – and when that skin has already been tortured with other instruments, it must be close to unbearable. Surely he must be near to passing out, or going mad with agony.

Should I call the police? The thought flashes into my mind and I look over at the telephone. What would I say? *Emergency, a woman is beating a man in the apartment opposite mine, you must stop her!* But he clearly wants it. Is it illegal to beat the shit out of someone if they want you to?

Something tells me calling the police would be the wrong move. It's obvious the man could stop this at any time if he wanted – at least, he could have before his hands were tied. He is consenting.

I close my eyes, aghast. *Dominic – is this what you want?* I remember that he went to boarding school. Maybe, when he was boy, he was beaten by someone and it started this incomprehensible desire in him. It's not much of a theory, but it's all I've got.

When I open my eyes, the breeze has sprung up and the sheer curtains are moving so much that the figures behind it become an indiscernible blur.

I'm grateful for it. I don't want to watch any more. I've seen enough.

I have no idea how I'm going to face Dominic tomorrow, after what I've witnessed.

THE SECOND WEEK

CHAPTER EIGHT

The next morning, I'm ready for Dominic when he knocks at the door at midday. The sun is bright in the sky overhead and it's another hot summer's day. I can't remember when it last rained, and the radio news this morning talked of possible drought precautions if the dry spell continues much longer.

Worrying about the weather is the last thing on my mind as I open the door to him. He looks fresh in a white linen shirt, light-brown shorts and a pair of white sandshoes. His eyes are hidden behind his black Ray-Bans, but he smiles broadly when he sees me.

'Oh, wow, you look gorgeous.'

I do a little twirl. 'Thank you. I hope it's all right for whatever we're doing today.'

'It's just right. Now, let's get going. I have a packed schedule for us.'

He seems in a good mood as we take the lift down to the ground floor but as I see the reflection of his back in the mirror, I can't help wondering what lies beneath that clean, cool linen shirt. Are the marks of the belt across his back? And his buttocks – are they bruised and sore from the hard punishment he got last night?

Don't think like that, I tell myself sternly. *You don't know that it was him.*

Then who was it? says a voice in my head. *It's his apartment, for goodness' sake. Of course it was him.*

I've been fretting over it all night, wondering what it could mean. What I didn't see was any sex. The man and woman appeared not to be involved in that kind of relationship at all. It seemed to be all about the giving and receiving of a severe beating, and that in itself was baffling me. In the night, as I lay thinking about it, I'd decided that the best thing to do was put it out of my mind and enjoy the day with Dominic. If the opportunity arose when broaching this kind of subject with him wasn't out of place or embarrassing – well, things would certainly have changed between us.

In fact, the minute we are together, the whole shadow play that I witnessed last night becomes dream-like and unreal. I can almost believe that I imagined it. The faceless man straddled over the stool with his wrists bound has nothing to do with the warm, handsome flesh-and-blood person standing next to me, his nearness making my skin prickle with excitement. A gorgeous summer's day spent with Dominic. I can't imagine anything more wonderful.

We walk to Hyde Park and as we approach it, I remember looking out at it on my first day in London. That Beth seems like a different person now, I think. Here I am, in a pretty silk dress and a vintage designer straw hat, walking beside an incredibly sexy man, about to be spoiled and entertained. My life has improved so much. And I've hardly thought about Adam for days.

'Do you know this park?' Dominic asks, as we enter by one of the gates.

I shake my head.

'It has lots of hidden treasures, and I intend to show some of them to you.'

'I can't wait.'

We smile at each other.

Just concentrate on the moment. Enjoy it. This may never happen again.

The park is huge and we walk a good way before I see the pale blue glitter of water, and then a boathouse with rows of little green boats with white interiors and blue pedalos in front of it.

'Oh wow,' I breathe.

'This is the Serpentine Lake, laid out for the pleasure of Queen Caroline. Now we all get to enjoy it.'

He has everything in hand and within a few minutes, I'm settled in one of the little rowing boats, my back to the prow so that I can face Dominic, who takes the oars, and begins to strike out into the middle of the lake.

'So all this is manmade?' I look at the great stretch of water, as long and snakelike as its name suggests, and the arched stone bridge spanning it in the distance.

'Yes.' A smile twitches Dominic's lips. 'The most effective pleasures often are. Nature gives us the pattern, and then we learn how to improve on it. And thanks to the whims and foibles of various monarchs, we get to enjoy all this.'

He pulls easily on the oars, obviously well practised at it, lifting the blades out of the water, smoothing them over the surface, then dipping them in with a clean motion and pulling back. We glide across the surface with only the faintest jerk when he puts his weight behind the oars. I put my hand over the side and dip my fingertips into the cold water.

'Do you know much about this place?'

'I always make a point of learning about the places I live,' he says. 'And the history of London is particularly fascinating. There's so much of it, for one thing, the place is drenched in it. It was Charles I who opened this park to the public – up until then it had been reserved strictly for royal use. And lucky he did. Half of London turned up here when the great plagues hit the city. They hoped to escape infection.'

I look out over the well-kept grassland, rather dry and yellow after the last rainless fortnight, with its beautiful trees and the elegant buildings visible at intervals. People sit outside a nearby cafe enjoying ice creams and cold drinks. I picture a vast crowd of poor seventeenth-century Londoners camping down in their thousands, living in desperate fear of sickness – there are squabbles and chatter, dirt and stenches, children and mob-capped women in grubby aprons trying to cook over open fires while men smoke pipes and plan how to keep their families alive.

On the sunny shore, there is a family, the mother

pushing an expensive buggy with a baby in it, the father trying to anoint his daughter with sun cream while she does her best to break free and escape on her pink micro scooter.

Different times, different troubles.

I turn my attention back to the boat. It's such a pleasure to watch Dominic row. The muscles on his arms bulge as he exerts his strength on the oars and as he leans forward, the white linen shirt falls open a little. I can see a patch of dark hair on his chest. The sight makes my heart quicken. I take a long breath and breathe out slowly. I have to keep control. I don't want him to know the effect he has on me, so I look away, hoping to hide my involuntary response to his nearness, his magnetic effect on me and the way he churns me up. As I trail my fingers in the cooling water, I become aware that he's watching me too. I can see from the edge of my vision that behind his sunglasses his eyes are on me. Perhaps he thinks I can't see that he's watching. The effect on me is electric; it's as though his very gaze has a laser-like quality and can burn my skin. The feeling is so incredibly intense, both pleasurable and almost painful at the same time, that I don't want it to end. For ages he rows on, pulling hard on the oars and we glide over the lake. Then he asks me if I'd like a turn, and the tension breaks.

'I don't think so,' I say, laughing. 'I'm not as strong as you.' I can't resist looking at him flirtatiously and saying, 'Do you work out a lot?'

'I keep myself in shape,' he replies. 'I don't like to let

myself go. I spend a lot of time sitting at a desk, I need to make sure I stay active too.'

'At the gym?'

He fixes me with an impenetrable look, those dark eyes looking almost black again. 'Wherever I can,' he says in a low voice, and the meaning he injects into it sends a delicious shiver down my spine. For the first time I begin to blossom under his gaze. Something about today is different. This isn't just a man taking a girl out as a gesture of friendship. I feel like a woman he desires and realise with a thrill of pleasure that this day already has a kind of tension to it, the kind that keeps everything buzzing and alive.

'I'm bushed,' Dominic says. A line of tiny sweat beads have broken out across his forehead and nose. I want to wipe them away with my fingertip but I resist the urge. Instead he takes off his sunglasses and wipes them away himself. Then he puts the oars straight in their rowlocks, and lets us drift for a while in the blazing sunshine. We sit in companionable silence and then he says, 'Well, I don't know about you, but I've worked up quite an appetite. Lunch?'

'That sounds fantastic.'

'Good. Then let's get back.' He sets the oars to the water again and pulls for the shore. It takes all his effort and he doesn't speak, allowing me the luxury of watching him at work. His rhythmic movements are setting off a memory inside me. Adam appears in my mind. His image, once so sharp and agonising in its clarity, is now strangely faded. It's as though I can hardly remember him. I recall that I used to feel something for him, but that all seems like a very long time ago. What I can't remember is him ever making me feel one fraction of this incredible desire. Our lovemaking was sweet and sincere and romantic, but it was never as tremblingly exciting as simply watching Dominic row. What would it be like if he actually touched me? It's an overwhelming thought that makes my groin heat and throb. I shift almost uncomfortably.

'Are you all right?'

I nod and say nothing, and Dominic, his dark eyes resting thoughtfully on me, says nothing more. Fortunately I manage to get control of myself as we reach the shore and return the little boat. The man at the kiosk says to Dominic: 'Your delivery arrived, sir. It's been laid out according to your instructions.'

'Thank you.' Dominic turns to me with a smile. 'Shall we?'

He leads me across the grass to a huge oak tree with spreading branches providing a circle of cool shade. Beneath it, on a pale plaid rug, has been laid out a fabulous picnic. A waiter stands protectively next to it, evidently waiting for our arrival.

'Dominic!' I turn to him with shining eyes. 'This is wonderful!'

As we approach, I can make out what awaits us: poached salmon, fabulous salads flecked with the jewel-bright colours of tomatoes, peppers and pomegranate seeds, pink tiger prawns in their shell, small speckled quails' eggs, a dish of glistening yellow mayonnaise, slices of rare roast beef, a melting brie and fresh baguettes. There are elegant dessert glasses full of something fruity and creamy. An ice bucket contains a bottle of what looks like champagne. It is all picture perfect.

The waiter bows to Dominic as he approaches. 'Everything is ready, sir.'

'It looks excellent. That will be all, thank you.' With a deft and discreet movement, he tips the waiter, who bows again and makes a subtle exit. We are left alone with the feast.

'I hope you're hungry,' he says to me, smiling warmly.

'Ravenous,' I reply happily, and sit down on the rug.

'Good. I like to see you eat. You've got a good appetite, I like that.' He pulls the bottle from the ice bucket. It is Dom Pérignon Rosé, which I know is a famous make of champagne. He pops the cork quickly and easily, and pours the foaming liquid into two waiting glasses.

He passes one to me, then lifts his own and says, 'To an English summer's day. And to the beautiful girl I'm spending it with.'

I turn red but I laugh, lifting my glass to his and meeting his eyes, and we both sip the fizzing liquid.

Could anything be more perfect than this?

We eat our fill of the delicious picnic and afterwards, sated and rather drunk on the fine pink champagne, we stretch out on the rug, and talk quietly. Dominic has picked up a piece of grass and is chewing it thought-fully. I watch him through half-closed eyelids. My whole body is alive to his nearness, but something is struggling to the surface of my consciousness, some-thing I don't want to think about but which I can't stop invading my mind.

It's the image of the man lying prone on that strange seat in his apartment while Vanessa, bold and strong, thrashes him with a leather belt, letting the ends thwack over his buttocks, hitting the flesh over and over until it's red and raw . . .

'Beth . . .'

I jump slightly. 'Uh huh?' I turn to look at him. He's rolled on his side and is now very close to me. I can smell a sweet citrusy cologne on the warmth of his skin. My stomach swoops with excitement and my fingers begin to tremble.

He stares deeply into my eyes, as though searching out my soul. 'That night . . . that night I found you crying in the street because you were lost. I've been thinking about it. Was that all you were crying about? Because you were lost?'

My mouth drops open and then I can't hold his gaze. I look down at the pale checks of the rug. 'Not exactly,' I say in a low voice. 'I'd just tried to go into a bar. A strange place called The Asylum.'

When I look up, his eyes have gone cold. *God, why did I say that? It's crazy to mention that place – and now look what's happened . . . !*

'Why did you go in there?' he asks sharply.

141

'I . . . don't know . . . I saw some people go down there, so I followed . . .' *It's not a lie,* I tell myself firmly. *It's what happened.* 'But the doorman was furious with me. He told me it was a private members' club and that I had to get out.'

'I see.' Dominic frowns at the slender stalk of grass that he's rubbing between his thumb and forefinger.

'We don't have many private members' clubs where I come from,' I say, trying to sound jokey, 'so it never occurred to me I couldn't go in.'

'And . . . what did you see there?'

I take a deep breath and shake my head. 'Nothing. People drinking and talking. I was only there for a moment.' I want to tell him what I really saw and ask him what it meant, but I daren't. The shutters have already come down, and I desperately want them back up again. I want the warm, sexy atmosphere to be restored, the delicious anticipation that something might happen at any moment.

'Good,' he says in a low murmur. 'I don't know if it's a place for a girl like you. You're so sweet. So incredibly sweet.'

He reaches out and then, to my amazement, he puts his hand over mine and strokes his thumb over my skin, making me burn with his touch. He stares into my eyes and I can see a conflict going on there. 'I shouldn't, I really shouldn't.'

'Why not?' I whisper.

'You're too . . .' He sighs. 'I don't know . . .'

'Young?'

'No.' He shakes his head. I wish I could run my fingers through that dark hair. 'Age has nothing to do with it. I've met teenagers wise beyond their years, and forty-year-olds as naive as Snow White. It's not that.'

'Then what?' My whole voice is saturated with longing.

He threads his fingers through mine. The touch is almost unbearable. I can hardly fight the impulse to reach for his face and bring it to mine.

His voice drops even lower and his eyes can't meet my gaze. My heart is racing as he speaks. 'I don't let myself go very often, Beth. But there's something about you – something so fresh and wonderful, impetuous and inspiring. You make me feel alive.'

Everything in me is responding to his words. I can hardly breathe.

'I haven't felt like this in a long time,' he says even more quietly. 'I'd forgotten how beautiful it is – and you've done that to me. But . . .'

Of course there's a but. Why is nothing ever simple? You just said I make you feel alive. But I daren't speak in case I break a spell.

'But . . .' He looks agonised.

'Are you worried I'll get hurt?' I say at last.

He shoots me a look that's impossible to read; then laughs with something like bitterness in his voice.

'I won't,' I say. 'I promise. I'm not here for long. Not long enough to get involved.'

Dominic lifts my hand to his mouth and presses it to his lips. The sensation is blissful, the most exciting kiss

I've ever had – and he hasn't even touched my mouth. He lifts his mouth away and turns his gaze to mine. 'Oh, we've got long enough, Beth. Believe me.'

Then it happens. He pulls me close to him and in an instant I'm in his embrace, pressed against the warmth of his chest, surrounded by his delicious smell and the strength of his arms. One hand is pressed to my shoulder, the other circles my lower back, as his lips meet mine. There's no question that I can do anything other than open my mouth to him. His lips are as delicious as I'd hoped but the kiss itself is more than I could have imagined: warm, deep, and all encompassing, so that I feel as though I'm drowning in the sensation of his tongue exploring my mouth. My body takes over, I have no conscious choice about what to do. My tongue meets his in the most exquisite touch. I know right away that I've never been kissed till now. This is the most perfect feeling of complete rightness, as though our mouths were meant to fit together.

My eyes are closed and I'm lost in darkness, aware only of the depth of our kiss, which is growing in intensity with every moment, and the way his hands press on my arms and back. As he kisses me, his hand moves down from the small of my back and over the curve of my bottom. He groans slightly as he touches me there.

At last, we pull apart. My breathing is coming fast and I know my eyes are shining. Dominic looks at me, his gaze burning with the intensity of what we've just shared.

'I've been wanting to do that since we first met,' he said with a smile.

'Since I dropped my ice cream?'

'Yes, then. I couldn't help noticing you. But it was afterwards as you lay on that rug in the garden – that's when I realised just how lovely you are.'

I feel awkward, embarrassed. 'Lovely? Me?'

'Of course.' He nods. I can hardly believe that some-one as gorgeous as he is would think me lovely. 'It's been hard to hold back, if I'm honest. And when I found you crying in the street, it was all I could do not to kiss you then and there.'

'I thought you were angry with me!' I say, laughing.

'No,' he says. He puts his hand under my chin and tips my face to his. 'My God, I'm really sorry, but I'm going to have kiss you again.'

He sinks his mouth on mine and once again the stars whirl in my head as I give myself over to the delicious sensation of his tongue caressing mine, the honeyed taste of his mouth and the sense of being utterly completed. We press against one another, pulling our embrace as tight as we can, and I can feel his hardness against my stomach. The manifestation of his desire is intensely exciting and my own desire floods my belly, making me throb and ache.

When we pull away this time, he says, 'I had some exciting activities planned for this afternoon, but I don't know how the hell I'm going to be able to do anything else but this.'

145

'Then let's just do this. Who says we can't?'

'We can't stay here all afternoon.' He clasps my hand again and stares hard at me. 'We could always go home . . . if you like . . .'

If I like? I can't think of anything I could possibly like more!

'Yes, please,' I say softly, the wanting clear in my voice.

We can read the desire in one another's faces and we leap to our feet. I gather up my hat and lace shawl. 'What about the picnic? Can we just leave it here?'

Dominic taps his phone briefly. 'They'll be here in about two minutes to take it away.'

'It was wonderful,' I say, hoping he's not reading my eagerness to be off as rejection of his day.

'Not as wonderful as what comes next,' he says, and my stomach clenches with that pleasurable pain that I've come to know so well lately.

I don't know how we get home so quickly, but in no time at all, we are in the lift on the way to Dominic's apartment. We kiss again, hot and passionate. I glimpse our reflections in the mirror: the way our bodies are entwined, our mouths pressed hungrily together – and it sends shivers of arousal shooting all over me. I want him desperately, my body screaming out for him, craving his touch.

My dazed mind wonders how far this is going to go, but I don't see how we can stop ourselves. The hunger that's possessing me seems to be even stronger in Dominic. He kisses me all over my neck, his dark stubble brushing against the soft skin, making me gasp at the sensation, before returning to my mouth. The lift doors are open for several seconds before we even notice.

'Come on,' he growls, pulling me through them and leading me towards the door of his flat. A moment later we are inside, the door shut behind us. At last we're absolutely private. My body is trembling all over with desire as we stumble towards the bedroom, unable to keep our hands off each other long enough to walk sensibly.

The bedroom is shadowed despite the bright sunshine outside. Dominic's bed is enormous, Emperor-sized, with a padded velvet headboard, immaculate white pillows and linen in a muted blue. A grey cashmere throw covers the foot.

Now that we're inside, he turns to me, his black gaze burning into me. I can read desire all over his face and it's unbearably exciting. I've never been looked at like that in my life.

'Is this what you want?' he asks huskily.

'Yes,' I reply, my voice coming out half as a sigh and half as an aching need. 'Oh my God, yes.'

He comes up close to me and searches my face intently. 'I don't know what you do to me . . . but I do know I can't fight it any more.' He moves his hands round to the back of my dress and slides his fingers over my shoulder blades as he finds the zip. Deftly, he pulls it down and I can feel my skin exposed as the dress falls open. With a quick movement, he unclips the belt that fastens behind, and now the dress slips gently down to the floor, leaving me standing there. I'm wearing simple underwear: a white bra with a lace edge and matching knickers, the front a demure white lace panel.

'You're so beautiful,' he says, smoothing a finger over my hip. 'Incredible.'

The extraordinary thing is that I feel beautiful: ripe and luscious and ready for him. More beautiful than I ever have before.

'I want you right now,' he whispers, and sinks his lips on mine, his tongue caressing my mouth as his hands roam over my body, across my back and over my bottom, where his hands linger for a while, savouring the full curves there.

'Your arse is made for me,' he murmurs against my lips. 'It's perfect.'

I can't help pressing it back against his palms, and he groans softly. He kisses a burning trail across my jaw and down my neck, then across my shoulder. It's my turn to moan now as his stubble grazes my skin. I'm desperate to touch him, to feel that warm brown skin under my fingertips and inhale his scent. I want to rip off his shirt and kiss the patch of dark hair on his dark chest, but he's now holding my arms firmly, stopping me from moving.

'My turn,' he whispers with a smile. 'Yours will come.'

Promises, promises . . . but oh God, this is divine . . .

His mouth is so tantalising, moving towards my breasts which are now rising and falling with my quickened breathing, but he's taking his time, kissing every inch of skin between my neck and the line of lace on my bra. My nipples have hardened and have become exquisitely sensitive as they strain against the cotton. I can't help lifting my head back, pushing my breasts forward, as, at last, his mouth reaches the edge of my bra. Then his fingers are there, those elegant, square-tipped fingers that hold so much promise of what they can do to me, pushing back the lace, letting my right breast escape from its confines, the nipple emerging hard and erect as though begging for the pull of his mouth on it. He moves slowly towards it, his tongue trailing over the soft curve until his lips meet it and he takes in his mouth. The effect makes me draw in a shivering breath, as a white-hot current flares out from my nipple and connects to my groin. I'm flooded by intense desire.

'Please,' I say beseechingly, 'please, I can't wait . . .'

He laughs and says teasingly, 'Patience, young lady, is a virtue.'

But I feel anything but virtuous: I'm lustful, abandoned, craving him, needing him. He's winding me so tightly, I can hardly bear it.

His other hand cups my left breast, his fingers tweaking my nipple through its fabric. My breathing is hot and heavy and I can't help small sighs escaping as the sensations of pleasure make my lids close and my mouth open.

I put my hands to his shoulders. 'Please, let me touch you,' I beg.

He gives my nipple a tug with his teeth, letting them graze over its tip, then pulls away. He takes a step back and looks at me, a smile curving his lips. Then he unbuttons his shirt, letting it drop to the floor. I marvel at the sight of his broad chest with its dark nipples, the brown skin and dark hair, the broad shoulders and the muscles of his upper arms.

Is this really for me?

He slides his feet from his shoes, and then all my attention is focused on his shorts. I can tell that he is hard but as he unbuttons his fly and takes them off, I gasp. His erection is incredible: beautiful in its smoothness, proud in its length, telling me frankly with its thick shaft how much he wants me.

Dominic takes a step towards me, his eyes hooded now with the power of his lust. He wraps his arms around me in an embrace and kisses me passionately. I can feel the rod of his erection between us, pressing against my belly. It's hot and hard, and my only thought is the incredible captivating need I have to feel him inside me.

He unclips my bra and it falls to the floor. My breasts press against his chest and at last I can wrap my arms around him, feeling the broad, smooth expanse of his back beneath my hands. I run my palms across it, savouring the feel of the muscled surface, and down over the hardness of his firm cheeks.

There's nothing there.

The thought pops into my mind unbidden. What do I mean? What is my subconscious telling me?

The beating you saw. There aren't any marks on him. You'd feel them.

Then it definitely wasn't him! I think with relief. *I don't know who it was, or why they were in his apartment, but it wasn't him . . .*

That thought releases something in me. My desire turns from something shivering and ecstatic into something that expresses a need I've never felt before. My arms wrap more tightly around him, my fingers scratch lightly on the surface of his skin, I let my face drop on his chest and run my teeth and tongue over his skin, biting gently at his flesh. I take his dark nipple into my mouth and tug on it.

'Christ,' he says, as I suck it, pulling it between my teeth. Then almost roughly, 'Do you want me to fuck you?'

There's a catch in his voice. I nod and let the small bud of his nipple slip from between my lips. It glistens from my saliva.

'Do you?'

'Yes!'

'Ask me . . .'

I've never said such a thing out loud, but I'm too far past caring about that. 'Yes, please, fuck me, I want you to so much . . .'

Suddenly, he releases his strength, lifting me up and carrying me to the bed as easily as if I weighed nothing at all, and putting me down so that I'm lying on my back,

151

my breast and belly exposed to him. The linen is cool beneath my heated skin.

He moves round to a small table, opens the door and takes out a condom packet. With a quick movement, he rips open the foil, removes the rubber disc and slides it down over his penis.

This is really going to happen.

I'm hungry for it, ready for it, desperate to feel him filling me up. He is back now, standing at the foot of the bed. He hooks his fingers under the rim of my knickers and begins gently to tug them down. As they reach my ankles and then are gone, he kneels down, gently parts my thighs and puts his lips to my small patch of pubic hair. I can feel myself opening like a flower as everything swells and fills with wet heat. I'm so needy, so eager. My body is begging for his.

'You're gorgeous,' he says in a low voice and the feel of his breath on my swollen clitoris makes me gasp and sigh. Then he runs his lips over its tip, letting his tongue drift over it, making it twitch in exquisite agony.

'I can't wait,' I pant. 'Please, Dominic . . .'

He lifts himself up and stands there for a moment, his magnificent cock rearing above me. Then he lowers himself onto me, pressing the hard shaft onto my clitoris, making me wriggle beneath him. His weight feels so good. My legs spread even wider to make it easier for him to enter me, my hips lifting up to meet him, and it all happens without my meaning it. My body is responding independently of my consciousness. All it knows is that it wants and needs his maleness, right now.

He pulls back a little and the tip of his penis is pressing at my entrance.

'Please, *please*,' I say, my voice almost a whimper, my eyes full of longing.

His own gaze is dark and intense. He's clearly savouring this moment and all of its deliciousness. I can feel my inner lips expanding with need, my body pulsing with excitement. I rise up slightly, reach out and put my hands on his firm backside, then pull him so that, at last, his shaft enters me, sliding in easily because I'm so wet but still moving with exquisite slowness, pushing forward to fill me up with a delicious sensation.

I moan and clutch at him as he pushes himself far inside me. There is a look of fierceness on his face, as though he's concentrating on holding himself back. He pushes hard into me, and my hips come up to meet him. I glory in the feeling of him pumping so deep into me. It's like nothing I've ever felt before. He's gathering speed now, and I'm finding my rhythm too, pushing up my hips and arching my back with every new thrust. Then he changes slightly, taking more of his weight on his knees, and slips his hands over the full cheeks of my bottom, grasping them and pulling me towards him. The sensation within me changes: it's sharper, more acute and makes me breathless every time he rams deep inside me. I gasp and cry out, and he squeezes my bottom hard with both hands, rocking fiercely forward so that he presses on my hot and inflamed clitoris. I can feel an incredible sensation swirling inside me: a feeling that comes in ever-increasing waves, building relentlessly. It is a blissful, unbearable feeling that takes me higher and higher as though I'm being carried inside a tidal wave towards my climax. I unwrap my legs and spread as wide as I can for him, my limbs stiffening with the need to come. I can feel Dominic increasing his pace, his need becoming heightened by my obvious closeness to orgasm, and the sight of his blazing eyes as he watches me as I tip over the edge. The spasms seize me and great judders of pleasure rock my body. I'm conscious of nothing but the exquisite delight of my release, and then I hear Dominic exclaim as his own orgasm boils up and spends itself. He falls forward on to my chest and we lie there for a long time, still joined, panting and exhausted.

At last he lifts his head, and he is smiling at me, bright and happy. 'Did you enjoy your day out, Beth?'

'I enjoyed my day *in*,' I reply, giggling.

'I enjoyed my day in you,' he responds, and we both laugh. We are so close, so intimate, so together at this moment. He pulls out of me, rolls over and deftly removes his condom and disposes of it. Then he takes me in his arms again and kisses me softly. 'That was amazing, Beth. You're full of surprises.'

I sigh happily. 'Well, I can honestly say that was extraordinary.'

'Do you want to stay the night?' he asks.

'What time is it?'

'It's after eight o'clock.'

'Is it?' I'm amazed. Then I nestle into the warmth of his arm. 'Yes please, I'd love to.'

'We'll get up and have dinner,' he says, but the bed is warm and delicious and before long, we've both fallen asleep, exhausted.

CHAPTER NINE

I wake in the morning to hear the shower going in the en-suite bathroom, and a few minutes later, Dominic steps out, wrapped in a towel. He's utterly gorgeous, with his black hair wet, drips of water falling on to his shoulders.

'Hi,' he says with a smile, his eyes bright. 'How are you? Did you sleep well?'

'Very well.' I have a Cheshire cat's grin as I stretch luxuriously.

'You look delectable,' he says as he gazes at me appreciatively. 'I wish I didn't have to get into the office today. I can't think of anything I'd rather do than get right back in there with you for a repeat performance.'

'Then why don't you?' I ask, giving him a coquettish look. Just the sight of him has sent my nerve endings into action again, making my skin tingle all over.

'I've got a job to do, sweetheart. And I'm late enough as it is.' He picks up a smaller towel and starts rubbing it over his hair. 'And don't you have a job to go to as well today?'

I don't know what he's talking about for a moment, then I sit bolt upright. 'Oh my God! The gallery!' I've completely forgotten about my new job in the whirl-wind of excitement I've been caught up in. 'What time is it?'

'Nearly eight. I have to get moving.'

I relax a little. 'Phew. I don't have to start until ten.'

He shakes his head, laughing. 'You arty types, you certainly have an easy life.'

I'm just thinking that I ought to get back to Celia's to get dressed when I slap my hand over my mouth with a gasp.

'What now?' Dominic asks, one dark eyebrow cocked enquiringly.

'De Havilland! I didn't feed him last night!' I scramble out of bed and reach for my clothes. 'Oh poor De Havilland! How could I forget him?'

'Don't worry, I have a feeling he'll still be alive. And I'm rather glad you didn't call a halt to proceedings because you were so busy thinking about your cat.'

'Celia's cat – that's why it's so dreadful!' I pull on my dress in double-quick time and then rush over to him. 'Thank you, thank you, for yesterday and last night.'

He pulls me close to his still-damp chest. I can feel the thump of his heart and smell a delicious concoction of soap, aftershave and his own musky warmth. 'I should thank you,' he murmurs and the sound rumbles in his chest. Then he leans over and picks up his phone. 'I haven't got your number, you'd better give it to me.'

I quickly reel off the number and he taps it into his phone. 'Great. I'll text you and then you'll have my number.' He drops a soft sweet kiss onto my lips. He tastes of mint and honey. 'Now off you go. Don't be late for your first day.'

De Havilland, of course, is furious with me. He's yowling crossly as soon as he hears my key in the lock, and as I come in, his yellow eyes seem to flash with anger at me.

'All right, all right, I'm sorry! I forgot you, it was wicked, but I'm here now.'

He runs ahead of me into the kitchen, his black fluffy tail straight up in the air as if to indicate his displeasure, then stands at his bowl, still miaowing, as I tip his biscuits in. Then he sets to, crunching them with relish as though he hasn't seen food in weeks.

I check the time. I'd better be speedy. I need a shower, and soon. But in the shower, I'm almost reluctant to wash away the scent of last night's activity. It was so wonderful, just the slight flash of replay can make my stomach swoop like a waterfall dropping over a cliff edge. It was like nothing I ever experienced with Adam, that's for sure. We made love, yes, but it was always the same: pleasurable, in a quiet way, but predictable. He never made me feel one tenth of that excited, uninhibited ecstasy that possessed me last night. The feeling I had as Dominic entered me was one of profound intimacy and the climax of our lovemaking was a kind of satisfaction I've never known. It shook me to the core. I look down at my body, the breasts covered in slippery soap, the soft belly, the mound below with its covering of fair hair, and I feel as though I've understood for the first time what I might be capable of.

Was that really me? And can I do it again? Oh my goodness, I do hope so.

I'm already craving him with a deep, inner need, like the thirst you feel on a hot afternoon.

Dominic.

His name makes me shiver with delight.

But you've got a job to do, remember? Time to haul your mind out of the bedroom, missy! Now let's rinse and get on with this thing.

I arrive at the Riding House Gallery on the dot of ten. I can see that James is already inside, and when he hears my knock, he comes to the door to let me in.

'Good morning! How are you, Beth? Nice weekend?' He's looking very smart in an English gentleman way, in khaki chinos, a pink shirt and a dark blue tank top. He's taller and thinner than I remembered, the glasses perched on his aquiline nose as he gives me a friendly smile.

'Yes, thank you,' I say cheerfully. 'I had a wonderful time.'

'Glad to hear it. Now, let me show you the ropes . . . Coffee first, that's the general rule. Whoever gets in first makes it – no takeaways, though, that's also a rule.'

'Are there lots of rules?' I ask, smiling, as he leads me through the gallery to a small kitchen at the back.

'Oh no, it's very relaxed. But I do have standards.'

159

I'm not surprised to hear it, he looks like a man who has particular likes and dislikes. Freshly ground Colombian coffee, a strong, spicy roast, is one of those likes, and there's a shining silver Gaggia coffee machine to make it. In a moment, he's handing me a delicious-smelling latte and sipping his own strong black coffee from a china cup. 'There,' he says, 'we're human again. Now we can get started.'

As the morning progresses, I know I'm going to like this job. Beneath his calm, elegant exterior, James proves to be witty and amusing, with an unexpectedly playful side, joking and laughing as he shows me round. My work is fairly undemanding. I have to answer the phone, help any customers that come in and sort out the general admin. Of course, as I know nothing, James has to do it all but I'm quick to understand his systems.

'I'm sorry this is all a bit junior,' he says apologetically. 'There is more interesting work to do, in time, I promise.'

'I don't mind starting at the bottom,' I say.

'Good girl.' He smiles again. 'I think we're going to get on very well.'

We do. In fact, we hit it off wonderfully. James is very easy to be around and he makes me laugh all the time. If I've got any suspicions about whether he might be flirting with me, they're put to rest in the afternoon, when a middle-aged blond man comes in, his weathered face looking rather battered in contrast to the smart white suit he's wearing. He goes straight up to

160

James, kisses him on the cheek, and starts talking to him in a language I don't recognise. James replies, then looks over at me.

'Beth, let me introduce Erlend, my partner. He's Norwegian, you must excuse him.'

Erlend turns and greets me very politely. 'How do you do, Beth? I hope you'll enjoy your time working with James. Don't let him be bossy, he always likes to be in charge.'

'I won't,' I smile.

So James definitely isn't flirting with me then.

As the two men chatter away easily in Norwegian, I look about the bright, clean gallery and want to hug myself with happiness.

I've got this job, and I've got Dominic. Could life be any better?

In the late afternoon, I get a text.

Hi, what time do you finish? Do you want to go for a drink after work? Dx

I send back a reply:

Sounds great. I finish at 6. Bx

The answer flashes up a moment later:

I'll meet you outside All Souls on Regent Street, by the BBC. 6.30 x

161

'Good news?' James asks, one finely shaped eyebrow raised over the top of his gold-framed spectacles.

I flush and nod. 'Mmm.'

'Boyfriend?'

I flush even deeper. 'Um . . . no . . .'

'Not yet,' he finishes with a smile. 'But you're hoping.'

I must be crimson by now. 'Sort of. Yes.'

'He's a lucky man, I hope he's treating you well.'

I have a flashback to just how well Dominic treated me last night, and get that rush of excitement, like I've just dived off a high board towards a pool very far below. I nod again, unable to trust myself to speak.

The gallery closes at six, and it's such a short walk to the church Dominic suggested – James tells me how to get there – that I'm there with plenty of time to spare. The church is obviously old, built in dark golden brown stone, and I loiter in the circular portico with its ring of columns, looking out at Regent Street. Traffic hums busily past the imposing facade of the BBC which stands next to the church. I'm quite happy watching people going past but I'm eager for Dominic to arrive all the same. It feels like waking up and remembering it's Christmas, or the day of a special treat – a delicious anticipation of pleasure.

In the end, I'm reading some of the information on the church noticeboard when he arrives, and I jump as I hear his voice say, 'Beth?'

'Hello!' I whirl round, beaming. 'How was your day?'

Dominic looks beautiful as usual, this time in a dark navy suit, elegantly cut even to my untutored eyes, and he smiles at me as he drops a kiss on my cheek, his hand touching the small of my back. 'Very good, thanks, how about you?'

I start to tell him about my first day at the gallery as he leads the way across Regent Street and westward into Marylebone. Dominic listens but doesn't ask much. He seems a little preoccupied.

'Are you all right?' I ask, concerned, as he leads the way into an atmospheric wine bar with a vaulted stone ceiling and tables tucked discreetly into alcoves. Candles flicker in mercury glass holders, casting strange shadows on the walls. He doesn't answer until we are sitting down in our own separate alcove, and he's ordered drinks for us both: glasses of cold Puligny-Montrachet. When he does speak, I realise at once that he's not really meeting my eye.

'I'm fine,' he says. 'Honestly.'

'Dominic?' I put my hand on his and for a moment he clasps it, but quickly releases it. 'What is it?'

He stares at the table, frowning.

'You're worrying me. Come on, what's up?'

The waitress arrives with our drinks and nothing is said until she's gone. My stomach is clenching with nerves. Why is he so cold and distant? Just this morning he was warm, flirtatious, intimate. Now he's put up a barrier, I can feel it. 'Dominic,' I say when we're left alone, 'please tell me what's wrong.'

At last he lifts his eyes to mine and I'm horrified to

see that they're full of sadness and apology. 'Beth,' he says slowly, 'I'm so sorry . . .'

I understand everything instantly, with a punch of horror. 'No!' It comes out before I can stop it. Fury races through me. He's not going to do this.

'I'm sorry,' he says again. He's interlaced his fingers and is staring down at them, his face creased as though he's in pain. 'I've been thinking about this all day and—'

'Don't say it.' I don't want to sound too pleading but I can't help it. 'You haven't given us a chance.'

He looks up at me again. 'I know, but that's the point. I can't give us a chance.'

'Why not?' I feel as though I've been caught by an avalanche, engulfed by a powerful force that's spinning me around, but I tell myself that I must stay calm. 'What we did last night was amazing, incredible . . . Am I just a stupid naive girl, or does that kind of experience happen all the time for you? I thought it meant something, that it was special to you—'

'It was!' he breaks in, looking agonised. 'Christ, it was. It's not that, Beth, I wish it was.'

'Then what?' The thought that's been lingering at the back of my mind, the one I've been steadfastly refusing to entertain, pops to the fore. *You know why*, it whispers to me, almost gleefully. *You've seen what he doesn't know you've seen* . . . 'Is there someone else, someone you haven't told me about?'

He closes his eyes and shakes his head. 'No. No.'

'Then . . .' *Come on*, whispers that evil little voice,

don't play dumb. You know more than he thinks. Tell him.

I want to shout back at it: *But I know it wasn't him, he had no marks on him!*

Perhaps she's very clever at not leaving marks, wheedles the voice.

Oh God, I never thought of that . . . Everything seems to be collapsing around me. When I speak, I sound tentative, almost afraid. 'Is it because of what you and Vanessa do together?'

Now I've shocked him. He freezes for a moment, then his mouth opens as if he wants to say something but can't think what.

I draw on all my courage and say, 'I saw it.'

'You've seen *what*?'

I thought he might be angry with me, but the look on his face is more baffled now. I stop, uncertain, but he's staring right at me, his gaze boring into me. He looks stern, his eyes taking on that icy quality I've come to dread.

'Beth, I want to know. What have you seen?'

The images flash into my mind: the crouching man kissing the implement, the rhythmic movement of the woman's arm, the vivid shadow theatre of the beating.

'I saw . . .' My voice drops low again, and now I'm the one who can't meet his eye. 'Saturday night. I saw from my flat into yours. The curtains were drawn but they're transparent with the light behind them and . . . I saw you and Vanessa. At least I think it was her. I don't know.' I look up into the beautiful depths of

165

those black eyes, flecked with gold light from the candle, and wish I didn't have to say what I'm about to say. 'I saw her beating you. First, over her knee like a naughty child, then in a different position and after that, I saw her whip you with a belt while you lay on that strange stool you've got.'

He's staring at me and I would swear that he's gone pale.

'I saw it,' I repeat dully. 'I know what you do together. Is that why you want to finish with me before we've even had a chance?'

'Oh, Beth.' I can see that he's searching for the words. 'Oh, God, I don't know what to say. You saw this in my apartment?'

I nod.

'And you assumed it was me and Vanessa?'

'What else am I supposed to think? It's your apartment. I've seen you in there together. Who else would it be?'

He thinks for a moment and then says, 'Okay, I think I know what's happened here. You're right about one thing. The woman you saw was Vanessa. She has a key to my apartment, you probably guessed that when she came in the other night. But . . .' he fixes me with a steady look '. . . the man was not me. I can promise you that.'

'Then . . . who do you allow to come into your flat like that, to be hit?'

'Well, I don't really allow it, as such. I mean, I don't like it. But Vanessa knew that I was away that night and she has a client whose particular fantasy is to be a wealthy tycoon dominated in his plush flat. She'll have taken him there to give him the scenery to play in.' He shakes his head. 'I haven't forbidden it, but I've told her I want her keeping work out of my home. She presumes quite a lot on our old relationship.'

I'm confused. 'Wait – her *client*? Her *work*? Vanessa's a . . . prostitute?' I can't believe it. Beautiful, polished, sophisticated Vanessa is a hooker? It doesn't seem possible. Why would she need to do something like that?

Dominic breathes out, a long whistling sigh, and leans back in his chair. 'Oh my goodness. The proverbial can of worms has just been well and truly opened. I can see that I'm going to have to be straight with you here.'

'I'd appreciate that, really,' I say, a touch of sarcasm in my voice.

'All right. I was going to tell you about me, but we'll start with Vanessa.' He picks up his wine glass and takes a sip, as though needing a boost of courage from the alcohol. I lift my own glass, cold and beaded with condensation, and take a gulp of the clean, minerally white wine. I have a feeling that I need courage too.

Dominic sets his shoulders, clasps his hands together, and looks at me. 'First of all, Vanessa isn't a prostitute, not in the way you think of a prostitute, anyway. She does charge for her services, but she rarely, if ever, has sex with her clients. She offers a different kind of service altogether. Vanessa is a professional mistress and dominatrix, and she specialises in offering people with certain needs a private and safe space in which they can live out and enjoy their fantasies.'

I don't say anything while I absorb this. I've heard of dominatrixes but only as figures of fun in films and stories. I've never really considered that they exist in the real world. That's what Vanessa does?

Dominic continues. 'Most people think of sex and romance in a very straightforward way – generally, it's one man and one woman, getting naked and have straight sex. Vanilla sex, as they say. Of course, you've probably seen the men's magazines in newsagents, the ones that deliver the fantasies pretty much accepted as male: big colour pictures of bare tits and open fannies for men to wank over.'

It's so odd to hear these words coming out of Dominic's mouth, and he says them with a kind of cold scorn that makes it even more disconcerting.

He leans forward and focuses on me entirely. 'But many, many of us are not like that. That isn't our fantasy at all. We need something else, and we don't want just to imagine. We want to live it.'

He's saying 'we'. He must mean himself. Oh my God. What's he going to tell me?

'You remember that basement bar, The Asylum?' he says suddenly, and when I nod, he continues. 'That bar belongs to Vanessa. In fact, the whole house above it belongs to her. It's where people go to enjoy their fantasies and satisfy their needs without fear. It's a safe house, really. She created it for people like her.'

I take this in, remembering the submissive people in their cages. 'She's a dominatrix . . .' I say, puzzled.

'All doms need subs, or nothing's going to happen,' he says and for almost the first time that evening, he smiles. 'The top and the bottom. The yin and the yang.' Then he looks thoughtful, evidently calling up scenes from his past. He continues after a moment. 'Vanessa and I met in Oxford when I was studying there. I liked her at once, there was an incredible attraction between us. I'd just come back from America and knew nobody, so I was delighted to meet a woman like her. And she was very unusual in her attitudes. It wasn't long before she introduced me to her . . . tastes. It started playfully enough. She began tying me to the bed during sex, getting me aroused and stringing me out for a very long time, tormenting me almost with her techniques – and I liked it very much. It wasn't long before she introduced objects into the bedroom: scarves, ropes, blindfolds. She liked to gag me, blindfold me, play her games with me. Then she introduced me to spanking. Gently at first – some sharp raps on the buttocks with her hands – and then more seriously. She brought in paddles and belts, she began to spend longer spanking me than she did anything else, and she loved it. God, she loved it.' His eyes glitter with the memory.

So he's no different to the man on the stool after all. I don't like the feeling I get when I imagine Vanessa and Dominic having sex: it's part burning jealousy and part secret arousal at the thought of him stretched naked on a bed, being taken to the edge of pleasure. 'And . . . you? Did you love it?'

He sighs again, and takes another drink. 'It's so hard to explain if you haven't done it. It sounds unbelievable, I know, but pain and pleasure are very closely linked. Pain doesn't have to be the worst thing in the world – it can stimulate and excite and make the pleasure very, very intense. When it ties in with certain fantasies or leanings that already exist in your psyche – the desire to be controlled, say, or punished, treated like a naughty child or a saucy girl who needs taming – well, then it can be simply explosive.'

I try to imagine this but still I can't understand how being hit, being hurt, can be fun. At least, I don't think it can for me. I don't think I have punishment fantasies. I'm sure my fantasies are love fantasies.

Dominic goes on, evidently keen to get the story off his chest. 'I was willing to go only so far along that road, but Vanessa wanted to go further. She had a desire to enact full-scale flogging on me, but I wasn't keen. I liked her games up to a point, and after that they did nothing for me. And then we found the Club.'

'The Club?'

He nods. 'A secret gathering of like-minded people. The Club met in an old boathouse near the river that looked nothing from the outside but inside was devoted to the art and practice of flogging. It had all the equipment that is difficult to keep in a private home: spreader bars, crosses, racks and so on.'

I gasp. *A torture chamber? My God, aren't we trying*

to stop this sort of thing, not encourage it? Does Amnesty International know?

Dominic sees my expression. 'It sounds bad, I know. But it's all consensual. Nothing is done without the floggee wanting it. My first experience there was mind-blowing. I saw a man flogging a woman, seriously flogging her.' He has a faraway look in his eyes and I know he's seeing it again in his imagination. 'She was chained to a St Andrew's Cross – you know, a cross like an X – fastened by her feet and wrists, and he used seven different instruments on her, beginning lightly with soft horsehair and ending with a heavy flogger they call the cat o' nine tails – except this had about twenty – by which time she was almost in pieces. It was amazing.'

I can see the image in my mind: a woman screaming in agony, her back a mess of welts and blood, a man crazed with power, thrashing out at her with all his strength. *And this is meant to be fun?*

'And when did they have sex?' I ask tentatively.

Dominic looks surprised. 'Sex?'

'This is some kind of sexual activity, isn't it? Or am I completely missing the point? So when did they have sex?'

'The rules of the Club forbid intercourse or penetration unless members are in private and agree that as part of their scene. But a lot of people get sexual pleasure without what you might think of as sex. Sex *is* flogging; flogging is sex. Or it isn't. It all depends. The relationship and the power exchange

171

between the participants is often enough to give the release they crave.'

I stare at him. He's right: I've never imagined some of the things he's telling me. 'So you became members of this club?'

Dominic nods. 'Vanessa adored it. It was the scene she'd been looking for, she'd found her family. The Asylum is an offshoot of the Club, but a little more elaborate because it caters for more than simple domination.'

'There's more?' I ask faintly.

Dominic laughs. 'Oh yes. There's a lot more. But let's not get side-tracked. I'm trying to explain why I would never be that man you saw in my apartment.'

'Why not?'

He looks me straight in the eye. 'Because when I saw that flogging, I knew then for certain that I did not want to be manacled to the cross, taking the bite and the sting, the vicious punishment of the instruments.' He pauses for a second and says, 'I wanted to be the man with the whip. I didn't want to receive it. I wanted to deal it out.'

I don't know what to say. I stare at him, my eyes wide.

Dominic sighs, his expression suddenly defeated. 'I didn't intend to tell you about it like this. It's come out all wrong.'

I hardly hear him because I'm busy making connections in my mind. 'So that's what you meant when you said that your needs and Vanessa's were not compatible.'

He nods, slowly. 'Yes. I'm afraid so. You can't have two dominant personalities in a relationship, not when it forms a vital part of the sexual dynamic. But, more to the point, we weren't in love any more. The relationship had run its course and we became what we were meant to be – friends. And our exploration of the scene bound us very tightly together.'

'With handcuffs, by the sound of it,' I say tartly, and am a little wounded when he starts to laugh. 'I wasn't trying to be funny. This is all very strange for me.' I lean towards him, looking intently at him. I should have known that a man this beautiful would be anything but straightforward. 'So you're telling me that you need to flog women?'

He takes another drink. *Am I making him nervous?* 'This is odd for me, Beth, because you know nothing of this world, and things that are quite normal for me are going to sound bizarre to you. Believe it or not, there are lots of women who get great pleasure from being submissive. And I get a great deal of enjoyment from controlling them.'

I don't know what to say. I'm trying to picture this man, so outwardly normal, wielding a whip across the back of a vulnerable woman. I'm filled with a mixture of anger and sadness, but I don't really understand where those emotions have come from. Before I've decided what to do, I'm stumbling to my feet, pushing my chair back across the stone flags with a harsh screech. 'So I can see why you want to end it,' I say, my voice trembling. 'I suppose last night wasn't enough for you. I thought it was amazing but I suppose that without beating me to a pulp, it just wasn't any good for you. Well, thank you for letting me know.'

Hurt springs into his eyes. 'Beth, no, it's not like that.'

I cut him off. 'No, I understand. I think I'll go now.' I turn and dash for the door. He stands up, calling my name, but I know he can't follow me without paying the bill, so I head out onto the street and hail a passing taxi.

'Randolph Gardens, please,' I say breathlessly, as I climb into the back, and all the way back to Mayfair, I'm shivering as though the temperature has just dropped to zero.

CHAPTER TEN

James notices the change in me at once when I arrive at work the next day.

'Are you all right?' he enquires, looking at me over the top of his spectacles. 'You don't seem quite as perky as you were yesterday.'

I try to smile. 'I'm all right. Really.'

'Ah. Boyfriend trouble, if I'm not much mistaken. Don't worry, my dear, I've been there. I can't tell you how pleased I am that Erlend and I are a comfortable old couple with no more of the woes of the courting days. It makes up in restfulness what it lacks in excitement.' His expression is sympathetic. 'But that doesn't mean I've forgotten how much it can hurt. I won't ask questions – I'll just take your mind off it.'

I'm not quite sure how James can make me forget last night's revelation. I've thought of nothing else since. Last night I lay in bed, my eyes wide and sleep elusive, as I imagined Dominic brandishing all manner of instruments, laughing maniacally as he brings them down over a woman's back.

A man who wants to hit women. How can he be like that? I don't understand. I don't even know that I want to understand.

175

I try to tell myself that, but the reality is that I can't stop the way I feel about him. I still long for him in every way and he fills my thoughts all day, despite James's best efforts to keep me busy working on the catalogue proofs for the next exhibition. I hear nothing from Dominic and as the hours pass by, I'm weighed down more and more by depression at the thought that I might not see him again.

In the evening, I go home, stopping only to pick up some groceries, and try to fool myself that I'm not watching the flat opposite, hoping that I'll see some sign of life there. I'm craving a sight of Dominic as badly as any addict craves a fix. In fact, I worry that if I do see him, I won't be able to stop myself going straight over there.

By eight o'clock, with the flat still in darkness, I'm in a frenzy, pacing backwards and forwards, picking up my telephone to text him but managing to stop myself, and all the time picturing where he might be and what he might be doing. I'm on the verge of going back to The Asylum to see if I can find him, when there's a knock on the front door.

I freeze. *Dominic. It must be. Unless it's the porter . . .*

I open the door tentatively, my heart beating wildly. He's there, resting one arm on the doorframe, looking terrible for the first time since I've known him. His chin is stubbled and there are bags under his eyes, which are tired and bloodshot. It looks like he's barely slept. He also looks sloppy, in rumpled jeans and a grey sweatshirt. He's staring at the floor but looks up as I emerge slowly from behind the door.

'Hi,' he says in a low voice. 'I'm sorry, I'm probably the last person you want to see right now. But I had to come and see you.'

'No.' I smile weakly. 'I want to see you too. I've missed you.'

He looks abjectly miserable. 'But the way you ran out last night. You were obviously horrified. Shocked. Disgusted.' He runs his fingers through his dark hair, making the ends stick up all over the place. It's an absurdly sexy look. I thought I liked the polished, stylish Dominic but maybe I like the messy one even more. The look in those black eyes is beseeching. 'It came out all wrong, Beth. I shouldn't have told you like that, the way I did. You've got the wrong idea.'

My throat is dry. I swallow and say, 'What's the right idea?'

'You think I just want to beat women up. It's not like that, I promise. Will you let me try to explain? Please?'

I stare at him for a long moment. There's no question that I could turn him away or refuse, but I am so stunned to be in his presence again that I'm processing everything at half speed. 'Of course. Come in.'

I step backwards into the dark hallway and he steps forward to join me. That's all it takes. The moment he is close to me, I inhale his gorgeous scent: sweet, lemony, musky, and utterly irresistible. Now that he's close to me again, my insides turn to liquid, my knees weaken and I stare at his mouth, my own lips parted with the rush of desire I'm experiencing.

'Beth,' he says throatily, and then his mouth is on mine, and we're kissing passionately, as though we can't get enough of one another. The feeling is bliss, like being taken up into a velvet tornado – powerful, thrilling, whirling, but soft and dark at the same time. His taste and the force of his desire awaken a lust in me I've never known before. I want him so much, and the moment his tongue touches mine, I'm instantly ready: hot, wet and full of need. I can tell from the hardness in his groin that's pressing against me that he's ready too. I feel as though we're both unable to control ourselves, acting under instinct, driven by the force of our desire for one another.

His hands are under my top, lifting it, taking it over my head, leaving me in just my bra. He drops his head to my chest for a moment and showers hot kisses over the soft mounds of flesh that rise from the cups, but he is back at my mouth in an instant, which I meet hungrily as I can't bear not to be tasting him. I'm lifting his T-shirt too, and he takes it from me, pulling it off in a swift movement and then our chests are pressed together, the flesh on flesh creating the most intensely pleasurable sensations.

His lips and tongue are busy at my mouth again, he's nipping at my lips, sucking my tongue. His passion is fiercer than it was before and mine rises to meet it. I drag my nails lightly over his broad muscled back, making him groan into my mouth, then I reach for the buttons on his jeans, and undo them quickly. The heat of his erection radiates towards me and I can feel the great shaft straining against the soft cotton of his boxer shorts. I slide my hand inside the opening and it's hot and hard and so velvety soft. I rub my hand along it, moving the skin gently under my palm, and he groans again. His own hand is busy at my skirt fastening and a second later it drops to the floor. His fingers are already delving into my knickers, reaching to my hot, damp sex. As he strokes my swollen lips and presses his fingers into the dark heart of me, I gasp as well and thrust my tongue into his mouth with rapture. His fingers slide up to my bud, and as he rubs over the little button, twirling it under his fingertips, it reacts with a force that makes me shudder and grip harder on the huge length of his penis. We're pleasuring each other now, and then he slides his fingers back down through my wetness to the entrance, and pushes first one and then the other inside me. I throw back my head and cry out with the exquisite feeling. He pushes again and again, thrusting his fingers deep into me.

'I've thought of nothing but you since we fucked,' he says. 'I can't stop wanting to feel you and taste you.'

In response I begin to tug down his jeans. He has to take his hand from my knickers to let me take his jeans and boxers down his strong thighs and calves. As I reach the floor, I kneel in front of him. I press my face against his groin, his cock hard on my cheek as I inhale the delectable soft scent of his pubic hair. I can feel his fingers on my head, stroking my hair, wrapping strands gently around themselves. His penis is incredible and I want to love it in the way I hope it will soon be loving me. I run my lips over the length of his erection, marvelling again at the sweet softness of the skin and the iron hardness beneath. When I reach the top, I hold it with one hand while, with the other, I cup the heavy balls below, stroking them gently. I can hear his breathing become ragged as I caress them with my forefinger, and then in a quick movement, I take the head of his penis in my mouth, sucking it, twirling my tongue around it and over the top, all the while moving my hand along the shaft. Dominic begins to move his hips, and his fingers clutch hard at my hair as I suck and rub, knowing that it's causing him intense enjoyment. His pleasure is turning me on even more and I'm not sure how long I can stand it when he pulls himself free and says throatily, 'You'll make me come.'

The next moment, he's beside me on the floor and then his mouth is against mine again. He's kissing me deep and hard, pushing me gently backwards until I'm lying on the cold marble. The contrast of our hot bodies and the cold floor is exhilarating, making me wriggle and sigh. Then I feel him pressing to enter me and in the next moment he slides inside, filling me up with that luscious, wanton feeling. I wrap my legs up over his back so that he can penetrate as deeply as possible; I want him – no, I *need* him right in the heart of me, pushing me onwards towards the racking pleasure I hunger for.

This is fierce, furious passion. He drives his hips

down to meet mine, and then thrusts again. Our tongues meet, part, then meet again in time to his movements.

Then suddenly, Dominic grabs my wrists with one hand, pinning them above my head. A surge of excitement passes through me. So this is what it's like to be restrained. Being locked under his body while he takes control is an incredible feeling.

'Yes, my beautiful girl, yes,' he says, his teeth gritted, his eyes burning into me with the fervour of his own sensations. 'Come on, come for me.'

His words arouse me even more. It's as though he's taking ownership of my climax, and even in the grip of this fierce, erotic moment, I wonder if this is a taste of being submissive to Dominic. If it is, then maybe it's more exciting than I realised. Each forward thrust brings his pubic bone grinding down on my clitoris, and pushes him deeper within me. I can feel the waves beginning, the rolling sensations of pleasure that begin in my groin and radiate out into my belly. Each wave lifts me higher and higher towards the apex of feeling, as the intensity I'm experiencing gets ever more excruciating. Then, as it becomes too much for me to stand, I feel the climax hit me, lifting me up in a tumble of magnificent pleasure. I cry out but there are no words, and as I stiffen and shudder, I feel him drive forward into me, pressing hard in several short, sharp thrusts and then, with a groan, he comes as well in long, intense strokes, pushing until eventually it's over.

We lie in a daze for a few moments, panting and

recovering ourselves, Dominic still inside me. As I smile luxuriously, running my hands over his back, he pulls out of me and I realise he's frowning.

'What is it?' I ask, feeling the wetness of his come on my thigh.

'I didn't put a condom on.'

'Well . . . actually, I'm on the Pill,' I admit. 'I've been on for it years and I didn't stop when Adam and I broke up. But . . .'

He nods. 'I know. Safe sex. It's important, I shouldn't have let myself get carried away.' He looks serious. 'Look, I get myself checked regularly as part of my medicals. I have a clean bill of health, so you don't need to worry about me.'

I want to say the same but I suddenly realise that, of course, Adam was secretly fucking someone else, and I have no way of knowing how many partners she had, or whether they used a condom. Tears spring to my eyes.

'What is it, sweetheart?' Dominic says tenderly, stroking my hair. When I explain, with a tearful catch in my voice, he says, 'I don't think you should worry but if it will set your mind at rest, you can get yourself checked by my doctor. He's nearby on Harley Street, and he's fantastic. I'll make you an appointment if you like. Or there's a female doctor at the practice, if you'd prefer. If it makes you happy and sets your mind at rest.'

I'm touched by his concern and kiss his cheek. 'Yes, maybe I'll do that. Then I can put Adam and everything about him well and truly out of my mind.'

'Good.' He kisses me lightly on the lips. 'Now – shall we get up? This floor is suddenly getting rather cold and hard.'

We take turns to shower and when Dominic comes back, dressed in his T-shirt and jeans again, I've got a glass of wine waiting for him in the sitting room, and I'm curled up on the sofa in the silk robe, my own glass clutched in my hand.

'I didn't actually have that in mind when I came to see you,' Dominic says, smiling, as he sits down opposite me. 'Although maybe I did, I don't know . . .'

I smile back at him. 'I've been so miserable today.'

'Me too.' His expression becomes sombre again. 'But there's still stuff we have to discuss.'

'I know.' I sigh. 'It's hard for me, Dominic. It's hard to understand why something like what we've just shared isn't enough for you. You want more. You want this strange other world that Vanessa introduced you to.'

He nods slowly. 'I can't really explain it, except that maybe it's a little like taking drugs. Once you get used to getting your kicks that way, it's hard to go back to being without it. At the moment, what we're experiencing with each other is incredible, just incredible. There's no denying that.' An expression of sadness flits over his features. 'But I know what will happen. After a while, I won't be satisfied with it, not in the same way. I'll want a little more, a little of that dangerous edge. I'll want to have the thrill of control.' He stares

183

straight at me, his gaze clear and piercing. 'And you don't want to be controlled.'

'You don't know that,' I protest. 'Maybe I do want to be controlled!'

He shakes his head. 'No. Most submissives have the urge for it from a very young age, it develops along with their sexuality. You see, it's not that I want to beat women, not exactly – I want to exercise control over submissive personalities who desire my correction, and because I'm heterosexual, I get pleasure from doing that with women. It's not about abusing anyone, it's all completely agreed and quite safe and boundaried. But you don't want that. If you had the desire to be flogged or spanked or punished, you'd probably know it by now.'

I return his gaze with a piercing one of my own. 'You didn't.'

He looks surprised. 'What do you mean?'

'According to you, you had no desires like that until Vanessa showed you what she wanted from you. And you didn't even know you wanted to be dominant until you saw the flogging.'

There's a long pause while he considers this, one hand absent-mindedly rubbing back and forth along the arm of his chair. Then, at last, he says, 'You're right. I didn't know. But I don't know if it's the same for subs, that's all.'

'But why can't we go on, and see what happens?' I ask almost forlornly. 'Perhaps this time you won't have those urges.'

'I can't make that promise, Beth, and the truth is, that's always happened in the past. I don't want to make you feel something for me, and then leave you because it can't work between us.'

'It's a little late for that,' I say quietly.

'I know. I'm sorry.' He plucks at the chair cover, not able to look at me.

I stare at the long handsome body, too big for Celia's delicate armchairs, and wonder how all this happened. 'So you mean, even after what we just did, that it's over, that it can't go any further?'

Dominic looks up at me, his dark eyes sad. 'I'm afraid so.'

I feel utterly wretched. 'So that was just a farewell fuck?' It comes out more cynically than I intended.

'You know it wasn't like that,' he says softly.

I feel angry and grief-stricken in equal measure. 'I just don't know how you can tell me you want me, that you've thought of nothing else but me, that you can come the way you did just now – and then walk out on me.'

He closes his eyes for a moment. When he opens them, he looks even sadder than he did before we made love. He stands up slowly and says, 'You know what? Neither can I. But it's for the best, Beth. I promise.'

He walks over to me, stoops down and kisses my lips. The nearness of him is intoxicating but I close my eyes, trying to shut him out.

'Beth.' His voice is hardly more than a low murmur. 'I would like nothing more than to take you into the

185

darkest part of me. I'd like to show you every last shred of the desire I have for you, and make you mine completely. But you can't come back from that place, Beth, and I couldn't bear to take you there and then lose you.' There's a heartbeat of a pause, then he whispers, 'I'm sorry.'

I keep my eyes shut, but I know he's pulled away from me, and his footsteps sound as he walks out of the room. Then I hear the front door shut behind him, and it feels as though my heart is breaking.

CHAPTER ELEVEN

'No, I'm fine, really, Mum.' I make a face at James, who's putting a cup of coffee down on the desk for me, telegraphing that I won't be long. He makes a 'take as long as you like' gesture and goes off to a discreet distance so that I can talk freely.

'Are you sure, darling?' My mother sounds anxious. 'I worry about you on your own in that big city.'

'I'm really all right. And I'm at work now, so I can't talk . . .'

'Promise you'll call me later? And I can catch a train to be with you any time if you need me.'

'There's no need for that, but I'll definitely call you soon. I better go now.'

'All right, then. Take care. Goodbye, I love you!'

'I love you too, Mum. Bye.' I put the phone down, comforted by the talk with my mother. Even though I didn't tell her what's happened with Dominic, her sharp mother antennae picked up some of the gloom I couldn't quite stop from coming into my voice.

James comes back over to see how I'm doing with the catalogue proofs. I show him that they're nearly finished.

'Good,' he says. 'You've got an excellent eye for

detail, Beth. That takes a weight off my shoulders, I can tell you. I'm not very good at that myself. Sometimes I get Erlend to double-check for me, but his written English isn't perfect, and he can make matters worse by putting mistakes in instead of taking them out.' He shakes his head, laughing. 'We're a right old pair. Now – once the proofs are done, I've got some things we need to start dealing with.'

We go through some tasks. I'll be helping to organise the next private view, which is happening in two weeks' time, and sorting out the taking down of the current exhibition and the installation of the next. There's plenty to keep me busy, and James has more time to deal with clients, which is his forte. I've already witnessed him at work, approaching a customer who came in off the street and talking to him about the art on the walls. Wary of a hard sell at first, the customer took a while to relax but with James's gentle guidance, he found a picture he liked very much and before long, a deal was struck.

I was impressed. It can't be easy to persuade someone to part with five thousand pounds just like that.

'In these difficult financial times, people are seeing art as an investment,' James explained. 'I spent a while reassuring him that this artist is going to hold his value and probably go up. That's what customers are most concerned about now – but, of course, they must love the art as well. It's an investment that can bring a great deal of pleasure.'

Now he looks me in that wise way he has, peering

over the top of his spectacles and reminding me of an owl in a storybook. 'You just don't seem yourself today. Is everything all right?'

'Yes, fine,' I say automatically, but the dullness in my voice gives the lie to it.

'Right then. It sounds like we need a good natter. The shop is quiet, the proofs are nearly done.' He pulls up a chair and settles himself opposite me, his elbows on the desk and his chin resting on his hands. 'Now. Shoot.'

I look at him. I can hardly believe I've only known him a few days. We're getting on so well, and he's amazingly easy to talk to, one of those people who are absolutely unshockable. I get the feeling James has had a lot of life experience and that along with his kindly nature has made him into the perfect agony uncle. Plus, he's really interested. *Can I tell him the truth?*

As if he can read my mind, he says, 'You can tell me *anything*.'

'Well . . .' I take a deep breath and it all comes out, right from the start and the night I first saw Dominic in his apartment, until last night and his adamant refusal to give our relationship a chance. It's a relief to let it all out and by the time I've finished, James is looking rather bemused.

'Beth,' he says at last, shaking his head. 'This is not the average boyfriend trouble, I'll admit that. This is a nice old conundrum, I must say.'

'I don't know what to do,' I say bleakly. 'I can't force him to be with me if he doesn't want to.'

189

'Oh, that's not your problem, darling, he definitely wants to,' James declares.

'Do you think so?' I sound so eager, so hopeful.

'Of course. He's clearly crazy about you but he's trying to do the right thing by you. He's sacrificing himself for you.'

'But he doesn't need to!' I wail. 'I don't want him to do that at all.'

'No – you're obviously wild about him as well, and when you're in the grip of an emotion that strong, you'll do anything. He foresees trouble ahead and he doesn't want to put you through it, but you're willing to take the pain later if you can have the pleasure now.'

I think about this for a moment, staring down at the blond wood of the desk, and the pile of brightly illustrated catalogue proofs, and then I say in a low voice, 'What if I take the pain now?'

James looks at me quizzically. 'What do you mean?'

'Dominic described his need for control as a kind of addiction, like a drug addiction. Perhaps I can go into that world with him, and together we can work out a cure, a way to come down and learn to do without it.' As I say it, it makes complete sense to me. I feel a rush of happiness, as if I've stumbled on to the perfect solution. Of course. If going into that world is what it takes to be with Dominic, then that's what I will do. I remember his hand gripped on my wrists as we made love, and his order to come that sent me whirling into orgasm, and a delicious thrill runs through me. Maybe the journey of discovery would reveal hidden pleasures . . .

'It's a serious thing, Beth,' James says, concern creasing his brow. 'Dominic has made it clear he doesn't want you in that part of his life. Perhaps it's an aspect of his character that, deep down, he doesn't like or doesn't want to share with you.'

'If he won't share it with me, we can't ever have a relationship,' I say firmly. 'And I want that so desperately. And . . .' I feel a flush over my cheeks as I say something I never imagined I'd say aloud to anyone, let alone my new boss '. . . a part of me is curious. I want to understand the power this world has over people. I've been half alive for years and I don't want to go back to that sleepy existence again.'

James raises his eyebrows at me. 'All right. That's different, then. If you want to do it for yourself, as well as for him . . . I can see that. It's less dangerous, let me put it that way. I'd be very against you doing it just to keep him.' He looks thoughtful. 'It's not a scene I've ever been drawn to – BDSM, it's called: Bondage, Dominance, Sado-Masochism – but a lot of gay men are. There are leather men, who are very into bondage, restraint and punishment. I had some friends, a couple, who lived a complete master-and-slave relationship whenever they were at home or with trusted friends.' James frowns at the memory. 'I found it highly weird, I must say. It wasn't something that appealed to me. Watching them enact that situation was uncomfortable – Gareth was the master and Joe was the slave, except that Gareth called him "it" or "1", and Joe lived as his literal slave, cooking, cleaning, serving Gareth in every way, often crawling about on his hands and knees. In their house they had a dungeon where they retired to play their games – Gareth torturing Joe for hours on end. To their mutual satisfaction, I might add,' he says hastily. 'But to be honest, it made me wince a bit. Made the little man run away and hide rather than stand up for business, if you know what I mean.'

My eyes are wide and I'm aware of nervousness fluttering around inside. 'Do you think that's what Dominic wants?'

'A slave?' James shakes his head slowly. 'I don't think so. A submissive is not the same as a slave, as I understand it. Gareth told me once that Joe was such a complete masochist, that he's what is sometimes known as a pain pig.'

'*What*?'

'I know – it sounds unpleasant. I think it means that even by BDSM standards, he was into the most severe forms of punishment, outside the scope of what is generally considered safe. It doesn't sound to me as if Dominic requires one of those people. In fact, the very healthy state of your sexual relationship before you've so much as sniffed the leather leads me to believe he's very far from being a dyed-in-the-wool sadist.'

I blush again, but all this is helping me tremendously. I feel I'm beginning to understand a little more of this curious, shadowy world. 'I'm so grateful for your help, James,' I say sincerely.

'You're welcome, darling, but I'm not sure what else I can do for you.'

'Actually,' I say slowly. 'There is something. I know it's a lot to ask of you but . . .'

He leans forward, interested. 'Go on. What is it?'

An idea has been forming in my mind, and now I hesitate for a moment to get my thoughts together, then I tell what I would like him to do.

At home later, I'm tired by the extraordinary upheavals of the last few days. I feel as though I've been through the emotional wringer, experiencing everything from unbelievable ecstasy to deep despair, and it's worn me out. Supper, a warm bath and a chat to De Havilland help to revive me. Besides, I'm titillated by the thought of what I'm about to do. When I think of it, butterflies swarm in my stomach and I can't believe what I've planned, but it's also exciting.

Clean and fresh from my bath, I slide on the silk robe, enjoying the cool slipperiness over my skin, and walk into the sitting room. For the first time, I'm half hoping that the flat opposite will be in darkness, but of course it's not. Tonight, the blinds are up, the curtains are drawn and I can see into the softly lit interior of Dominic's flat, although he isn't there. It's a beautiful sight, at once bringing me closer to him. Usually I would leave the lights off in Celia's flat, so that I'm relatively invisible to him, but not tonight. I move around the room, switching on the lamps until the room is illuminated by a gentle glow. The silver lacquer panels come alive in the electric light, shining and shimmering like the surface of water.

Then, as I hoped he would, Dominic comes into his sitting room. He's holding a tumbler of something that looks dark and strong – whisky or brandy or something like that, I suspect – and he's got that just-back-from-work look, as though his jacket and tie are abandoned on the bed but he's too exhausted to change completely. My heart swells when I see him and I'm flooded by the desire to hold him, kiss those perfect lips, stroke his tired face and run my hands through that dark hair. I can also smell that delicious fragrance his skin holds in its pores. But the reality is, we're separated. As he comes into the sitting room, he looks over towards Celia's flat, and stops at once as he realises that I'm there. I know he can see me clearly, but I make sure that I do not look directly at him. Even though I'm intensely aware of him and exactly where he is and what he's doing, I pretend that I have no idea he's watching.

Like an actress on the stage, seemingly oblivious to her audience.

I walk around the sitting room, organising small things, rearranging photos and ornaments, picking up books and looking at them. I know that Dominic has moved closer to his window now. He's standing directly opposite, watching me, his tumbler held against his chest, the other hand in his pocket. He's waiting for me to look out, to communicate with him. But I'm not going to.

Not in the way he expects.

First, to help me, I switch on the CD player. Celia

left a disc of classical guitar music in the deck and it fires up and begins to fill the flat with gentle strains. It might not be the best soundtrack in the world but it will do. I move around the room, getting the stiffness out of my limbs, relaxing. On the table is a glass of wine I put there earlier, rich and red, and I sip it, feeling the heat in my stomach and the alcohol in my blood almost at once. This will help.

Dominic hasn't moved. He's still watching me. I make sure I'm close to the window and begin to caress my own arms and run my hand over my neck and chest, moving it inside the neck of the gown. It slides over my skin, my fingertips cool on my breasts. I am rose-scented from my bath oil and it's left me soft and smooth. I lift my hair up and let it fall.

Is this sensuous? I wonder. *Is this sexy?*

But I know I'm going to have to forget my self-conscious and lose myself in the moment if this is going to work. *Do it for yourself.*

I close my eyes and forget about the Dominic standing across the way, watching. Instead, I summon up the Dominic who fucked me so well. I imagine his face in the grip of his hot desire, the intense expression as he pushed himself into me with forceful thrusts. I remember taking his erection in my mouth, sucking his tip and making him groan out loud. I shiver all over and at once feel that spread of arousal, the tingling of nerves coming alive and juices rushing to the surface, making me ready for whatever lies ahead.

I slide my hand back into my gown again, but this

time I cup my breast, rubbing my thumb over the nipple that is already puckered and stiff, the tip dark red and thrusting. It responds to my touch, lighting small fuses in my groin and making me sigh. I do the same to my other breast, awakening it with a rub and a pinch, letting it add to the spin of excitement in my stomach. Then, slowly, I let the gown drop open and shrug it down over my shoulders. Now the gown is held up by the belt, but my chest is entirely exposed and under the gown I'm wearing a black lace bra, cut low and underwired so that my breasts form soft globes that are held in two wispy lace cups.

My eyes are only half closed, so that I can see Dominic at the opposite window. I know he's watching. I imagine his breath coming harder and faster as he realises what I'm doing. Then, suddenly, he moves and a moment later, his flat is plunged into darkness. Then he is back at the window but now I can only see his outline, a shadow, and he is standing further back so that I can hardly make him out at all.

Now, the usual situation is reversed. He's the one in the dark looking at me, in the light.

But I know exactly what I'm doing. I know that he's watching.

I feel a fresh wave of arousal and rub my hands over my breasts again, playing with the nipples as they strain and rub against the textured surface of the lace. I run my hands over my arms, shoulders and neck, play them over my belly, and then return to my breasts again. This time I release them from their cups, setting them free so that the nipples are exposed, pushed upwards by the bra. I reach for my glass, take a sip of wine, then dip my fingertips into it and rub the red wetness over the nipples.

This delicate play is doing its work for me. I'm breathing faster and my sex is swelling and pouting, filling with a delicious hot wetness. My body has been awakened by Dominic and is hungry for more, eager to feel those transports again. My instincts are driving my hands downwards. I let one disappear into the folds of the gown, playing it over myself, letting it linger and feel the heat between my legs.

Are you watching, Dominic? Is this exciting you?

Slowly, I pull at the belt holding up the gown and it slides free. As it loosens, the gown slips down my legs to the floor, leaving me only in my lace knickers and bra. As one hand rubs and caresses my breasts, the other pushes its way down inside my knickers and down to my secret place. I push a finger into my hot wetness. Oh my goodness, I feel so ready down there, hungry for touch, ready to yield up pleasure to me at the slightest touch. I run my finger over the full lips, sliding it through the honey there, and bring it to my clitoris, that sensitive bud that sends those exquisite messages out to all my nerve endings.

I lick my lips as my fingertip rubs against it and it quivers deliciously. It wants more and more. I rub it again hard, twirling over it with more pressure. It's begging me to be rougher, to be firmer. It wants to be brought to its peak, my whole body needs it . . .

Dominic. I imagine he's touching me, those big square-tipped fingers exciting me, plunging into me while the pillow of his thumb presses hard on the dimple above.

I can't fight the urge now. My legs tremble as I gather pace, rubbing hard in long strokes across my most sensitive place.

'Dominic,' I gasp aloud, and then it comes, the orgasm crackling and shaking me. I have to reach out with my other hand and clutch the table to prevent myself falling over, as my limbs respond to the intense sensations. I'm quivering with the force of it as it grabs and shakes me in several violent motions, and then it recedes, leaving me gasping.

My head droops, my eyes are shut. I take a long breath, then bend and pick up my gown. I wrap it around myself and move about, turning out the lamps.

I do not know what is happening in the flat opposite. It's in darkness and I do not look anyway. I've shown him myself in the most intimate way. Now he knows that I can go further than he thought possible.

And this, Dominic, is just the beginning.

CHAPTER TWELVE

'Are you ready for this? Are you sure?' James searches my face anxiously, wanting to be certain that he's not helping me down a path better left untrodden.

'Absolutely,' I say with determination. I've dressed up in the sexy black dress I bought on my makeover day, and used all the make-up techniques I learned then to make myself look as sophisticated as possible.

'All right.' He puts out one arm for me to slip mine under. 'Well, you look lovely. I'm very proud to have you on my arm.'

With that, we start walking through the fading evening light towards Soho. I hope I'm doing the right thing. Despite what happened last night, I haven't heard from Dominic. I'm sure he watched every second of what took place, but my phone has remained silent all day. No text, no call. I just hope that I didn't have the opposite effect to the one I intended.

Well, it's done now.

But this is different. It's taking myself, uninvited, into his world. It's risky and dangerous because I have no way of knowing how Dominic will react to it. His character in his other existence might be quite different to the one I think I know.

James talks on, helping take my mind off the thoughts churning in my head.

'So I've done a little research into this place,' he confides as we walk along, looking like any other smart city couple on our way, perhaps, to the theatre or an expensive restaurant. The truth is very different to what any observer might suppose.

'What did you find out?'

'It wasn't easy. There's a website but it's extremely vague and most of it is members only. How you become a member isn't really explained. I suspect it's a question of who you know, as it so often is. However, I made a few calls and managed to find someone who's a member.'

'Oh?' My interest pricks up. 'What did they say?'

'Full of praise,' James says laconically. 'Loves it. He joined when he found true love with his girlfriend. He's not yet told her that his particular pleasure involves enemas and golden showers, so he goes to the club every now and then for that. Worth every penny of the very expensive membership, he says.'

My mouth drops open and James notices and laughs.

'Oh, my dear, you really have no idea, do you?' He pats my hand in an almost fatherly way. 'Your innocence reminds me of happier times. Never mind. Don't worry, we're not going to see people doing that kind of thing out in the open. It's far too sophisticated for that. You'll see when we get there.'

James knows exactly where we're going, which is good because I'm beginning to feel sick. If he weren't striding confidently beside me, with every intention of seeing this through, I would be lagging and getting ready to change my mind and head for home. Soon, too soon, we've passed through the busy Soho streets and have found the turn off into that strangely quiet place where the tall Georgian houses have their windows shuttered against the outside world. The old-fashioned street lamp glows and the iron railings glimmer in its light. It's easy to imagine we've stepped back in time, and that any minute I'll hear the clip-clop of horses' hooves and the creak of carriage wheels, perhaps see a mysterious figure in a long frock coat and a top hat.

'Well,' James says as we come to a halt outside the house. 'Here we are. The Asylum. Shall we go and join the Bedlamites?'

I take a deep breath. 'Yes,' I say firmly. And we descend the metal staircase towards the black door below.

Inside, the man I saw before is sitting at the table. He looks as weirdly frightening as I remembered, with dark tattoos swirling over one half of his entire face and over his skull, and with those curiously pale, almost white eyes. He looks up at us as we enter, his gaze going immediately to James. I hope that he's forgotten the brief visit I made here last time, but just in case, I keep my eyes lowered.

'Yes?' he says, his tone unfriendly.

'Good evening. I'm not a member, unfortunately,' James says, sounding far more confident than I ever could have, 'but my friend Cecil Lewis is, and he said he would arrange for us to be welcomed here this evening.'

'Cecil?' The doorman cocks his head at us, still frosty but a little less hostile. 'Of course we all know Cecil. Just a moment.' He stands up and disappears through a dark doorway off to the left that I guess must lead to vaults underneath the pavement. James and I swap glances, mine worried and his amused, and he raises his hand to show me his crossed fingers. A moment later, the doorman is back. 'All right, Cecil's arranged it. I'll need to issue you with temporary cards and there will be a charge for tonight's entertainment.'

'That's no problem at all,' James replies smoothly, reaching for his wallet.

'We don't do money here,' the doorman says, as though such a thing would be hopelessly vulgar. 'You will be invoiced. I'll need your details in this book. As Cecil is standing for you, you understand that he will be charged if you neglect to pay.'

'Of course. My own club has exactly the same rules,' James returns, refusing to be ruffled. He bends down, picks up the old-fashioned silver nib pen and dips it into the inkwell. He writes his name and details, the pen scratching over the paper in the silence. 'There. All done.'

The doorman turns to me. 'Now you.'

I take the pen obediently and write my name and the address of Celia's flat, then hand the pen back.

The doorman produces two cards of heavy ivory

paper. They are engraved in black script with the words *Temporary Member of The Asylum* and underneath *Your discretion is required.* I take mine and clutch it. My entry card to this secret world.

'You can go in now,' the doorman says, nodding towards the doorway off to the right. I know where it leads. Into the club itself.

'Thank you.' James steps forward and leads the way and we pass through the doorway and into the dark interior that awaits us. As we venture inside, it looks the same as it did the last time I was here but now there is more time to look around. I try not to stare, but my eyes are drawn at once to the cages at the back of the room. They are there, but now they hang empty, looking like vast round birdcages. Chains inside hang limply.

'There were people in those before,' I hiss quietly to James, nodding towards them. 'Girls in bondage gear.'

'I wonder why they're empty tonight?' he says. He's leading the way between the tables and finds us an empty one. 'Let's sit down here.'

The room is very dark. The only illumination comes from tiny red glass lanterns on the tables and some heavily shaded wall lights. The atmosphere is very louche. Around us, people are sitting at other tables and waiters dressed in black polo necks and black trousers move between them, serving drinks from their trays. No one seems to be eating. I get the impression that different sorts of appetites are sated here.

A waiter comes up to us and hands us a drinks

menu. James peruses it for a moment and says, 'A bottle of Chateau Pichon Longueville Comtesse de Lalande '96, please.'

'Yes, sir. And . . .' The waiter looks at us impassively. 'What sort of room will you be requiring later, sir?'

'Ah . . .' James seems disconcerted for the first time. 'Er, well, I'm not sure, actually. We haven't decided.'

The waiter looks surprised. 'Really?'

'That is – we're temporary members, I'm not sure what's on offer.'

'Ah, I see,' the waiter says, his face clearing. 'I'll fetch you the menu, sir, so you can see our range.'

'Now we'll find out,' James murmurs to me as the waiter heads off. I look around at the other people. They seemed normal at first glance, well dressed and relaxed in these unusual surroundings, drinking expensive wine and cocktails, but as I watch, I see that unexpected dynamics are being played out. One table seems to be two women drinking together but I soon realise that one of the women is in fact a man, dressed in women's clothing and in full make-up. He keeps his eyes lowered at all times and only moves to fill up his companion's glass or speak when he is spoken to.

'Look,' I say to James and he glances over discreetly. 'Is he a transvestite?'

James whispers back. 'I don't think so. But don't ask me what they're up to.'

At another table, a woman appears to be drinking alone, but a movement catches my eye and I see that a man is underneath the table, crouching over her feet. It's then I realise that he is assiduously licking her leather boots, as carefully and rhythmically as a cat cleaning its paws.

The waiter reappears with our drinks and the room menu. As he puts the bottle on the table, he says, 'It's cabaret night tonight, sir. A great favourite with a certain section of our membership. Afterwards there is usually a high demand for rooms, so it's best to book early.'

He leaves us with the open bottle of wine and the menu. I take it and read it as best I can in the semi-darkness.

'The nursery wing,' I read just loudly enough for James to hear. 'Two chambers are available, each fully equipped for baby's every need. The schoolroom: suitable for the education and chastisement of pupils. The throne room: a luxurious chamber fit for a queen. Mount Olympus: a heavenly boudoir, designed for a goddess and her minion but suitable for gods and their slave girls too. The wet room: suitable for all kinds of play. The dungeon: three separate underground chambers superbly supplied with tools, where masters and mistresses can give their slaves the richest of punishments.' I put the card down, feeling a little faint. 'Oh my God. What is this place?'

'Didn't Dominic tell you about it?' James asks, one eyebrow raised.

'He said it was somewhere safe for people to live out fantasies. I just didn't realise what those fantasies can be.'

James shakes his head. 'There's no limit, darling. No limit at all.'

'But . . . *a nursery*?'

'I'll bet you'll find the biggest, butchest babies you ever saw in there,' James remarks with a laugh. 'But think about it this way. Some Alpha males crave a little time off, when they don't have to bestride the world, take on the massive responsibility that comes with their jobs or their money, when they can return to the safety of childhood.'

'I can see that, I suppose,' I say haltingly. 'But to dress up as a baby . . . and do they find it sexy too?'

'You'd be surprised what people can get sexual enjoyment from. I suppose some could even get it from doing their tax return. I did have a friend who got highly aroused every time she did a sudoku puzzle. She kept piles of those puzzle books by her bedside and got in a panic when she ran out of Biros.' He laughs. 'I'm exaggerating, but you see what I mean.'

James pours out glasses of the wine. It glints ruby red in the candlelight. 'I think you'll like this, it's rather good,' he says, admiring the liquid in his glass. He takes a sip. 'Oh, fabulous.'

I sip as well. He's right. I don't know much about wine, but I can tell this is something special, it's so smooth and delicious.

As we're enjoying the wine, some lights come up and I notice a small stage at the front of the room for the first time. A pair of pale blue spotlights are trained on the stage and into their cool glare steps a woman. She's beautiful and curvaceous, wearing an exquisite red flared dress and high heels. Her hair and make-up are like a vintage screen goddess's. Music plays and she starts to sing in a low husky voice about wanting to be loved, just a little. It all seems like ordinary cabaret until she begins slowly to strip away her clothes. The dress comes away in two separate pieces, revealing a corset tied tightly around a tiny waist and thrusting up a large bosom, silken underwear, a garter belt and stockings.

'She's a looker all right,' James murmurs.

It's a burlesque performance, the kind of thing that's been popular for a while now. As she sings the sultry nightclub number, the corset comes off revealing a pair of larger than expected breasts. She writhes prettily, swinging her hips and posing delicately in her heels. Then the shoes come off and she peels away the stockings too. Only the silk pants are left, and as the song reaches its climax, the singer unbuttons something at the back and the pants drop away, revealing a large penis nestled up over a pair of shaven balls. There's a sound from the audience like a gasp mixed with a sigh. The singer tugs on the penis for a moment so that it hangs large and pendulous, then smiles at the audience as though asking for their admiration of her appendage.

'Oh,' says James in a surprised voice. 'Now I wasn't expecting that.'

I giggle.

Another corseted woman comes out and begins to berate the singer, who puts on a good act of looking astonished, and then ashamed. This woman – who seems like the real thing as far as I can tell – produces a riding crop, which makes the singer cower and pretend to be frightened. She drops to the floor and the other woman starts laying about her with the whip, bringing it down with hard smacks across the white back and shoulders, all the time scolding the singer's outlandish exhibitionism.

The audience are evidently enjoying the show. Perhaps this act is why there seem to be plenty of dominant woman and their vassals here this evening.

'I've no idea what we're going to say when they ask which room we want,' James murmurs, pouring some more wine.

'Perhaps we can just make our excuses,' I say, still watching the performance onstage. Someone is approaching us through the gloom. 'I think the waiter's coming now,' I mutter to James. 'Better get the excuse ready.'

But as he nears, I see it is not the waiter at all. It's Dominic, his face white and set, and his eyes icy cold. My insides clench with a mixture of pleasure and fear, and I'm frozen as he approaches.

'Beth,' he says in a low voice, 'what the hell are you doing here?' He glances at James, a horrible, hostile look. 'And who the fuck is this?'

'Hello, Dominic,' I say, trying to be cool, though it's hard with him so near. He's wearing a black cashmere jumper and dark trousers and looks gorgeous. 'I didn't know you'd be here tonight.'

'Well, I am,' he says, his voice almost trembling. I can see he's trying hard to hold in his emotions.

Why is he angry with me? He's got no right! He doesn't own me, for Christ's sake, and as far as he's concerned, it's all over.

The thought helps me to be strong.

'How did you know I'm here?' I ask boldly.

'Your names came up on the system,' is his brief explanation, though I still don't know how that information reached him. Dominic looks over at James again. 'Who is this?' he growls.

'A friend,' I say quickly.

Dominic's black gaze flickers at me. He knows I don't have friends in London, but he won't ask me more in front of James. He stares at me for a while, and then says coldly, 'I don't want you here.'

The words wound me horribly but I pretend that they bounce off me. 'I don't care what you want,' I reply, my voice cool. 'I'm a free agent.'

'Not to come here. This is a private club. I can ask you to leave.'

'We can leave,' James breaks in, 'but do you mind if we finish this bottle? It's rather good, you see . . .'

Dominic looks at him as though a worm has just spoken, then says, 'All right. Finish your drink and go.' He turns to me. 'Beth, are you all right with this man? I can put you in a taxi home.'

I stiffen my shoulders and raise my chin defiantly. 'I don't need your help. I can look after myself.'

Dominic opens his mouth, then closes it again. He

209

stares at me again, one more burning gaze, and then says briefly, 'All right.' Then he turns on his heel and strides back across the club. We watch him go as the rest of the audience concentrates on the beating being meted out on stage.

'Well, there's one thing I'll say about that,' James remarks, lifting his wine glass to his lips. 'That young man is clearly not over you in any way, shape or form. Quite the reverse, in fact.' He smiles at me. 'If you wanted to set the cat among the pigeons, I think you've succeeded.'

James and I share a taxi home, even though he's going in a completely different direction.

'I don't mind,' he says, 'I can take the long way round to Islington. Are you sure you're going to be all right on your own tonight?'

I nod. 'I'll be fine. I'm used to it, and I've got De Havilland to keep me company.' A black cloud of depression has fallen on me and now I can't really remember what I expected to get out of the whole exercise. If I had thought that Dominic was going to greet me with open arms, then I was sadly mistaken.

'As long as you're sure,' James says, and he gives me a kiss on the cheek and a squeeze of the hand as I climb out of the taxi. 'I'll see you tomorrow. And ring me if you need to.'

'I will. Goodnight.'

I go upstairs slowly, feeling the full weight of my misery. My experience at the club has made me unsure about everything I thought I'd decided. I wanted to take my own first tentative steps towards Dominic, to see if he might meet me halfway, but I've no idea how I can go any further. There's only so far James can help me, and there's no one else I can turn to at all.

Unless . . . Vanessa's face floats before my consciousness. She's the only other person I know in London, and she must be the only one with that much influence over Dominic. Could she . . . would she help me? It's unlikely, I suppose, but then again . . . But how will I reach her?

In the flat, I go to the window of the sitting room and look out but of course the flat is in darkness. I know where Dominic is. I remember how I stood here last night, and what I did.

Did I humiliate myself?

I sigh. I have no idea. But it seems that gaining entry to Dominic's world is going to be harder than I thought.

CHAPTER THIRTEEN

The next day is busy at the gallery and James has me stay late to oversee the removal of the current exhibition. The artist comes in to check that all is going well and that his pictures are being treated with the appropriate care, so James opens a bottle of white wine and we end up having a fun evening. This is definitely the kind of career for me, I think. Schmoozing artists and getting a bit tipsy with the boss? Fine with me.

I try not to think about Dominic and instead concentrate on my plan to get hold of Vanessa. The only thing that I can think of is going back to The Asylum and demanding to see her – but Dominic could well be there, which would ruin that particular plan. I don't know her surname or anything else about her.

Later that evening, I feel more depressed than ever. I'm approaching halfway through my stay, and time feels as if it's speeding up. I love my job but how will I be able to do it if I can't live in Celia's flat? It doesn't pay very much and I'll need to start planning now if I intend to stay in London. Right now, I can't think of anything I'd rather do. The idea of going home is awful. I've taken the steps towards a new life and I can't imagine turning back.

And then there's the fact that I haven't got any further with locating Vanessa.

The only bright spot is that James has invited me out over the weekend. He's going to take me to the theatre and then on to one of his favourite restaurants where he's promised we'll see someone famous, as there's always a celebrity or two eating there.

I'm settling down to watch a DVD, which I bought in my lunch hour to watch on my laptop. With no television, I've stocked up on some films to entertain me during quiet evenings in the flat, and today I've opted for an old favourite, *The Lady Eve,* a black-and-white movie from the forties with Barbara Stanwyck and Henry Fonda. The razor-sharp dialogue always makes me laugh.

I've just settled down and the opening credits are playing when there's a knock on the door.

Instantly my heart starts pounding. I pause the film and pad over to the front door, hardly able to breathe. I open it, and there he is. He's in jeans, a pale shirt and a dark grey cashmere sweater, and the smoky colour makes his dark eyes even more intense.

'Hi, Dominic.' My voice comes out in a whisper.

'Hi.' He looks cold, his eyes flinty. 'Have you got a few minutes? Can I talk to you?'

I nod and stand back to let him in. 'Of course.'

He strides through to the sitting room and regards the computer with its frozen frame. 'Oh. You're watching something. Sorry to disturb you.'

'Don't be silly. You know I'd rather talk to you.' I

213

go over to the sofa and sit down, wishing I'd known he was coming so I could have brushed my hair and checked my face.

He says nothing but goes over to the window and stares out. His profile is stark against the glass and I admire the long straight line of his nose. I can tell from his mouth that his jaw is clenched. He looks stiff and tense.

'Is something wrong, Dominic?' I venture. De Havilland has jumped up next to me and is roosting on his paws like a long black fluffy chicken. I run my fingers through his soft fur and his purr rumbles away.

Dominic turns to look at me and his eyes are flashing. 'I've tried to keep away,' he bursts out. 'But it's killing me. I have to know who that man is and what you're doing with him.' He crosses the floor towards me, reaching me in two strides. 'Please, Beth. Who is he?'

I stare up at him, keeping calm by concentrating on the slow steady purr under my fingertips, De Havilland sitting unperturbed beside me. Am I going to lie or am I going to tell the truth? I have a feeling that what I say now will influence the course of everything.

'He's a friend,' I say softly. It's hard having Dominic so near to me and yet unable to touch him. 'A friend who's promised to help me.'

He pounces on my words. 'Help you do what?'

I wait for a long time before I speak, staring at his face. I've known him such a short time and it already means so very much to me. I don't know if what I'm about to say will change everything, but I do know that I don't want things to stay the way that they are. Then I say very softly, 'He's going to help me enter your world.'

Dominic's face drains of colour. His lips are pale and hardly move when he says, 'How is he going to do that?'

'You don't think I can.' All my emotions boil up to the surface, and I fix him with an intense look. 'But I can, and I want to, and he's going to help me.'

'Oh my God.' Dominic sinks down into an armchair and puts his face in his hands. I know what's racing through his mind: images of James and me, together. In his head, I'm letting James do all the things to me that he has sworn he'll never do. It must be torturing him; I can understand that. When he looks up at me at last, his dark eyes are tormented. 'You'd let him do that.'

I lean forward towards him, desperate to make him understand. 'I want to be close to you, I want to be with you. If this is what it takes, then I want to do it.'

'No,' he says, sounding broken. 'Not that. I can take giving you up, but I can't stand this.'

I get up and go to him, sinking to the floor and putting my hands on his legs, as if in supplication. 'But you don't have to,' I say pleadingly. 'It doesn't have to be him. It could be you.'

Slowly he uncovers his face and looks at me, half desperate and half reluctant. 'You really mean it? It's what you want?'

'Yes. It's true. And if it's not you, I'll find someone else, if that's the only way.'

Our eyes are locked on one another. I've never felt more complete than when looking at him. He leans down and lifts me slowly towards him. 'Beth,' he says throatily. 'God, I want you so much. You don't know what you're asking. But it kills me to think of you with anyone else.'

'Then let me be with you.' I lift his hand to my mouth and kiss it. I take one of his fingers in my mouth and suck it gently, wrapping my tongue around it, loving it. He watches, his eyes becoming hooded as desire fills them. I move closer to him, release his hand and let it slide behind my head and pull me towards him. Slowly, tantalisingly, our mouths touch and press together. I feel the warmth of his tongue slide over my lips, and I automatically part them to grant him entry. His tongue explores me, and I breathe in his familiar, delicious taste. I press back into his mouth and we are lost in our kiss, his hand on my head pulling me ever closer to him.

At last we part, breathless. Our eyes are locked, the heat between us incredible, and then he says, 'I saw you. That night. In here.'

'You mean . . .'

'Yes. When you were alone.' His eyes glitter darkly. 'It was extraordinary.'

'Did it . . . make you happy?'

'Happy?' He strokes my hand. 'I've never known anything like it.'

I smile, embarrassed but pleased. 'It was only for you.'

216

'I know. It was a beautiful gift.' He laughs and adds, 'Let's hope old Mr Rutherford on the floor above me wasn't looking out, or he'll have finally had that heart attack he's been talking about.'

In that moment, we both relax.

'Will you stay?' I ask.

'I don't know how I could leave,' he replies, his eyes glazed with lust.

'Then come on.' I stand up, take his hand, and we go together to the bedroom.

He undresses me slowly, stopping all the time to kiss the skin that he is uncovering. The feel of his lips brushing mine, the tip of his tongue lapping gently against me sends my nerve endings haywire. When I'm in my underwear, I can't resist the need to touch him in return any longer.

'Let me,' I say, running my hands up under his shirt and sweater, and he does. I pull his sweater up over his head, then unbutton the shirt slowly, kissing his torso where each loosened button reveals his bare chest. I can see from the shape of his jeans that his erection is standing proud, eager to be free, and I unbutton those too, sliding them down over his long, firm thighs.

When he is in just his boxer shorts, I take his hand and lead him over to the bed. We lie down together, stroking our hands along the shapes of one another's bodies, me taking in his muscular hardness and he the soft curves of my breasts and yielding belly.

I slide my hand downwards, brushing it lightly over the trail of black hair that leads from his navel to the waist of his boxers. When I touch the velvety top of his penis, it throbs and moves under my hand.

I run my hand up and down the hot shaft for a moment, then slowly I bend to kiss his stomach, licking the skin gently as I descend towards his erection.

He moans slightly. 'Oh, Beth . . . that's so good.'

I move so that I can pull the boxer shorts down, sliding them down his calves and over his ankles. Then I edge my way slowly up his body, until I am straddling his thighs. His eyes are glazed, taking in my breasts still confined by my bra and the knickers concealing my sex from his gaze.

I bend down over his length, letting my hair drift lightly over his skin. I grasp the shaft in both of my hands, moving the skin gently.

'You're so big,' I say softly.

He says nothing but his lips are parted as he draws a ragged breath.

'I want to kiss you, take you in my mouth and suck you,' I say throatily, gazing straight into his eyes and seeing his lust spark up a level as I speak. Then I stoop downwards and breathe lightly on the tip of his penis, its softest, sweetest part. I put my tongue out and lick around it, curling my tongue round its head and then I take it between my lips and let the head fill my mouth as far as it can. One hand keeps hold of its hard length, while the other slips underneath him and plays lightly with his balls, my forefinger rubbing at the spot beneath them, the place that makes him gasp when I touch it.

He moans, and his hips buck lightly, pushing his

penis deeper into my mouth. For long minutes, I suck and play with him, revelling in the effect I'm having on him, the mounting desire in his eyes, and the way his hard thigh is pressing against my hot, damp sex and stimulating my clitoris.

'Beth,' he says huskily, 'I can't take much more, I'll come in your mouth . . .'

Part of me wants him to come, but I'm also greedy for myself. I take my mouth away from him and move so that I can take my knickers off, then I straddle him again, sliding myself further up him. I take my weight on my knees and position myself over him, holding his penis straight up, away from his belly. His eyes are heavy, lidded with anticipation of what I'm going to do, as I bring myself down to his tip, letting it play in the slippery wetness of my sex. I'm hungry for his swollen shaft, everything in me demanding it, but I'm also enjoying this tantalising moment.

Dominic puts his hands out onto my hips, running them around and over my bottom.

'Do it,' he says, 'I need you.'

At his words, I press myself down, plunging him into my depth, engulfing him. He fills me up and for a moment I think he's pierced something in me, he's so far and deep inside. I gasp and shake my head, arching my back at the voluptuous sensation. His hands move my hips in time to his movements and we are in perfect synchronisation, my body meeting his thrusts so that we both draw in fierce gasps as he hits a sweet spot inside me.

The power begins to build within me and I can feel Dominic's speed increase. My long oral worship of his cock has put him in the grip of an explosive orgasm, and he's pounding towards it. His excitement has an incredible effect on me. Every time he hits home, the feeling grows more intense, a strong, vibrant, electrical thrill; and then his thighs stiffen underneath me, his face contorts with the intensity of the physical sensation pulsing through him, and his orgasm rocks him, bursting out inside me and instantly I'm tipped over the edge, my climax convulsing me with pleasure and wringing me out, so that I fall onto his chest as it leaves me.

Dominic sighs as he comes back to himself, wraps his arms round me and strokes my hair.

'That felt like coming home.'

'I don't want you to leave me again,' I say, running my hand over his skin. It's damp from our exertions. 'I want to be with you. I'll do anything. So, will you show me? Will you let me in?'

He clasps my hand tightly in his, and runs his mouth along my shoulder. Then, looking deep into my eyes, he says, 'Yes, I will. I'll take you there. I promise.'

A feeling of deep calm fills me, even though I know that I've won a battle that may not bring me happiness.

'Thank you,' I say softly.

He stares at me with dark, dark eyes, and says nothing.

THE THIRD WEEK

CHAPTER FOURTEEN

Beth

Thank you for a wonderful night.

I'm away this weekend on business, but we'll start on Monday. I'll collect you after work and we'll go to dinner.

D x

I find the note on the empty pillow next to me when I wake. I read it several times, then hold it to my chest, staring at the ceiling. Here is the proof that I've succeeded in the task I set myself. Dominic is going to take me down that dark path into a place I can't really imagine. I have no idea what awaits me. I've never even been smacked, not seriously. My parents didn't spank me, and my brothers fought with each other rather than me.

Now I've asked the man I want most in the world to do that to me. And I have no concept of what that really means.

I get up and pad towards the bathroom. Until it begins, I have the weekend. James is taking me out, the weather is still hot and sunny, I'm young and it's summertime. And there's a delicious man in my life. So all in all, I think as I climb out of bed, life could be considerably worse.

The whole weekend is permeated by the knowledge of what awaits me. Even while I'm enjoying the theatre and the glitzy restaurant, or soaking up the sun and taking a river trip, the sense of dark, excited apprehension is always with me.

James wants to know what's going on with Dominic – 'Quite a fiery character, I thought,' he says, 'but such a looker! No wonder you're head over the proverbial heels' – and although I don't tell him exactly what's happening, I hint at it and James is quick to understand.

'Just be careful, Beth. Don't forget we can never separate our hearts from our bodies. Your emotions are the strongest part of you. Whatever you think your body can stand . . . well, it's what you yourself can take.' I know he's sincere when he tells me that he's there for me if I need him.

I just hope I'm not going to.

Monday comes, and with it, the feeling of fearful anticipation grows. I can hardly keep my mind on my work at all during the day, and I have to have a good talk with myself in the lavatory mirror.

As I face my reflection, I look different somehow. Perhaps it's the stark quality of my work outfit of crisp white shirt, black skirt and belted, black cardigan, and the way my hair is pulled back into a tight and glossy ponytail, but I know I seem older and wiser than I did just a few weeks ago. A little more ready to be brave, perhaps.

'Now come on, Beth,' I say firmly to myself in the mirror. 'He's not going to say hello, pull out a whip and start laying into you. It's not going to be like that.'

Whatever I might fear, I have confidence that Dominic will be a good and gentle guide. I have to relax and put my trust in him. I need to put myself entirely in his hands.

Perhaps that's what it's all about. Have I already agreed to surrender and given him the control he loves?

I'm struck by the paradox that it's taken my strength of will and determination to bring me to a place where I yield it up entirely to another person. But I realise that I trust Dominic to protect me, and that feeling is deeply comforting.

And I'll know more tonight.

My eyes have a shining quality. I know I'm excited by this strange turn things have taken. And there are only a few hours left to wait.

Dominic arrives promptly as James is putting the closed sign up in the gallery. I feel a rush of pride as he walks in, so tall and handsome and so beautifully turned out in a dark grey suit and gold silk tie. As ever he looks immaculate, but his expression turns to astonishment when he sees James and recognises him from The Asylum.

'Charming to see you again,' James says, imperturbable as ever. 'Have a lovely evening, you two.'

'Thanks, James, goodnight,' I say, picking up my bag and joining Dominic by the door.

'He's your *boss*?' Dominic says as he drops a kiss on my lips.

I nod, smiling a little mischievously. 'We bonded very quickly.'

We walk out of the gallery together and on to the street. Dominic frowns and I can see a flicker of jealousy in his eyes. 'Not too closely, I hope. Was he really going to have some kind of relationship with you?'

'I'll tell you a secret,' I say, pulling him down so that my mouth is close to his ear. 'He's gay.'

Dominic looks a little mollified but he still growls, 'That doesn't necessarily mean anything in my world, I can tell you that. You'd be surprised what can happen when all the barriers come down.'

'Where are we going?' I ask, slipping my arm under his and snuggling close to him as we walk. For some reason, I feel more affectionate with him than ever, longing to touch and hug him. For a moment, I wonder if I can call this all off and we can just go home and cuddle on the sofa. Then I think: *Dominic's not a simple cuddle-on-the-sofa guy, remember? It's this way – or not at all.*

'We're going to The Asylum,' he replies. He seems a little distracted but perhaps it's just the desire to be off the busy after-work streets.

'Oh.' I feel obscurely disappointed. I'd imagined some new ground but perhaps it makes sense. It is a place that seems to feature large in Dominic's life, so

I'm going to have to get to know it.

We are soon making our way down the metal staircase to the door. It's so early that the place has a deserted feel to it. The desk at the entrance is unmanned, but Dominic leads me confidently inside. The tattooed man is behind the bar, writing something on a clipboard, and he looks up as we enter.

'Evening, Dominic,' he says in a friendly way, quite at odds with his aggressive appearance.

'Hi, Bob,' responds Dominic. 'Is she here?'

'Upstairs. I'll just buzz her down.' The tattooed man reaches for a telephone and makes a quick muttered call.

'He's called *Bob*?' I say quietly but incredulously. I giggle.

'Yes. What's so strange about that?'

'Well . . . he doesn't look like a Bob, that's all.'

'Mmm, I suppose he does look quite odd,' Dominic admits, smiling. 'I'm used to him, I guess.'

'Bob,' I say again, and laugh.

I'm looking about the empty bar and thinking about how different a place can be with no one in it, its character quite changed, when a door towards the back of the bar opens and in strides Vanessa.

She looks amazing in a scarlet trouser suit, ice-white silk shirt and high heels. Her lips are painted to match her suit, and her short wavy hair is loose, softening the look. Her eyes, though, are not exactly welcoming as she approaches.

'Darling,' she says brightly, smiling at Dominic as

she kisses him on the cheek. Then she turns to me with an altogether colder look. 'Hello. We meet again. It's an unexpected pleasure.'

I nod, shy suddenly. She seems so far away from anything I could ever be.

'We'll go to my apartment,' she says, turning back the way she came. 'Follow me.'

So this is it. I'm being taken beyond the safe zone.

I follow her, Dominic close behind, and we go through a dark baize door and into the most private part of the club. At first, there's nothing to see. A corridor, a staircase, closed doors. We ascend to the first floor and Vanessa turns to Dominic.

'Would she like to see any of the chambers?'

'Why don't you ask her,' Dominic says quietly. 'She's right here.'

Vanessa turns her cold gaze to me. 'Would you?'

I take a deep breath. *Why not?* 'Yes. Please.'

'Right.' Vanessa strides to the nearest door and opens it. 'We're quiet tonight. This one is empty. It's part of the nursery wing.' She stands back so that I can step inside, and I venture in a few steps and look around.

It looks like the archetypal baby's bedroom from years gone by, with blue and pink gingham everywhere, a white chest of drawers decorated with cute bunnies, a toy box and a cot with ruffled bedding, except that everything is on a massive scale. The cot is big enough for an adult male; a giant potty with a ruffled skirt concealing its base sits in one corner. A large table that can accommodate an adult lying flat also holds supplies of baby wipes, talcum powder and a basket full of enormous disposable nappies. On a shelf, along with teddies, rattles and baby books, is a tray of dummies and a selection of baby bottles.

I look around in astonishment. So this really happens. People actually want to enact this fantasy.

'The nursery is very popular,' Vanessa remarks. 'Our other room is in use at the moment and I'm afraid that from the sounds of it, baby is being very naughty indeed. Shall we go on?'

I follow her out, seized for a moment by a wild desire to laugh. But I also find something strangely comforting in the idea that if someone truly is seized by the need to return to the nursery like this, then here is a perfect place to come.

'You may as well see this too,' Vanessa says, and leads me to a door on the opposite side. She opens it and we both look in. It's a vintage schoolroom, with a blackboard, old-fashioned desks and chairs, a bookshelf with text books and exercise books, pots of pens and pencils, an old tin globe and so on. But also very present are the instruments of correction: a dunce's hat, a long cane, a large paddle hanging up by a leather loop, and a leather strap. There is also a wooden device that looks a little like a tunic, which I guess is another tool for punishment.

'Very popular. Extremely popular,' remarks Vanessa. 'My real problem is getting enough governesses. Well-trained ones are worth their weight in gold.'

She closes the door and we go on. I look at Dominic with a questioning look but he shakes his head with a smile and I understand: all this is interesting but it's nothing to do with us.

'I think the other chambers are in use,' she says. 'We'll go straight to my place.'

We climb another flight of stairs and come to the very top of the house. Vanessa stops outside a green door, unlocks it and we go inside. Here is something else altogether: a neat and beautiful living space, a penthouse apartment with breath-taking views over the city rooftops. She leads us in and gestures that we should sit down, while she goes to get some drinks.

'Why are we here?' I whisper to Dominic as we sit down on the dark green velvet chesterfield sofa.

'I want Vanessa to accept you. And there are questions you'll want to ask her too. She knows more about this from a woman's point of view.' Dominic lifts my hand to his mouth and kisses it, gazing at me with a sweet warmth in his eyes. 'I want to do this right, Beth. This seems like a way in.'

Vanessa returns with a tray loaded with a wine bottle, glasses and a dish of salted almonds. She pours the drinks and hands them out before sitting down with hers in an elegant brown suede chair opposite us. She regards me with a look that is now not unfriendly but more guarded. 'So, Beth, Dominic tells me you're interested in becoming a member here.'

I nod.

'What has brought you to our happy world?' she

asks with a lift of her eyebrows. 'Do you wish to become a mistress?'

I'm not clear what she means by that, so I say, 'I'm not sure.'

'Not sure?' Her gaze slides to Dominic. 'Oh. Then I think we can safely say you don't. A mistress is usually pretty sure of what she wants.'

Dominic breaks in. 'Beth is more interested in being a submissive.'

'Ah. I see. Well, then, the mistress world is probably not for you. There are female subs within it but it tends to be more about female domination and male submission. You'll have seen from the play areas I showed you that it is about the male taking on a role in which he is chastised and corrected by a powerful woman. In which he is controlled and finds release and satisfaction in punishment – not just the punishment but in acts of rebellion, fear of reprisal, and eventually the joy of submission to what he must endure.' Vanessa sighs, almost happily, as if recalling pleasurable moments. Her fingers play about her wine glass and I notice that the nails on one of her hands are long, and on the other, short. Then she looks at me again and continues. 'The mistress environment is about punishment and discipline. It is dressed up in costume and playful in its props and scenery, but it is also harsh. Naughty boys suffer punishments that will make your eyes water just thinking about them. Naughty girls however . . .'

Her eyes glitter and she leans towards me and says

in a low, caressing voice, 'What punishments do you think naughty girls should get, Beth?'

I feel strange, as if the world is moving faster and I'm spinning with it. 'I . . . I don't know,' I stutter.

She goes on in that hypnotic voice. 'I think that there are girls who want to feel the sting of their master's anger. Girls who know that they're only truly themselves when they're surrendering to the delightful bite of the crop, the crack of the cat slapping down across their backs, the extraordinary journey that flogging will take them on. There are girls who need to feel ropes tighten round their wrists and ankles, to have their hungry pussies filled with naughty toys, who want their pain to turn into the most intense pleasure.' She puts her head on one side and gives me a smile of enormous sweetness. 'Is that you, Beth?'

My heart is racing and my breathing is coming fast, but I try to hide it. My voice comes out cracked. 'I don't know. Perhaps.'

Her smile fades and she turns to Dominic. 'I hope you know what you're doing,' she says in a flat tone. 'You know what happens when—'

Dominic breaks in quickly. 'It's fine, Vanessa, really.'

She thinks for a moment, and looks over at me again. 'I want to make sure you understand something, Beth. There are things grown adults want to do that society regards with distaste, or even abhorrence. It doesn't fit in with the accepted narrative of sexuality and it tells us some uncomfortable things about ourselves. But I believe every human has the right to live as happily as they can, and if it takes something as simple as the occasional spanking, then I think it should be possible for them to enjoy that. I provide this place as a haven for those people, a space where they come and live out their fantasies in safety. Safety and consent is key to everything that happens in this house, Beth. Once you understand that, you'll feel more secure about the road you're travelling on.'

'I do understand,' I say, and I feel suddenly that it is a kind of privilege to be here, listening to such an experienced practitioner of her art.

'Good.' She takes a gulp of wine. 'I must be getting on, I'm very busy this evening. I think Dominic wants to show you something else.' She puts down her glass and stands up. Smiling and almost friendly she says, 'Goodbye, Beth. It was nice to talk with you.'

'Goodbye. And thank you.'

'Dominic – we'll talk later, no doubt.' Then she heads for the door and is gone.

I turn to Dominic. 'Wow.'

He nods slowly. 'She knows her stuff. Now come on, there's one more place to visit.'

We go back to the basement level, pass the entrance to the bar, and go through a thick, reinforced door. Another door waits beyond that. I don't like the sight of it at all. It's studded with knobs of harsh-looking metal. Dominic goes first and opens it to a pitch-blackness beyond. He switches on a light and spotlights in the ceiling spark to life.

I gasp. I can't help it. What lies beyond looks like a

medieval torture chamber. I see a large wooden frame contraption with manacles and chains to bind hands and feet to it. Against a wall is a large X-shaped cross, also with loops for the attachment of restraints. Chains stretch from the ceiling to the floor, for what purpose I can't guess, at least, not right now. There are strange deformed benches, on which people must lie in a variety of positions. In the corner is something that looks like a large upright box with holes pierced in it. All this is bad enough, but then my gaze is drawn to the wall and I see that hanging in a row on hooks is a wide variety of instruments, all of which appear terrifying to me. They are flogging tools. Some have thick handles and a big bush of leather tails. Some have just a few strands of leather that are thicker and heavier-looking, with knots at the ends. Some look soft, almost fluffy, with slender handles and long strands of horsehair. Others look as though they have more bite, with braided tails, or a single, serpentine plaited length with an evil-looking forked tongue at the end. Then there are the ones like riding crops: slim lengths of taut, bouncy leather that look as though they'd be agonising flicking down on bare skin; and whips, with thick handles that taper to a long single length. There are canes, strong and hard, and paddles of all sizes, some two-headed, some pierced with holes, others quite plain and somehow those frighten me the most.

'Dominic,' I say, clutching at him. 'I don't know . . . I'm not sure.'

'Hush.' He takes me in his arms and hugs me,

stroking my head. 'It's meant to look scary. It's a place where the imagination goes to a space that's usually your worst nightmare. But it's not that bad, I promise. You come here willingly, you stay willingly, and nothing happens that you don't want.'

I can hardly believe this, but he's smiling sweetly down at me.

'I promise. I don't want to hurt you – not the way you're imagining it. And don't worry, we're not going to start here anyway.'

I'm trembling and fearful, worried about what I've done, what I've agreed to. I don't know if I can do this.

Dominic takes my hands and kisses them. When he speaks, his voice is low and throaty. 'Trust me. That's all you have to do. Trust me.'

CHAPTER FIFTEEN

I don't say much on the way back to the apartment building. I feel strange and rather sick. I can't wipe the image of that place out of my mind, or bear to think of what goes on there. I see maddened eyes, foaming mouths, hear screams and the slash of the whip on soft flesh. It makes no sense to me. How can this be connected to love – to the urge to love and comfort someone, to be gentle and sweet with them?

Dominic senses my fears and lets me take the time I need to process what I've seen, but all the time he keeps his arm around me and his head close to mine. I feel as though I can soak up his strength and confidence, and that helps a little.

'I've got something to show you,' he says as the taxi pulls away from Randolph Gardens, leaving us on the pavement outside. 'Something just for us.'

I'm puzzled.

'Come on.' He looks pleased and excited, and he holds my hand as we go inside and up in the elevator that takes us to his side of the building. But we don't go to the fifth floor this time. It is the seventh, the very top.

'Where are we going?' I ask, surprised.

He smiles, his eyes bright. 'You'll see.'

On the seventh floor, he leads me along the corridor to a door, takes out a key and opens it.

Tonight, I've been amused, surprised and horrified by what I've discovered behind closed doors, but this is something else altogether. Now I'm mystified as we step inside. It's another flat, familiar enough in its layout but a little smaller than Celia's or Dominic's. It's plain enough and simply furnished, from what I can see.

'Here,' Dominic says, and he crosses the small hall and opens a door to the bedroom. I go forward and look within.

'I made this for us,' he says, as I take in the scene. 'I had it done over the weekend.'

Beyond lies a beautiful boudoir, dominated by a vast bed: an old-fashioned iron bedstead with fresh white sheets, a mountain of pillows and a lavender silk counterpane. The textures in the room are all soft and sensuous, from the velvet armchair to the white fur rug and the row of what look like small feather dusters on the table next to the bed. There is an antique chest of drawers and a cabinet of dark-golden wood. I see a strange chair like the one in Dominic's apartment, but large and longer, upholstered in soft white leather with what look like leather reins attached beneath the seat, and a low footrest.

'Look at this.' Dominic goes to the wardrobe and opens it to reveal a row of exquisite lingerie, wisps of lace, mostly in black – and other things too: long loops

237

of silk and leather than look more like equestrian equipment than clothes. I see hoops and buckles and small steel rings but nothing makes any sense on the hangers. There are also stiff corsets with long laces, and wide leather belts with buckles and zips. A silken negligee adds a touch of softer luxury.

I look at him in disbelief. 'You bought all this for me?'

'Of course.' He gestures about him. 'That's the point of all of this. It's just for you and me. It's all fresh and new, with no associations, just for us to play with.' He turns to me eagerly. 'Do you like it?'

'I like it a million times more than the dungeon,' I reply fervently, which makes him laugh. 'Did you really do all this over the weekend?'

I can't believe the organisation needed, let alone the cost of acquiring another flat in the building, as well as furnishing it like this.

He nods and comes towards me, his eyes full of meaning. 'Amazing what can be done when it's important.' He reaches me and turns my chin upwards so that my face is tilted to his. 'I want you to know the pleasure we can bring one another, what heights we can reach.'

Liquid lust floods my stomach and the images of fear and pain vanish. All is beautiful, playful and tender again.

'All this is new to me,' I say huskily. 'But I want to learn.'

'The lessons will be easier and more delightful than you think,' he returns, 'and we'll go one slow step at a time.' His lips brush mine, soft as a butterfly wing, and then just when I don't think I can stand it any longer, he presses down, pushing my mouth open with his tongue, taking possession of it. We kiss eagerly, and the desire that has been building between us floods into life. I'm excited that we're here – not in Celia's flat, or in Dominic's, but in this, our place.

He undresses me quickly between kisses, and I help him. Soon I'm standing before him naked, my nipples already hard and sensitive, as he runs his appreciative gaze over me.

'You're amazing,' he says almost wonderingly. 'You're made for pleasure.' He runs his hand over my behind. 'This is glorious. Just the thought of it makes me hard.' He pulls my hand to his crotch and I feel the hardness there. 'See?'

Oh God, I want it. I want it right now. I start to push his jacket from his shoulders and he quickly takes it off and then sheds the rest of his clothes just as swiftly. We're standing, naked together, our excitement obvious from our rapid breathing, drinking in the sight of one another.

'Is this where it begins?' I ask, my heart pounding hard. Down below I'm aching just as hard. I never knew I was capable of feeling want in such a painful, physical way.

He smiles. Leaning down he nuzzles my neck and runs his tongue lightly up it, reaching my earlobe, which he tugs and bites lightly before whispering in my ear, 'It's a taster. Just a little tiny taste.'

The feeling of his breath in my ear sets off sensations that are almost unbearable, making me squirm with delight and gasp.

He takes my hand and lifts it to his mouth, taking the top of my forefinger and index finger between his lips. I can feel the warm wetness within as his tongue plays over the tips and the grazing of his teeth. A sense of danger tingles through me: he could clamp down painfully on my fingers at any time, and although I'm sure he won't, the possibility is there. The sucking is more arousing than I could have guessed as his tongue runs all over my fingers, taking them further into his mouth. Then I feel his other hand is at my crotch, moving so gently across my pubic hair that at first I'm hardly aware of it, then stroking me a little harder and with more intention. One of his fingers slips inside me, unexpectedly hard and fast, pushing upwards. It's delicious, but not enough. I want more at once. The tantalising tongue playing over my fingers is making me so hot. My head goes back and I sigh with longing. Dominic seems to understand, for he pushes another finger up to join the first and I feel my inner wall stretch deliciously to accommodate him. Oh, but it still isn't enough. I know what I want. With my free hand, I reach for his hard, hot length, but he won't let me touch it, moving just out of my reach.

He releases my fingers from his mouth and guides my hand downwards. Delighted, I think that he's going to let me touch his penis and reach out for its beautiful smooth heat, but he's pushing my hand somewhere else. I gaze into his eyes and he's staring back, intense and strong, as he moves my hand over my own downy hair. I can feel where his other hand is pushed up hard against my crotch and its movement as he thrusts his fingers deep into me. It turns me on even more to feel the mechanics of the delicious sensations he's giving me. Then he pulls his fingers out, running their wetness over my belly, and urges my own hand to take its place.

'Touch yourself,' he murmurs.

I remember how he watched me bring myself to orgasm through the window. How can I have any embarrassment now? I move my fingers over the hot wet lips below my triangle of hair.

'That's right.' He's watching my fingers as they trail across my own sex. 'Go inside yourself.'

I push one finger in the heat between my legs, and run it up inside.

'Now take it out and taste it.'

I hesitate.

'Go on,' he says and I hear the first hint of sternness in his voice. Is this a test?

I take my finger slowly to my mouth. He's watching me intently as I part my lips and put my finger inside.

'Suck it,' he whispers, and I obey, closing my mouth over it and letting the taste spread over my tongue. It's tangy, almost sweet, and most definitely tastes of sex. 'You're delicious,' he says. 'Now. Go to the bed.'

I turn and walk over to the bed. 'What now?' I ask, but a look from him silences me.

'No talking, I'll do the talking,' he says.

Oh God, so it really has started. But he'd said this is just a taster. I don't feel afraid. My first step towards surrendering control is easy enough – so far.

'Lie on the bed, on your back,' he says. 'Put your arms above your head. And close your eyes.'

I do as he says. The crisp cotton and shiny silk covers provide a cool and pleasant texture under my naked back as I lie down. Closing my eyes, I rest my arms above my head, slightly bent across the pillows.

I hear him come near to me, then the sound of a drawer opening and closing.

'Something simple to start with,' he says. A wisp of soft and slippery fabric drifts down onto my face, and the next moment, he's pulled it tight across my eyes and is lifting my head so he can fasten it. The world becomes very black, and I feel a small stab of panic. *I can't see. I didn't choose this!*

'Relax. This is all for you,' he murmurs as if reading my mind. 'You're safe, you'll see.'

One of my wrists is lifted and I feel a soft woven fabric bind it to one of the iron bars of the bedstead. Then the other is tied too. The bonds are not tight or uncomfortable but the feeling of being restrained is very odd. I pull lightly on the bonds and find I can move my wrists only a centimetre or two.

'Trust me,' he breathes. 'This is for your pleasure, I promise. Now. Open your legs.'

I feel uncertain now I cannot see him, vulnerable opening my legs to expose my most private self with-out any sense of where he is or what he is doing. But every sensation is heightened with my sight gone. I'm more aware even of the air in the room as my hot sex is opened to it. The room goes quiet but I sense him moving around. I hear the snap of a match being lit and smell the faint cordite smell of its hot flame. A moment later, I smell a heady incense sweetness of jasmine and cedar.

So that's it. He's lighting a scented candle. That's okay, that's nice.

So far I've liked everything about this experience: the luxurious room, the beautiful fabrics, and now the delicious aroma. But I'm also puzzled. This lull in proceedings is making my arousal falter a little. I'm coming back to myself, and that lost-in-the-feeling mind-set is easing off.

Then, suddenly he's beside me again. The bed moves as he climbs on to it and kneels in the space between my open legs.

'Are you ready?' he asks in a low voice.

'Yes, I'm ready,' I say. The minute I say that, I'm buzzing again, my blood pounding round my body. I'm lost in darkness, vulnerable and open. My hands are bound.

'Good.'

A pause, and then a strange sensation. A drip of heat on my breast that instantly becomes a pleasant warmth. Then another on my other breast. Another hits my belly and then another. What is it?

His fingers scroll over my breast and begin to slide easily over the warm place. I understand. He's dropped

243

some kind of oil on me, and is now beginning to rub it in. The feeling is luscious, voluptuous, as his fingers work on my skin, spreading the oil over me, making me smooth and slippery. He draws the oil over my nipples, tweaking them with his fingertips. The oil makes the traction harder to achieve, so he rubs them harder, pinching them and squeezing them, making desire pull hard in my belly.

Why are nipples directly attached to the groin? I wonder hazily as I begin to writhe with the intensity of the feeling. He's squeezing harder and harder and I can feel that my nipples have swollen and become hard as bullets. The harder they get, the wetter and more slippery I become.

'Stay still,' he says, and I try to stop moving, but I'm panting hard and it's difficult not to respond to the intensity of the sensations he's giving me. He begins to massage my breasts, cupping them, smoothing them, returning to the nipples, then leaving them to caress the soft mounds. Then he works his way down my belly, rubbing the oil into my skin, making me so smooth and lubricated.

'You're very beautiful, Beth,' he says as his large, powerful hands rub my belly, getting ever closer to the place that's dying for his touch. 'I love to see you stretched out like this, just for me. Your whole sweet body surrendered to me.'

I shiver at his words but I can't speak. All I can concentrate on is his fingers, rubbing, swirling, approaching my open legs, where the ache for him is building hard and strong. I want those fingers plunged back into me again. More than that, I want his cock, I want to feel that hard shaft pushing deep inside me *now*.

'Please,' I moan. 'Dominic, I can't bear it.'

'You're going to have to learn some endurance,' he says, sounding amused.

To my tingling frustration, he bypasses my groin altogether and instead hot oil drops upon my thighs and legs. Slowly and painstakingly, he massages the oil into my skin, working his way down my legs and right to my feet. He concentrates on first one, then the other, rubbing each toe and the balls of the feet, and massaging the instep. It's beautifully stimulating. I never knew my feet had such hidden possibilities, but just as I'm relaxing into the pleasure of the foot massage he returns swiftly and smoothly up my legs to my hips.

Now I wish I could see his face but I forget all about that in the next moment, because he's smoothing oil down over my pubic hair. He spreads his fingers over my hips and uses his thumbs to roll down gently, ever closer to where my clitoris is hungry with need. It feels as large and hard as one of my nipples and I'm intensely aware of it throbbing as I anticipate his touch. I want to move, to gyrate my hips and arch my back, but I remember Dominic asked me to stay still and I want to try my best to obey.

Then, when I don't think I can stay still a second longer, the pad of his thumb strums over the top of my clitoris, making me cry out and buck without meaning to.

'The rules aren't strict today,' he says throatily. I can hear in his voice how turned on he is by my strong arousal. 'So you can move now if you want to.'

Then he begins to stroke my bud harder and harder, sending out shudders of pleasure. The feelings are building more intensely in my pitch-black world and as I move on the bed, I feel the restraints tugging my wrists and it heightens my excitement. I can't do anything. I need him to do all of it. Without him, I can't get myself to that peak of ecstasy that I now need desperately.

Then he pulls away. 'There was more,' he says, 'but I can't wait any longer myself.'

I sense him rising up. God, I wish I could see that magnificent cock! Then he's between my legs, holding his length at my entrance, making it play in the oily, slippery depths.

I buck against him, trying to urge him in, but he lingers there for a moment longer.

'You're so ready,' he murmurs. Then, with a huge thrust, he rams into me.

I cry out. *God yes, yes.*

It feels deeper than it has before. He pulls out slowly then pushes again, hard, fast, deep. A slow retreat and then that same gorgeous, slamming advance. He begins to find his rhythm, a solid, delicious thrusting, meeting my pubic bone with every inward thrust and giving my clitoris the grinding pressure it wants so much.

'I want you to come, right now,' he growls. Then his mouth is on mine and our tongues meet in a wanton delicious kiss.

I'm making a sound I don't recognise as anything like I've made before; this is the most intense feeling I've ever had. As his penis hits secret spots deep within me, I'm lost in the velvet darkness of the blindfold and the extraordinary climax that's whirling up to grab me.

'Come,' he commands.

It takes me and crashes me down in a huge wave of blissful euphoria, moving me with its deep force for what feels like minutes, and then I feel Dominic tense, pause deep in his thrust, push hard again as his penis swells even larger, then his orgasm floods out of him with exquisite force. Without seeing it, I can feel it all the more intensely and I love the sensation of him throbbing within me. Then he is lying beside me on the bed, panting.

I'm still fighting for breath myself, still astonished by the force of what happened to me, as Dominic unties me from the bedstead and removes my blindfold.

He is smiling as he takes it away, then kisses my lips. 'So,' he says tenderly, 'how was the first lesson?'

'Earth-shattering,' I say with a satisfied sigh. 'Truly . . . mind-blowing.'

'It sounded it and felt it. You gripped me very tightly during your orgasm. It was amazing.' He drops another kiss, this time on the end of my nose. 'I think we can consider the bed well and truly christened.'

'Mmm,' I wiggle happily. 'It's lovely.'

'I'm glad you like it. It's all for you. This place is ours to do what we like in.' He fixes me with a searching look. 'And tomorrow, we'll begin in earnest.'

CHAPTER SIXTEEN

The next day, I'm still euphoric. James doesn't ask me outright but he takes to calling me Puss. 'Because you look like the cat that's got the cream,' he says with a knowing smile.

It's true, I'm practically purring all day. Everything about my experience the night before was enjoyable. I'm beginning to wonder what I've been missing all this time.

But it's only because it was Dominic.

We're going out tonight, I know. He told me last night that before we could go any further, there were things to be discussed. It sounded ominous and he must have seen the expression of worry on my face because he said it was all very straightforward and nothing to be concerned about.

At seven on the dot, my taxi draws up to the restaurant where Dominic told me to meet him. I don't know this part of London but I recognise the Tower of London and Tower Bridge as the taxi goes past. I must be out to the easterly side of the city.

The restaurant is by the Thames, in a converted warehouse with magnificent views up and down the river, and over to the South Bank.

The maître d' stands and bows as I explain that I've come to meet Mr Stone. As I say it, I realise that I don't even know if this is Dominic's surname or not. It is simply the name he told me to ask for.

'Very good, madam. This way please.' The maître d' leads me through the crowded ground floor to a lift that takes us up several flights to the airy, glass-fronted extension on the warehouse roof. Here the view is even more astounding, as it reaches up over the diners' heads.

'Mr Stone is on the private terrace,' the maître d' says, and a moment later he is leading me out onto a pretty area, open to the evening sky but enclosed on either side by its own glass walls which are further insulated with a lining of green hedge set in granite planters. A cool breeze ruffles the hedge tops, and the briny scent of the river is strong.

Dominic is sitting at the table, a glass of white wine on the table before him. He gets up as I approach, a smile twitching his lips. He looks more gorgeous than ever in his dark navy suit, this time with a pale blue shirt and a silver silk tie.

'Miss Villiers. What a pleasure.'

'Mr Stone. How nice to see you.'

As the maître d' pulls out my chair and waits for me to take my place, we kiss politely on either cheek.

'I'm so pleased you could make it,' Dominic says.

The maître d' gently pushes my chair in as I sit. He fills my glass from the bottle of white wine in the ice bucket by the table, then bows and leaves us.

As soon as he's gone, Dominic leans forward, his eyes dark and glittering, and says, 'I've been tasting you on my fingers all day.'

I giggle at the contrast between our polite selves and our dirty, sexy selves. 'You had a shower this morning, I expect,' I said, 'so that statement is wildly untrue.'

'I must be dreaming it then,' he says. He raises his glass. 'Here's to our new discoveries.'

I lift my glass as well. 'New discoveries,' I say happily, and we both drink. I look about at the darkening summer evening, enjoying the view as the lights come on. Further up, I can see the illuminated bridges over the Thames, and all the bustle of the riverside. The world is humming and moving all around us, but as far as I'm concerned, the universe is here on this terrace. All I want and need is here. Dominic has everything I could dream of in a man: he's clever, educated, witty, and gorgeous. He's kind and loving, and takes me to a plane of bliss I didn't even suspect existed. The rapturous feeling that fills me whenever I think about him is surely falling in love. It's deeper and more exciting than what I felt with Adam. That now seems like a sweet but superficial teenage romance, understandable at the time but now just a shadow of what was waiting for me further down the line.

'I've ordered for us,' Dominic says.

'Okay.' I'm slightly surprised. He's never done anything like that before.

But I've taken the first step, remember? And this must be part of all that.

251

Fine, I think, shaking off my mild annoyance. I trust Dominic. It's not as though I have any allergies or anything – not that he asked, anyway – the main thing is, he's a source of education for me. Whatever he orders will be worth having.

He's staring at me, his eyes slightly hooded. I wonder if he's remembering last night and our frenzied encounter. I hope so. Small ripples of pleasure race through me at the memory.

'So,' he says. 'We need to discuss our ground rules.'

'Ground rules?'

He nods. 'You can't embark on a path like ours without them.'

I remember what Vanessa said: *Safety and consent is key to everything that happens in this house, Beth. Once you understand that, you'll feel more secure about the road you're travelling on.*

'All right,' I say slowly. 'But I don't know if we need them. I trust you.'

A smile twitches Dominic's lips. 'Words a man like me thrills to hear. However, ground rules are necessary. Only the most extreme of relationships function without them, and I'm not drawn to those. I may be dominant but I'm not an out-and-out sadist.'

'I'm glad to hear you say there's a difference,' I say. I'm still grasping all these terms, but of course I've heard of sadism. A student at college had a party trick of reading out the writings of the Marquis de Sade at parties and it usually only took a few minutes before I was so sick to my stomach that I had to leave.

Dominic says, 'I inflict pain but I have no desire for the gruesome torture of true sadism. Almost no one does.'

I don't want to think about that, so I say a little impatiently, 'Well, let's agree the ground rules then, shall we?'

'Very well.' He leans towards me. 'The first thing you have to understand is that the Dominic you meet in our lovemaking, or whatever you want to call it, will be the controlling master that you've agreed to obey. Outside that room, we function in reality where normal rules of behaviour are obeyed. Inside, things will be different. To signal that this scenario has begun, I'd like you to wear a collar.'

'Oh.' I'm surprised. 'Like bondage gear?'

He nods. 'A collar is a very resonant symbol of submission.'

I think about it. He's right. A collar signals possession. Animals wear collars. Slaves wear collars. It is a sign of being tamed. *Is that what I want for myself? To be tamed?*

'I've never considered myself needing taming,' I say aloud, almost without thinking.

Dominic looks instantly concerned. 'You're missing the point,' he says, worry in his voice. 'It isn't about you in your real self. It's about your fantasy self. I don't want to break you, or tame you in the real world. But in our special world, you'll agree to be submissive to me. Do you understand?'

I nod slowly. It makes sense. I can see suddenly that

the things I do with Dominic in our sex life won't necessarily reflect my real self. That makes me feel relieved, though I don't quite know why.

'So you agree to the collar?' he presses.

'Yes.'

'Good. I have a beautiful one waiting for you at the flat.'

I remember the gorgeous flat he's made for me and something melts inside. 'I wish we were there right now,' I say softly.

The wind ruffles his hair. He presses his fingertips together and looks thoughtful. 'So do I,' he murmurs. 'But not before we've worked out these boundaries . . .'

At that moment, the door to the terrace opens and a waiter comes out with what looks like a large metal cake stand except that the tiers are full of seafood.

He places it on our table and says, 'Your *fruits de mer*, sir.'

Another waiter appears immediately, with finger bowls, tiny forks and what look like nutcrackers, as well a glass dish of mayonnaise, and another of purple liquid with chopped onion in it, lemon halves wrapped in muslin and a bottle of Tabasco.

When everything has been placed before us, one waiter tops up our glasses, and they both leave.

'Oysters,' Dominic says, raising one eyebrow at me. 'Lots of selenium and zinc. Very healthy.'

But it isn't just oysters. Each tier has a bed of ice on which lie a variety of seafood: langoustines, lobster claws, periwinkles and prawns.

Dominic sips his wine. 'This Riesling is a perfect match for this course,' he says, satisfied. 'Now. I think we should begin.'

I follow his lead, using the little forks to spear out the winkles, and the crackers to snap the lobster claws, so that the sweet white meat can be pulled out with the fork and dipped in the thick mayonnaise. The shallot vinegar, sprinkled over the oysters, brings out their briny, metallic flavour as they slip down. I can understand why this is regarded as an erotic meal: the rituals of extraction and the enhancement of salty, tangy flavours, makes this a peculiarly arousing meal. I've never eaten oysters before, but I follow Dominic's example and swallow down the slippery frilled ovals in their acidic bath of vinegar or lemon, or with the spicy heat of Tabasco. They're strange – almost creamy – but delicious.

'There's more we need to discuss,' Dominic says.

'Is there?' The pleasure of the food, the river air and the aura of luxurious indulgence has made me very relaxed – not to mention the effect of the bone-dry Riesling, which, I decide, is easily one of the nicest wines I've ever tasted.

'Yes. First, I want you to understand that this is all about you. People seem to assume that this is all about the pleasure of the dom. That's completely wrong. You will be the centre of my world when we are in it. You'll be the focus of all my attention, and your reward will be an intensity of experience, a fulfilment of fantasy and . . .' a smile twitches at the corner of his lips '. . . some very powerful orgasms.'

My stomach flutters at the thought. *Hard to say no to that.* 'But you get your pleasure too, don't you?'

He nods. 'It comes from mastering you, enforcing your submission. I want you in my power, doing as I please. I get my own intensity of experience through fantasy. The beauty is where our fantasies meet and enhance one another.'

'I see.' I really think I do see. My experience in the boudoir has already shown me how everything can be more heightened with the introduction of suspense.

Dominic dips a langoustine tail in mayonnaise and eats it slowly before continuing. 'In the chamber, once you're wearing your collar, you'll have to call me sir. It's another signal that you're prepared to obey me.'

'And what do you call me?'

His eyes flash a little. 'Anything I like. That's the point.'

I feel chastened but nevertheless say, 'But that doesn't sound fair.'

'I probably won't use your name,' Dominic concedes, 'but I'll call you whatever I see fit at the time. Now, the next thing is something all relationships of this type employ. Whenever we enter the world of fantasy, there is the risk that we'll live it so strongly we'll get carried away. So there is something called the safe word. It means "stop, I've had enough".'

'Can't I just say "stop, I've had enough"?'

'There will be times when you say "stop" or "no" or "I can't stand it" but you mean something else entirely. We need a word that breaks into the fantasy at once and brings it to a halt. The usual choice is the word "red" but I want something different for us, so I think we'll go with "scarlet". Do you think you can remember that?'

I nod. 'Of course. "Scarlet" means stop.' But I don't expect to use it. I can't imagine that I'll ever want Dominic not to do the blissful things he does to me.

'Now, we could also agree various limits on what you'll do and what you won't do, but in this instance, Beth, I want you to trust me, that I'm going to take you slowly along the path and not do anything too extreme.'

'Like what?' I frown. 'You mean, like the things in the dungeon?'

He nods. 'I have a sense of your past experience and what your nature is like already. I think you're very open to many of the things I'd like to do for you. A great deal of my pleasure will come from introducing them to you – and if there's anything you don't like, the safe word is your safety net. Will you agree to that?'

I think about this for a moment. It all seems very vague, but the equipment in the boudoir was so different from what I saw in the dungeon. It was sexy, feminine, erotic. Without that unpleasant promise of agony that the tools in the dungeon held. 'I think I will agree to that.'

'Good.' Dominic smiles. 'Then there is one more thing to agree. I want you to give me three nights, for the rest of this week, starting on Thursday night. The agreement will come to an end on Saturday so you'll have Sunday to recover, and we'll both have the option to renegotiate our terms.'

I stare at him, surprised again. When did our relationship become a business deal like this? I thought we were moving, rather deliciously, towards being a couple. It sounds suddenly as though all that is over by the weekend with an option to renew.

'It's for you,' Dominic says softly, seeing my expression. 'It's all for your protection. Once you agree to submit to someone, you might feel powerless, but the truth is that your power is only on hold. You still have everything you started out with. It's important to remember that.'

'All right,' I whisper. I might supposedly have power, but I don't really see how I can say no.

'Good. Then our ground rules are established. Let's enjoy this delicious meal. Then I'm going to send you home to get some sleep.'

Disappointment rushes through me. 'We're not going to spend the night together?'

He shakes his head, laughing gently. 'Not tonight. I'll see you on Thursday night. I think a little bit of anticipation will do us both good. Besides, I'm away on business tomorrow and I'll be leaving before dawn.'

'Where are you going?' I say, interested.

'Just to Rome.'

'What to do?'

'A business meeting. Very dull, I promise.'

'Rome doesn't sound dull,' I say longingly.

'It's not Rome that's dull. It's the meetings.'

'I still don't really know what you do . . . '

'That's because I can think of other things I'd rather

talk about.' He picks up his glass, and changes the subject. 'Tell me about this new artist you're exhibiting in the gallery. I'm very interested.'

We carry on talking as though we are just a normal couple, enjoying dinner on a terrace in the breeze of a summer evening. Not as though we've agreed our strange erotic contract of power exchange. But the knowledge of what awaits sends a dark snake of excitement curling round my belly.

Where will he take me? Can I really let him?

I will know all too soon.

CHAPTER SEVENTEEN

I know that Dominic has gone to Rome, so the next day I'm surprised to receive a letter, hand-delivered by a courier to the gallery.

I sign for it just as James comes out from the back. 'Is that for me?' he asks.

'No.' I gaze down at the thick cream envelope with my name typed on the front. 'It's for me.'

'Oh.' James looks puzzled, then his face clears. 'It's from the delectable Dominic, is it?'

'I suppose it must be.' I open it. There's a key and a folded piece of paper which I open and read.

Beth,
I want you to be at the flat on Thursday evening. Here is the key. You must be freshly showered and neat. Put your hair up so your neck is bare. I wish you to wear the collar you will find beside the bed. On the bed is the underwear I have selected for you. Be ready for me when I arrive at 7. 30. I want you kneeling on the floor by the bed when I come in.
Dominic

I blush and fold the letter up again quickly.

'A love note?' James says. He's on his way out to an appointment, so isn't really paying attention, for which I'm grateful.

'Yes . . . that's right.' It sounds rather ridiculous, but I suppose this strange, terse little note does have a certain tenderness to it. It certainly holds the promise of something strange and exciting.

'How sweet,' James says.

That's one word for it.

I stare at the letter and realise that I've undertaken a serious thing. He has given me warning that I have time to prepare myself, mentally and physically. Dominic knows what he is doing.

Thursday night

I am in the flat well before the appointed time, and I've obeyed the instructions to the letter. I've scrubbed and scrubbed in the shower, and shaved my legs and armpits, oiled them with lotion until they are completely smooth. My hair is pulled back into a high, tight bun so my face and neck are clear. I feel ritually cleansed, as though I've been purified before this new stage in my life.

On Wednesday, I visited a discreet doctors' surgery in Harley Street, where, in a calm and rather luxurious environment, I was given a full check up and had blood tests taken. The results were through the same day: I have a clean bill of health.

It feels appropriate somehow, as though the tests have purified me inside as well.

261

On the bed, which has been stripped down to one sheet, I discover a set of black underwear has been laid out for me: it looks deceptively simple, barely there, just scraps of slippery black silk. I pull on the knickers, which are made of silk and mesh, with transparent panels going over my hips, their edges making an open diamond shape over my crotch, which is exposed. When I turn to look in the mirror I see that while my buttocks are covered, the lowest part of my curves are not, and my bottom is also accessible. The cheeks peep through, white and soft against the black. The bra is little more than a set of black silk straps. The cups are shallow, made only to push and frame my breasts and not to cover them. When I've put it on, the effect is stunning. Slender jet-black lines run over my skin and hug my breasts, emphasising their curves and offering them up like delectable morsels.

This lingerie is certainly a cut above anything I've worn before, and its discreet sophistication is very sexy. There is the hint of strictness in the stark black lines, but only a hint. My eyes are drawn to the way my sex pouts through the space at the front of the knickers, and my nipples are already pink and proud. I run my hands over my stomach and breasts, shivering a little. The anticipation is already making me hot.

On the table beside the bed, I see the collar. I go over, pick it up and stare at it. This is not the studded dog collar of my imagination. It's latex, punched with tiny holes like filigree lace, with a small latex ribbon at the front and a popping stud at the back to fasten it. I lift it up and put it around my neck.

My stomach swoops as I feel it touch my skin and the power of its symbolism hits me. This is the sign of my submission. I surrender myself when I wear it. That feeling is, to my surprise, shiveringly erotic.

Maybe this is part of my innermost self after all, I think. I press the stud so that the collar is on. It fits me snugly, prettily, like a black lace necklace.

I glance at the clock on the wall. It's almost seven thirty. I remember my instructions. I'm dressed as I was told, so I go to the white fur rug at the front of the bed and kneel down. I feel self-conscious at first, even though I am alone. I spend the first long minutes wrapping strands of the fur rug around my finger and freezing whenever I think I hear the slightest sound. Seven thirty comes and I wait, still and anticipating, but nothing happens.

Is he late? Has he been delayed?

I don't know whether to get up and text him to see if he's all right, or whether I should stay where I am.

I can hear the clock ticking slowly, and I stay kneeling. Five minutes pass, then ten, and I can't stand it any longer. I get up and go to the hallway where I've left my bag so that I can check my phone for any message from Dominic. No sooner have I walked on to the cool marble floor of the hall, then I hear the turn of a key in the lock. My heart thuds and a drenching feeling of fear races over me, making the palms of my hands prickle. I turn, spring back into the bedroom

263

and am kneeling on the floor in no more than a second. I hear the front door open, and slow footsteps advance into the hall. There are long pauses, the sound of movement and footsteps but he does not come into the bedroom immediately. I am grateful for the pause, hoping that my heart rate will drop and my breathing steady before he comes in, but I can't seem to control it. The guilt of disobedience is still flooding me, making my fingertips tremble.

What the hell is he doing? This wait is agonising!

Then the footsteps come to the bedroom door. He is standing in the doorway but I do not look up.

'Good evening.' His voice is deep, low and layered with power.

'Good evening,' I say, raising my glance only enough to see his legs. He's wearing jeans. There's a long pause and then I remember. '*Sir*.'

He walks towards me. 'Have you obeyed my instructions?'

I nod. 'Yes, sir.' I still haven't looked up into his face. I'm nervous of this new Dominic, a Dominic I've agreed to obey.

'Have you?' His voice is even softer now, but with unmistakeable steeliness inside the mellow tones. 'Stand up.'

I raise myself up, aware of my naked breasts pushing up wantonly from the shallow cups of the bra, and the brazen invitation of my crotchless pants. But I also know I look beautiful and from the harsh breath that Dominic draws in, I can tell that he thinks so too. I lift my eyes to his face for the first time. He is different: still sublimely handsome, but those black eyes of his are hard and his lips have a set to them that could almost be called cruel if it weren't for the fact that there is tenderness to them too.

'Did you obey me?' he says.

'Yes sir,' I say again, but colour floods my face. I'm lying. He must know I am. My heart is racing again, my fingertips trembling and my knees feel weak.

'You have one more chance. Did you obey me?'

I pull in a long shaky breath. 'No, sir. I went to the hall when you were late.'

'Oh. I see.' His eyes flicker with pleasure and his mouth twitches. 'Disobedience, so early. Dear me. Well, you need to learn your lesson quickly, so we can nip this insubordination in the bud. Go to the cabinet and open the right-hand door.'

Trying to calm my breathing and the fluttering nervousness in my stomach, I go over to the polished cabinet and do as instructed. There is a wide variety of strange-looking things on the shelves.

'Take the red rope.'

There is a coil of scarlet rope on the bottom shelf. I pick it up. It's soft and silken in my hand, not rough as I'd imagined.

'Bring it here.'

I take it over to Dominic. He looks strong and powerful in a black T-shirt and jeans, his hair slicked back. He doesn't smile as he takes it from me.

'Disobedience is very naughty, Beth,' he breathes.

He holds up one end of the rope which is sealed with scarlet wax and begins to trace it down over my body, circling each nipple with it and then running it over my belly.

Excitement clenches inside me and I feel my sex awakening and dampening. *Oh God, this is hot already.*

Then he turns me around. 'Kneel by the bed post.'

I walk a few steps to the bed and kneel down, wondering if he is going to hit me with the rope.

'Put your arms around it and clasp your hands together on the other side.'

When I've done this, he comes forward and in a moment he has bound my wrists together with a few twirls of the rope and a skilful knot. Then he runs the rest of the rope to the floor.

'Spread your legs,' he orders.

I do it, knowing my white cheeks are exposed, my whole bottom open to him and the pouting lips below. I know they're already wet. I'm sure he can see the glistening traces of my arousal and that makes me even hotter and wetter. I rest my hot face on my forearm, which is tightly pressed to the bedpost, my bonds making it impossible to move.

I feel something against my sex. For a moment, I think it's Dominic's finger but it's too big and thick, and it's not hard or hot enough to be his cock. Then I realise he's trailing the waxen end of the rope across me, letting it play in the slipperiness. The feeling is delicious.

'Oh,' I murmur.

'Quiet. No noise. And no movement.'

I feel a light whip across my buttocks. It's the silken part of the rope. It doesn't hurt but it's a definite expression of intent. I try to keep still.

'Now. A little something to begin your punishment.'

He walks away from me and from the corner of my vision I see him go to the cabinet. He takes something out and puts it on the bed where I can see it. It's a large and rather beautiful glass object, smooth and slightly bent, about five inches long. When he knows that I've seen it, he lifts it up and comes around behind me. Suddenly, he's kneeling close to me, I can feel the heat of his body on my back. He puts his face close to my neck and runs his finger over my collar.

'I like this,' he whispers. 'This is lovely. It suits you very much.' He drops his face and kisses my neck, nipping lightly at the skin with his teeth. I want to sigh with pleasure but I remember my instructions and keep as still as I can.

Now something new is playing at my entrance, something cold and very smooth. I know it's the glass object.

'This is a dildo, Beth,' he says. 'I'm going to press it inside you. I want you to keep it there for me. Don't let it come out.'

As he speaks, I feel the cold thing push up inside me. The sensation of being filled is delicious, the cold bringing an extra dimension to the stimulation. But it's slippery smooth and I'm very wet. Dominic pushes it deep, holds it there and then removes his fingers and instantly I feel a drag as the dildo begins to slip back out.

'You naughty girl,' he scolds as he sees it begin to emerge. 'What did I say?'

He pushes it back up again with a firm thrust that makes me want to sigh out loud again. I clench around it, tightening my pelvic muscles, willing myself to hold it.

'Very good. You are trying hard,' he murmurs. 'Now. Your arse is begging me for attention.'

His palm smoothes over my bottom, caressing the smooth surface, revelling in the transition from the silken mesh of the knickers to the soft flesh. Then suddenly he smacks down on me, not hard but with a sting. I jump and the glass dildo jumps inside me, giving me a delicious sensation of inward thrusting. Dominic rubs my cheeks again, then delivers another smack that judders through me. It doesn't hurt so much as cause an internal shudder, and again the dildo presses upwards inside me.

Oh God.

'Your bottom is so beautiful,' he says in an uneven voice. He smacks me again. *Oh God, I can feel it building.*

I rest my face against the bedpost, my bound hands just below me. The sight of the scarlet rope around them is exciting. My breasts, eager and sensitive, press again the cold metal of the bedpost, the nipples rasping it. Below, the dildo, warm now, threatens to slide out.

I pull all my muscles to stop it, and again the delicious heat throbs in my belly.

'Oh dear, you can't hold it for me, Beth,' he says in a voice of playful menace. 'I didn't think that was so much to ask. Well, for that . . .'

He delivers three hard slaps in quick succession that send a hot glow racing from my buttocks to cover my whole body. Then he begins to run the dildo in and out of me hard. It's a startling but delicious feeling, as I kneel before him, open, letting him fuck me with the glass toy. His other hand comes round to where my clitoris is buzzing so hard I'm wondering if I will actually come without any other stimulation, but as he begins to thrum it with his fingers, running down into my slippery depths and returning to it, hard and strong, it responds by washing strong euphoric waves of pleasure over my entire body. My legs are losing strength, I would be sliding down the post if I weren't lashed to it, and I'm shuddering all over with the force of my building climax.

'As you're a beginner,' he whispers harshly in my ear, 'I'm going to let you come, but only if you come as hard as you can. Come on, give yourself up to me.'

It's all I need. I cry out as the climax seizes me and releases me in a huge, rocking, all-encompassing orgasm.

'Oh yes,' he says. 'That was what I wanted to see. Now. We're not finished quite yet.' He pulls the dildo from me. It slides out easily and he drags it up behind me, so that it runs between my cheeks. He holds the oiled tip at my other entrance, pressing it gently for a moment, and just as I am wondering if he is going to try and penetrate there, half worried and half curious, he takes it away.

A moment later he is untying my wrists, but if I think it is all over, I'm mistaken.

'Lie on the floor,' he orders. 'Put your bottom high in the air, rest your head on your arms.'

I crawl onto the rug and obey, feeling utterly shameless as I thrust my bottom as high as I can, knowing what I'm displaying to him: my swollen lips, wet and glistening with the spending of my climax. I feel his fingertip trace around it, running over the hair there and smoothing over the slippery skin.

'What a delightful sight,' he says, his voice thick with desire. 'And all mine.'

I hear him unbutton his trousers but he doesn't take them off. Instead he kneels behind me, grips his hard erection and presses it to my entrance. 'I'm going to fuck you very hard now,' he says. 'You may make a noise if you wish.'

I'm glad he says that because as he slams into me, he seems to penetrate my very core, and the cry is forced from me. I couldn't keep it in if I wanted to. His cock thrusts hard, over and over, each time reaching that spot where the pleasure is teetering on the brink of pain, but I want more of the sweet agony. I want him to feel the kind of intense pleasure he's given me, I want to offer myself up to him, every bit.

I feel the roughness of his trousers against my bottom as he presses against me, and that in itself feels hot. He holds my hip with one hand, seizes my breast with the other, squeezing and fondling the nipple, his breathing racing hard. In, and in again, and in, his shaft swelling further, filling me up, and then I feel the stiffness of his body as his climax begins boiling up, and with a final thrust he explodes inside me.

We are both panting now as the effects of our activities begin to wear off. Slowly, he pulls out of me. He gets up and goes over to the bedside table where he gets a tissue and wipes himself. Once he is out of me, I fall down on the rug, still breathing fast, my heart rate slowing and the juices of our climaxes trickling down my thigh, warm and wet.

'Dominic,' I say, 'that was amazing, really.' I smile at him. I feel so close to him, and I yearn to hold him, inhale his beautiful scent and kiss his mouth tenderly.

He turns and gazes at me, almost impassively. Then he returns the smile and says, 'Thank you, Beth. I enjoyed administering your first punishment. You took it bravely but it was just the beginning.'

I watch, surprised, as he walks over, buttoning up his jeans.

Is it because I'm still wearing the collar? I wonder, and I reach up to unbutton it.

He kneels down beside me and lifts my hand to his mouth. He kisses it. 'Thank you,' he says again. 'I'm anticipating our next encounter with great pleasure.'

Then he gets up and walks out, leaving me lying there on the floor, with his semen still gushing out of me, quite alone.

271

I lie there astonished and hurt. *Is this how it's supposed to be?* I think, horrified. I want to hold him and be held, to kiss and be tender with him.

But I promised to obey him. This is just the first night. I have to wait and see where he plans to take me. Dominic knows what he's doing. I have to trust him.

Friday

I wake very early in Celia's bed. It is just after four o'clock in the morning. I don't know why I've sprung awake like this, I ought to be exhausted after what happened last night. It was emotionally draining as well as physically demanding. De Havilland is asleep on the bed beside me. I don't know if Celia permits him to sleep in the bedroom but I find his nearness a comfort. I reach out and put my fingers in that soft warm fur and after a minute, he responds, his little engine running with its rolling purr.

'You need me, don't you,' I whisper to him. 'I make you happy, don't I, pusskins, just by stroking you.'

Why is love so complicated? Why, of all the men in the world, did I have to fall for this one, the one with the tender outside and the steely core? Because I am falling in love, I know that. Only love could make me feel this desperate and confused, full of yearning and in that sweet does-he-doesn't-he agony. I know he desires me. I know he thinks I'm beautiful and fuckable, and that I give him pleasure – so much that he's willing to take on another flat and furnish it just for me.

How much did that cost? For a week's worth of fucking?

Another thought slides into my mind. *Unless he plans on this going on for more than a week.*

I don't know how I feel about that. I like this game so far, but I also like the fact that there's a limit to it. I might feel very differently if this were to be our life permanently. Because . . .

Because I need love, not punishment . . . ?

Because I want to give as well as receive . . . ?

Because . . .

Something dark and horrible lies just outside my conscious. I sigh and turn over, disturbing De Havilland, who stretches out his limbs, and flexes his claw with a tiny mew, then curls back up to resume his purring.

I want to go back to sleep but I can't. I stare wide-eyed at the Chinese wallpaper, counting the parrots and tracing their plumage with my gaze until my alarm goes off and it's time to get up.

As a result of my lack of sleep, I'm groggy and tetchy during the morning.

'Is everything all right, Beth?' James asks, when I swear at the computer for being slow.

'Yes, yes, sorry,' I say, shame-faced. 'Bad night. I couldn't sleep.'

'Excellent time for catching up on reading,' he remarks lightly, but he treats me a little more gently during the morning, fetching me coffee and making sure I've got plenty of the thin ginger biscuits he knows I like so much.

During the morning, a courier arrives with another cream envelope addressed to me. I read the letter within.

Dear Beth

Congratulations on your initiation last night. I hope you enjoyed it as much as I did. Tonight, you must be at the flat by 7.30 pm, ready for me. Wear what you find on the bed. Before I arrive, you must wash the implements on the table and apply lubrication, and lay out the instruments of correction. Kneel on the floor as before.

Dominic

I read the letter over twice. Excitement flutters in my stomach again but not as joyously as it did yesterday. The spanking Dominic administered to me yesterday did not hurt particularly, but I know that was because of my heightened state when he administered it. I understand that I was already in a place where pain and pleasure are close allies, and the stinging blows on my bottom were intended to enhance my enjoyment. But I'm not sure how I cope when he wants to go further.

And I'm sure he will want to go further.

'Beth, you're looking very pale,' James says, coming up to my desk. 'Are you all right?' He inspects my face closely. 'Is everything going well with Dominic?'

I nod.

He looks at me thoughtfully. His usual habit is to make a joke of everything and ever since I confided in him about Dominic's urges, he's teased me all the time with small jokes and puns about bondage and punishment. I have the feeling that he would normally say something along those lines now, but something stops him. Instead he looks me straight in the eye.

'Beth, you're on your own, far from home. If Dominic forces you to do anything you don't want to do, or you stop enjoying whatever it is he's doing, then I want you to tell me. I'm your friend, and I worry about you.' His eyes are tender. 'You're just a little thing.'

His kind words send a whirl of emotion spinning inside me. Tears sting my eyes, even though I don't want to cry.

'Thank you,' I say in a high, tight voice.

'You're very welcome, sweetheart. It's a big bad world out there, but you don't have to suffer alone. You can call me any time, weekend or not.'

As he walks away, I can't help a tear trickling down my cheek. I wipe it away hastily, fold up my letter, and concentrate as best I can on my work before it's time to keep my appointment with Dominic.

That night in the apartment, there is a new set of underwear waiting for me. This almost doesn't qualify as a garment at all. It is a kind of harness but rather than leather, it is made of soft black elastic ribbon. It takes me a while to understand how to put it on but when I've worked it out, it makes a daring pattern on my white skin. Two black straps make a long V from my shoulders to my crotch, passing over my breasts and leaving them totally exposed. There is a double strap over my hips, one of which is wide and has hanging straps to attach to stocking tops. Everything connects just below my navel, where a small zip holds it on. From there two straps disappear under my crotch, one on either side of my sex, to connect the back. When I turn to look at my back reflection, I see a criss-cross effect, the straps passing round my hips with the long attachments for stockings, and a single strap disappearing between my cheeks like a thong. Tiny black bows mark the place where the straps meet at the back. The effect is rather beautiful, in a geometric sort of way.

When the harness is on, I put on the stockings that have been left on the bed and attach them. A pair of black stilettos also sits on the bed, so I put those on too. They fit perfectly.

Then there is the collar. It is not the sweet latex affair of last night. This time it is in glossy black leather and it fastens with a buckle at the back of my neck. It is studded with shiny black raised sequins that mimic studs but are altogether more glamorous. I look at it in the mirror. The symbol of my submission.

I remember my instructions and return to the bed. A long blue latex vibrator, not quite in the shape of a phallus but close, lies on the covers next to a purple bottle. I pick up the vibrator and examine it. It's rather beautiful with its clean lines and delicate curves, and the colour takes away the creepiness of the kind that are made to look like human flesh. At its base is a little outcrop that I guess must be intended for clitoral stimulation.

I take it to the bathroom and wash it carefully in water, though I'm certain it has never been used before. After patting it dry with a towel, I take it back to the bedroom and sit on the bed. I pour some of the oily lubrication from the purple bottle onto the palm of my hand and begin to rub it all over the blue shaft. I'm surprised to feel myself responding as I massage the oil onto the latex. This is an inanimate object and yet I find the anointing of it an intimate act, as though I'm bonding with it, getting to know it, learning to anticipate the pleasures I will experience with it. I begin to feel something like affection for its gentle curve and upward thrust, and as it becomes shiny and oily, I even feel as though it has become aroused itself, in preparation for me.

Then I glance at the clock and realise that Dominic is due here in only a few minutes. I lay the now well-oiled vibrator on a towel on the bed, and look at the other instruments of correction. Like the vibrator, they are far from the ugly torture instruments I saw in the dungeon. They are stylish and beautiful, as if meant for display rather than to be shut away. One is a kind of whip with a short, stout black leather handle, a steel ball mounted on the end of it, and a head of dozens of suede tendrils. I run my fingers through them. They are soft and remind me of the waving tentacles of a sea anemone. Beside the whip is a long slender shape of a riding crop, in black leather, with a loop at its light, springing end.

Oh. Oh my God.

I shiver. I don't know if I can take it.

If I'm loved I can take anything. The thought springs into my mind and I have no idea where it came from. *I want to show Dominic I'm worthy of his love. And I will.*

Dominic is only five minutes late this time, but I have learned my lesson. I stay kneeling on the floor until he arrives, and when he comes in, I do not look up. I stare hard at the white rug, seeing his jeans and black Paul Smith shoes from the edge of my vision.

He stares at me for a while without speaking and then says softly, 'Very good. I know you've obeyed me this time. You're learning. How are you tonight, Beth?'

'Very well, sir,' I whisper, keeping my head down.

'Are you looking forward to tonight? What did you think about when you cleaned the blue tool?'

I hesitate for a moment then say, 'I thought about what it would feel like, sir, when you put it in me.'

There's a sound like a long soft sigh. 'Very good,' he murmurs. 'But don't get too complacent. There are other surprises awaiting you too. Stand up.'

I rise to my feet, a little unsteady in my unaccustomed black stilettos. I keep my eyes lowered but I hear his ragged gasp.

'You look amazing. Turn around.'

I turn so that he can see the criss-crossing ribbons over my back, the ribboned lattice at the base, the strap that disappears between my cheeks, and the enticing stretch of white thigh between the harness and my stocking tops.

'Beautiful,' he says throatily. 'Turn back. And look at me.'

I obey, lifting my eyes demurely. He's wearing a black T-shirt that defines his muscles and the broadness of his shoulders. Is this the uniform he needs for his mastering of me? The sight of his face sends a quiver of passion through me. It's a beloved face, not simply because it is so handsome but because it is his. I want to feel it close to me, kissing me, loving me.

He reaches out a hand and strokes the collar at my neck. 'This one is lovely,' he says almost meditatively. 'It works very well.' He hooks his finger underneath and pulls me close to him, then he put his lips on mine and kisses me hard, probing my tongue with his, pressing into my mouth.

It's the first kiss we've shared for what feels like an age, but it is not as tender as the last one. He's hard and fierce in his possession of my mouth, hardly seeming to care what I feel.

Then he pulls away, his mouth curving into a smile. 'Now,' he says. 'Your first task. Take the things off the bed and put them on the bedside table. Then lie on your back with your arms above your head and your legs apart.'

I'm feeling the familiar fluttering in my belly, the quickening of my pulse. Now what? What will he make me suffer now? I fear the pain but I'm also anticipating a torrent of exquisitely agonising pleasure.

I lie on the bed as directed.

'Close your eyes.'

I close them and he approaches. A moment later a silken blindfold goes around my eyes. I'm sightless again. My wrists are lifted and each one is placed in a kind of softly lined bracelet, then I feel them being attached to the bed railings. *Handcuffs*. He moves to my feet and I feel similar restraints being put on my ankles and then buckled to the foot of the bed. *Ankle cuffs*. I can't help tugging lightly on them but I can barely move my arms or legs except to rock very slightly.

'No moving,' snaps Dominic's stern voice. 'This is your only warning. No movement, no sound. Or you will regret it. Now, hold still.'

He approaches me again. I can feel the warm heft of his body coming close to me and I yearn to be able to touch it. I want to feel his skin under my fingertips. The hardest part of this agreement is that he doesn't seem to want me to love him back. I never expected this when I became submissive.

Now I feel his fingertips at my ears. He's pressing something into them – two soft foam pads that quickly meld to the shape of my inner ear and at once the sound is blocked out. Now all I can hear is a rushing sound which comes from within my own body, the thudding of my heart and the hiss of my own breathing. This is very strange. The sounds are very loud and this makes me fearful. Will I hear my own voice if I make a sound? I daren't test to see, Dominic's warning is ringing through my mind.

I'm alone in this strange dark space full of whooshing and thudding noises. Dominic's heat and weight has moved away from me now, and I have no idea where he is. I'm not sure how long he leaves me in that place, but with each second the suspense grows greater. With each second, the sense grows that something is about to happen – some feeling, some sensation, which may be pleasure or may be pain – until I'm almost overwhelmed with the anticipation and want to cry out for something, anything to happen.

When I think I can bear it no longer but I must speak or move, I feel something. It touches my chest in a spot above my breasts and it *burns*. Something hot. Oh no, wait . . . it's not burning. It's freezing cold. My skin seems to pucker underneath it. *Ice.*

There is another burning sensation on my belly, which wants to contract and wiggle under the feeling. It takes all my control to stop myself. The ice makes my skin prickle and burn. I desperately want to touch it but even if I let myself I can't move an inch. Then an unseen force moves the cube above my breasts, trailing it over them, rubbing the nipples with it. The ice performs its strange two-faced trick of freezing and burning me at the same time, but the effect on me as my nerve endings respond is acute. My belly sends a fiery message to the heat between my legs, telling it to intensify, and I can feel the wetness flooding out. *All this from an ice cube.*

The one on my belly is melting and it begins to slide over my skin, leaving cold trickles in its wake. It hits the strap of my silken harness and moves slowly along its edge towards my hip. It's all I can do not to buck and arch to make it slide off entirely and stop tormenting me.

Then, very lightly, something probes at my swollen lips. I've felt this before, when Dominic used the dildo on me, but this is a little different. It's warm, thick and slippery. I know it's the vibrator. He's going to use it on me. A tingling thrills round my groin, making my sex twitch with anticipation. I expect him to play with it at my entrance for a while, working me up, but he doesn't. Instead, quite quickly, he pushes it into me, filling me up with it. I imagine its sweet shaft sitting neatly within me, soaking up my warmth, ready to move within me. But once it's buried in my depths, the little outcrop nuzzled against my clit, nothing more happens. It is left there for minute after minute, until I cannot resist clenching my muscles around it, drawing it up further into me by my own efforts, but this is clearly not allowed, for a stinging slap comes down upon my belly. I freeze at once.

Have I gone too far? A kind of fear mixed with excitement races through me. *What now?* The answer takes a while to come, and unexpectedly, the object inside me whirrs into life and begins to pulse within me. *Oh, that's good. That's very good.*

It's a deeply sexy feeling, as the shaft pulses and throbs, the little outcrop whirring against my clitoris. Without sight or sound, it is almost as though I can hear it as deep in my chest as a cat's purr. I am staying still and letting the sensations flood outwards from the vibrator but any moment now, it will begin to be too strong for me. I will have to move, and even if I don't, I will end up coming, I'm sure of it. I grit myself to stay still and obey the orders I've been given.

Then, without any apparent outward force, the vibrator changes speed, increasing its pace and also its activity. It begins to rub and pulse inside me as though a small hard ball is moving up and down against the wall of my vagina, stimulating me in a way I've never known before.

Oh God, it's glorious. I don't know if I can stop myself coming.

The little outcrop is now thrusting itself against my clitoris with unbearable pressure, without a pause or a change in tempo, making me begin to ascend the heights towards a crashing climax.

Stop it, I can't think . . .

My brain is in a whirl, blackness scattered with coloured stars filling my mind. Before I can stop myself I've begun to thrust my hips upwards to meet the beautiful rhythm inside me and I hear, as though from far away, my voice sounding in my throat. I'm screaming, I realise in my black daze.

Suddenly the pulsing stops. With a rough movement, the vibrator is taken from my body. I'm bereft, I'm desperate, I'm shuddering with the power of the orgasm waiting to give me the release I crave.

Then the earplugs are gone and I can hear myself panting hard in the real world.

'You naughty girl. You moved. You screamed. You wanted to come, didn't you?'

'Y-y-yes,' I manage to say.

'*Yes, what?*'

'Yes, sir,' I whisper.

'You are a wicked, voluptuous girl with a hungry, gluttonous, pleasure-seeking body that must be punished.' I can hear the pleasure in his voice as he unbuckles the cuffs at my hands and feet. He leaves my blindfold on. I'm disoriented, as though I've suddenly found myself back in a place I thought I'd left.

His hand lands on my arm. 'Get up. Come with me.'

I follow his lead and move myself off the bed. My limbs are like jelly, hardly able to hold me up. He guides me across the room and I follow blindly, not even sure which way I'm facing. Then he puts my hands down on a smooth, sloping leather surface. I know where we are now. We're at the leather seat, the strange white object with the low footrest and the leather reins.

What's going to happen now?

I ought to be scared but I'm not. He is touching me gently, helping me in my blindness, and I trust that he knows what I can take, how far he can go. His anger with me is a fantasy, designed to bring us closer and take us to delicious, forbidden places.

Safe in that knowledge, I shiver with apprehension of what is to come.

Dominic places me on the seat so that I'm straddling it, facing the long reclining back with my back open to him, my wet sex pressed against the chair. Within a few moments he has tethered my wrists to something behind the frame so that I'm almost embracing the seat's smooth surface like a lover. The tops of my stockings graze against my thighs where they meet the edge of the chair. He is busy with the straps of my harness for a moment and then he pulls them away so that they hang down, leaving my back clear and naked.

'Oh, my darling,' he breathes. 'I wish I didn't have to hurt you, but when you've disobeyed me so flagrantly, I have no other option.'

I hear him walk back to the bedside and return. There is a long moment, while I wait, hardly able to breathe, and then I feel the first slow tickle of the many-tailed whip.

It doesn't hurt at all. If anything, its teasing is a pleasant, sweet play on my already sensitive skin. It sweeps over me, the tendrils making a figure of eight, moving so fluidly that I think of seaweed wafting in an underwater current. I begin to relax, my fear ebbs a little. Then the figure of eight stops and it flicks down me, still so soft and with hardly a sting. Flick, flick, flick. The feeling is almost invigorating as my skin tingles beneath the little nips of those soft suede tails. I prickle as the blood rushes up to the surface of the skin.

'You're turning rosy,' Dominic murmurs. 'You're answering the kiss of the whip.'

I can't help flexing my back a little, stretching, as the whip comes down a little harder. It bites just a little more into my skin, but we're very far from anything I would describe as real pain. I find it strange to admit to myself, but I like this sensation, the feeling of my back exposed, the swoop and flick of the tails stimulating my nerve endings, my groin pressed hard against the velvety smoothness of the leather. Perhaps it is because everything in me is still burning and throbbing from my recent near climax. A vision pops into my head: I recall the man in Dominic's apartment, the one who was spanked over a chair very like this. I remember my horror, my bafflement, at such a thing. And here I am, thrilling to my very own taste of punishment.

Now the whip is coming down in sharper movements, sweeping first to one side of my back, then the other. It's beginning to sting now and for the first time when one hard stroke hits me, sending a million tiny bites all over my skin, I gasp out loud. The sound brings another, harder stroke. I clench my thighs as it hits, gasp again and feel myself pressing into the seat, rubbing my engorged clitoris and puffed sex hard onto it. My skin is beginning to feel fiery hot, and where the tails are striking me is tender, stinging, hurting. Each blow is now making me pull in a sharp breath and release it on an 'Ah!'.

'Six more for you, Beth,' Dominic says, and he lands the half dozen, each one a little gentler than the last as though he is working me down. My back is alive with red-hot pain, stinging all over, but God, I'm excited and ready for something to drive me to ecstasy.

'Now,' he says. 'Your naughty bottom.'

I don't know what he means until, sharply and unexpectedly, a hard blow from the riding crop lands on my exposed cheeks. Now that hurts, horribly.

'Ahhh!' I scream. 'Ow!'

It's like red-hot metal has been pressed to my skin. My whole body vibrates with a sick feeling as the pain radiates out. Then, to my horror, another blow comes down. I scream again. This is not like the gentle tender touch of the suede whip, this is real pain, thwacking down across my bottom, burning, hurting. I cannot, I *will* not take much of this.

Then it stops and Dominic says tenderly, 'You've taken your punishment well. You'll remember not to come without permission next time, won't you? Now, you'd better kiss the rod. But not with your mouth.'

I feel its thick leather handle probe my sex. Dominic runs it up towards my bottom, stopping again at the entrance and pushing it just a little harder into that other place. I gasp. Then the handle is gone. My wrists are being untethered, my blindfold is taken off. Dominic puts his strong hands round my waist and turns me round to face him. He's naked, his huge length rearing proudly up, almost pressed against his stomach in its arousal. I have no idea when he took his clothes off but I suppose it could have been any time that I was cut off from the world. His eyes are a denser black than I've seen, as though the whipping has taken him to a different plane.

I'm reclining on the seat, the leather cooling against my burning back. 'Now I'm going to kiss you,' he says. He lifts my legs and I notice for the first time that there are slender stirrups extending from the lowest part of the chair. He puts a leg into each one so that I'm open to him. Then he kneels on the footrest, his face at the same level as my crotch. He inhales deeply.

'You smell divine,' he murmurs. Then he leans forward, his arms wrapped round my thighs and nuzzles into my pubic hair.

I gasp. It's electric, pulses of pleasure throbbing through my body.

His tongue flicks across the top of my clitoris. *Oh. Oh . . .*

I have no words, I can do nothing but respond with my body. I know that I will not be able to stop myself no matter what my orders are. His tongue is lapping at me, licking long slow strokes across my entrance and up to that most sensitive place where he tickles unbearably with the tip of his tongue. The golden, liquid electricity flows through me, shaking my limbs, stiffening me, and I know it's coming. Then he takes the whole of my bud in his mouth and sucks hard on it, pressing his tongue down, licking, tantalising and . . .

Oh I . . . I can't . . . I . . . !

My fists are clenched, my eyes screwed tight, my mouth open, my back arching.

I've got to do this, I can't wait, I . . .

The orgasm explodes around me as though I'm in the middle of a giant firework. I do not know who I am or what is happening, only that bliss is flowing through in great heartbeats of ecstasy.

Even while I'm pulsing, I feel Dominic's huge penis pressing at my lips, then he's filled me up so that he can feel the last of my convulsions around his shaft. He's holding on to the armrests of the chair, using them to pull himself deeply into me. He's darkly aroused, his face flushed, his eyes glazed. He says nothing but lets his weight fall forward on me and kisses me hard as the torrent of his orgasm is finally released.

He lies on me panting for a while, his cheek pressed against the leather of the chair. Then he runs his hand over my body, turns and kisses the side of my face.

'You've done so well,' he whispers.

I thrill to hear him say it. I want to please him, I want to earn his love.

'I found the riding crop very difficult,' I reply humbly. 'I didn't like the pain.'

'You're not supposed to like it,' he says, pulling out of me and standing up. 'But you get your reward after-wards. Don't you feel better?'

I look at him. He's right, I feel an extraordinary sense of satisfaction, of post-orgasmic languor. But . . . I'm not sure that it's enough. I gaze at him, aware that my collar is still around my neck and we are still in the boudoir. I do not know if I'm permitted to say that I long for him to be sweet and tender with me. I am fascinated and aroused by Dominic the master, but I want my other Dominic too, the one who was the sweetest lover I can imagine. That Dominic held me in his arms and caressed me. I need that now, in the aftermath of his strictness and the punishment he's meted out to me, more than ever.

Please. I try to send the message with my eyes. *Please, Dominic. Come back to me. Love me.*

But he's already looking for something to dry himself with, and he walks away from me. I have a view of his magnificent broad back and his firm bottom and strong thighs, which only serves to make me long for him more desperately. I want to run my hands over that skin, receive reassurance from his body and the way his strength can be used to comfort me as well as hurt.

'I'll see you in the morning,' he says, turning and smiling. 'And I want you to sleep well tonight. You'll need all your strength tomorrow.'

He turns back and continues preparing to get dressed. He is still in the room but, as I lie on the chair, watching, I feel as though he has left me already.

Saturday

In the morning, I look at my reflection in the mirror. There isn't a mark on my back – Dominic must know exactly what he is doing with the whip – but across my bottom I can see two faint red stripes where the riding crop hit me. I suspected they would be there, I've always bruised and marked easily.

There is no pain but I run a bath and soak for a long time, easing my muscles which feel stretched and tired from being held in position by the cuffs. As I lie in the scented water in the silent apartment, I wonder why my body is fine but my heart feels sore. It should be the other way around: I have what I wanted, after all. Dominic is doing as he promised, and taking me down the path, as deep into his world as I'm willing to go. He is giving me ecstatic pleasure every day and taking his own with me.

So why am I crying? I wonder, as tears begin to well up and flow down my cheeks.

Because I'm lonely.

Because I don't know this Dominic, the one who orders me around and beats me.

But you asked him to do it, I remind myself. *He didn't want to and you forced the issue. You can't regret it now and you can't back out.*

I don't want to back out, I'm sure of that. But when I made the agreement, I didn't realise that this Dominic would replace the one I knew and loved. I realise that I miss the tenderness and affection that we used to share. The things that happen to me in the boudoir, when I put on that collar and signal my obedience, may bring me exquisite sensation but they also have the capacity to humiliate and degrade me. When I allow myself to be treated as a naughty girl who needs punishing, a part of me is ashamed that I can abase myself like this.

I need Dominic to tell me that he still loves and

respects me, and that in the outside world, I'm still the Beth he treasures and values.

But I never see him in the outside world! Not any more.

Today is the last day of our agreement. I have no idea what will happen next. But before then, there is whatever test Dominic has planned for me. I want to feel excited but there is a cold emptiness inside me.

Of all the ways I thought I'd feel about Dominic, I never suspected I might feel nothing.

I get dressed and do some chores around Celia's flat, restoring it to its usual pristine state. Even though it now feels like home, I can never shake the knowledge that it belongs to Celia first and foremost. I'm checking my mobile for a text from Dominic when there is a knock at the door.

I open, expecting to see him standing there, but it is the porter. 'Hello, miss,' he says and holds out a large package sealed in brown paper. 'I've been asked to deliver this. It's urgent, apparently.'

I take it from him. 'Thank you.'

He looks at it, curious. 'Is it your birthday?'

'No,' I reply with a smile. 'Just some things from home, I expect.'

When he's gone, I kneel on the marble tiles of the hall and rip off the outer wrapping. Inside is a black box tied in soft black satin ribbon, a cream envelope tucked into it. I take the envelope, open it and extract the letter.

You are required to rest this morning. Your lunch will be delivered at midday and you must eat all of it by 1pm. At 2pm you are permitted to open this box. Further instructions await you inside.

Each letter, I realise, is more controlling than the last. Each has dictated just a little more of my actions, going beyond my sexual being and into my life as an autonomous person.

Today, even when I'm not with him, Dominic is dictating what will happen to me. And he knows that I will obey him. I have the sense that he knows exactly what I do, as though his gaze can extend beyond the sitting room and into the entire flat.

I wouldn't put it past him to have the place wired up, and secret cameras installed.

The thought is an extraordinary one, and as soon as it enters my head, I dismiss it. And yet, the idea that this new Dominic might be capable of such things stays with me.

I stare at the black box, wondering what lies inside it.

'Oh well,' I say, 'there's no point in dwelling. I'm not going to open it until two o'clock. For all I know, he might have some kind of timer in there that will tell him when the lid is lifted.'

And I don't want to give him excuses to punish me. After all, today is the day when we will go furthest.

At the thought, a kind of cold excitement grips me.

For the first time I can taste real fear inside my desire for Dominic.

Obeying my instructions, I have a quiet, restful morning. My mother phones me to see how I am and even though I think I sound perfectly normal, she picks up at once that I'm not myself.

'Are you ill?' she asks, worry in her voice.

'No, Mum. Just tired. I've had a long week. London life does take it out of you, I find.' *Along with all the sex.*

'I can tell you're down. Be honest. Is it Adam?'

'Adam?' I sound genuinely surprised. I haven't given him a thought in days. 'No, no, not at all. London has been the perfect cure as far as that's concerned.'

'I'm pleased to hear it.' Mum sounds relieved. 'I always thought you could do better, Beth, but I didn't want to say so when you so obviously loved him. He was perfectly fine as a first boyfriend but I'm glad you'll have the chance to spread your wings. You need a more worthy man than him, someone to expand your interests, broaden your experience and share your zest for life. I want my Beth to have the best man in the world to love her.'

I can't speak. My throat has closed around a hard object blocking it, and hot tears have sprung to my eyes. They begin to drop down my cheeks and I can't stop a stifled sob.

'Beth?'

I try to speak but it comes out as another sob.

'What is it?' she cries. 'What's wrong, baby?'

I wipe my eyes and manage to damp down my sobs enough to speak. 'Oh, Mum. Nothing's wrong, really. I'm just a little homesick.'

'Come back, darling, come and see us! We miss you too.'

'No, Mum, there are only two weeks left in the flat. I don't want to miss out on this opportunity.' I sniff wetly and give a weak laugh. 'I'm being silly! It's just a little weep, nothing serious.'

'Are you sure?' She's still anxious.

Oh Mum, I do love you. I'm still your baby girl, no matter what. I clutch the phone tightly as though it will bring me closer to her comforting embrace and familiar motherly warmth. 'I'm fine, I promise. And I'll come home if I get too miserable. But I'm sure it won't come to that.'

At exactly midday there is a knock on the door. When I open it a man in the uniform of a smart hotel or expensive restaurant is standing there holding a large tray loaded with dishes covered in silver cloches.

'Your lunch, madam,' he announces.

'Thank you.' I stand back and he brings it inside. I direct him to the kitchen and he puts the tray down, deftly dresses the table in a linen cloth he produces from somewhere, and sets it with silver cutlery, a wine glass and a tiny bud vase holding a dark red rose. Then he uncovers the dishes and lays out my lunch: an enormous char-grilled steak with tarragon butter melting over it, new potatoes speckled with fresh herbs and

295

steamed green vegetables – broccoli, beans and wilted spinach. The aroma floats up. It looks and smells delicious and I realise how hungry I am. The waiter puts a dish of fresh raspberries with a large blob of whipped cream on the table, pours a glass of red wine for me from a small bottle he produces from a pocket, and stands back with a smile.

'Your lunch is served, madam. The dishes will be collected this evening. Simply leave them outside.'

'Thank you,' I say again. 'It looks wonderful.'

'You're most welcome.'

When I've shown him out, I return to the kitchen. The clock tells me it is ten past twelve. I sit down to my solitary lunch.

It is, as I expect, delicious, the steak pink in the centre and everything just as it should be. I have the distinct feeling I'm being given a hearty helping of all the major food groups, to ensure I have stamina for whatever is to come. I finish well before one o'clock but there is still an hour until I can open the box.

I'm definitely learning the effect of anticipation and delayed gratification. Every minute seems to tick by slowly but I don't know whether I yearn to open the box or dread it. It sits in the hall, waiting for me, and its pull is so strong I almost feel as if Dominic himself is concealed inside.

I wander about, restless, sometimes looking from the sitting room window to the flat opposite and wondering what Dominic is doing at this very moment, and what plans he has for me today. There is no sign of life behind the darkened windows.

At two o'clock I return to the hall and stare at the black box.

Okay. It's time.

I pull the black satin ribbons and they drop silently to the floor. I lift the lid. It's tight-fitting and the box beneath is heavy, so it takes a little while to shake the lid free. I put it down and look inside the box. All I can see is a mass of black crumpled tissue paper and another of those cream envelopes. I open it and remove a piece of thick cream card on which is printed in black lettering:

Put on what is in here. Wear everything you find inside. Come to the boudoir at precisely 2.30 pm.

I put down the card and push back the tissue paper.

Whoa. Okay. The next level.

Inside the box is a harness, not in slippery soft silk this time, but in thick, black leather. It is not embellished with tiny ribbons but by buckles and hoops of silver metal. I lift it out. As far as I can see, it will sit over my shoulders and buckle beneath my breasts. At the back, the thin straps meet between my shoulders, and then are joined by a single straight strap to a large metal ring that sits in the centre of my upper back. The straps that go under my breasts continue round also to join the ring. It's a simple but effective design.

I take another leather object out of the box. It looks like a large belt, and it takes me a moment to realise

297

that it is a cross between a belt and a corset – a waist cincher. It looks tiny. Am I really going to fit it?

And then there is the collar. This is the most daunting of the three: it is thick black leather, designed to cover my neck completely. It buckles at the back and at the front is a silver metal ring.

Oh my goodness.

I remember that I have to wear whatever is in the box. What else in here?

There is a pair of black stilettos, like ones I wore yesterday, and two small purple boxes. I open one. Inside are two pretty silver butterflies.

What are these? Hair clips?

I look at them carefully. Each one has a little clamp behind it; when the wings of the butterfly are squeezed, the clamp opens. Suddenly I understand.

Nipple clamps.

I open the other box. Inside is a small oval of pink silicon with a silver base and a black cord. It has a tiny control beside it. I flick the switch and the little pink egg begins to vibrate.

I see.

So these are the props that will begin my journey to meet Dominic in the world he loves so much.

Time is moving swiftly. I have to get ready now.

Ten minutes later, I am wearing my harness, buckling the slender strap under my breasts. The waist cincher is buckled tightly around my middle, constraining me. I have no other underwear as there was none in the box. I have on the stilettos but my lower body is completely bare and fully exposed.

I must go. He's going to be waiting. He'll be cross if I'm late.

I pick up one of the butterflies. Is this going to hurt? I tug on my nipple and it springs to life under my touch as though it knows that something interesting is about to happen. I open the clamp with its pretty-looking silver fingers, and attach it to the rosy tip of my nipple. It locks on, the butterfly looking like it has landed there to suck nectar from my breasts. The sensation is tingling and not unpleasant, its grip is not as tight as I'd feared, but I have a feeling it will increase as time goes by. I pick up the other clamp and put it on in the same way. The delicate silver butterflies look incongruous next to the leather harness, but somehow it works.

Now for the egg.

I part my legs and put the little oval at my entrance. I'm already slippery there, as the time for my appointment with Dominic comes closer. Pushing with my forefinger, I press it up through the entrance and it nestles inside me, giving me a pleasant, full sensation. The black cord hangs downwards, ready for when the little egg has finished its work. I pick up the control and move the switch. The egg begins to throb and whirr inside me, though there is no noise and no outward sign of it. It is my secret internal massager.

Now how am I going to get to the boudoir? I can hardly walk through the building like this.

It's not in the instructions but I'll have to wear a

coat. Surely Dominic can't expect me to go outside virtually naked. I take the trench coat from the hall cupboard and slip it on. I'm decent again. Except for the thick leather collar around my neck, no one would know that under my coat I'm ready for submission. I slip the key to the flat into my pocket and go.

It is more arousing than I could ever have dreamed to walk through the building, knowing where I am going and what I am wearing. The little egg keeps up its internal throbbing as I ride down in the lift and walk across the lobby to the other lift that will take me to the seventh floor.

'Nice surprise was it?' the porter asks as I pass his desk.

I jump. I'm so intent on where I'm going that I haven't even noticed him. 'What?'

'Your package. Nice was it?'

I stare at him, aware of the clamps around my nipples beginning to hurt just a little, the movement of the egg and that I'm almost naked. 'Yes, thank you. Very nice. A . . . a new dress.'

'Oh, that is nice.'

'Well, goodbye.' I carry on quickly, heading for the lift, desperate to be on my way. I know I have only a minute or two left until 2.30. The lift doesn't come at once, and I can feel my anxiety growing as I wait for it. *I'm going to be late!*

At last the doors slide open and I dash inside, pressing the button for the seventh floor.

Come on, come on.

The lift climbs slowly to the seventh storey and slides open again. I hurry down the corridor, awkward in my high heels and knock at the door of the boudoir, panting.

Please let me be on time.

The door does not open. I knock again and wait. Still nothing. I rap again, loudly.

Suddenly it swings open. He is there, in a long black robe. He has eyes of icy steel and his mouth is set hard. 'You are late,' he says briefly, and my stomach turns to liquid fear.

'I . . . I . . .' My lips are stiff and I'm shaking. I can hardly get the words out. 'The lift . . .'

'I said two thirty. There are no excuses. Come inside.'

Oh shit. I'm frightened, my heart pounding in my chest, adrenalin prickling all over me. A voice is telling me to run away. To tell him to get lost, I'm not playing these games any more. But I know I'll obey. I'm too far in to climb out of all this now.

'Take off your coat. Which, incidentally, I didn't give permission for.'

I want to protest but I know now he wanted me to disobey him in some way. I've managed to make him particularly angry by being late. The coat drops off my shoulders and I'm standing there in my harness, my nipples a vivid red and now stinging hard with the pressure of the clamps and the fact that my treacherous body is responding to him, heating up and tingling.

301

The little egg in my depths is still pressing away, revving me up with its humming caresses.

Dominic's eyes glitter beneath his straight black brows. 'Very good,' he says. 'Yes. That's what I wanted. Now. Get on your hands and knees.'

'Yes sir.' I drop down as instructed. He bends down and does something at the front of my collar. As he stands up, I realise he's attached a long leather lead to it.

'Come.'

He walks towards the bedroom and I follow behind, crawling on my hands and knees. He doesn't tug on the lead but I know it's there, symbolising that I am his. In the bedroom, the lights are dimmed. A long low bench has been put at the foot of the bed. Once we are inside, he bends down again and removes my nipple clamps. It is a huge relief when they are off, but they leave the nipples elongated, throbbing and hypersensitive.

'Go to the bench,' Dominic commands, standing up again. 'Kneel in front and stretch out along it.'

I obey his orders, wondering what is going to happen now as I crawl to the bench and along the smooth wood, my knees on the floor, my bottom exposed.

'Hug it.'

I wrap my arms around the bench, my sensitive nipples hurting as I press down on the surface.

Dominic begins to pace around behind me. I can't see what he's doing but I can hear a rhythmic slap as he hits something against his palm.

'You disobeyed me,' he says in a voice of utter sternness. 'You were late. Do you think a submissive should keep her master waiting, even for one second?'

'No, sir,' I whisper. The anticipation of whatever he's going to do to me is terrible.

'It was your duty to be here before two thirty so that you could be in the boudoir as I ordered on the *stroke* of the half hour.' At the word *stroke,* he slaps his hand again.

What's he holding, for Pete's sake?

His voice drops to a whisper. 'What should I do to you?'

'Punish me, sir.' My voice is small and humble.

'What?'

'Punish me, sir,' I repeat, more loudly.

'Yes. I need to teach you some manners. Are you a naughty girl?'

'Yes, sir.' The words are arousing me, making me hotter. I wonder if he's forgotten about the egg, which is still throbbing away inside me.

'What are you?'

'A naughty girl.'

'Yes. A very naughty, disobedient girl. You need six of the best to teach you a lesson.'

He stops pacing and thwacks whatever he's holding through the air. It makes a whistling sound and I guess it is the riding crop. I feel a rush of fear. I don't want this, it hurts. *Stay strong,* I urge myself. *Don't show him you're afraid.*

There is a long silence and I feel my buttocks tingling

303

with the anticipation. I can hardly bear it. And then, thwack!

The whip lands across my buttocks. It stings but doesn't deliver the sickening blow I've been fearing. I stay still and try not to move.

Thwack!

It lands again across the plumpest part of my buttocks, a little harder this time. I gasp. Before I can regain myself, it lands again, harder still and then again. I cry out. My whole bottom feels aflame, the skin red hot and sensitive. The crop cuts into me again with a biting, stinging slice that sends sizzling agony across my skin. I don't like this feeling of burning pain at all. The little egg is still whirring inside me but I'm hardly aware of it. All I can feel is the agonising cut of the whip as it lands on me for a fifth time. The pain makes me sob out and tears rush into my eyes. I steel myself for the last blow and it comes, harder than all the rest, cutting into my tender skin with the burn of a red-hot poker.

I feel a shuddering sob rising up in my chest but I summon all my strength and suppress it. I don't want him to see me cry.

It's over. Over.

But I'm going to tell him that I don't want that feeling again. I can't bear the feeling of the crop, not just the pain it inflicts but the sense of debasement I feel from having my bottom whipped like that.

He bends down and tugs on the black cord between my legs. The little throbbing egg comes out with a tiny pop. He switches it off.

'Well done, Beth,' he says softly and rubs his hand gently over my bottom. 'I was hard on you. I couldn't resist the sight of your gorgeous skin turning so hot and red for me. I wanted to tear into it with all my strength.' He draws in a breath and sighs. 'You've made me very hot. Get up.'

I lift myself off the bench, my bottom throbbing with pain. I can barely stand.

'Come to me on your knees.'

I obey, and as I reach him, he lets his robe fall open, displaying his nakedness underneath. His penis is standing, huge and hard, evidently fired up by the excitement of what he's just done. His eyes are dark with lust as he watches me moving towards him, my breasts pushed upwards by the harness. I'm holding the lead that's clipped to my collar so I don't trip over it.

'Give me the lead.'

I pass it up to him, keeping my eyes lowered so that I don't offend him with a direct gaze. He takes it and tugs on it gently, pulling tight until I'm forced to press against him, his erection hard against my face. My breasts are against his legs, my collar pressed against his thighs.

Desire moves inside me, counteracting the painful stinging of my bottom. The smell of him is gorgeous, familiar and comforting. At last he's going to let me love him the way I want to. I can touch him, caress him, show him how I feel about him.

'Take me in your mouth,' he commands. 'But do not touch me with your hands.'

Disappointment floods through me. *But at least I get to kiss him, lick him, and taste him . . .*

I run my tongue along the shaft: it's hard and radiating inner heat. When I reach the top, I take it all between my lips, twirling my tongue over the smooth surface, sucking and licking. His fingers curl into my hair, holding on firmly as I let his penis fill my mouth, taking in as much as I can. It's difficult at the angle I'm at, and my jaw already feels stiff as I open wide to take in his girth, but the joy of being able to love him like this makes me determined to ignore the discomfort. Oh, I adore licking him, smelling him and tasting his musky, salty flavour.

As I suck him, the fingers in my hair tighten. He moans. Then he pulls himself free of my mouth and walks over to the white leather chair, tugging on my lead so that I follow. He sits back on the chair, his legs open, and pulls me up onto the footrest, so that I can lean forward as he did to me yesterday and return to my task.

I hold on to the side of the chair and take him in my mouth again, sucking and licking. He moans more loudly. I want to hold his shaft and move the skin, to bring him even more pleasure but I remember that it is forbidden, so I concentrate on working hard with my mouth, titillating him with my tongue, sometimes smoothing him long soft laps and sometimes using the tip to play around its top.

'Yes, that's beautiful,' he murmurs. He's watching me as I service his penis, his eyes half closed. I imagine how I must look to him in my collar and harness, paying homage to his huge erection with my mouth. I can feel my own arousal now, the wetness between my legs, the growing hunger to be filled by this great thing of his.

He growls again, and draws in a broken breath. I can feel him swelling even further in my mouth. His hips are moving now, pushing his length into me, fucking my mouth. I want to touch him, I need to – I'm half worried that he'll push too far down my throat and choke me and that I'll need my hands to stop him. He thrusts harder in, and I fear that I might gag, but his pleasure is about to erupt now. He gives several sharp, hard pushes and a hot gush erupts in my mouth, full of salty liquid whirling around my tongue. I feel it swim in my mouth, then I swallow it down. It leaves a strange burning trail. Without thinking, I put my hand to Dominic's penis as he pulls it from my mouth.

'That was lovely, Beth,' he says in a voice that is velvety yet menacing. 'But you touched me. And I believe that I strictly forbade such a thing.'

I stare up at him, nervous. Of course I am still his submissive. I must obey. Does this mean more punishment? I'd been hoping that he was going to do something about the heat between my legs and my growing desire.

'I . . . I apologise, sir—'

He ignores me, cutting me off. 'Get up and go to the hall. Put on your coat when you get there and wait.'

I do as I'm told, wondering what on earth we're

going to do now. A few minutes later Dominic emerges from the boudoir. He is dressed in his black T-shirt and jeans.

'Follow me.' He leads the way out of the flat and I follow him along the corridor to the lift. My lead is hanging down inside my coat. We take the lift down to the lobby. I look at Dominic who ignores me, tapping messages into his phone instead. At the ground floor, he strides across the lobby and I hurry after him, my shoes tapping on the floor, to where a long black Mercedes is waiting outside. He opens the door and climbs in, leaving me to follow in behind. The driver is invisible behind a darkened screen. I sit next to Dominic on the smooth leather seat and the car pulls smoothly away.

I want to ask where we are going but I do not dare. Dominic continues to say nothing but is busy with his phone.

This day is proving to be very strange, and Dominic himself even stranger. I look over at him discreetly and he seems so very distant.

This isn't what I want.

The voice comes into my mind. I try not to listen. It is what I want. I asked for it.

I try to gather my strength for whatever is lying in wait for me at the end of this ride.

I am not surprised when the car pulls up in the small Soho street outside The Asylum. I have suspected that somehow or other I am going to end up here, and now I know that the moment has come.

A rush of fear goes through me.

'Get out,' Dominic says.

I obey and he follows. Then he leads the way down the metal staircase to the front door. Taking a key from his pocket, he quickly unlocks the door and goes through it. When I have followed him into the small inner hall, he shuts it behind us. I can tell that the place is deserted. Now he pushes my coat from my shoulders and takes my lead. Without a word, he strides off though the empty bar and I am forced into a half run to keep up as he pulls me after him. I know where we are going.

I've always known.

Sure enough, he takes me to that metal-studded door, and pushes it open. He turns to look at me for the first time since we left Randolph Gardens.

'Now you will learn the true meaning of punishment,' he says.

I'm terrified. This is real, choking fear I can feel rushing up inside me. I step into the darkness, and Dominic flicks a switch that brings to life what look like real candles in metal sconces on the wall, but they must be electric.

Now I can see those implements again: the crosses, the bars, the row of evil-looking floggers. My stomach crashes downwards with a nasty sick feeling.

But I must do it. I have to go through with it.

I remember the decision I made to trust Dominic. He won't go too far with me, he said that.

He takes me over to the bars stretching horizontally

across the far wall, then he unbuckles my harness, and slips it over my arms. He lets it drop to the floor unheeded, and makes me stand with my front against the bars, my back to him. He lifts one of my arms and puts my wrist in a manacle level with my shoulder and positioned so that I can move and flex my arm. He does the same with the other. Then he opens my legs and puts one ankle in a restraint and then the other. I can hear his heavy breathing. This is exciting him.

'Now,' he says softly, when I'm completely restrained, 'we will begin.'

I close my eyes tight and clench my stomach. I will bear this. I will do it. And later I'll explain that the dungeon is not my scene no matter what.

Why did he bring you here? asks my inner voice, *when he knows that this place frightened you?*

I don't want to listen. I don't want to hear it. I've got to concentrate right now on enduring whatever is coming my way.

The first touch is light and sensuous, the tickle of long coarse horsehair over my shoulder blades. Dominic seems almost to be drawing something over my back, as though marking out his territory, learning the contours for when he begins to strike.

'This is your punishment for disobedience,' declares Dominic. I can feel him behind me, drinking in the scene: the manacled girl, the flickering light, the whip ready to strike.

The first blow is soft and gentle and so are the next few. He is warming me up. The blood rushes to my skin, making the blows feel like dozens of sharp little cuts. The horsehair is scratchy and scrapes across my already tender skin. I keep my eyes tightly shut and try to control my breathing, but my heart is racing and fear churns in my stomach.

The heat is spreading as he begins to deliver harder, more regular blows.

So this is a flogging. I'm being beaten with a whip in a dungeon.

I fear, then, what is going to happen. I'm outside myself, considering my predicament. And that means my inner fantasy life is flickering and dying.

But it's too late.

The blows stop and I hear Dominic's footsteps move to the rail of instruments, and then he returns. He's holding something else, I can sense it. He turns it through the air a couple of times in swinging practice strokes and then it comes down, flying over my back, dozens of tails with cruel knots at the end biting into my skin.

I throw my head back and scream with surprise and pain. But before I can think, the tails hit me again hard from the other direction. He's sweeping his instrument back and forth, hitting me on each swing.

Oh my God, this is unbelievable!

On it goes, the heavy strokes landing with metronome regularity. The pain is intense and with each blow I cry out loud, unable to keep the control I'd fought for under the onslaught. And with each strike, Dominic hits a little harder, as though my screams are inciting him to put more strength behind the blows. His breathing is heavy and laboured.

The tails spray pain across my back, biting cruelly into my poor, tender skin. It's vicious. It's more than I can stand, I'm shaking and, between my screams of agony, I'm crying.

The safe word. I have to use the safe word.

I've lost all faith that Dominic can see what a state I'm in. He's flogging me hard, and through the haze of pain and confusion in my mind, I think that he may be losing control.

Now I really am terrified – I'm desperately scared, my crying is getting stronger and more intense as the evil instrument rips into my back again and again, left, then right, left then right. Sometimes the biting tails flick round and nip at my breasts and stomach.

What is the safe word?

I'm in such agony, my head rolling round across my shoulders, my back arched inwards away from the blows, my arms tense, that I can't think at all. All I can do is dread the next blow.

The ... safe ... word ... is ...

I gather all my strength and howl, 'Red!'

He hits me again, wham! Hundreds of blades slice into my fervid skin.

'Red, Dominic, stop, stop!'

It's not red ... it's ... oh FUCK, the PAIN ... it's ... something else ... it's ... HOLY HELL ... I'm dying, I'm dying ...

'Scarlet!' I scream. 'Scarlet!'

I tense for the next blow and when it doesn't come, I start shuddering uncontrollably, sobbing wildly. I've never felt such pain, inside or out.

'Beth?' It's a voice I've not heard for days. It's Dominic's normal voice. The voice of my friend, my lover, the man I've been yearning to see again. 'Beth, are you all right?'

I can't talk, I'm crying too hard, tears streaming down my face, my nose running. The sobs are shaking me all over.

'Oh God, baby, what is it?' There's panic in his voice. He drops the flogger and dashes forward to unbuckle my restraints. As my arms are freed, I flop down and sink to the floor, taking my head on my knees and rocking back and forth as I cry.

'Beth, please!' He puts his hand on my arm, careful to avoid the agonised tenderness of my back.

'Don't touch me!' I spit, enraged through my tears. 'Don't come near me!'

He holds back, shocked and uncertain. 'You used the safe word . . .'

'Because you were beating the shit out of me, you bastard, you utter bastard, after everything I've done for you, everything I've offered you and endured . . . My God, I can't believe . . .' The big sobs are racking me now but I manage to speak through them. 'I've been such a fucking idiot. I trusted you, you bastard, I put my faith in you and look what you've done to me . . . !'

I'm so desperately hurt, from the physical pain and

from the sad remnants of my broken trust, and all I can do is weep.

For several minutes Dominic watches me in silence as if at a loss how we came to be in this situation, or how to comfort me. Then he quietly gets my coat and wraps it round me. Even the soft cotton of the trench hurts like hell as he drapes it round my poor back.

He helps me gently to my feet, and leads me out of the dungeon, through the empty bar and out. The car is still waiting for us on the road above. We climb in. I'm still crying, unable to rest my back on the seats, as we return to Randolph Gardens.

I weep all the way. Dominic does not say a word.

THE FOURTH WEEK

CHAPTER EIGHTEEN

That Sunday is the worst day of my life. I'm in agony, for one thing, my back covered in a mass of livid red welts that make me gasp in horror when I see them in the mirror. I haven't got any way of anointing my back with lotion, either, so I spend a long time in a cool bath, trying to draw the heat out of my skin.

I am also in a terrible state emotionally, unable to stop weeping at the memory of what Dominic did to me. It feels like an awful betrayal. He asked me to put my faith in him, and I did. He asked me to trust him to know my limits and I did. I told him that I did not like the dungeon but that is where he took me, to inflict unspeakable agony on me.

And I let him.

That is what hurts too. Dominic may have wielded the whip but I let myself get into that situation. Then I remind myself that it's Dominic who lost control and took the whole thing to a level beyond my capability. He must have forgotten in the heat of the moment that I'm a novice at this – but it was his responsibility to look after me, and be aware of what I could take. He failed at that.

It's also deeply painful that Dominic has not been in touch with me to talk. He has gone silent. I receive one text message that reads simply: *I'm sorry Dx* and nothing else.

Does he really think one text is going to make up for that . . . that assault?

He'll have to do better than that.

On Monday morning, I ring James and tell him I'm ill and can't come into work. He sounds a little wary, as if he can tell that I'm not being honest, but he says all the right things about looking after myself and not coming in until I feel better. I spend the day alone, thinking obsessively over the days I spent with Dominic, trying to analyse why it went so very horribly wrong. I curl up with De Havilland on the sofa and take all the comfort I can from his soft, purring warmth.

At least the cat still loves me.

The welts on my back are still vivid and sore, but the pain is dying down a little. The heat, which kept me awake on Sunday night, is now ebbing out of my skin. I can imagine a time now when it won't hurt, when I'll be healed.

On Tuesday, I call in sick again and now James sounds worried.

'Is everything okay, Beth?'

'Yes,' I say, 'well . . . sort of.'

'Is it something to do with Dominic?'

'Yes and no. Listen James, I need one more day. I'll be back in tomorrow, I promise. I'll tell you then.'

'All right, sweetie. Take the time you need. I understand.'

I know how lucky I am to have a boss like him.

By Tuesday afternoon, I'm feeling a little better. My back continues to hurt but it's definitely improving. I'm still sick at heart, though, at not hearing from Dominic. Whenever I think of it, I feel devastated that he could treat me so badly and then abandon me. Surely he must know that he left me an absolute wreck?

It's late on Tuesday afternoon when I hear the knock at the door. My heart begins to quicken at once as I think instantly that perhaps it's Dominic.

No, I tell myself sternly, as I go to the door. It's bound to be James, calling round with chicken soup and chocolate for me. But I can't help hoping as I reach the door and open it.

To my astonishment, the man waiting for me outside the apartment door is not Dominic or James. It is Adam.

'Surprise!' he cries, grinning all over his face.

I gape at him, unable to believe my eyes. He looks so different to me now, even though he's exactly the same as I remember. His clothes are shabby and totally lacking in style: he has a cheap checked shirt on under a grey sweat top with the name of some sports team on it, and baggy blue jeans that sit under the swell of his belly. He's wearing large white trainers and has a sports holdall over one shoulder. He stares at me, obviously delighted with his surprise arrival.

'Aren't you going to say hello?' he says, when I remain speechless.

'Ah . . . ' I'm still finding it hard to process the evidence of my own eyes. It doesn't make any sense. Adam? Here, at Celia's flat? 'Hello,' I manage limply.

'Can I come in? I'm dying for a piss and a cup of tea. Not at the same time obviously.'

I don't want him to come in but as he needs the lavatory, I feel I can't refuse. I step back and let him inside. It's so weird seeing this part of my life, one I thought was a closed chapter, walking into my new existence. I don't like the way it feels one bit.

'There's the loo,' I say, pointing to the bathroom and his dash inside gives me the moment I need to gather my thoughts. When he comes out, whistling happily in the way I once thought sweet and loveable and now makes me grit my teeth, I say, 'Adam, what are you doing here?'

He looks surprised at my clipped tone. 'Your mum told me where you were and I wanted to come and see you.' He spreads his hands as though asking how I could question such a simple, natural thing.

I stare at him. I have a vague memory of having loved this man once, of being devastated when he broke my heart, but it seems ludicrous now. He looks pallid and half-formed compared to Dominic, with his non-descript messy hair, plump face and pale blue eyes.

'But Adam,' I say, trying to sound measured and reasonable, 'last time I saw you, we broke up. You were fucking Hannah, remember? You dumped me for her.'

Adam makes a face and waves his hand in an impatient gesture. 'Oh that. Yeah. Listen, I came to say sorry. That's all over. It was a mistake and I regret it. But the great news is, I really want to give us another chance!' He beams at me again, and waits, as though expecting me to scream and whoop with joy.

'Adam—' I stare at him helplessly. I don't know what to say.

'What's a guy got to do to get a cup of tea around here?' he asks, and starts opening doors. When he finds the kitchen, he says, 'Bingo' and goes in. I follow, hating the way he's intruding into my ordered life. I remember now how he always used to barge in and help himself to anything he wanted, leaving a mess in his wake.

'Adam, you can't just show up like this. You should have called.'

'I wanted to surprise you,' he says, looking a little hurt. He takes the kettle to the sink and starts to fill it. 'Aren't you pleased to see me?' He gives me the little-boy look, the one that used to melt my heart.

'To be honest, it's not a great time.'

For goodness' sake, don't try to spare his feelings! He didn't do the same for you! Just tell him to sling his hook and get out!

'You don't look too busy. Your mum said you might be at work and to wait till later or call you, but I thought I'd swing by and see what's happening, and here you are! Fate, you see.' The kettle is back on its cradle and switched on.

Okay, one cup of tea, then he's out.

I make two mugs of tea while he tells me of his trip to London on the train and his experience of the Underground. I take him through to the sitting room, where De Havilland is sitting sentinel at the window, gazing out at the pigeons as he often does. He turns his yellow stare to us, blinks and returns to the window, his tail tucked round his legs.

'This is a bloody nice place,' Adam says, looking around the room. 'Whose is it?'

'My dad's godmother. She's called Celia.'

'Oh. Well, play your cards right and you might inherit it.' He gives me a knowing look. 'That'd be nice.'

We sit on the sofa. I wonder what on earth I'm going to say to him. Then I remember the recent past. 'So. Hannah. It hasn't worked out?'

He wrinkles his nose as though he's just thought of something distasteful. 'Nah. We just didn't gel. It was more of a physical connection, you know? Which was all very nice for a bit, but it got boring.'

I see the image of them in bed together, but it doesn't hurt or appal me now. In fact, they seem well suited. I have a flashback to Adam making love to me, panting hard in my ear as he pumped away, in, out, in, out, in exactly the same way every time. It was perfunctory and quick. Sweet, because I loved him, but darkly passionate? Stirring and exciting? Did he push boundaries and help me discover aspects of myself that I didn't know existed?

Of course not. Dominic did that.

I suddenly realise that I've been changed forever by my experience with Dominic. I can never go back to someone like Adam now. Dominic might have some kinky tastes and unusual pleasures, but at least he wasn't boring.

Adam is gazing at me now, his hands wrapped round his mug. 'That's why I wanted to come and find you. Because what we had was really special. I was an idiot and I hurt you, but I've put all that behind me now. I want us to get back together.'

'I . . . I don't . . . think . . .' I take a deep breath and say, 'No, Adam. That isn't going to happen.'

His face falls. 'It isn't?'

I shake my head. 'No. I've got a new life now. A job.'

'A boyfriend?' he asks swiftly.

'Well, not really. No.' *It looks like Dominic and I are over, after all.* 'But that doesn't change anything. There's no future for us now.'

'Please, Beth.' He gazes at me winsomely. 'Don't write me off just like that. I know that me turning up here like this is a shock. Take some time to think about it.'

'It isn't going to change anything,' I say adamantly.

He sighs and sips his tea. 'Well, we can talk about it later.'

'Later?'

'Beth, I've got nowhere to stay. I thought I could stay with you.'

'Why would you think that?' I cry, exasperated. 'We broke up!'

'But I want you back.'

I shrug and sigh with exasperation. We're back where we started.

'I can't go home tonight,' Adam says. 'Let me stay here? Please?'

I sigh again. I don't have much choice in the matter; I can hardly throw him out in the streets. 'All right. You can sleep on the sofa. But only for one night, do you understand? I mean it.'

'Message received!' he says cheerfully, and I can read all over his face that he's confident one night is all he needs to win me back.

Once I've got used to Adam's presence, I quite enjoy having him to stay, in an odd way. He's good company and is soon chatting away, telling me all the gossip I've missed and what his crazy brother is up to now. I cook us a simple pasta supper and we share it while he natters on. It's weird to hear so much noise in Celia's apartment, it's usually so quiet.

Later, we return to the sitting room and Adam tries to sweet talk me a little by reminding me of happy times we spent together and the promises we made to one another. I don't mind reminiscing but it's not going to have the effect he wants. When I bring him a pillow and rug and leave him to settle down, he makes an attempt to kiss me but I firmly rebuff him, which he accepts with seeming equanimity.

I'm sure he thinks it's just a matter of time before I cave.

I go to sleep in Celia's room, still bemused by the thought that Adam is next door right now, perhaps even planning how he's going to sneak his way into my bed. Luckily I hear nothing from him all night.

The next morning, I'm feeling a great deal more cheerful and I'm keen to get back to work.

'Are you off later?' I ask Adam, as I gather my things together after breakfast.

'Well . . .' He looks a bit cunning. 'I thought I might hang around actually, if you don't mind. I'd like to see a bit of London while I'm here, as you've got the room . . .'

'Adam,' I say warningly.

'Just one more night?' he pleads.

I stare at him. I suppose it can't do any harm. 'One more. And that's it.'

He grins. 'Agreed.'

It's lovely to see James again. I've missed him.

'Puss, you're back!' he calls as I come into the gallery. 'I've been so worried.' He comes over and makes to hug me, but I pull away, wincing. 'Ah.' He looks knowing and a little sad. 'Oh Beth, did he hurt you?'

I nod slowly. It's a relief to confide in someone at last.

'That bastard. Was it against your wishes?'

325

I nod again, feeling like a traitor to Dominic.

'That's forbidden,' declares James, his expression serious, looking over the top of his spectacles in that way of his. 'I'm sorry, Beth, I don't care how much you feel for him – safe, sane and consensual, that's the rule for BDSM. If he's broken it, don't go near him again, do you hear?'

Something in me deflates in despair at his words. But perhaps he's right. I just wish it were easier to bear.

We spend a happy morning catching up, and laughing about Adam turning up and trying to wheedle his way back into my affections. I tell James I fully intend to chuck him out tomorrow, no matter what.

At lunchtime, I'm on the sushi run, so I head out to cross Regent Street to our favourite place to get some takeaways for us. As I leave the gallery, I pass an old church, tucked away from the world behind red brick walls and an iron gate, open so that passers-by can pop in for a look. To my astonishment, someone darts out of the small courtyard as I pass and grabs my arm.

I gasp and look up to find Dominic, gripping me hard, his eyes wild and looking unusually unkempt. 'Dominic!' My insides clench in excitement at seeing him again.

'I've got to talk to you,' he says urgently, and pulls me through the gate into the courtyard.

He's going to apologise! My heart leaps at the thought. *Maybe there's hope . . . ?*

He's staring at me almost angrily, his expression fevered, as he says, 'Who is he, Beth?'

'What?'

'Don't play the innocent – I've seen him! The man in your apartment! Who the hell is he?'

I reply without thinking. 'It's Adam.'

He draws in a sharp breath, gives me an intense look that is almost despairing, then he lets go of my arm and strides out of the courtyard and away without looking back.

'Shit!' I curse as I hurry after him. He's already disappeared down a side street. Why did I say that? Why didn't I pretend he was my brother? Now he's going to assume that I'm back with Adam. I curse again. I'll have to call him later and explain.

Then again, why should I? He still hasn't apologised for what he did to me. Maybe it will do him good to stew.

I still haven't decided what to do when I return with our sushi.

I'll think about it later.

Adam has managed, in the course of one day, to spread everything in his bag all over the flat, plus the detritus of whatever food he bought or made himself. I feel a surge of irritation to see how carelessly he's treated the place, and at the same time feel relieved that I'm not facing a lifetime of clearing up after him.

'How was your day?' he asks solicitously as I arrive home. 'I thought I might take you out for dinner tonight.'

'That's sweet of you, Adam, but why don't we go out for a drink first and see how we go from there?' I've already made up my mind to be completely frank tonight, tell him there's no chance and explain that he has to go first thing in the morning. The pub seems like a good place to do it.

'Okay, great. Let's go.'

Out of the apartment building, we stroll together through the hot streets. The air is very close now and the sky is hazed over with white clouds for the first time in ages. I think I can feel a storm building, but it's probably what we need after days of blue skies and heat.

'You know what, Beth,' Adam says conversationally as we walk along. I'm heading for the place Dominic took me that night. 'You're different, you know. You seem more . . . I don't know . . . more grown up. More sophisticated. And sexier. Definitely sexier.' He gives me a look that I think is supposed to be flirtatious, but it comes over as slightly leery.

'Really?' I'm interested, despite myself. I have wondered if my experiences in the last few weeks have changed me at all. It seems they have.

'Yeah,' he says graciously. 'You're really attractive.'

'Thanks,' I say with a laugh, then remember I'm going to be dumping a bucket of icy water on his hopes any minute now. 'But, Adam, while that's very nice it doesn't mean that anything's going to happen between us.'

We stop. He looks me straight in the eye. Then he smiles a little sadly. 'It's really over, isn't it?'

I nod. 'Yes. I don't love you. It's well and truly finished.'

'Is there someone else?' he asks.

I flush bright red and say nothing.

'I thought so,' he says with a sigh. 'Oh well. It was worth a try. I've been an idiot, Beth, I know that. I didn't know what I had until I wrecked it. He's a lucky guy, that's all I can say.'

I smile back at him, feeling a little choked. 'Thanks for saying that, Adam. Really. You've put a lot of things to rest for me. We can still be friends.'

'Yeah, sure,' he says heartily. 'But something tells me we're not going to see you back at home very much in the future. I could be wrong, of course, but it's my gut instinct.' He thinks for a moment, and says, 'Shall we still have that drink? For old times' sake?'

'Yes. I'd like that.'

'Good. And I'll be on my way in the morning.'

We look at each other a little longer, acknowledging what we once meant to one another and the end of that time of our lives. Then we walk on, towards the pub.

When we get back much later, I unlock the flat to let us in. Adam, a bit drunk after four pints, is talking loudly and doesn't notice the cream envelope waiting for me on the floor.

My heart skips as I see it and I scoop it up quickly. While Adam chatters on, I slip into the bedroom and open it with trembling hands. It reads:

To My Mistress,
Your slave humbly requests one night with you. Honour
him with your presence tomorrow night in the boudoir.
He will be waiting from 8pm.

I clutch it to my chest.
Oh my God. My slave? What does he mean?
I'll go. Of course I will. How could I not?

CHAPTER NINETEEN

The next day I say goodbye to Adam, and watch as he heads off to the train station, back to the world I've left behind. Soon Celia will be home and what will I do then? Worry is beginning to niggle at me. I'll have nowhere to live and, once James's assistant gets out of hospital, no job either.

I'll send Laura an email, I decide, and tell her that I'm interested in sharing a flat with her, and maybe James will find a way to keep me on as well at the gallery.

One thing is for certain. I can't go back to my old life. Not now.

I spend the day in a heightened state of anticipation but I'm not sure how I feel about the forthcoming encounter. I keep it to myself, mulling over what it might mean, alternately excited and fearful. The physical pain on my back may have faded, and the weals are almost gone, but I'm still hurting very badly at the way things turned out. I tried my very best to be what Dominic needed and in the end, he took more than I could give. And the fact that there has been no apology from him wounds me most, much more than the flogging itself. I loved him and offered myself to him, and he has simply vanished out of my life as if he were never there.

I remember the wildness of his eyes when he asked me about Adam. He must think we're back together. Well, he'll find out soon enough when Adam is no longer visible in the flat.

I am also intrigued. My slave? Dominic doesn't do submissive. I know he began that way, as Vanessa's plaything as she learned her dominating skills, but he turned his back on that.

Something is going to happen. I just can't be sure what it will be.

When I get home, I take a long bath, letting the hours slide by. I dress carefully, not in any costume this time, but in my black dress. I may not be wearing crotchless panties or harnesses today, but I make sure I am wearing my prettiest underwear.

Just in case.

Secretly, I hope that he is waiting to take me in his arms, kiss me and tell me that he made a terrible mistake, he is not a dominant at all, but just a normal hearts-and-flowers-and-fantastic-only-mildly-kinky-sex guy, and that he wants to be with me. That would sort out all our problems at once. But I have a feeling that's unlikely.

It's after 8.30 as I make my way up to the boudoir. I know it's childish to make him wait, but I can't help relishing that I can get a little of my own back for the way he made me wait for him. When I knock on the door, my pulse is rattling away and my palms have dampened. A fluttering nervousness settles in the pit of my stomach. I long to see him, the old Dominic who once belonged to me, but I'm also afraid of what might happen in the boudoir. I promised to be a submissive when I was in there.

But I'm not wearing the collar, I remind myself.

After a moment the door swings open into darkness. I peer in and then step forward. 'Dominic?'

'Beth.' His voice is low and husky. 'Come into the bedroom.'

A muffled light shows from within the room across the hall. I walk towards it. In the boudoir, the low bench has gone, though the white leather seat remains. There are two armchairs at the foot of the bed, angled to face one another. The bedroom lamps are on low. Dominic is sitting in one and he stands up as I come in, his head bowed as though he's staring at the floor.

'Thank you for coming,' he says in sombre tones. 'It's more than I deserve.'

'I want to hear what you've got to say,' I reply, my voice sounding stronger than I feel. 'I was wondering when, if ever, you were going to speak to me again.'

He raises his eyes, and they are so drenched in sorrow, I want to rush to him and hold him and tell him it's going to be all right. But I manage to control myself. I'm desperate to hear whatever he's going to tell me.

'Come and sit down, Beth. I want to explain everything.' He gestures to the chair next to his. When we are both sitting, he says, 'I've been through a very bad time since I last saw you. What happened between us on Saturday – that dreadful thing – has caused me a great crisis. I had to leave for a couple of days and see someone to whom I could confess what I'd done and ask for advice.'

'A therapist?' I ask.

'No, not really. A kind of mentor, I suppose. It's someone who has occasionally guided me on this path, whose wisdom and experience I respect and admire. I won't talk further of this person now, except to say that I was made to understand the gravity of what I did.' His head bows sadly again, and he clasps his hands in his lap as if in supplication.

My heart goes out to him. He looks so beautiful in this half-light, silhouetted by the lamp behind him, and I long to touch him, to run my finger along his face and whisper that I forgive him.

But do I?

Not yet. There are some things I need to tell him before that can happen.

He looks up at me, his black eyes looking liquid coal in this light. 'There are rules governing this kind of relationship, Beth, as you know. I was very arrogant. When we laid out our ground rules, I told you that I thought I would be able to read you and know when you reached your limit. I didn't allow you to set your own limit, even though I knew you didn't like the dungeon. I can see now I was determined to take you there, no matter what you felt. I . . .' he pauses and grimaces '. . . I've been told that I have been acting out the loveless relationships of my past, where my subs have been in my life solely to give me sexual pleasure. But this – us – is something else entirely. I know that you gave yourself to me for love, not your own pleasure. It curdles me up to think how I took that precious thing and used it so selfishly.'

'You weren't completely selfish,' I say gently. 'Many – no, most – of the things you did to me, I loved. I had a wonderful time. You gave me such pleasure, of a kind I had no idea existed. But there was something very wrong.'

He nods. 'I think I know what it is. But you go ahead. Tell me.'

I know what I'm going to say. I've been framing the thoughts in my head for days now. 'When you became Dominic the master, you lost all trace of the other Dominic. You never kissed me – not with any feeling or tenderness – and you hardly touched me. I could bear that while we were acting out the scene, while I was your sub. But afterwards, when I felt so strange – when I felt so close to you but so vulnerable from all the things you'd done to me, especially when you beat me and hit me – that was when I needed you to love and nurture me. I needed your kiss and your arms around me, and your reassurance that I'd done the right thing.' Tears spring to my eyes. 'Most of all, I needed to know that I wasn't really your worthless slave, but your precious girl.'

'Don't, Beth,' he says. His voice is harsh, as though it's painful to hear what I've got to say. 'I've fucked up so badly and I know it was wrong. It's hard for me to admit, because I've never lost control of a scene before, never, I thought I was too good at it for that, a practised master of my art.' He laughs grimly. 'It turns out not to be the case. And I don't know why it happened. All I can think is that I'm not used to being so emotionally involved with someone.' He stands up, goes to the cabinet, opens the door and takes something out. He returns with it and places it on my knee. 'That's why I want you to use this.'

I stare down at it. It's the cat o' nine tails that he used on me in the dungeon and I feel sick as I look at it. 'Dominic, no, I can't . . .'

'Please, Beth. I want you to. I can't forgive myself until I've suffered a little of what you suffered.' He is staring at me intensely, begging me to do this for him.

I want to throw the goddamned thing across the room. 'Why can't we be normal?' I shout at him. 'Why can't you just apologise? Why does it all have to include *this*?'

'Because it's my penance,' he says in a low voice, as though repeating something he's learned. 'I have to do it.' He takes off his jacket and then his top. He is bare to the waist.

Oh, my beautiful Dominic. I want to love you. I don't want to hit you.

'No,' I say, barely above a whisper.

He gets up and comes to kneel at my feet, bowing his head. I run my eyes over the tanned expanse of his back, the soft dark hair at the back of his neck, the muscled curve of his shoulders. I want to feel him, touch his intoxicating mix of hard muscle and soft smooth skin. I put out my hand and ruffle the surface of his dark hair. He says softly, 'I want to apologise to you, Beth, for the dreadful, unforgiveable thing I did to you. The most important part of our relationship was the trust, and I took your trust and abused it. I'm so, so sorry.'

'I forgive you. I don't want to punish you.'

'Beth, please . . .' His dark eyes turn beseechingly to mine. 'I need it. I need to suffer as you did. It's the only way.'

I look again at the whip on my lap. It looks so harmless, almost innocuous. But with the force of human desire behind it, it can flay you alive.

'Please.' That one word is so freighted with need.

How can I refuse him?

I stand up, taking the flogger in my hand, feeling its weight. Is this, I wonder, my most submissive moment of all? My beautiful, controlling, masterful Dominic wants me to give him a taste of what he inflicted on me. He has demanded it, and I will obey. 'All right. If it's what you want.'

Relief floods his features. 'Thank you,' he says, almost happily. 'Thank you.'

He gets up and goes to the white leather seat. I

337

remember the ecstasy I felt there, as Dominic made me soar to the very heights of pleasure. Now he lies on his front, taking his hands below the seat and holding onto the frame. His back is exposed to me from the nape of his neck to the waist.

'I'm ready,' he says.

I approach and stand by the chair, feeling the heavy whip in my hand. Its handle is a little too long for me to hold comfortably, and I guess that this is not the instrument a loving domme would use to begin a flogging. I remember how Dominic always warmed me gently with delicate strokes and softer materials before he laid on the sterner instruments.

Am I really going to do this?

It's what he wants, I tell myself. And, despite everything, I love him.

I lift the whip and bring it down on Dominic's back with a circular stroke. It's an ineffective blow, hardly grazing him, but the sensation of using the flogger is so strange I can't do it with any real force. I try again and again, but still I'm not able to put any true strength behind it. I am afraid that it is because I do not want to.

'Try a different stroke,' Dominic says. 'Take your arm back and follow through in a straight line so the tails flick over me, then back in the same way. Don't swing your whole body, keep the power in your arm and wrist.'

Lessons from the master, I think wryly, but I do as he says and the first blow with any meaning lands across Dominic's back. I gasp as I feel the reverberation in my arm.

'Yes,' Dominic says in a firm voice. 'Carry on. Harder.'

I do it again from the same side, pulling back and pushing through. Now I see a darkening of the skin where the tails have bitten, and I sweep back from the other direction, landing them again in the same place.

'Very good, Beth. Well done. Please continue.'

I begin to find my rhythm as I become accustomed to the weight of the whip and the feel of the tails slapping down on Dominic's back. I begin to listen for the sounds, and the way they are forming a kind of beat to my actions. I start to forget that the crack of the tails on his back are causing him pain, even though I know this to be the case.

The strokes are growing in intensity. Dominic's back is reddening, the skin puffing up under the blows. I realise that I'm beginning to feel a sense of what that power can feel like, of how the urge to rip into the willing victim can begin to possess with a dark, primitive strength. Maybe there is a brutality in me after all.

So perhaps the person the controller most needs to control is themselves. Their desires must be governed by what their submissive can take.

I understand now that this is how Dominic has failed himself. And me.

As I think this, any desire to relish the pain I am inflicting dies. The sight of the reddened skin, and the stripes of red and white that appear where the tails land cause an awful sadness to rise up in me.

But I go on.

Instinct tells me to change my stance and I stand almost side on to Dominic, taking my arm back and powering through like a tennis player hitting a strong forearm shot. Just before the whip strikes, I hold back the power so that the impetus drops and the tails bring their greatest force to the skin, and don't continue on.

As the first of these hard blows hit, Dominic cries out. The sound rends my heart. He shouts again and again as the whip strikes with its flock of teeth. I notice that the skin on his back has begun to weep clear fluid, and the sight makes tears jump to my eyes, hot and sharp. Sobs begin to rise in my chest and I feel them break in my throat in time to the blows I am raining on his back. This is becoming too much, but I grit my teeth and force myself on.

Dominic is containing himself now. His eyes are shut and I can see the fierce set of his jaw as he fights to absorb the agony and not cry out. I know that every strike is cleansing him, giving the redemption he craves.

But I don't know how much longer I can stand it. This is merciless, this is barbaric.

'Don't stop,' Dominic orders, through gritted teeth. 'Keep going.'

Keep going? Tears are dripping down my face now as I obey, pulling my arm back, forcing it forward and round in a thwacking sweep, cutting the flogger into his back. The stripes are now indistinguishable from the mass of swollen redness on his back. It's weeping too, the clear liquid sticky and shiny on his skin.

'I can't,' I say, 'I can't.' The sobs are beginning to choke me.

Then I see it. The ruby drops breaking through the surface of his tortured skin, erupting like miniature volcanoes. They speckle his back, and begin to flow. Blood.

'No!' I cry, and I let the flogger drop down, the power seeping from its tails. 'No, I can't do it.' I start to cry in earnest. 'Your poor back, it's bleeding.' Overcome I sink down onto my knees, the whip falls from my hand, my head droops and I start to cry. How has it come to this? I'm beating the man I love until he bleeds.

Dominic shifts and slowly raises himself. He is stiff with the pain, and when he turns to look at me, his eyes are wet too. 'Beth, don't cry. Can't you see? I don't want to cause you pain.'

This seems so bitterly ironic, that I cry even harder.

'Hey, my girl, my girl.' He gets off the seat and comes to me, kneeling close and takes my hands. 'Don't cry.'

But his own face is full of sadness, his eyes glittering with tears. I can't even embrace him, his back is far too tender for that. Instead, I reach up and cup his beloved face in my hands. 'How did it come to this?' I whisper. Then slowly I stand up. 'I can't do this any more. I know you need to work through your guilt or whatever fucked-up thing you're feeling, but I can't be your instrument any more. It hurts too much, Dominic. I'm sorry.'

Then I turn for the door and leave him there. I don't want to abandon him, but I know that if I don't go now, my heart will burst.

CHAPTER TWENTY

At work, James is gentle with me. He can tell my emotions are all over the place and that I'm working through something important. He must be regretting taking me on, I think, I've been nothing but a basket case since I started.

But I manage to turn my mind to work – it helps, in fact, because while I'm doing the exhibition organisation, I can forget about last night's awful scene. When I do remember it, it's with a kind of dull horror. I feel as though I'm caught up in some kind of nightmare, where love and pain are deeply, inseparably entwined, and for the first time I don't know if I can stand it.

I think of Adam – placid, predictable Adam – waiting for me back at home. Perhaps that's the answer after all. Perhaps the world of grand passions and high drama is not for me.

But it seems that there's no solution: heartbreak if I carry on, and heartbreak if I don't.

In the afternoon, James brings me a cup of tea and says, 'I've had a bit of news from Salim.'

Salim is James's usual assistant, and, from what I

can glean from the files, he's amazingly organised and efficient.

'He's out of hospital next week,' James continues, looking a little sheepish. 'And after that, he'll be coming back to his job here.'

'I always knew he would,' I reply. 'You've never pretended anything else.'

James sighs and takes off his gold-framed spectacles. 'I know. But I've loved having you here, Beth. You've added quite a bit of spice to my life, for one thing. I wish we could find some way to keep you on.'

'Don't worry,' I say with a smile. 'I have to leave Celia's flat next week. I always knew this was just a temporary life.'

'Oh Beth.' He puts his hand on my arm. 'I'll miss you. I hope you'll always consider me a friend.'

'Of course I will. You won't be able to shake me off that easily!' I'm trying very hard to sound normal but inside I'm in a whirl of uncertainty. What on earth can I do next? Even if Laura wants to share a flat in the autumn, I'll have to go home in the meantime. With no place to stay and no job, what can keep me here?

Dominic?

I close my mind to that. It's too painful to think about either of the alternatives: being with him and being without seem equally painful.

'If anything right for you comes up, I'll let you know,' James says.

'Thank you, James. I'd appreciate that.'

'How are things with Dominic?' he asks tentatively.

'Any change?'

I'm silent for a moment, wondering how much I can tell him. Then I say, 'I don't think it's going to work. We're just too different.'

'Ah.' He sounds knowing. 'It's a bit like a woman falling in love with a gay man, I'm afraid. You might think you can change him, but the reality is, you can't.' He rubs my arm comfortingly again. 'I'm sorry, hon. You'll find someone else, I promise.'

I can't trust myself to speak so I just nod. Then I have to bow my head and get on with changes to the client database before he can see that my eyes are filled with tears.

London is bursting with Friday evening jollity as I walk home, even though the sun has now well and truly disappeared under a thick grey haze of cloud. It's still warm, though, almost muggy, and the air feels thinner than usual.

I sense something different as soon as I head up in the lift, and by the time I'm opening the door to the flat, I know for sure that there is a change in the atmosphere. For the first time, De Havilland doesn't come trotting out to me, his tail in the air. Then I see the two large suitcases in the hall.

'Helloooo,' comes a voice, and a moment later, a smart older woman is standing in the doorway of the sitting room. She is tall and elegant, dressed in a blue printed silk wrap dress, her skin is lined but baby soft and her hair is a chic silver crop. It's Celia.

I gape at her in astonishment.

'I know, I know,' she declares, coming towards me with her hands outstretched. 'I should have called! I meant to, but when I wanted to call, my phone didn't work and when it did, I was too tied up with passports and airports and what have you.'

I'm still processing everything as she clasps my hands and kisses me on both cheeks. 'Have I got it wrong?' I ask. 'I thought you were back next week.'

'No you're right, but I couldn't bear that wretched retreat a moment longer! I've never been locked up with so many frightful bores for so long. I can't believe I managed as long as I did. And the food . . .' She raises her eyes to heaven. 'I must be spoiled, darling, but I believe there's no moral imperative that means food should taste ghastly! In fact, I behave a great deal better when I'm able to eat delicious things three times a day. Now, don't be disappointed because I'm home early.'

'Of course I'm not,' I insist, but I am. Horribly.

'You don't have to leave, you can stay here till the time is up but I'm afraid I shall have to reclaim my bed. Little old ladies of seventy-two must have their luxury mattresses and supportive pillows, I'm afraid. But I've been told my sofa is more comfortable than many a hotel bed. So you can have that.' She smiles at me. She really does have the most amazing skin: it looks as soft as tissue.

'Well, if you don't mind,' I say hesitantly. I don't have anywhere else to go, after all, and I still have a week left to work for James. Perhaps I can make some other arrangement next week, although I can't think what.

'Of course I don't. The flat looks wonderful and De Havilland is positively glowing. You've obviously taken care of my little angel. Now, do you have plans for this evening, or will you let me take you out for supper?'

I had no real plans, except to see if I could see Dominic in his flat across the way. That will have to wait now, I suppose.

'Supper would be lovely, Celia, thank you,' I say brightly.

'Excellent. We'll go to Monty's Bar. They do such wonderful food and I really feel I deserve it after all I've suffered.'

Monty's Bar and the dinner Celia buys me is wonderful, but I can't help wishing I was back, alone in her silent apartment, able to see whether Dominic is at home or not. She is very interesting and amusing, and she asks me plenty about my time in London and my job at the gallery, but I feel as though I'm supposed to be somewhere else. By the time we get home that evening, it's late and when I at last have the opportunity to look out of the sitting room window, the flat opposite is in darkness.

Celia makes up the sofa with sheets, blankets and a pillow, and I snuggle down there, but for a long time I can't sleep. All I can do is watch the darkened windows opposite and wonder where he is and what he's doing.

On Saturday it's obvious that Celia wants to be busy in the flat, sorting out her things and settling back in, so I leave early in the morning and go for a long day out on my own. It's as though I'm almost back where I started in all of this, as I walk around London with all the other tourists, queuing for the British Museum and the V & A. Every half an hour, I check my phone, hoping against hope that Dominic will get in touch but it seems unlikely. I told him when we parted that I couldn't do what he wanted any more. He's probably given me up as a lost cause, and now that he's received his strange idea of penance, he doesn't need me any more.

Still, I can't help hoping against hope that he wants to fight for me, perhaps even try to change. But hour after hour goes by and still no message comes.

I get home hot and tired in the late afternoon and Celia is waiting for me, calm and relaxed now that she has unpacked.

'Tea for you, I think,' she announces, and makes a pot of Earl Grey which she serves with delicious little apricot biscuits. While we are sipping at our tea, she chatters on about things and then says, 'Oh, yes – while I remember . . . When I came home yesterday, there was a letter for you on the hall mat. I put it on the table and meant to tell you all about it, but I quite forgot. I saw it just after you left this morning.'

I put my cup down quickly and rush to the hall. The familiar cream envelope is there addressed to me in Dominic's writing and I rip it open with trembling hands. There is a handwritten card inside.

Dear Beth

I will never stop respecting your courage and bravery. It took a lot to do what I asked for last night. I know I've pushed you to the limits and I understand completely that you've gone as far as you can ever go. If anyone needs to compromise their needs, it's me, Beth, not you. I've been very selfish but I've learned that it isn't going to bring me what I need more than anything else, and that is you.

I've had my chance, I know that. You stuck with me for longer than any other woman would. I still managed to fuck it up. It's more than I dare hope after all that's happened, but I will be in my apartment tonight if you want to talk.

If I don't hear from you, I will understand that you don't wish us to be in contact any longer, and I will respect that.

I hope you and Adam will be very happy together.

All my love

Dx

P. S. The boudoir is at your disposal. Use it as long as you need it.

I gasp in horror. He was waiting for me *last night*. While I was out with Celia, he was in the flat, wondering if I would arrive there.

And his note makes it sound as though he wants to change, as though he's willing to try a different way.

Oh my God. Am I too late?

I hurry to the sitting room and look across at the flat opposite. The gauzy curtains are drawn but I can see a figure moving around inside.

He's there. There's still time.

I turn to Celia, who is watching me with faint surprise from the sofa. 'I have to go out. I don't know when I'll be back.'

'Whatever you must do, darling,' she says, stroking De Havilland who is curled on her knee. 'See you later.'

I don't even say goodbye to her in my haste to be gone.

CHAPTER TWENTY-ONE

It takes me a few frantic minutes to get from one side of the building to the other, but at last I am racing along the corridor to Dominic's flat. I bang hard on the door.

'Dominic, are you there? It's me, Beth!'

There's an agonising wait and then I hear footsteps approaching. The door opens and swings back to reveal the tall, slim figure and high cheekbones of Vanessa.

What's she doing here?

'Ah, Beth,' she says coolly. 'Well, well.'

'Where's Dominic?' I gasp. 'I need to see him.'

'It's a bit late for that, isn't it?' She turns on her heel and walks back inside. I follow her, panting.

'What do you mean?'

She turns around and fixes me with a hard look. 'Haven't you caused enough trouble?' she asks in a cold voice. 'You've turned everything upside down. Everything was going very nicely before you arrived.'

'I . . . I . . . I don't understand – what have I done?'

Vanessa strides into the sitting room and I go after her. It's horrible to be in there without Dominic. It seems to be lacking its lifeblood without him.

'Well, you've certainly caused an upset, that's what you've done.' She fixes me with her stare. 'Dominic's gone. He's left.'

'Left?' The blood drains from my face and I feel faint. 'Where's he gone?'

'It's really none of your business but if you must know, he's on his way to Russia. His boss needs him there and he'll be gone for some time.'

'How long?'

Vanessa shrugs. 'Weeks. Months. I don't know. When his boss says go, he goes. From Russia, he might go to New York or Los Angeles, Belize or the Arctic Circle. Who knows?'

'But . . . he lives *here*.'

'He lives wherever is necessary. And if he needs to be elsewhere, there is plenty to keep him busy.' She is walking around the room, collecting bits and pieces and putting them in a canvas bag. 'So I'm afraid it looks as though your little holiday romance is at an end.'

I stare at her, still uncomprehending. How much does she know about what's gone on? I know that she and Dominic are close, but are they so close that he's confided in her about our intimate relationship?

Vanessa stops walking about and turns to face me. Her face is stony as she puts one hand on her hip. 'I think you're a fool, if you must know. He was willing to do more for you than he ever has for anyone else. He was willing to try and change. And you threw it away.'

'But it's a mistake,' I say breathlessly, finding my voice at last. 'He thinks I'm with Adam, but I'm not. And I was meant to see him last night but I didn't get the note until just now.'

Vanessa shrugs as if all this detail is too tedious for words. 'Whatever the reason, you've missed your chance.' She smiles grimly. 'That little bird has well and truly flown. Most women would have done anything to have Dominic, no matter what little foibles he might enjoy. I don't think you'll get a second chance.'

Her words pierce me painfully. Have I really been so stupid?

Suddenly, she leans towards me, her expression almost kind. Her eyes soften and she says, 'Go home and forget about him. It's for the best, really. It wasn't meant to be, that much is obvious. You've had your fun. Go back to where you belong.'

As I stare at her, the fight suddenly goes out of me. *She must be right. She knows Dominic better than anyone.* If we were meant to be together, then we would not have made such a royal mess of it. The way the note was lost . . . it must be fate. What's the point of fighting it, now that he's gone?

'All right,' I say quietly. 'I understand. Will you tell him . . . Tell him that I wish it could have been different for us. And that I'll never be sorry that I met him. What we shared meant so much to me.'

'Of course.' She smiles at me, as if glad our little interview is at an end. 'Goodbye, Beth.'

353

'Goodbye.' I turn and walk out of Dominic's apartment for what I suspect will be the last time.

Celia is listening to Handel and sipping a glass of white wine as she reads a book when I come in. As soon as she sees my face, she pours another and hands it to me.

'Poor Beth,' she says sympathetically. 'Life can be miserable, can't it? I take it it's to do with love.'

I nod, still shell-shocked as it starts to sink in that Dominic has gone.

'You don't have to tell me anything, my dear, but I'm here if you need me.'

I sit down and take a gulp of the white wine. Its cold flintiness brings me back to myself a little. 'I thought . . . I thought I was going to be with someone, but it hasn't worked out. He's left.'

Celia shakes her head. 'Oh dear. Is it all based on a misunderstanding?'

I nod again, and my eyes sting. I do all I can to damp down my emotion. I don't want to lose control, I'm not sure how I'd ever regain it. 'I think so,' I say. 'I'm not even sure any more. I thought it was too painful to be with him, but now I don't know how I'll manage without him.'

'Oh dear.' Celia sighs. 'Yes, that sounds like it.'

'Like what?'

'Like love, my dear. Many people prefer to shun love. They settle for something easier, less all consuming, less dangerous. Because, as Shakespeare observed, violent delights have violent ends. Great passion brings

354

pain with it. But to live without it . . . well, is it worth it?' She fixes me with a bright look. 'I'm not sure. Not all of us are granted the chance to feel that sublime passion for someone else, or the agony that comes with it. I was lucky to know it more than once, and that's why I live happily alone now. Knowing I've tasted at that magnificent cup, I'd rather survive on the memory than accept anything less.'

I stare at her, imagining that young Celia, lost in rapture with her lover, living, as I have lately, on a knife edge of delight and despair.

'It was all a very long time ago,' she says with a twinkling smile, 'and I expect it's hard to believe that an old woman like me ever felt what you're feeling.'

'Oh no, of course not,' I say quickly.

'I have just a little wisdom to pass on to you.' She leans towards me. 'Don't be satisfied with a quiet life. Youth slips away more quickly than you can ever guess. Take your strength, your vigour, and all the life within you, seize it, enjoy it, feel it. Even the pain reminds you that you're alive and without it we wouldn't know what pleasure is. Don't forget that golden lads and girls all must, as chimney sweepers, come to dust. We shall be a very long time dead.'

Her words stir something within me.

She's right, I know it. The idea that I'd ever wanted to reject Dominic and all he'd given me and made me feel was absurd. He went too far but I know with absolute certainty that he would never have let it happen again. He was prepared to listen to me, and to

355

compromise. I can see that now. But my chance has slipped through my fingers. He's gone.

There isn't pleasure without pain. There isn't passion without suffering. I'd rather feel alive than safe.

Dominic – where the hell are you?

It's only when, much later, I'm curled up on the sofa and trying to sleep that I remember what Dominic wrote about the boudoir. The key is in the pocket of Celia's trench coat and I slip into the hall and retrieve it. It sits in my hand, smooth and cold.

Apparently it's now mine for as long as I want it.

It's an extraordinary gesture that I can't really take in. It means, I realise, that my accommodation problem is solved. I can go there whenever I want. Now, if I want to.

The problem is that it's all too raw. I can't go there at the moment, knowing it's the last place I saw Dominic and recalling all the things we did. Is all the stuff still there? The underwear, the toys, the seat? I don't know if I can bear to see them. I tuck the key away safely. I'll decide later what to do.

The next day, the storm breaks over London and the rain crashes down, accompanied by great rolls of thunder and the crack and flash of lightning. It's been building for days and now the pressure is released in torrents.

I stay inside watching the rain coming down and wondering about the boudoir. I'll have to tell Celia about it, and she's bound to question how I came to have sole access to a flat in her building. She'll probably tell my parents and that will lead to yet more tricky questions. But I don't want to lie to her, either.

When my phone rings, I rush to it, hoping that it's Dominic but it's James.

'Hello, darling, forgive me bothering you at the weekend, but something's come up that I thought you should know about. Can you meet me?'

'Yes – is everything all right?'

'Everything's fine, but I'd like to see you if I can. Meet me at the Patisserie Valerie on Piccadilly in an hour.'

I go out with an umbrella, sploshing my way through the shiny streets on my way to Piccadilly. It only takes a few minutes to walk there and I enjoy the distinct Sunday feeling in the air. It might still be busy but it's down a gear from the usual weekday madness.

James is waiting for me when I arrive, his nose buried in a newspaper, an espresso steaming gently beside him. He looks up when I get there and smiles.

'Ah, you made it. Splendid. Let me get you some coffee.'

When I'm settled with a latte and a *pain au chocolat* to dip into it, he says, 'I know this is strange, but I simply had to see you. I had a breakfast meeting this morning with a particularly interesting client of mine. His name is Mark Palliser and he happens to be the personal art dealer for a very rich man indeed. Mark had some things to discuss with me, and as he is a busy man who occasionally spends a great deal of money at my gallery, I naturally made myself available to him.'

I dip my *pain au chocolat* in the coffee and nibble at it, letting the pastry melt on my tongue. So far, I can't quite understand what this has to do with me.

'We had our charming breakfast in the morning room of his Belgravia house. Mark, as you'd expect, has exquisite taste. Incidentally, he's looking for an assistant and I mentioned your name to him. He would be an excellent man to work for, you'd learn a lot.'

'Really?' That's interesting – a possible job is good news. But is that why he wanted to see me? It couldn't wait until Monday?

James goes on, 'We were just discussing some business when another visitor arrived and Mark asked me to wait in the sitting room for a few minutes. Well, his sitting room is connected to the breakfast room by a rather pretty arch, so I was able to see who his visitor was and hear everything that they said.' He looks straight at me. 'It was Dominic.'

I gasp. 'Dominic? But it can't be – he's left. He's gone to Russia.'

'Not yet,' James says. 'I believe he's going this evening. A private jet is flying him there. From what he and Mark discussed, he's going to be away some time.'

My heart is pounding and my breathing quickens. 'I thought he'd left. That's what Vanessa said.'

'I wondered if you knew. I got the feeling from the general atmosphere of black misery that surrounded him this morning that you might not.' James smiles at me. 'Beth, I thought long and hard before I told you about this. You know I've got reservations about whether Dominic is playing by the BDSM rules. But I also know that you don't need me making decisions about what you should or shouldn't know. You love him, I can see that, and I had to tell you what I found out and give you the choice about what to do. I still want you to be careful though. Do you understand?'

'Of course I do, and thank you for telling me. I appreciate your concern so much. But didn't he see you?'

James shakes his head. 'I don't think so. I have a feeling that he wasn't aware that there was anyone in the next room, and anyway, a giant Chinese vase stood rather conveniently in his eye line. At least, I made sure it did.'

I pull in a long breath, my eyes wide. 'But, James, what am I going to do?'

'Do you want to see him before he leaves?'

I nod, my eyes filling with tears. The idea that I might have a chance to see Dominic, to tell him how I feel and that I made a mistake leaving him the other night, makes my heart swell, and adrenalin surges through me.

James leans forward. 'I don't know if it helps, but he happened to mention that he's returning to his flat at three o'clock today. He's being collected from there by his driver to take him to the airport.'

Excitement explodes in my chest. 'Thank you, James! Thank you so much.'

'You're welcome. I wanted to see your face when I told you the news. Now, go and see if you can make that naughty leopard change his spots.'

CHAPTER TWENTY-TWO

I hurry back to Randolph Gardens, stopping at a stationery shop on the way back to buy some cream card and an envelope. I don't have a great deal of time to put my plan into action.

The rain doesn't seem so bleak and depressing any more. Instead, I splash joyously through the puddles, not caring that I'm getting soaked because I haven't bothered to put up the umbrella. No matter what happens, I've got the chance to see Dominic again, to steal a few moments with him and tell him what I so desperately need him to hear.

I knock on the door of Dominic's apartment but no one answers, to my relief. Vanessa must have gone.

I wonder why she felt she had to lie to me, and why she so obviously wants me off the scent, but I don't have time to dwell on that now. Instead, I hurry upstairs to the boudoir. It feels strange to be unlocking it, knowing that there is no one inside. I switch on the light. The hall looks the same as it did before, plain and bare. I walk across to the bedroom and put that light on too. The room is different. The leather seat has gone, and the cabinet is locked. In the

361

wardrobe, the bondage gear is gone, but the lacy lingerie and the negligee remain. He has removed anything that might shed a light on the more unusual activities we got up to in here, but he's left the things he supposes I might still like.

Hmmm. Well, there are still things that can be done ... After all, exquisite custom-made bondage gear isn't the only option ...

Before I do anything, I write my note to Dominic. It says simply:

Come to the boudoir at once. It is urgent.
B

That should be enough, I think, and take it downstairs. I slide it under the door, and then return to the boudoir to start getting ready.

At three o'clock, I'm a mass of nerves, pacing around the boudoir. I've had a chance to look around now, and it's a plainly furnished but very serviceable flat, smaller than the ones on the lower floors but plenty big enough for one. Is this really mine to use as I want?

I'll try and remember to ask Dominic, but I'm too shivery with anticipation to keep my mind on any one thing. I'm wearing some of the beautiful black underwear from the wardrobe, the pair of stilettos from my second night here, and the trench coat, which I borrowed to wear to meet James. I've put my hair up and done my best to enhance my face considering I've only got a lip gloss and a compact in my pocket.

In the bathroom mirror, I look all right, considering. My eyes are bright and excited and my cheeks have little spots of pink – nature's blusher. I stare at my reflection and then say, 'Good luck.'

At ten minutes past three, I hear a loud rap on the front door. I jump wildly and gasp. So he's come. He's here. It's my last chance. Whatever happens, I must get this right.

I take a deep breath, do my best to quell the nervous riot in my stomach, and walk to the front door. I open it and Dominic is standing there, looking heart-breaking in a beautiful black suit, his dark hair ruffled and his eyes anxious.

'Beth? Are you all right? I got your note.' I can hear the worry in his voice.

'Come in,' I say, my voice firm but neutral.

He steps inside, frowning. 'What's this about? Just tell me you're okay . . .'

I push the door shut behind him and lean against it in the darkness. 'There is something wrong,' I say, my voice low.

'What? What is it?'

I speak again, putting a steel edge into my voice. 'I'm very . . . *very* . . . angry with you.'

'What?' He's puzzled, I can tell. 'But . . . Beth, I—'

'Be quiet,' I rap out. 'Don't say another word. I'm furious with you because you were planning to leave without telling me. I know exactly what you're about to do. You're going to be collected in a short while, taken to the airport and from there you'll travel by private jet to Russia.'

'How on earth do you know that?' Now he's surprised. I'm wrong footing him at every step.

'Don't ask questions. The point is, you are running away without permission and that makes me very, very cross.' I lean forward and I can see that realisation is dawning in his eyes. 'And now I'm going to make sure you remember that you must never *never* do such a thing again. Do you understand?'

He stares at me for a moment and then says in a low voice, 'Yes, I understand.'

'Good. Now follow me.' I walk ahead of him into the bedroom where the blinds are drawn and the lamp is set low. Then I turn, and slowly slip the trench coat from my shoulders, revealing my underwear. He draws in a breath as his eyes travel down from my full breasts encased in black silk down my hips and over my belly to the silken knickers. 'Do you like it, Dominic?'

He nods slowly, looking me straight in the eye.

'Excellent. Now. Take your clothes off.'

'Beth . . .'

'You heard me. Do it.'

He looks as though he is going to protest but then he stops, pauses for a moment and obeys me. He takes off his jacket and trousers and everything underneath until he is standing in just his boxers. I can see that his penis is already pushing at the cotton as his erection begins to swell.

'Oh dear. Didn't I tell you to take your clothes off? Are your boxer shorts not part of that?'

He nods.

'Then take them off *now*.'

He slides them down and takes them off. Now he's revealed to me in all his glory, the broad chest, flat belly and long, muscular legs. His erection is now hard and strong as his hot gaze rakes me.

'And now, you'll have to understand what it means when your mistress is cross with you. Go to the bed.'

He turns away from me and I nearly gasp out loud. His back is a mass of red stripes that have only just begun to heal. I want to run to him and kiss his wounds, the ones that I inflicted, smooth them with cool cream and make them better. But that isn't my plan, not right now. I want to show him that I can inflict a different kind of torment.

'Lie on your back,' I order, hoping he will tell me if that's too painful. But he says nothing and doesn't appear to be in pain as he lies down. I come to the bed with the silken belt from the negligee, take his wrists and wrap them together, then tie the belt to the bars of the bedstead.

He watches, his gaze becoming more intense as he feels his power being surrendered.

I lie down beside him on the bed and touch him gently, running my fingers over his chest, circling his nipples and down his belly. I can smell him now, that musky sweet scent with the citrus tang. Oh, it's beautiful. It's making liquid desire pour through my core, hot and delicious.

'I want to punish you with my own kind of

torture,' I whisper, 'so that you think twice before leaving me again.'

Then I devote myself to his body, kissing every inch of it, working my way down to his feet, where I suck and nibble his toes, and back up, leaving the swelling erection entirely alone as I stroke and caress the rest of his body, gently tickling where he is most sensitive, licking and tugging on his nipples as his breathing grows heavier. When he is ready for a little more, I raise myself and straddle his stomach, then slowly I unclasp my bra, let it fall away and lower my breasts for the attention of his mouth. He is eager for them, pulling each nipple into his mouth and sucking hard, grazing them with his teeth until they are stiff and rosy. Then I spend long, lazy minutes kissing his neck and jaw, biting on his earlobes and tantalising him with my mouth until he is desperate for my kiss, which eventually I let him have, so that he can slake his thirst for me at last.

I've left his glorious length alone for long enough. I'm eager to give it my own variety of torment, with my fingers, lips and tongue. It's waiting for me, the twitch as I bring my mouth close showing the delicious anticipation that's making it stiffen even more. I run my tongue up and down the iron-hard shaft, letting my fingers play in the patch of hair at its base, and travel gently downwards to his balls, where I know he's sensitive and where the touch of my fingers can make him stiffen and sigh and groan. I let my tongue play softly all around him, leaving the tip to endure its own agonising wait for the soft wet touch of my mouth. When I myself can't wait any longer to enjoy the pleasure of wrapping my tongue over the hot smoothness, I take him into my mouth while my hand works hard on his shaft. He's beginning to crave more force now, more pressure, to intensify the glorious sensations I'm giving him.

All this is having its effect on me too. I'm eager for some attention myself, my body, aroused and wet, needs it own adoration.

I shimmy my knickers off and lie along his body, my breasts pressed to his chest, his cock hard against my belly. He groans into my hair and says, 'Beth, you're so beautiful. I love you like this, so seductive, so gorgeous . . .'

'I want you to make love to me,' I say. 'We've done lots of fucking, amazing fucking. Now, give me loving. I'm going to untie your hands, and I want you to show me how beautiful I am and what my body makes you feel.'

I reach up and pull the silk belt. It slides apart and Dominic's hands are free. He takes my bottom in his hands and groans as he feels the soft cheeks in his palms. He rubs and squeezes them, saying, 'This is so fantastic . . . I can never get enough of your gorgeous bottom.'

'Do as I say,' I whisper. 'You know what I want.'

'Your wish is my command,' he replies, his gaze burning as he turns over onto his side. 'Open to me, Beth.'

I let my legs fall open so that he can see what waits for him there. He immediately drops his head downwards so that he can kiss the swollen lips and lick at the slippery wetness, running his tongue over the sensitive bud of my clitoris and making me sigh with the delicious sensation.

'You taste of honey,' he murmurs. 'Sweet . . .'

Just as I'm getting greedy for more of the gorgeous licking and nibbling, he changes his position, pulling me underneath him. Now he is strong and imposing as he uses his weight to push my thighs further apart, and get himself into position.

'Do you want me?' he asks, between hot kisses on my lips.

'Yes,' I say longingly.

'Put your arms around me.'

I hadn't wanted to touch his back, but now I obey, feeling the slight roughness of his wounds under my fingertips.

'You're making it all better,' he whispers. Then he brings the head of his erection to the sweet place and begins to push his way in. 'Your sweet loving is making it better.'

I can't say anything because everything in me is focused on the blissful feeling of his thickness pushing slowly in and filling me up. I bring my hips up to meet him, urging him on deeper inside me. For long minutes we lose ourselves in the rhythm of his hip meeting mine, the back-arching moment of his cock going as far as it can into my depth, and the deep tonguing kisses.

Then, without our saying anything, our speed

increases, the thrusts become longer and hard, as the desire to reach our climax begins to possess us. I wrap my legs around him so that I can push him even further within me, and make him grind against me in the way that is going to bring me the best kind of orgasm, where I am shaken both inside and out.

We don't mean to reach our peak at the same time, but the mounting excitement building in each of us transmits to the other and drives us on to the next level. Dominic is breathing hard, his jaw is set in that particular way that means his orgasm isn't far off.

'Dominic,' I say, my voice coming out like a moan. 'Please, yes, don't stop doing it just like that . . .'

'I want you to come, my beautiful girl,' he says.

That is all I need and as I stiffen around him, and my head goes back, my mouth opening in a cry of ecstasy, I know that he is coming too, releasing his hot orgasm into my centre. I convulse and shudder in wave after wave, until at last it dies away, leaving me breathless and dazed. Dominic is prone on my chest, panting hard after the strength of his climax.

As we recover, he says, 'Oh my God, Beth, that was amazing.' He laughs and runs kisses all over my face and neck, and for the first time in a long time, he looks truly happy. 'Thank you.'

'Thank you.' I look at him and I know my eyes are shining.

He laughs again. 'That was a most unexpected pleasure. I didn't know I had a determined little mistress waiting for me up here.'

'You don't have to leave now, do you?' I say, snuggling into him and relishing his delectable body. 'Isn't your driver waiting?'

Dominic checks his watch and sighs. 'Yes, probably. I don't want to go. I want to stay here with you.'

A delicious warm feeling spreads over me. This is what I'd wanted from him – the loving to soothe the hurting.

'But . . . I can't. I'm sorry, my darling. I'll have to leave in a minute.'

My heart sinks. 'Do you really have to go?'

'Yes. And I don't know when I'll be back.'

'So – what does this mean . . . for us?'

Dominic slides me a look. 'I take it you're not back with Adam, then.'

'No, no!' I shake my head. 'I never was. He came to see me and I told him it was all over. Honestly!'

He stares up at the ceiling for a moment and then says slowly, 'You know, Beth, all this is hard for me to take in. About an hour ago, I thought it was all over for us, and I was trying to get to grips with that, and with everything that's happened. I know you've been in a lot of pain over it, but so have I.' He turns on his side and looks at me. 'To be honest, I still am. What happened between us, and what I did – well, it's really shaken me.'

I reach out and stroke his hair. 'But . . . it's all right now, isn't it? Now you know I still want you?'

He clutches my hand in his, and laughs, a tender, almost wistful laugh. 'Oh, Beth. I wish it were all that simple. You see, I was terrified by what I did to you. I had no idea I was capable of that, of losing control in the way I did. I need to find out why it happened before I can trust myself around you again, do you understand?' He comes closer to me and I see that his eyes are rich and chocolatey, not black at all. The long dark lashes around them are so beautiful, even more so when his eyes are sad as they are now. 'If I don't find out what made me act that way, and fix it, then there's a very real danger I could do it again, and if I did that ... well, I couldn't bear it. I need to be sure you'll be safe if you have a relationship with me.'

'Of course I will be!'

'I'm touched by your faith in me. But I don't know if I share it.'

Anxiety flares inside me. 'What do you mean? What are you going to do?'

'I'm not sure. But before I come back here, I've got to face my demons and overcome them. I believe the darkness in me needs to be healed.'

'You mean, your desire to dominate?' I frown. 'Is that the darkness?'

He shakes his head. 'No – it isn't that simple. It's so complex I can't understand it myself. Sex and love have been separate so long for me that it feels as though putting them back together has been seismic. It's shifted something within me. I need to make sure everything is safe before I try again.' He sighs. 'You see, even when I made you punish me, I was making you do something you didn't want to do. I understand that now, and it's a hard truth to accept. My controlling impulse dominates me to such an extent that it's beyond my control.' He laughs softly at the irony. 'I hope I'm making sense. It's hard to explain. I don't want to make promises to you, Beth, but, if you'll wait for me while I sort these things out, perhaps we can find out together if there's a future for us.'

'Of course I'll wait,' I say, though I can hardly bear the thought of our being separated. 'But how long?'

He draws a pattern on my palm with his finger before he says, 'I don't know. Can you wait, Beth?'

'Yes. As long as I have to.'

'Thank you.' He drops a kiss on my forehead. 'We'll stay in touch while I'm away. Look after yourself, won't you?'

I nod. So the parting is coming after all. He's leaving, going far away to somewhere I cannot follow. Perhaps he'll come back changed. And if he overcomes that darkness he's so afraid of, will he be the same Dominic? Or someone else entirely? I wrap my arms around him, suddenly frightened. 'Don't go! Please.'

He kisses me, very long and very sweetly. 'I wish I could stay. But we'll be together again, I promise.' Then, gently, he unwraps my arms and slips away from my embrace. He gets up and stares down at me, those beautiful eyes full of tenderness. 'I will be back, Beth. Don't forget me, will you?'

Forget you? As if I could.

'I'll never forget you,' I breathe. 'Goodbye, Dominic.'

Then I close my eyes, because it's too painful to

watch him dress and leave me. I feel the weight shift as he climbs off the bed, and hear him as he moves around the room, collecting his things and getting dressed. There is a painful ache behind my eyes and I know it's the tears I'm fighting to keep in. When he's ready to leave, he comes to the bed and kneels down. He takes my hand and wraps it in his own large one, and brings his face so close that he's pressing his cheek to mine. I draw a small, shuddering breath and a tear escapes my tightly shut lids and runs down my nose.

'Don't cry, my Beth,' he says, so softly and gently that I have to use all my strength not to break down. He kisses away my tear and then brushes my lips with his. 'We'll speak soon.'

I can't open my eyes. It's too painful to watch him go. He lets go of my hand and I feel him move away from the bed and stand up. Then he is leaving, and my eyes open just in time to see his broad back and dark hair before the door closes behind him. After that, I hear the front door close with an awful finality.

So it's happened. I close my eyes again, and blank out the boudoir. Instead the image of him standing next to me in the garden floats into my mind: he's strong, happy and smiling. He's telling me that something told him to come and find me, and here I am.

But he's gone.

And now, my wait begins.

ACKNOWLEDGEMENTS

My thanks to all those at Hodder & Stoughton, particularly to my editor, Harriet, and copy-editor, Justine. Their encouragement helped so much.

My thanks to my agent and all at David Higham Associates.

I have been inspired by those who have the courage and imagination to live the lives they want, and who do so with respect for others. We all have a wonderful gift to enjoy: let us do so with careless restraint, sensible rapture and mindful pleasure.

If you fell in love with

fire after dark

then tell us what you think on Twitter
@HodderBooks using #afterdark

The best books live on in your head long after they are finished. As you read, you are turning the pages faster and faster to find out what happens next, only to feel bereft when you reach the end.

If that is how you feel now, you might like to join us at www.hodder.co.uk, or follow us on Twitter @hodderbooks, and be part of our community of people who love the very best of books and reading.

Whether you want to find out more about this book, or a particular author, watch trailers and interviews, have the chance to win early limited editions, or simply browse our expert readers' selection of the very best books, we think you'll find what you're looking for.

And if you don't, that's the place to tell us what's missing.

We love what we do, and we'd love you to be part of it.

www.hodder.co.uk

 @hodderbooks

HodderBooks

HodderBooks